BRITTANÉE NICOLE

LOVE & TEQUILA MAKE HER CRAZY

Copyright

This is a work of fiction. Names, characters, places, and incidents either are the product of the author's imagination or are used fictitiously. Any resemblance
to actual persons, living or dead, events, or locales is entirely coincidental.

Love & Tequila Make Her Crazy © 2022 by Brittanee Nicole

All rights reserved. No part of this book may be reproduced or used in any mannerwithout written permission to the copyright owner except for the use of quotations in a book review.

First Edition March 2022

Cover Design by Cover to Cover Author Services
Editing by Happily Editing Anns

DEDICATION

John,

You're my first, my last, my everything…and I'm your favorite person.

Thanks for sharing this life with me. I love you.

Brittanee

PROLOGUE

Nate
Nine Years old

"Shhh. Stop giggling or they are going to find us." Covering Amelia's pink lips with my hand, I pull her lower into our hiding spot, the smell of chocolate overwhelming me. "Did you bring a cookie with you?"

Amelia's eyes grow wide, and she shakes her head, but I know better. The seven-year-old goes nowhere without chocolate. Chocolate chip cookies to be exact. Her cheeks are constantly smudged with dark black and I'm never sure if it's chocolate or dirt. She's not a girl who likes bows or playing with Barbies, but chocolate and chasing after us boys, those are her two favorite things. I glare at her, letting her know that I don't believe her, and she timidly pulls the telltale blue Chips Ahoy! bag out of her pocket. It's crinkled and missing a few cookies, but she offers them to me anyway. I laugh and shake my head. "Put them away before we get caught."

Amelia shrugs and takes a cookie out before stuffing the bag back in her pocket. "It's been a while. I don't think they're coming."

I lean back against the bed and cross my ankles like my dad does when he relaxes after a long day at work. "We picked a pretty good spot."

She giggles again, and her white-blonde hair falls wispily in front of her face. She needs a haircut. Badly. "They know the boat is your favorite spot. I'm not sure how Jack never figures out this is where we hide."

They probably just figure I'm not about to bring Jack's seven-year-old sister onto my dad's boat. Or they are using this excuse to play basketball while Amelia is missing. Jack hates having his little sister trailing us all the time. I feel bad for the kid. There are only boys in the neighborhood, and she's harmless. Besides, she's always got chocolate, and I happen to love chocolate.

And she laughs at all my jokes. *No one laughs at my jokes.* I'm not even sure I'm funny, but she sure thinks so.

"Give me a cookie, Cookie."

Amelia smiles at her given nickname. I'm the only one who calls her that, and never in front of the boys. I'm not asking for a beating. I'm pretty sure Jack and Peter would tease me relentlessly if they knew I actually liked spending time with Amelia. And then Jack would probably punch me. It's not like I like her, like her. She's seven.

Pulling the blue bag out of her shorts, she grabs a cookie and hands it to me and then lies down next to me in the bed which sits behind the seating area of the boat.

The boat has bunk beds, a master bedroom, and this sneak-away bed in the back. It's my favorite spot because it gives me privacy. When Jack or Peter come for an overnight trip with my parents, we stay in the bunks, but when it's just me—the only child—and my parents, I like this spot better.

And it makes an excellent hiding spot. Although, I'm almost positive the boys are no longer looking for us.

Amelia turns her greyish-blue eyes to me. "Do you think I'll get seasick?"

I consider her question seriously. "No. I mean we're on the boat now and you're not sick."

"Right. But we aren't moving."

For the first time, Jack's parents are coming to Block Island with my family, and we are taking our two boats. My dad has been spending the past few weekends with Jack's dad teaching him everything he knows about boating. And I get to help him. The other boys don't get to come when we go out for the day, but since I've been boating with Dad since I was in diapers, he lets me come along, and I've got to be honest, I think even Dad would admit I'm more help than Jack's dad. This trip to Block Island is definitely going to be a test for him.

"You'll be fine, Cookie. But to be on the safe side, I wouldn't recommend eating any chocolate before you get on the boat."

She cocks her eyebrow up at me. This is an impossible ask. The girl eats Cocoa Puffs for breakfast, Nutella and peanut butter for lunch, and cries if her mom doesn't give her strawberries with chocolate to dip them in for snack. Amelia and chocolate go together like peanut butter and jelly.

Footsteps on the dock take my eyes off the chocolate which stains Amelia's upper lip. "Shhh." I hold my finger over my mouth, excited that they finally found us. Or at least they think they have. I bet it will take them another fifteen minutes to realize we are hidden within the boat.

Feeling pretty cocky, I lie back down and think of what I want once we win this bet. Jack, Peter, and I are pretty competitive, and we bet on everything. I told them there was no way they'd find us within ten minutes, and it's definitely been longer than that.

"Hey Scout, you down here?" My dad's voice echoes into the cabin, and I throw my fist in the air. Jack wasn't even the one to find us! I totally won the bet.

"Oh no." Amelia squeezes my hand and pinches her eyes shut. I look down at her tiny hands which are covered in speckles of chocolate and stare. Why is she holding my hand? And why do I like it?

"Yeah, Dad, we're in here." I squeeze Amelia's hand and let go, surprised when I already miss the feeling of her tiny fingers twisted with mine.

Love & Tequila Make Her Crazy

My dad's face peers around into my secret alcove, and he laughs. "You guys gave your mothers quite the scare." He holds out his hand for Amelia who climbs into his arms and nuzzles in. She's not a very cuddly girl around us boys, always trying to show her tough side, but when she's around adults, I notice she's always getting the extra snuggles. Probably because she's the only girl.

"Sorry, Mr. Pearson."

My dad shakes his head at her. "What did I tell you kids about that? Call me Paul. Mr. Pearson sounds so old."

Amelia giggles when I respond, "You are old, Dad." He leans in and pulls me toward him, tickling me before I have a chance to block him.

"Alright, you two, dinner's on the table. Let's go get you washed up, and Amelia, make sure to scrub extra hard so your mom doesn't see the chocolate on your lips."

Amelia smiles wide which is almost a gift. The girl barely ever smiles. She's always holding her face so stiff, trying hard to fit in with us boys. Every secret smile she gives me makes me feel like I've won a round of Horse.

Amelia goes into the bathroom on the boat to scrub her face, and Dad grabs my hand before I follow. "Nate, I know you like hiding on the boat, but she's too small to come down here without a life jacket. As the older one, I expect you to watch out for her."

I lower my head sheepishly. "Sorry, Dad."

He slaps his hand on my back. "It's okay, Scout. I also don't think your mom would be too happy to know that you had a girl in your bed."

I roll my eyes. "She's not a girl, Dad. She's *Amelia.*"

Dad chuckles. "Right. And right now, it's innocent. But you just wait, that girl in there…" He doesn't finish his sentence, and I stare at him confused. "Just, no more girls in beds, son."

I shrug my shoulders. Keeping Amelia out of my bed will be easy.

CHAPTER 1

Nate

The music blares over the radio in the pastel-colored van I drive, causing heads to turn when they notice my tattooed arm hanging out the window. I smile when I see shock on people's faces at spotting me in the driver's seat rather than the blonde sugary personality they assume should be driving the flowered vehicle.

The contract sitting on the seat next to me flutters with the wind. I wouldn't mind if the papers took off into the breeze, flying out onto the highway and relieving me of the discussion we'll soon be having.

Do I even want to give it to her? After years apart it would seem to be a no-brainer, but nothing is ever simple when it comes to Amelia. It's been almost three years since I last set eyes on her, but I imagine my body will react the same way it always did.

Heart pounding, skin buzzing, unable to stop smiling—just being in her vicinity sets my skin on fire.

If that hasn't changed, I'll have my answer. Although even if I know what *I* want, there is no saying that Amelia will take me back.

The ringing phone interrupts my thoughts. I know it's Grant even before I pick it up. I'd programmed the phone to play "Friends in Low Places" whenever he calls. He doesn't find it funny, and for some reason that makes me laugh even harder whenever I hear it. I take one hand off the wheel and slide the bar to accept the call. "Hi, Grant."

"How's the ride going?"

I bounce my left foot against the floorboard and keep my eyes on the road. "Almost to New York."

"Damn, you made good time."

"Just want to get this over with," I reply brusquely.

"Right. Well, the label needs the forms signed ASAP. When are you going to see her?"

Her. Such a loaded word. "Soon."

"Does she know you're coming?"

His questions tire me. I don't want to discuss her with him. "Listen, I gotta go. Cop up ahead. Don't have a hands-free device in this thing."

Grant laughs. "Yeah, I can't imagine that the seventies regularly fixed their Volkswagens with cellphone devices."

I hang up rather than responding. I don't want to shoot the breeze with him. To be honest, if I have to go back to Nashville, I don't know how I'm going to record with him. But what choice do I have? If Amelia doesn't want me, that's the only life I have left.

Or if I don't want Amelia.

Love & Tequila Make Her Crazy

The words taunt me. It's certainly possible my feelings have changed. I blow out a breath of air, shaking my head. I can lie to a lot of people, but I certainly can't lie to myself. The girl lives in my bones. For the last twenty years there hasn't been a day that I haven't thought about her. If she gives me the chance, if the fire is still there, I'll know exactly what to do with this contract.

Crossing the Mount Hope Bridge is like taking a portal back to my childhood. Practically every memory I have growing up takes place in Bristol or on the bay I'm currently driving over. Weekends spent on the boat, floating, tubing, fishing, or seeing who could do the most ridiculous donuts. Afternoons spent on the baseball field, or riding our bikes through Colt State Park, another spot that coincidentally sits on the water. You really can't go anywhere in this town without the sea being within view, the salt air tickling your lungs. It was a hell of a way to grow up.

I slow my vehicle as I get to the spot where my dad rests. The gravel crunches under my boots as I walk toward the open spot where he's been memorialized. Nothing about this trip home is easy. But this moment, although I've been in this spot countless times, takes my breath away. I'll never get used to seeing those words.

Paul Nathanial Pearson. Loving Husband and Father.
January 16, 1956- September 11, 2001.

So fucking unfair.

I dip my head and lean my arm against his grave. Over three thousand children lost a parent on that day. But I'm more than a number—so was he.

"Hey, Dad, I'm back in Bristol," I say numbly, lowering myself to the ground but continuing to hold on to the cold rock. "I'm home to see Mom. I'll make sure to give her a kiss for you. I think I'll stay on the boat. I still can't quite get myself to sleep in my room. It's just so odd. Even all these years later…it's too hard being in that house without you. Maybe that's why I left as soon as I could…"

I smile wryly at the sentiment. There were so many reasons I left, but wanting to get away from my mother was never one of them. But *needing* to get away from the interested stares, the apologetic eyes, the "I'm so sorrys" from strangers and from people you'd known all your life, and unwilling to always be the boy who lost his dad on that tragic day—all of those were reasons for moving to Nashville. Music was just the most obvious one.

"I've got a big decision to make," I tell him, then correct myself, already knowing the answer. "I *thought* I had a big decision to make. But let's be honest, you always knew Amelia was it for me. So, I guess it's not a decision so much as I have to get a plan together. I got off course the last few years. I'm so sorry you had to watch me screw up, time after time, and you couldn't do anything. But I'm going to make this right. I promise."

I lower my head against the tombstone.

Loving husband and father.

He was so many other things. Businessman, fisherman, boater, lover of baseball, tickle monster, boo-boo healer, best friend, hero, rule follower, but the most important roles—the things he would have wanted to be remembered as—loving husband and father, are the two things I want to become.

The two things that I know without a doubt would make him proud.

I steal another moment alone with Dad and then walk back slowly, allowing the sound of gravel below my feet to settle my nerves.

It doesn't take long to drive to my parents' house, now Sam and Mom's house. She's standing in the doorway waiting when I pull up. Her face lights up when she sees me, running out barefoot and throwing open my van door before I even have my seatbelt unbuckled.

"Oh, Nate, you're a sight for sore eyes."

She wraps her arms around me, and I laugh against her shoulder. "Miss me, Mom?"

She smacks my chest softly. "Don't tease me. It's been too long since I held my baby in my arms."

I roll my eyes. "Men in their thirties aren't babies, Mom."

She laughs. "You'll always be my baby. Even with all those tattoos on your arms."

I wince. It's not that I don't like my ink. I love it. But I'm sure it's a shock for her since the last time she saw me she could see actual flesh on my arms. Now that's hidden below the full sleeves I've been working on. "Yeah, I'm sure it will take some getting used to."

She smiles. "Actually, it suits you. Now come inside; Sam wants to say hello."

I get out of the truck and look back toward the house. "How's he feeling?"

She shrugs. "Good days and bad. But the doctors are hopeful, so that's how we are as well."

It sounds like something she says to herself every day. A mantra she uses to get from moment to moment.

A widow's curse.

"I can stay for dinner but then I have to get down to the bar." We walk slowly to the house.

"So, you're really doing this?" she asks, stopping at the door and staring me down.

"Yes, Mom. It's time."

She sighs. "I hope you're ready for her. She's not the same girl you left behind."

I don't expect her to be. It's been three years. "I'm ready. It's time to take my life back."

Amelia

Stuffing the chocolate into my mouth, I close my eyes and breathe. Another shift on the roof-deck bar, and the sun beating down on my skin reminds me that I forgot to apply sunscreen before coming in today.

"Hey, Hailey, you got any sunscreen?"

Hailey tosses me the pink tube which I easily catch. "Sparkles?" I raise my eyes to hers as I read the words on the bottle.

She shrugs her shoulders. "Caris left it on the boat yesterday. Sorry, I don't have anything else." We both roll our eyes because neither one of us would ever wear sparkles, but the fact that it's her older sister's makes perfect sense. Hailey and Caris couldn't be more different if they tried. Where Caris is tall and lanky, with perfectly coiffed blonde hair and blue eyes that could bring a grown man to his knees, Hailey is short, with wide hips, killer curves, and freckles. She has auburn hair which has never been touched by a bottle of dye.

Hailey is also my boss and one of my best friends.

Without another option, I spray the pink bottle and watch as my usually plain, pale skin is covered in a shimmer.

"Oh, sparkles," Shawn says as he walks up and watches me lather my legs.

Looking up, I meet his eyes and glare at him. There are no words necessary; he slaps his lips closed.

"Hails, want me to grab another keg to prepare for the crowd?" Shawn asks, looking at Hailey like she hangs the moon. She obliviously nods and I offer him a sad shake of the head. Poor man has been trying for the past few weeks to get Hailey to even look at him, and she's not budging. He's easily got eight years on her and he's a genuinely nice guy. Although, that might be his biggest strike when it comes to Hailey.

Around us, I consider the things I still need to prep before the afternoon crowd arrives. It's the last Friday in August, and we're experiencing an unexpected heatwave in New England.

The bar is located on the water in Bristol, and as one of the only bars with actual waterfront double decks, we are constantly slammed even in the fall. Since it's a hot day on the last weekend of summer, we are going to be too busy to think.

But let's be honest, thinking is overrated, which is why I keep myself busy. This is my third job. During the week, Monday through Wednesday, I work at the flower shop, Fridays are reserved for boat charters, and in the evenings and all weekend I bartend here. The only day I have to worry about is Thursdays. Hailey is a good enough friend that she normally goes drinking with me or lets me sit at this bar and drink while she works.

Love & Tequila Make Her Crazy

Not exactly the life I imagined for myself—or one that my poor mother pictured, as she likes to tell me all the time—but it's my life, and most of the time I happen to love it.

And when I have a weak moment, well, that's what chocolate is for.

My mind goes blank as customers arrive and order the first beer of the day. We'll be serving more beer than I'd like because of the heat. Pulling a draft beer for someone takes zero brain power. I much prefer when the customer gives me a challenge—even a mixed vodka requires a little talent—but pouring a beer, my brother Jack could handle that.

The day wears on, and as predicted the most ordered drink is beer. Even I'm starting to eye the cold Blue Moon with the orange slice I'm currently plopping in front of a brunette. I down a cup of water and stare out at the bay in front of us, happy that the sun is finally beginning to set. The magic hour is upon us.

"Hails, where's the music?" I look around, trying to find the local guitarist she usually hires for Friday evenings. He normally likes to have a whiskey before he sets up. While he annoys me with his constant ogling of my breasts, I do like his songs, and more importantly, the crowd likes his music which means they remain at the bar after dinner and continue to put money in my tip jar.

Hailey looks up from the cooler she's sitting on. "Oh, Jimmy had a wedding tonight. But boy, do I have a surprise for you! Wait 'til you see who I hired for tonight! He is a hottie!"

My eyes perk up. New talent. Wouldn't that be nice. Everyone in this town knows everyone else. Having grown up here, there are very few men to meet that I don't already know who they went to prom with, who they lost their virginity to, and more importantly, who they wished they lost their virginity to. It's an incestuous town in my opinion, which is why I prefer to date only people who aren't from Bristol. When I date at all.

Shawn looks at Hailey longingly, and I hip check him. "Stop being so obvious, dude," I mutter under my breath.

He coughs and looks away. "I don't know what you're talking about."

I cock my brows at him. "Shawn, we're family; don't bullshit a bullshitter." Shawn's sister is engaged to my brother.

He laughs nervously. "Don't mention this to Charlotte, please. I'll never hear the end of it."

I zip my fingers across my lips and throw away the key. "Lips are sealed. But seriously, why don't you just ask her out?"

As if on cue, Hailey jumps up. "Oh, he's here! God, look at the muscles in his back. And wait until you see his tattoos—they're what wet dreams are made of."

Keeping my eyes on Shawn, I watch as he winces again. Poor guy. He's hot. Dark hair, broad shoulders, and deep brown eyes. Why doesn't Hailey see what's right in front of her?

"Sorry, Shawn," I whisper.

He rolls his eyes. "It's fine. She doesn't see me...I've got tattoos too," he grumbles.

I laugh as my eyes skate up his arms. They're bare. "Maybe she just needs to *see* them," I tease, imagining Shawn has them hidden in spots that Hailey could explore. When he shrugs, I place my hand on his shoulder, comforting him, and turn to look in the direction of the newest musician. I spot the ink on his arms first—oh God, that's a weakness I didn't know I had.

His hands open the guitar case, and they hold me entranced. Perfectly strong hands, they don't so much as quiver as he moves them expertly around the case, taking out his guitar. That's when the breath hitches in my throat. I'd know that guitar anywhere. In all honesty, I should have known those hands. But the ink, the full sleeves on his arms—that never existed.

Not before.

But that guitar, the one his dad bought for his twelfth birthday—the last birthday gift he ever received from Paul—I would know that guitar anywhere. I'd watched him fumble his fingers over those strings, then sat front row as he wowed crowds with those same hands. My eyes had glazed over watching him string that guitar before he serenaded me with the first song he ever wrote. The night when I finally gave in, or maybe the night when he finally gave in—either way it was the night of my first kiss.

With those lips.

My eyes grow wide as he looks up and spots me, but I can't remove my gaze from his lips. The ones that kissed every inch of my body, and also, so callously broke my heart.

"Ow," Shawn says, removing my hand from his shoulder. "What the hell, Ames, you okay?" He rubs his shoulder where I'd just squeezed so hard I left red marks.

"Ugh, yeah. Sorry." I look back to the area where Nate was just sitting but find him gone.

Oh, thank God, it was just my imagination. Clearly, I conjured up the man, and he isn't playing guitar in Bristol, Rhode Island. I laugh at myself, and Shawn looks at me like I'm crazy. I'm not a big laugher. Or smiler. I'm better at the grimace or cold stare. So I'm sure my maniacal laugh is freaking him out.

"I thought I saw a ghost. Just losing it."

Shaking the memories from my mind, I pull three shot glasses onto the bar. I need a reset after that little moment. I mix three of my favorite shot—chocolate cake—and place three lemons on the edges. "Bottoms up," I say to my two friends and go to hand them each one.

Before I can grab them, fingers circle the tiny glass, and my eyes remain on the ink on the forearm which belongs to the hand. "Don't mind if I do," the voice I know better than my own says.

Squeezing my eyes shut, I whisper to Shawn, "Please tell me there isn't really a man with blue eyes standing in front of us."

The voice interrupts my conversation with Shawn. "Oh, chocolate cake. Shoulda known, Cookie. You always needed your chocolate."

I open my eyes and glare at him.

Love & Tequila Make Her Crazy

Nate Fucking Pearson.

God, why does he have to be so damn good-looking? If I were the type of girl to go weak in the knees, now would be the moment for that. But I don't have the capacity to indulge in moments like this. He'd stolen that ability from me.

Behind me, Hailey laughs. "Did he just call you Cookie? Oh dude, that's not going to end well for you."

I feel Shawn inching away from me, and I grab his hand, pulling him close. There is no way I can make it through this conversation without other people around. I can't be trusted alone with this man. Even after all these years.

He's a man. When did that happen? Last time I saw him he was still a boy. I mean, I'd been twenty-seven and thought we were grown-ups, but the man before me is different. He's hardened. The scruff on his face is light but it makes him seem older. Sexier.

Fuck.

And the lines around his eyes. They're new. There was a time when he couldn't get a pimple without me knowing. I knew every inch of that face. But not anymore. The years we've been away from each other are written all over his face. I wonder what he thinks of how I look.

Dammit, Amelia, no you don't. You don't wonder anything about him because he's nothing to you.

Nate chuckles as he puts the shot glass back down and looks up at Hailey. "I'd call her my wife, but she'd probably throw something at me. So, Cookie sounds safer, right, wifey?"

My chin stiffens, and my knees begin to betray me. *Not now,* I tell my inferior body parts. *Keep it together.*

The hardest words to mutter burn my tongue on the way out. "That's ex-wifey to you."

CHAPTER 2

Amelia

Nate's eyes flash, but he recovers quickly. "Aw, is that any way to speak to your best friend?"

Words are powerful. If you ever want to hurt someone you should give them silence. Silence is indifference. A lack of caring. Fighting with someone, granting them a piece of your soul through words, shows they still have power over you. That they still have the ability to light your fire. Silence shows nothing. I learned this from the master of pain. He hasn't spoken to me in three years.

I gulp down my response. He doesn't deserve my words.

Why is he back here? I honestly don't think I can handle this. Finally sensing that I'm about to lose it, Shawn loops his arm around my shoulders and pulls me close to him. I shrink into his embrace and bite back the emotion threatening to pour from my eyes. "Can I get you something, man? Amelia was just about to take a break."

Nate's eyes narrow in on Shawn's hands. "Nah, I'm all set. Don't take too long, Cookie, I've got a song just for you." He winks and walks off.

"Oh my God!" Hailey screeches behind me. "You were *married* to that?" Motioning to Nate's retreating frame, her mouth is practically on the floor.

"I wasn't married to that," I say, looking away from the muscles which are visible even under his tight black shirt. "The boy I married is gone." I breathe in, begging the air to reach my brain. Or maybe to wake up and find that this is all some sort of hallucination, and the man who walked out of my life years ago isn't standing here in my bar acting like nothing happened.

I slink to the floor, cradling my knees, and Shawn leans down to look at me. "You were married?"

My head snaps up. This all just happened in public. "You can *never* tell Jack."

Shawn frowns. "Jack doesn't know you were married?"

My shoulders slump. "No. And he can never know because I was married to his best friend."

"Woah. You need to back up. Jack and that hot guy are best friends. How come I never knew him growing up?" Hailey asks as she hands me a shot of Fireball like the good friend she is, and does one herself as well.

"Because he was in school with Caris. You were probably too young to remember them." Hailey is a few years younger than I am, so she definitely wouldn't remember my brother's friends who were even older.

Hailey shrugs and offers me another shot, but I shake my

head. "Probably best if I don't have any more to drink. I don't make good decisions around Nate."

It's an odd statement to be honest. He was the one person I was always myself around. The person I trusted more than anyone else. And I always thought I was that to him. Apparently, I never really knew him.

How could he walk back into this town and act like I mean nothing to him? Act like nothing happened.

He was *everything* to me.

I hear the first chords, and like everyone else in the bar, my eyes turn to the guitarist, infatuated with the way he strums the guitar even after all these years. His blue eyes look at me below his long black lashes. His hair is buzzed tightly against his head, and he annoyingly looks a lot like Colin Farrell.

Nate was always good-looking, but with the buzz cut, his eyes pop and his cheeks seem more chiseled. The scruff on his face does something to my insides, and those damn tattoos have me all screwed up. They snake up and down the arms that used to wrap around me on the boat.

Back then I would keep my nose close to Nate's skin and inhale. It was the only tell I ever gave that I was interested in being more than friends. For years I held him, listened to him talk, and pretended we were just friends.

It was only when we were on the boat, in our secret spot, that I'd let myself get anywhere near him. Using the excuse that he needed me, I allowed myself to touch him, never making it known that I needed him just as much. And now those arms look different. The skin color I'd memorized is all but a memory, just like our relationship. Would he still smell like him, or would that be different too?

Into the microphone he introduces himself. "Evening, everyone. I want to thank Hailey for letting me play for you guys. It's been years since I've been back here, but I'm just a Bristol boy at heart and I'm so happy to be back home. I'm going to start off with one of the first songs I ever wrote, right here in this little town, about a girl of course. Not just any girl though; she was *the* girl. She still is. This one's for you, Cookie."

He winks at me as he starts to strum our song, and my knees buckle. Shaking, I lean against the bar, wondering who the hell the guy singing to me thinks he is, and if he's ready to deal with the woman that I've become.

Nate

Seeing Amelia for the first time leaves me with so many thoughts. Some things are so familiar about her, and some are so jarringly different. Even with a bar between us I can still smell her; the chocolate sugar scent that *is* Amelia filters through the air. And from across the room, even without looking at her, I feel her presence. She is staring, connecting, relearning every inch of me just as I am with her.

She's lost weight, likely skipping out on full meals and eating toast with Nutella instead. It hurts to know that she isn't taking care of herself. Probably drinking too much, not sleeping enough, and pushing herself too hard just to forget. That was a problem I used to have. Now that she's standing in front of me though, I know for certain that all I want is a clear head, a clear schedule, and the opportunity to remember everything. Most importantly, I want to do all of that with Amelia by my side.

Her grey eyes look more worn, tired even. They're missing the fierce light, the effervescence that she'd always carried. *I'd* done that to her.

But she is still by far the most beautiful woman in the room, with her pink pout, small nose, and the breasts I dream about nightly. My hands ache to reach out for her, to take her in my arms and crush her against my chest, whispering how sorry I am and how much I still love her. But I lost the right to do that. So instead I acted like a jackass, hoping to light a little fire in her, to bring back the spark to her eyes. Even if it's anger, it's better than her resignation.

Anger I can handle. Anger I can work with. And, damn, is my girl angry.

To be fair, it's been almost three years. I try for the puppy dog eyes but she shakes her head, unwraps her apron, and walks out of the bar. It was probably wishful thinking to believe the song would work twice. I'll have to come up with another plan to win back my wife.

Money gets placed in the tip jar, and requests come in. I focus on the crowd and the feeling of the strings below my fingers. It's the only thing that's kept me going since Amelia walked out of my life. I play until my mind goes blank and am surprised when the male bartender that had his arms wrapped around Amelia walks up with a shot. "Figured you could use one of these after your night." I nod in his direction and take the smooth shot down. Not tequila like my girl's favorite, but it will do.

"How long have you known Amelia?" I ask.

He sighs, probably worried that she'll come back and spot him conversing with the enemy. It's a punch in the gut if I'm honest. I was always the guy who protected her, the one who knew everyone in her life. Now I'm practically a stranger. "Her brother is engaged to my sister."

My shoulders relax. He's not a potential boyfriend. Or a current one. He's Jack's future brother-in-law. *That* I can handle. I know I don't have any claim to her, not after the way we left things. Still, I don't know what I'll do if I find out she's dating someone.

"I heard your sister makes Jack very happy."

Shawn smiles. "Right, Ames said you were best friends with Jack. He know you're here?"

Love & Tequila Make Her Crazy

"Here as in at the bar? Or here as in back in Bristol and driving his sister crazy?"

With the crowd clearing out, Hailey looks in our direction waiting for Shawn to help her clean up. He looks back at her and pauses for a moment and then turns back to me again. "Here as in back in Bristol driving his sister crazy."

I laugh. "Yeah. He knows I'm here. Listen, I'll let you go clean up. I'm just going to pack up, and I'll be on my way." He nods and heads back to the bar. It's not like Amelia to leave the cleaning up to others. She must really have wanted to avoid seeing me to have left her shift early.

Too bad, my pretty girl, I'm not going anywhere. Not going to make that mistake again.

Moments later, Hailey stands before me, hands on her hips with her lips pursed. She looks like a firework that exploded with her red curly hair in all different directions and the same amount of energy bursting at the seams. "Did you know Amelia worked here?"

I sling the guitar over the back of my shoulder. Unsure of the appropriate response, I try the truth. "Yes."

Her brown eyes remain trained on mine. "And are you here to win her back?"

Easy answer. "Yes."

Hailey's face opens wide with a smile, and she sighs. "Oh, thank God. I was worried I'd have to kick your ass, and I really would have hated to do that."

I chuckle. "Kick my ass?" I stand about a foot taller and have at least a hundred pounds on her. I don't think she has a shot.

She puffs her chest and holds up her arm. "I'll have you know I have one hell of a left arm."

I smirk, glancing down at her skinny limbs. "Well, thank goodness I'm not on your bad side then, huh?"

"Exactly." She laughs. "So, what's your plan?"

My plan. I scratch the back of my neck. The furthest I got in planning had been coming home to Bristol. "Chocolate cake?"

Hailey shakes her head. "Yeah, I don't think this is a chocolate cake apology."

"You're probably right. Any ideas?"

"I can offer you the weekend spot. Friday, Saturday, and Sundays. Our regular guitarist normally stops after the summer, because he's got a grown-up job and all that jazz." She rolls her eyes like she can't believe anyone would rather work in an office than at a bar. I happen to agree with her though, so I suppose she's in good company.

"Every weekend?" I ask.

"You planning on sticking around?"

I nod as I make my decision. "Yes. I'm back for good. I never should have left."

Hailey smiles in understanding. "Then the job is yours. If you want it. But don't come back for her unless you're ready to catch her."

I reach out my hand to shake hers in agreement. I'm not

going anywhere. Amelia is my family. I'm going to fight like hell to show her that.

CHAPTER 3

Nate
Twelve Years Old

"You think Caris will be at the baseball game?" Peter asks as I stare down at my guitar, trying to tune it as his nonstop talking interrupts my concentration.

I grimace. "Why do you care if Caris is at the game?"

Peter's cheeks turn the same color as his hair. "No reason. Just wondering."

"Well, are you wondering if Jack's gonna be there?" I ask like a wiseass. He pushes against me, almost knocking the guitar from my hand. "Hey, watch it."

Peter reddens. "Sorry. Of course, Jack is going to be there. He's playing. I'm asking about fans."

Still focused on my guitar and not worried about hurting Peter's feelings in the least bit, I mutter, "If Caris comes it's because she wants to watch Jack play. Sorry, buddy." I don't even know why he cares about girls. All I care about is my

Love & Tequila Make Her Crazy

guitar and baseball.

Peter tosses a ball in the air and catches it in his glove. "Not all of us have a personal cheerleader at every event," he says bitterly.

I turn my attention to him, unaware what he's referring to. "Yeah, Jack's everyone's favorite. But who cares, you're the best catcher this town has ever seen." I guess I do care a *little* bit about his feelings.

The compliment goes straight to his head, and he grins. "Yeah, and have you seen my curve ball? I could teach Jack a thing or two." Rolling my eyes, I turn back to my guitar now that Peter is his usual happy-go-lucky self. "But I wasn't talking about Jack. I was talking about you. Amelia is at every game cheering you on. She's practically your personal fluffer. Whether you're practicing guitar, playing basketball with us, or up at bat, that girl is screaming like crazy for you."

"That's because I'm the only one that's nice to her. You guys can be such dicks. And she has to be at all of those events because her parents are there to watch Jack. If it wasn't for him, she wouldn't be around."

Peter laughs. "Yeah, whatever you say."

I round the base, running as fast as I can, and as I slide into home, her screams are the first I hear. "Pearson! Woohoo!" Peter flashes me a grin, and I dip my head below my hat.

"Personal fluffer, Pearson," Peter says out the side of his mouth as I walk by the guys, accepting everyone's high fives.

I shoot him a look, embarrassed. Does everyone on the team think Amelia likes me? It's not like that with her. We're just friends. She's Jack's little sister, and she's ten. I kick the clay, shooting orange dust into the air, and don't dare look at her in the stands again.

"Maybe if you stopped spending time with her on the boat she'd get the hint," Peter says, recognizing how uncomfortable I am.

"Maybe if you hadn't made it weird this afternoon this wouldn't be a problem," I mutter. Coach makes us line up and high-five the other team, and I keep my head down as I walk back to the dugout to collect my stuff.

Blonde hair flashes in front of me, and Amelia beams as she throws herself against my body. "Great job, Pearson! You totally won the game today." I keep my hands at my sides, grimacing at her touch. She pulls back and looks at me, biting her lip. "You okay?"

Not meeting her eyes, I lean down to pick up my bag. "Yeah. Just going with Peter and Jack to play video games. I'll see you later." My stomach pinches when I see her blank face and watch as she realizes we're ditching her. *I'm ditching her*. But before I can give it a second thought, I run after the boys, leaving Amelia staring after us.

Hours later I'm still replaying her reaction as I sit at dinner with my mom and dad. "That was a great game, Nate. Your swing is getting strong, son."

I nod at my father, finding it hard to take his compliment when I know I'd been so cold to Amelia. She was just being nice. Why did Peter have to say those things? He made me feel weird about being friends with her when I'm just being nice.

My dad isn't the type of person to miss when something is wrong. He always has a lesson or a joke. He *always* knows what to say. This time is no exception. Placing his fork down, he looks at me and gives me a soft smile. "Don't beat yourself up. Just apologize, and don't do it again."

Mom looks on, unaware there was even a problem, but because she knows Dad misses nothing, she doesn't interject.

"How do you know what happened?"

My dad chuckles. "Son, she's your biggest fan. It's hard to miss. She screams like a banshee. Don't take it for granted. Also, what did I tell you? As the older one I expect you to watch out for her. As should Jack and Peter. That's what boys do. They cherish those who care about them, protect them, care for them. It's what will make you a good man someday."

I swallow uncomfortably. I hate disappointing my dad. "I'm sorry, Dad."

He grins and slaps my back. "No need to apologize to *me*. I know you're a great kid. That's why you feel bad about what happened. I have to go to New York this week, but how about when I come back, I take you and Amelia out on the boat? I'm sure she'll accept your apology if you have Mom make some of her famous cookies."

We all laugh. Amelia loves her chocolate. "Would you do that for me, Mom?" I really want to invite the boys too. I don't want to give them a reason to say anything else. But Dad is right. I owe this to her. Amelia has always been my friend. I could be hers.

"You know how much I love Amelia. She's like a daughter to me," my mom says, sipping her wine and smiling wistfully.

Feeling better, I thank my parents and we finish dinner. That night, Dad and I head down to the boat while Mom cleans up in the kitchen. We stare at the stars like we do every night, and he asks me to play him the new song I'm learning on my guitar. It's not as good as I want it to be, but I play it for him anyway. "I'll try to practice this week and have it down by Saturday. Maybe I can play it for you, Mom, and Amelia when we go boating."

"Oh, your mother will love that. What's better than Bob Marley on a boat?"

I laugh. "Three Little Birds" is Mom's favorite.

"Nate, everyone is looking for you." Amelia climbs into the small alcove, and I wipe the wetness from my face.

I just needed a minute. That's all. I can do this.

"Well, you found me." I huff out a sigh and stare down at my black shoes. My dad would kill me if he saw I was wearing shoes on the boat. Not that it matters anymore.

Amelia slips her tiny fingers into mine and lays her head down on my shoulder, saying nothing else. The feel of her fingers, the smell of chocolate, and her weight on my chest sets me off. Shaking, my body betrays me, and the tears pour out. "Shhh, I'm right here," she whispers against my chest, using her other hand to rub circles on my stomach, soothing me without ever looking up. She knows enough to know I can't look her in the eye. I can't see anyone else's pain. Mine is too consuming. She knows enough not to tell me it's going to be okay because it never will. Never again will it be okay because my dad, my best friend, my superhero, is gone.

Sobs rack my body, and Amelia holds me, her hair wet from my tears, her hand weak from mine squeezing hers so tightly. I give myself another five minutes, taking everything she's willing to give me, and then I sit up. "I have to go check on my mom." I straighten my tie, still not meeting her eyes.

"Meet me back here tonight?" Amelia offers, fully aware the nights are impossible. It's been weeks since my dad last spent a night in our house, but we are only now able to have a funeral. We had to wait for them to find a body. To confirm that Dad really was one of the unlucky ones who didn't make it out of the towers. We'd all been walking around like zombies. I honestly believed that my dad would just show up one day. How did this happen?

I nod, unable to voice how much the nights mean to me. Amelia sneaks onto the boat after her parents go to bed. I'm sure they actually know where she's going. Who lets their ten-year-old out of their sight? Everyone is probably just allowing it. Looking the other way. Doing whatever they can to help the poor boy who doesn't have a dad anymore.

Don't let a girl in your bed, especially that girl, Dad told me. But how can I not allow her to hold me when she's the only one that says nothing. She doesn't try to make it better. She doesn't tell me it will be all right. She just lets me cry.

I'm sorry, Dad. Shoes on the boat, girl in my bed. Sneaking out of Mom's house. I keep breaking all the rules. I promise I'll do better.

I hang my head in shame. I'll do better, but not tonight. Tonight, I'll be back with Amelia. *Tomorrow, I'll do better, I promise.* But even as I make the promise, I know nothing will ever be all right again.

Amelia
Eleven Years Old

The daffodils at the Pearsons' are just starting to sprout. With the early spring weather this April they are going to look beautiful. It is odd how alive they make the house feel, with their bright yellow cheeriness in such a contrast to the way everything else feels.

It has been seven months since Mr. Pearson died, yet the house still stands exactly the same, as if everything had frozen that warm September day. On the front door, the Labor Day red, white, and blue wreath hangs. Mrs. Pearson hadn't changed it out for her typical Halloween wreath, or Thanksgiving, and definitely not Christmas. No Easter decorations hang in the windows. There had been no Christmas tree, and Mr. Pearson's shoes still sit in the hall next to the front door. But these daffodils are going to disrupt the bubble wrap that has so tightly enclosed this house, as if trying to preserve every memory that lay inside. If Mrs. Pearson sees them, it will be another reminder that the seasons keep changing, and everything keeps moving forward, even if she and Nate are stuck in September.

I stand staring at the flowers, shears in hand, gloves hanging from my back pocket, trying to decide the right thing to do. Should I remove them? Try to protect the bulbs and perhaps replant them next year? Or I could let these tiny reminders bring them forward, slide a little of the bubble wrap off, see if letting the air in makes anything brighter. The noise of the front door opening jolts me from my place, and I fall forward into the beautiful flowers. Darn. Might not have a choice now.

"Amelia, what are you doing over there?" Mrs. Pearson looks absolutely stiff watching me try to lift myself up off her gorgeous flowers.

Shoot. Shoot. Shoot.

Before I can stop them, tears of anguish fill my eyes. I'm making it worse for her. For them. And it's the last thing I want. I can't even explain what I'm trying to do because that will only put into words the one thing we don't talk about. Mr. Pearson is dead, and I don't know how to help them move forward.

When she sees the tears falling from my stupid eyes, she lowers herself to the ground and speaks softly, "Oh, Amelia, it's okay. Don't cry." As she pulls me against her, the tension from not wanting to cry on her only makes me cry harder and I sob. This isn't me. I don't cry. I control my emotions. I control everything.

Righting myself, I look up at her, wiping away my tears, ready to apologize. "I…I just didn't want you to see the flowers." I point to them feebly.

Her eyes crease in understanding and then she sighs. "It's time, huh?"

I breathe out as if I've been punched. "I don't know. Just… that's up to you. But I wasn't sure if you wanted the flowers or not."

She looks down at the smushed flowers and shakes her

head. "You know what? I think I do. Do you think you can help me bring these back to life?"

I nod. Mrs. Pearson is the one with the green thumb, but I'd love if she'd teach me. I'd love to do anything to spend time with her. To help her.

She gets up and comes back with her own gardening gloves, and we quietly get to work, weeding her garden and fixing the daffodils. She even brings out some of her Easter decorations, including the little bunnies she always liked to set up around the flowers. "What do you think?" she asks as she places the last one.

I admire the front yard; it's bright and cheery, the way I always found Mrs. Pearson to be.

Before.

"It's beautiful," I tell her.

She squeezes my hand. "Thank you."

I shrug my shoulders. "Oh, it's no big deal. You did most of the work."

Mrs. Pearson looks down at her hands, pulls off her gloves, and then meets my gaze. Her blue eyes, which look so much like Nate's, shine with fresh tears. She shakes her head. "No, thank you. For being there for Nate. For being *here*. It's easier when you're around. It doesn't feel like it's just Nate and me. Like something is missing."

Or someone, is really what she means. And although it makes me feel good to think that I can make it even a little less hollow,

I know that isn't true. We all feel the loss of Mr. Pearson in every breath we take. No one is helping ease that ache. No matter how hard we all try. "He won't touch the guitar," she says quietly.

I nod. "I know."

"I can't go on that boat," she admits, twisting the gloves in her hands.

I nod again. "I know."

"You're the only one he lets in."

Once again, I know. But I'm eleven. I'm not sure how helpful I am to any of them. But I'll try. If I can do anything for these two people who I love as much as my own family, I'll try.

I leave Mrs. Pearson on the lawn and make my way down to the boat. That's where he always is. Every day after school that's the first spot he goes. Nate no longer plays sports or video games with the boys. He doesn't do anything but sit on the boat in our little alcove and stare at the ceiling. And I've let him do that, offering him my hand when I sneak next to him, as I rattle off facts about what went on during my day. Telling him about the rumors swirling about Jack dating Claire, or Peter getting pantsed during gym class. Sometimes I even get him to laugh. But just as quickly as the sound rings out, he quiets himself, as if it's a betrayal for him to so much as smile.

Today I'm going to do something different. As Mrs. Pearson said, it's time. He's a thirteen-year-old boy and he's lost so much, but someone has to get him to move again. I'm nervous that what I'm about to do will cause him to turtle further into himself, that he'll retreat so far that even I won't be able to get him out, but I know I have to try. I promised her.

With me, I carry the guitar case Mrs. Pearson let me grab from Nate's room. I hope this doesn't backfire. Slipping off my shoes at the edge of the boat, I hop over the side and lower myself into the living compartment. Nate silently shifts around in the berth, likely moving over to make room for me, expecting that I'll do as I always do and slide in next to him and start talking. But that isn't the plan today. Instead, I open the guitar case and stare at the beautiful wooden instrument. Mr. Pearson had gifted it to Nate for his birthday last year. His last birthday present from his dad. Ever.

I am treading into dangerous territory.

I run my hand over the smooth surface, and my fingers hit against the strings, making a clunking sound. It almost sounds like the heaves the Titanic made in the movie, stretching and breaking as it sank.

This moment has the ability to sink more than a boat.

The sound of Nate sitting up pierces my nerves. His legs scratch against the fabric and then he leans out of the alcove, peering at me with confusion, and then…anger. Fury. A coldness

I'd never seen. "What are you doing with that?" he manages to grit out.

"The town is holding an event…to honor your dad," I choke out.

Nate's eyes slice me. "Yeah, I'm aware. Put the guitar back, Amelia."

I hold his eyes with my own, willing myself not to break. "Your mom wants you to play a song. 'Three Little Birds.'"

His eyes nearly break me, the flash of something so painful, so filled with anguish, it's worse than if he actually hit me with his fist. He says nothing though.

I don't back down. He needs this. *He needs me.* "I'll do it with you…teach me."

Nate slams his fist against the wall, then cries out when the pain registers. Does it hurt less than his heart? Or more?

"Please, Nate. Teach me."

He sneaks back into the cubby, and I hear him grumble, "Go home, Amelia."

Although I know I am doing the right thing, hearing the resignation in his voice, the broken empty person he's become, makes me want to give up. I walk off the boat, leaving him to his privacy, but I leave the guitar too.

The next day when I show up, the guitar is in the same place and so is Nate. Rather than pushing, I slide next to him in the alcove, lean my arm next to his, knock his elbow, and when he finally looks down at me, I whisper, "I'm sorry."

Love & Tequila Make Her Crazy

Nate nods but he doesn't say anything. He just snakes his hand into mine, and I start talking to him. Nervously at first but then we settle into a rhythm—him quiet and me talkative—until it's dinner time and I leave again, staring at the guitar wistfully as I go.

We follow this pattern for a few more days until one day I come in and he's sitting there staring at the guitar. Not touching it. Just staring. It feels like he needs me to say something. To ask again. So I do. "I really want to be able to help your mom with the event. Could you teach me?"

Nate lifts the guitar tentatively and for the first time in months, holds it. It almost looks like he's holding a hundred-pound weight. It sags in his arms, but when he finally adjusts it against his chest and presses his fingers onto the strings, I watch in amazement as his face softens. And just like that he's *Nate* again.

CHAPTER 4

Amelia

Lucky for me I don't have time to focus on my ex-husband's appearance because I agreed to bartend an event at Linden Place. Like Bristol, the town where I have spent most of my life, this mansion has an incredible history. Once owned by the famed DeWolf family, who were slave traders in the 1800s, the mansion is as beautiful as its history is ugly. And unfortunately for me, so is the outfit they've picked for me.

"What in the hell is this?" I grimace, pointing at the 1800s dress Hailey has on.

Hailey shakes her hips and yet the wide skirt barely moves. She's short, and the dress practically swallows her whole. "Don't be jealous, yours is in the back room. Hurry and go change. The event is starting in fifteen minutes, and we still have to prep the sangria."

"Nuh uh." I shake my head. "You said nothing about a costume, Hails. *Nothing!*"

Love & Tequila Make Her Crazy

She beams at me. "That's because I knew you'd say no, and I needed you."

"That's ridiculous. Utterly preposterous. I cannot believe you would do this to me. After what I went through last night, you should take pity on me."

Hailey raises her eyebrows. "Oh, are we finally going to talk about the hot guitarist who also happens to be your ex-husband? Because if so, I will totally not make you put on the costume."

My shoulders slump. I'd rather wear the damn dress. I huff in the direction of the closet prepared for my latest humiliation. First, it was my failure of a marriage, which came at the same time as the loss of my business, then momentarily I had to move back in with my parents. Not something any twenty-seven-year-old wants to do after living on her own since the age of eighteen. Fortunately, my luck was looking up. Until this week at least.

I scored an awesome apartment, my bartending job was bringing in enough savings for me to start thinking about focusing on my business again, and I even started to date. Okay, I started to consider dating. But still. Progress. Finally, at thirty, my life was starting to feel normal.

That is of course until Nate Pearson appeared again. Shaking the memory of his hands, or his voice, or the new tattoos that snake up his arm, I come face-to-face with today's attire. The sleeves are white and poufy, the skirt is navy blue and wide, and the top is almost a turtleneck. For a girl who doesn't wear dresses, this is so not my style. Or you know, the style for anyone from the twenty-first century.

I drop my jean shorts and tank top to the ground and shimmy my body into the parachutesque monstrosity, then sidle my way out of the room so Hailey can corset me into this trap. "Seriously, how did women survive the summers in these outfits?"

Hailey shrugs. "Truth." She squeezes the strings on the back of the dress, pulling tight and leaving my waist the size of a Barbie doll. "Let's do something with this hair of yours." She points to my always messy blonde hair, which hangs listlessly around my face.

"Do your worst," I instruct, watching in the mirror as she twists my hair into a bun. Sadly, with fine hair like mine, it barely makes a tiny pebble on my head and looks absurd. "Okay, not your worst. Do better. So much better." Hailey meets my eyes in the mirror and pulls the hair-tie out. Then she pulls a few pieces back, leaving half my hair down, and does a simple braid on each side, sweeping my usually messy hair off my face.

"Thank you." I nod in her direction. She doesn't deserve a smile for putting me through this, but at least she won't get a glare.

We make our way into the courtyard which has tables set up for the event, but there is a lack of decorations. Before I have the opportunity to consider what type of floral arrangements I would have put together for this event, a cart is pushed into the courtyard with ten arrangements covering it. While the flowers are all pretty, they are missing the oomph, the special something, that I know they need.

I type a quick message to my boss, asking her to quickly meet me here. I have an idea that not only will make this event look so much better but will also help her brand-new business. The business that I'm helping build and that I hope will give me a name in our tiny town as the go-to florist for events. I'd recently purchased gold leaves and flanked the edges with small pearls. If placed with these bouquets, they will make the entire arrangement pop.

Karen responds almost immediately to my text. "Give me fifteen minutes."

Excellent. Now all I have to do is get the okay to touch the bouquets from the event coordinators. As I grew up in this town, I know just about everyone who works here. I spot Lucille and sashay my way over to her, trying hard to own this dress. I'm pretty sure Martha Washington owned it though, so I'm failing miserably.

"Lucy, can I have a moment?"

The woman looks up at me under her signature red hair—cliché I know—and regards my outfit. "Well, I never would have thought we could have gotten *Tom Boy Amelia* in a dress like that."

I shrug my shoulders. "It's for a good cause, right? I'm a team player." I try for a smile. "Speaking of good causes, did you know that Karen opened a flower shop on Hope Street?"

Lucille doesn't miss my swivel to what I'm really after.

"Yes. Unfortunately, we've been getting our flowers from the same store forever. But maybe for the next event I can talk to her." She goes to walk away, but I can't give up that quickly.

"How 'bout I do one better for you? I asked her to drop off some fillers that will make your current flowers pop. Really make the event stand out among all the other events. You know, it will probably make them even better than what Macy did for the Fourth of July Ball." I'm devious. Macy is her sworn enemy. Okay, frenemy. Not that women of a certain age should still have frenemies but for Macy and Lucille we'll make an exception. They volunteer on every town committee, each vying for who gets to handle the biggest events. The Fourth of July Ball is the cream of the crop. The event of the year. For a town whose sole focus is on the tradition of hosting the longest running Fourth of July celebration in the country, the Ball is the flag that shoots out of the cannon. And this year Macy had been the lucky one to host it. Lucille was scandalized.

She raises her eyebrows to me. "You'd do that for me?"

In this town everyone has a side, and I've always been on Macy's. She's good friends with my mother. But this is business. I give her a firm nod.

"Well then,"—she pauses as if she's really taken aback by my offer—"okay. I'll make sure to let everyone know that Amelia Fitzpatrick was behind the design as well."

I blush. "Just let them know it was Pearson's Events that did it. I'll have Karen drop off cards as well."

Love & Tequila Make Her Crazy

She nods and I walk over to the flowers, preparing the arrangements in my mind. I hope Karen brings ribbon and lace as well. I have an idea that will work perfectly with these hideous outfits we're wearing.

"Amelia Pearson, as I live and breathe," Nate's low voice drips with sarcasm.

Rolling my eyes before I dare spin around and let him see me in this monstrosity, I arch my back and growl, "For the last time, I'm *not* a Pearson."

Nate doesn't wait for me to turn. He grabs me by the shoulder and spins me toward him. "Sure you are, sweet cheeks. Now where do you want this stuff?" Before I can react, his eyes travel the extent of my body, taking in every inch of the humiliation that is known as my life. "Oh." He lets out a low laugh and meets my eyes.

"Not a word, Pearson. Not. A. Word."

He throws back his hands. "Oh, come on, even you have to admit I get to comment on this. I mean…you didn't even wear a dress to the prom…or our wedding." His eyes soften at the memory.

I bite back a scowl. "Wedding? I'm surprised you even remember it occurred, given how flippantly you treated our '*marriage.*'" I mime quotation marks around the word marriage and his eyes flash.

"We're not doing this here. My mom asked me to drop these off to you. I didn't realize you'd be so well…dressed, or I

53

would have come in costume." He smirks again and my stomach clenches. I've missed that smile. The way one lip turns up while the other one remains flat when he tells a joke. The crookedness that seemed so perfect, giving him an edge, and almost always only for me. I close my eyes to forget, to remove myself from this moment, to control my temptation to launch myself into his arms.

"Right, great, thanks." I take the box filled with the decorations and walk away. Unfortunately, my ex-husband does not take the hint.

"So, what are you going to do with these?"

It's hard enough to move around with the skirt billowing in front of me, knocking into the table every time I shift. Add in Nate's breath on my neck and his eyes caressing me with his stare, and I'm just about worthless.

"Please, Nate," I say breathlessly, begging him with my tone to let me be. This is a big deal for us. Pearson's Flower Shop, I mean. This could help launch Karen's business into events and give me something to do outside of stuffing flowers into vases. It would give me back a little piece of my life that had been stolen from me years ago. And once again the man who stole it is standing in my way.

He presses his body against my back, so close that I can feel the outline of his arms, the hardness of his chest, and the sway of his hips, and then he leans down and brushes the softest of kisses against my neck. The feel of his lips sends a flurry of fire to my cheeks, warming me in areas that have been frigid for years. "Anything for you, Ames," he says softly and then he walks away before he can feel me arching my back into him, reaching for the past, for the people we used to be, and to the last time I felt whole.

Nate

"How did the drop-off go?" Sam asks me at dinner. My mom raises her gaze to me, interested in the answer as well.

"It was good. I saw Amelia."

My mom shakes her head. "I'm sure I'll hear all about it tomorrow."

"You need help at the flower shop?" I wiggle my eyebrows at my mother, but she just throws her napkin at me.

"You stay away from my shop. I don't need you scaring away my best employee."

Sam casts a sideways look at me. "Son, how was it seeing her?"

My shoulders tense at his term of endearment. It's not that I don't love Sam. He's been wonderful to my mother for the last fifteen years. But he's not my dad, and I am most certainly not his son. Seeing as how he is one of the reasons I am finally back in this town though, I give him what he asks—the truth. "Hurt like a bitch. And it's also the most alive I've felt in the last few years."

My mother blows out a breath. "She hasn't been sitting around waiting for you, Nate. She moved on. It's going to take a lot more than you singing a few songs to get her to look in your direction again."

Don't I know it.

Cockily, I reply, "Oh, she was definitely looking. And I think she liked what she saw."

Sam laughs, and my mother rolls her eyes. "What are you boys going to do tomorrow when I go to work?"

"Maybe we'll stop by the flower shop and take you to lunch?"

My mother gets up and kisses me on the cheek. "Let me see how Amelia is doing before we decide that. If she doesn't seem like she's going to take off my head for hiding that you're back, then maybe." She winks as she walks out, leaving me and Sam to clean up.

"So how are you really feeling about everything?" he asks me again, once my mom is out of earshot.

Nervous. Scared. Wishing I'd never gotten myself into this position. Angry. Hopeful. "Eh, okay, I guess."

"Well, do you have a plan?"

I look around my childhood home at the kitchen table I used to sit at with my mom and dad and the picture of the three of us still sitting on the mantel—*the three little birds*, as my mom always called us. Next to it is one of Sam and my mom as well. It's odd how time just continues forward even when you don't want it to. What I would do to go back to the moment that picture was taken—on the boat with my dad and mom, on vacation in Block Island, Amelia still my friend, Jack by my side, and Peter…Peter still alive. I don't think I've had a plan since he died. But it's about time that I make one. "Get my girl back. Start living again. Give her forever like I promised."

"Maybe start with Jack?"

"One step ahead of you. Meeting him for drinks this week." I slide out of the chair and force Peter and my dad from my mind. They'll always be in my heart, but right now I have to focus on the living. It's the only way I can move forward. And if I have learned anything over the last few years without Amelia, it's that living with her is the only way I want to move forward.

That evening as I lie on the boat, trying to concoct a plan, I hear footsteps padding down the dock. For years that sound would fill an excitement in me that I could barely contain. It was always Amelia. Mom never came out to the boat after Dad died, and Jack and Peter knew this was *our* spot—Amelia's and mine.

But I'm positive it's not her. She could barely look at me this afternoon, so she certainly isn't seeking me out on the boat. That would be too personal for her. When my mom peeks her head around the corner, I'm both momentarily relieved and disappointed.

Is it still hard for Mom to be in here? Does this hurt? It's only been three years since I last held Amelia in this exact room, and it shreds me being in this space again without her.

Does the fact that Mom hasn't been with Dad for twenty years make this harder or easier? Does the fact that he didn't walk away from her—he was taken, murdered, unable to come back—make it so that she could justify his loss? God knows the fact that Amelia gave up on us without so much as a fight makes it almost impossible to forgive. But I'm working my way through it. In the end the anger isn't worth it. The only thing that will ever make me happy is being with her again. I have to forgive. Myself and her.

"Hey, sweetheart," Mom says, looking at me nervously as she steps onto the boat. "Permission to come aboard?"

I give a nervous laugh. "Always."

Her eyes move around the cabin, taking in the wooden walls and decorations which are the same as the last time she'd been on here. I wonder if it smells the same to her. If it feels the same in the way it sways. Is it like putting on an old sweater? *Dad's sweater.*

Finally, her eyes rest on mine, and she lowers herself onto the bench in the corner, the one that turns into a bunk where Peter and Jack used to sleep. Memories exist in every crevice.

"How are you doing, love?" she asks, a quiet resolve taking

over the room.

I give her a false smile. "Oh, you know me. I'm great. Happy to be back."

Her eyebrows rise in the knowing way that only a mother's can, telling me she knows I'm lying and that it's unnecessary. What it would feel like to be a boy who could just cuddle into her lap, to allow her to kiss this boo-boo away. Unfortunately, broken hearts don't work like that. "I brought you something."

My eyes raise to hers, perking up from my comfortable position. "Yeah?"

She blows out a breath of air, and I notice how her hands shake as she reaches behind her, picking up a small book, black and worn, with simple gold writing on it. "Your father was a practical man." She smiles as she looks down at the book. "Not like you."

I try to control my offense to this statement, but she catches my scowl. "It's not a bad thing, Nate. He was a rule follower, a rule maker. He belonged in an office as much as he belonged captaining this boat. In places where there was structure—you tie a knot a certain way, you file a patent a certain way. You have to go slow through a no wake zone." She smiles at some memory. "You're like me. Soft. Strong-willed. Hopelessly devoted."

I smile at this admission.

"Your dad knew we'd fight. We were so different. He tried to control too many things. Didn't make time for the extras in life. He was always worried about providing for us, doing right by us. And while we were dating, I told him I thought it made us incompatible. I tried to break up with him."

My eyes widen at this. I never heard this story, and I crave stories of my father like a starved animal, reaching for every morsel of Dad, wishing for one more piece of him. "Really?" is all I can manage.

She meets my gaze and nods. "So in your dad's typical fashion he came up with a list of rules. His *Rules of Promises*. They're all in here." Her fingers tap lightly on the back of the black book. "All the promises he made to me, set down as rules, so I knew he'd follow them. He never broke the rules." She smiles, shaking her head.

"Why are you telling me this?"

It feels like this is significant. Like she had waited for the perfect moment to share this, or maybe not the perfect moment, but a moment when she knew I'd need it. She'd come onto the boat she hadn't stepped foot on in twenty years to deliver me another piece of my dad—it was monumental.

My mom's lashes flutter closed for a moment, then she looks up at me, her blue eyes that match mine conveying how heartbroken she is to *have* to give it to me. "You never seemed like you needed it before. He'd imparted so many of these promises—or rules—on you when you were little, I didn't think you needed it. *I* needed it. I needed to remember how much he loved me. That he had set out to put us back together when he had the opportunity." Her voice breaks at this, because he had

Love & Tequila Make Her Crazy

the opportunity when they were engaged but not later when she so badly needed him to put us all back together.

"But now you think I need it?"

My mom nods. "You and Amelia… Oh, Nathan, you and Amelia are soulmates. I think your dad and I knew it even when you were children. Or at least we hoped you would be. The way she loved you so fiercely, cheered you on, supported you. What else would a parent want for her child? But you are also very different. She's slow to trust where you're an open book. She's stone-faced where you're always smirking. And she follows the rules while you break them."

That's hard to hear. I always wanted to follow the rules, to make my dad proud, but my mom was right—I consistently let him down. My mom seems to notice the sadness in my eyes as she says, "It's not a bad thing, Nate. People like you and me bring people like them out of their shells. We make them live. And man did your father *live*."

She laughs, and I flash back to moments with my dad on the deck of this boat, cruising fast over the waves, not quite following the rules and him laughing at the excitement on Mom's and my face as we landed hard wave after wave.

"So here are the rules that I think even *you* can follow. Use them to win her back. To remind you of what Dad would say if he were here. I know Sam isn't Dad and sometimes it's hard having him act that role." I wince at the truth. "And I don't know what to tell you to do because I'm like you. But Dad always knew what to do, or at least he did for me. I'm hoping he can help you too, one more time."

My throat grows tight realizing that it's one more piece of Dad—probably the last piece of him I'll ever have. But twenty years later, to have found something, to have any connection to him at all, that I hadn't had before—it's a gift. I squeeze out the words, "Thank you." My mom gets up and leans over me, kissing my forehead lightly, then she presses the book into my hands and walks off the boat without another look.

CHAPTER 5

Amelia

Sunday morning I walk into the flower shop prepared to have words with my ex-mother-in-law. It's not easy working for someone who is the mother to your ex. Actually, that's not true. It has been nothing but easy since she opened this shop. But that was before she decided to butt into my marriage. Or my divorce. Or whatever the relationship Nate and I have—it's a very complicated one. But her butting her head into it is a problem.

Sending Nate to deliver the decorations yesterday was cruel. It was confusing. Seeing him leaves me wishing for things I can't have. A future that isn't mine. It's completely unfair, and I expect her to know better.

"Morning, Amelia," Karen says with a smile. Her face falls when she sees mine. "Okay, maybe not a good morning."

I plop my purse on the counter and grimace. "No. Not a good morning at all. Which honestly stinks because yesterday was amazing—outside of seeing he who shall not be mentioned. I really think the event will spark interest in the business plan you and I were discussing."

I try to remain hopeful about that fact at least. Yesterday *was* amazing. Everyone loved my design, Lucille lived up to her word and told everyone it was our shop who did the décor, and I could hear the murmurs of interest. But in the back of my head, I couldn't stop thinking about Nate. What is he doing here? And more importantly, when is he leaving?

"Do you want to talk about it?" Karen's blue eyes soften.

Never in my life have I wanted to disappoint Karen. In fact, I've probably spent the majority of my life trying to keep her smiling. We've *never* had a confrontation. Not even when I came home and told her it was over with Nate. It's a balancing act we've maintained for over twenty years. She's not my mother. I fight with my mother. She's…it's hard to put into words… but she's more than a friend, and certainly more than a mother-in-law. That's not always a welcome term or a good term to many women. I guess some people have bad relationships with the women who raised their husbands. But that was never my issue. We were family before we actually legally became family. I have been part Pearson—an honorary Pearson—for as long as I can remember. Even before Paul died.

But at this moment, as I stare into eyes so much like the man who broke my heart, I'm angry with her. I deserved a heads-up. After all we have been through, I deserved her honesty. Yes, Nate is her son, and he comes first, but I'm not just his ex-wife. I'm something—*someone*—to her too.

"When is he going back?"

Love & Tequila Make Her Crazy

It's the safest question. It doesn't matter why he's here; I just need to calendar his departure date so I can put myself on overdrive until he's gone. Avoid Nate Pearson like the plague and then return to the regularly scheduled programming on that date.

Karen's lips twitch, and she looks away from me. Why is she looking away from me?

"Karen," I say sternly.

She sighs. "He's not."

"He's not what?"

Faithful? My husband? The person I thought he was?

Yeah, all those things go with "he's not," but I doubt she's talking about that.

Karen leans her arms against the counter, slouching over and taking a breath before looking back up at me. "He's not leaving, Amelia. He's back. *For good.*"

Nate

Not surprisingly, my mom does not want us to meet her for lunch. Amelia is in rare form, she texts. Give her some space.

Frustrated, I have no choice but to listen. Sam wasn't wrong. I need a damn plan. I'm a thirty-two-year-old musician without a real career. At least not a career that I can make work in Bristol. I can't pick up random gigs and expect that to impress Amelia. She needs to know I'm serious about staying here. Which means I need to find a job. I throw myself onto the bed in the boat. This definitely felt a lot bigger when Amelia and I were in school. We spent our fair share of nights in this exact spot, first as kids cuddling and eating cookies, and then as horny teenagers.

My mind wanders back to the later years. The memories are enough to put a smile on my face and leave me hard with need. It's been so damn long since I've been with Amelia. And I haven't gone near another woman. *Ever*. I made a promise, and I kept my word. My stomach turns knowing the same probably can't be said about her. But I can't hold it against her since she doesn't exactly know that she's mine. *Still mine*. Forever mine.

She looked so damn good yesterday, even in that ridiculous costume. I didn't love how she had her hair back off her face. I always preferred it messy and down—casual and barefaced Amelia was always my favorite—but obviously that wouldn't have been the right look for the event. Perfect for my bed though. And her eyes. Her grey eyes searched mine as if trying to decide if I was real when I showed up at the bar. As bad as I wanted to peruse her whole goddamn body, I kept my eyes focused on her face. While she was looking my way, at least. I can't help that when she talked to customers my eyes trailed her body like she was my own personal buffet. Her breasts seemed bigger, more than a handful, just like she is. Her small curves and her tiny hands, as always, did me in. And those luscious pink lips—it took everything in me not to hop over the bar and kiss them.

Remembering how those lips used to tease me, I close my eyes and prepare to take the edge off. Footsteps on the dock still my fingers. The sound of shoes being dropped and the feet landing on board force me off the bed and standing at attention. Who the hell is here? My mom visiting twice in twenty-four hours seems almost impossible.

"Mom?" I call out.

Amelia's pursed lips greet me. She's wearing shorts that barely cover her ass. They're frayed at the edge and show off her incredible legs. The day before, they'd been hidden under her dress, but now my tongue practically wags from my face. "Eyes up, Pearson."

I meet her eyes and try a casual smile. "Hey, Cookie, look at us, settling back in like old times." I reach out to grab her and pull her to my chest, but she pulls back.

"Don't."

Running my hands against my head, I try to recover from her rejection. Her eyes trail down to my belt where my shirt lifted from reaching out to her. *Hm, apparently, I'm not the only one affected.* Noted.

"Can I get you a drink? I don't keep it stocked like I used to, but I'm sure I can find something." I turn around and look at the cabinets, avoiding her angry eyes.

She breathes fire. "Nate, turn around. I'm not staying for

a drink."

Turning, I look at her sadly. "Come on, Cookie, for old times?" I jump into our alcove and wait for her to follow. When she doesn't, I peer around the corner and look back at her. Her head is lifted to the ceiling and her eyes are closed. "Amelia, please." She opens her eyes and looks at me.

"We're not kids anymore, Nate. I'm not crawling in there."

I sigh. "Fine. Sit down though. Somewhere. Please. You're making me nervous."

I scoot out of our spot and wait for her to sit. She plops down on the bench. "Happy?"

Sarcastically, I reply, "Overjoyed. So to what do I owe the pleasure of Amelia Pearson on my boat?"

She glares at me. "Amelia Fitzpatrick."

"Tomatoes, tomahtos." Unable to sit still anymore, I stand up and look in the refrigerator, grabbing a beer for myself and offering one to Amelia. She shakes her head, and I pop the top off mine.

Fuck, this conversation is harder than I thought it would be. We'll have to agree to disagree about the name.

"So, to what do I owe the pleasure of having you on board?"

"What are you doing here, Nate? It's been three years."

I sip my beer. "Can't a guy come visit his family?"

She folds her arms across her chest, and my eyes dip to her left finger, the one without the wedding ring that I placed there so many years ago. The ring that I now wear around my neck on a chain. Her diamond is in the safe, but her wedding band is always by my heart. Mine is still on my finger.

"Your mom says you're not visiting. You're moving back. Why?"

Stupidly, I reply, "To win my girl back," having been too focused on her bare finger. That was definitely not the right answer though. Her eyes harden. Sighing, I say seriously, "It was time, Amelia. Nashville was never permanent. You and I always planned on coming back."

She laughs sarcastically. "Could have fooled me. Last time I checked, we both came back to Bristol and only one of us stuck around. You went back to Nashville and made it clear we were done."

She is definitely rewriting history. But that isn't a fight I'm willing to have right now. There's no winning if we're fighting, and I desperately want to win. "Please, let's not do this. I'm back. There's no undoing what we both did. But I'm here and willing to work on us."

Her eyes grow wide. "Us? Us? There is no us, Nate. There hasn't been an us since we signed the divorce papers. There's a *you* and there's a *me*. And seeing as how we are both living in this town for the time being, I just wanted to make that clear. I'm no longer your home, Nate, and you most certainly aren't mine." Hitting me right where it hurts, she uses my words against me.

I shake my head at her clear attempt to hurt me. "I'll stay out of your way."

"Good. Because my boyfriend won't like it if you show up at the bar when we're working. It's not fair to him. Or me. And I'm sure you don't want to see me all over him. But since it's hard to keep my hands to myself, I make no promises. So, you know, just leave me alone."

She stands up and gives me one last once-over before she prepares to head out.

"You're dating Shawn?"

She flinches at his name, and her entire body stiffens as she turns back to me, not quite meeting my gaze.

Yeah, she's not dating him. Nice try, sweetheart.

She nods her head. "Yup. We've been keeping it a secret from Jack and Charlotte, so I'd appreciate it if you didn't mention it to anyone. It's new. But serious. *Really* serious." Her fingers pinch together as she walks. It's her tell, the thing she does every time she lies.

"I won't say anything."

"Right. Because you don't talk to Jack. Because you blame everyone for everything. How silly of me." She hops off the boat before I have a chance to respond or defend myself. Just like last time, she thinks she has everything figured out. She's quick to judge, easy to anger, and willing to throw away everything just so she can prove she's right. And fuck, that hurts more than anything.

CHAPTER 6

Nate
Seventeen Years Old

"What time did we tell him to meet us here?" I ask impatiently, staring at my phone for the fifth time, wondering where the hell Jack is. We'd planned to meet a few of our friends at the cove, and I want to get there before all the boats tie up and we end up without a spot on the mooring. Peter's dad agreed to let us take his boat since mine is too big for this type of day. We just need the little speed boat to get over to Potter's Cove which is just across the bay.

"He just texted; he's parking now."

"Great," I say, jumping onto the boat and starting to remove the lines. "Let's get everything ready so we can pull out as soon as he jumps on."

Peter gets to work on the dock while I turn on the engine. When I look up, I spot Jack with a pissed-off grimace. Behind him, the familiar wisps of Amelia's blonde hair blow in the wind. My heartbeat speeds up, and I grip the wheel tightly.

What is *she* doing here?

Under his breath, I hear him mutter, "Just get on the boat, and you better not tell Mom and Dad about Claire being here."

Amelia glares at him. "You don't have to be such a dick."

She's right. But I also don't blame him. Amelia goes out of her way sometimes to let it slip when Claire has spent time in Jack's room. She finds it hysterical when he squirms—him not so much.

"Hi Peter, Pearson," she says, lowering her eyes without looking at me. She always acts so strange when the boys are around. Maybe I do too. It's like our friendship is some secret, but if it is, it's the worst kind because everyone knows Amelia spends an insane amount of time on my boat, alone with me.

It's not weird at all though. Or at least that's what I keep telling myself. These feelings swirling in my chest, the clammy hands when she's around, the hardness in my pants, it's all just hormones. I'll get over it as soon as I get a girlfriend. I'm sure of it.

"Hey, Cookie. Didn't know you were joining us for the day." I give her a relaxed smile.

Amelia graces me with one of her rare grins. "Yup, Dad said Jack could only go if he took me."

Jack rolls his eyes. "Just remember the deal."

She salutes him. "Aye aye, Captain." Then as if she remembers where we are, she glances at me and winks. "Actually, I guess that's you. *Captain Pearson*." Her voice takes on a seductive drawl, and I have to pinch the sides of my legs and focus on baseball stats.

The boys finish untying the lines, and we pull away from the dock. Jack stands next to me while Amelia sits up front, her long legs splayed out in front of her with Peter on her opposite side. As they talk, her laughter dances over the wind.

"Are you even listening to me?" Jack asks, drawing my attention away from the front.

I shake my head. "Sorry, I was focused on the wind."

Jack laughs. "Yeah, no. You're focused on my little sister's legs. Nice try, though."

My eyes dart to his. I can't even lie to him, but I definitely don't know what to say.

Yes, I'm in love with your little sister. I have dreams about those legs wrapped around me every night.

That probably wouldn't go over well. And since Jack is my best friend, I can't possibly think of Amelia like that. But I also don't know how to stop. "I, uh…" I stumble for words.

He laughs again.

Fuck.

Knowing that I'm not ready to have this conversation—and definitely not when Amelia is just a few feet away—I focus on driving the boat. Fortunately, my best friend becomes distracted by his phone. It's likely Claire wondering why we're so late.

It only takes about fifteen minutes to get over to the cove, and after quickly throwing the lines, we are tied up and ready for an afternoon of lounging in the water. Jack hops off our boat, making his way over to Claire, and Peter catapults himself over the side screaming, "Cannonball!"

I fiddle with the gears and do basically anything to avoid looking in Amelia's direction. It would be a dick move to leave her by herself on the boat, but staying also doesn't seem like an option. Not if I want to keep my hands to myself and my friendship with her brother intact.

"Nate, can you do my back?" Amelia's soft voice sends an electric shock through my body, and my shoulders tense. I need to turn around and look at her. *Respond to her.* But I can't get myself to move. "Nate?" she asks again.

Sighing, I prepare myself and turn around, looking at her feet before raising my eyes slowly, trailing her legs up to where her jean shorts used to be. But fuck, instead she's wearing a tiny yellow string-bikini bottom, and my eyes grow wide as I study the way she's looped the strings, not nearly tight enough to protect her from teenage boys. Like me.

Eyes up, Pearson, I reprimand myself. But my eyes continue to move slowly up to the top of the bikini below her belly button, over her smooth skin, and then to the bottom of her bikini top which barely covers breasts I had no idea she had. She's always in a T-shirt. I've never even seen cleavage.

When did she get those? It's like they sprouted overnight. It's literally impossible for me to stop looking. To stop myself from staring at the soft curves and the obviously hard nipples which are pebbled against her flimsy top.

"Nate," she says again, but this time her voice is softer. Breathier. I swear she can see my thoughts.

I meet her eyes. "Yes."

"Yes, what?" she asks, as if she's just as lost as me in this moment. Her normally grey eyes are blue like the ocean, reflecting off the sea, and hazy with desire.

I blink, removing myself from this moment with my best friend's little sister. *This is so wrong.* "Yes, I can put lotion on your back. Turn around."

Please turn around so I don't keep ogling your boobs.

Oh shit, Amelia has boobs. What the hell am I going to do? I'll never be able to sit in the alcove on the boat alone with her again. Before it was bad, but this is tragic. I won't be able to stop myself from touching her, from lying on top of her and kissing her, from running my hands over her body. This is fucking impossible.

Like the jackass that I am, I relish taking the lotion from her, watching as she turns around, lifting her hair off her neck. It takes everything in me not to lean down and kiss the center of her neck—it looks so soft and it's like my damn body is being pulled toward her. Like I was never meant to be any more than a few inches from her.

There is a buzz between us, an electric current that always sizzles just at the surface. We've somehow managed to keep enough distance through the years to keep from getting burned, but I know the minute I touch her today, it's over.

I'll never get her out of my system. And like a damn fool, I don't stop myself. I don't call out for someone else to lather her. I willingly move closer, pressing my hands against her shoulders, and rub circles over her back, up across her angel wings as my mother always calls them, down to just above her ass, which my eyes now dart to.

Obviously, she needs to have the backs of her legs done, so I get to work, lowering down, smoothing the lotion down her legs, dangerously close to areas I have no right to be fantasizing about.

Amelia is silent the entire time, maybe as lost as I am in the feel of my hands on her. Hopefully, that's how she feels. Or else this will have just crossed a line from friendly to creepy.

Amelia doesn't pull away. She doesn't smack me. Instead, she turns around, and because I'm on my knees from lathering her lower legs, I'm now face-to-face with her bikini bottom. I look up and meet her eyes. They are wide in surprise.

"Here, let me help you up," she says, offering me her hand. I stand up easily and stare down at her. Just like my dad told me I would, I have shot up to over six feet this year. Amelia is tiny in comparison.

We stare at one another in silence, and I feel like an understanding passes between us. Things have changed. There is no going back. I either have to figure out a way to be friends with this girl and not spend time alone with her on my boat like we always have, or I've got to talk to Jack and then make my move.

Love & Tequila Make Her Crazy

There is no more teetering. No more skimming the surface. I've relied on her friendship for years. Relied on her to make so many things in my life right. I can't imagine not having that anymore. But it scares me to take things further. Either way I risk losing her.

I glance to the side, looking at the boat filled with girls my age, and I make a decision to keep Amelia as a friend. I'll get a girlfriend. These feelings will subside. They have to. I *can't* lose her. She means too much to me. Her friendship and support are everything.

When she bites her lower lip, I shake my head. Amelia doesn't even flinch. She simply nods as if she gets it.

Of course she gets it. She gets *me*.

Without a second thought, she hops off the boat, propelling herself into the water and freeing me to go spend time with someone else. For a moment, I consider throwing it all away. Throwing caution to the wind and jumping in after her. But something stops me. And her name is Heather. As I stare off after Amelia, Heather hops onto the boat and gives me a flirty smile.

Here's to trying to make it work with someone else.

Amelia
Fifteen Years Old

"Oh, did you hear Jack asked Claire to prom?" The girl at the locker next to me whispers to her friend. As if it's a secret. Jack and Claire have been making out in his room for the last two months. Who else would he have asked to prom? These girls are clueless.

"Yeah. I'm just wondering when Nate is going to ask someone. I tried to hint to him at the party last week that I didn't have a date, but it's so hard to tell if he's interested or not."

My heart races at the mention of Nate's name. He was at a party with these girls?

"He's had a tough time. Cut him some slack. I'm sure he wouldn't have kissed you if he wasn't planning on asking you."

I slam my locker shut and both girls jump. When the blonde looks at me, she smiles. "Oh, Amelia, didn't see you there. Hey, you're always around Jack and his friends, right? Did they happen to mention if they're going to prom?"

I don't force a smile. "Nope. You'll have to ask them yourself." I turn on my heel and stalk out of the building.

Love & Tequila Make Her Crazy

I race home, avoiding Jack and his offer to drive me. I'm not surprised that he didn't tell me about this party that they all apparently went to. It's no secret that Jack doesn't want his sister following him around everywhere. But Nate's betrayal cuts deep. I can't be mad that he kissed another girl. Of course he did. He's a seventeen-year-old male, and it's not like I have any claim over him.

Cursing under my breath, I keep running until the docks come into my line of vision. I'm mad because he hid the fact that they went to a party without me. Nate and I don't lie to each other. He invites me to everything. He never makes me feel like I'm just Jack's little sister.

Embarrassment heats my cheeks as I realize that he was just being nice all these years. Now that he's older, of course he doesn't want to hang out with me. He wants to spend time with girls his own age.

Girls he can *kiss*.

My stomach turns from the images teasing my stupid brain. Slipping my shoes off my feet, I hop onto the boat. This is my sanctuary. Nate won't be here. He's probably off with Jack somewhere. Possibly kissing Heather.

There'd been a moment a few weeks ago on the boat where I thought maybe he was looking at me like he wanted more than friendship. Like maybe he wanted to kiss me. But what do I know? Clearly nothing.

The truth is that even without him, this space calms me. I

grab the cookies from my backpack and scoot my body onto the alcove berth. The first bite of chocolate leaves me still shaking, but by the time I eat the second cookie, my heart rate settles.

I take out my sketch pad and start to draw. I discovered I'm pretty good at this when we started using charcoal in art class. Since then it has become something just for me. Something that soothes me. I don't usually take out my pad anywhere but home, but seeing how even chocolate isn't doing the trick, sketching it is.

The boat creaks, and I hear Nate call out to me, "Cookie?" His voice grates on me in a way it never has before. Stupid nickname. How could I have thought he felt anything for me other than friendship?

Cookie. It's a damn child's name. Or a dog's. Or a blonde twenty-five-year-old who marries the seventy-year-old millionaire.

"Yup," I manage to grit out, but I don't bother sitting up. He can come to me. I listen as Nate slips off his shoes and makes his way onto the boat.

When he peers around the corner of the bed, my heart crumbles.

Why does he have to be so good-looking? Why do I have to have these stupid feelings for my brother's best friend?

His blue eyes sparkle the moment they meet mine, and his face lights up in a smile. I push my artwork behind me, hiding the one piece of me he doesn't know about. Looks like we both have secrets. Mine just doesn't happen to be blonde with big boobs.

"What are you doing here? Jack was looking for you after

school to drive you home."

Anger comes flooding back. He wasn't coming to find me because *he* wanted to see *me*. He knew if Jack couldn't find me, I'd be here. He's just doing his friend duties again.

"Just wanted some time alone," I mutter before stuffing another cookie in my mouth so I don't have to talk anymore.

"Alone from everyone else, right? Not me." He says it with such conviction. As if he knows I would trade my own arm for time with him. Obviously, I never *don't* want to be with him. It's pathetic.

I'm pathetic.

Rather than responding, I move over to the side so that he has room to slide next to me. When he doesn't make a move to sit, I stuff another cookie in my mouth. This is unbearable.

Nate eyes me and smiles. "You think you can take a break from your cookie eating and pouting to come over here for a minute?"

How does he know I'm pouting? Is it that obvious? "I'm not pouting," I say with a full mouth.

He laughs. "Sure. Whatever you say. Please? I brought my guitar. I finally got the song I've been working on finished. I want to play it for you."

Seeing his blue eyes pleading with me, there's no way I could ever say no. I roll my eyes though because I don't want him to know I'm a total pushover for him. "Fine, you can play me your song."

Nate pulls the guitar out of the case, and my heart flutters.

There was a time I thought he'd never look at that instrument again.

He settles himself against the table and props his leg up on the bench, holding the guitar with tenderness. Then he looks up at me and gives me a small smile. He almost seems...*nervous*. Which is ridiculous. It's just me. Smiling back at him, I give him a rare piece of me and hope he knows just how special he is.

God, I'm such a pushover for him.

When he starts to sing, I'm surprised by the deepness of his voice. So much stronger than the boy who played songs for me over the last few years. When did he grow up?

"She doesn't know what she does to me. She doesn't know she's my world.

With her blonde hair, and long legs, and the smile she reserves for me, she makes my emotions swirl.

Oh, she made me better. She's the best friend that I'll ever have.

But she doesn't know what she means to me. One day she'll see that we're meant to be.

But until then, it's just me, asking her to trust that I'll always be, the man that's in love with her."

Nate's eyes remain on mine as he sings. Imagining he's actually singing the words to me, that it's *about* me, is the greatest feeling in the world.

I'm not sure how I missed that he'd fallen in love with someone. *With Heather*, I remind myself by saying her name. If I wasn't so lost in his eyes, I'd probably feel like an idiot right now.

Love & Tequila Make Her Crazy

I manage to clear my throat. "Wow, Nate. That's beautiful."

Nate exhales a shaky breath. "I've been dying to play that for you." He puts the guitar down and stares at me. "So, what are you thinking?"

What am I thinking? Um, that I want to sink below this boat and stop imagining him kissing the blonde from school that he's fallen in love with. Yeah, that's about the only thought going through my mind.

"Just, uh, she's a lucky girl." I choke out the words, trying hard not to register my disdain for Heather.

Nate laughs.

He *laughs.*

"I'd say I'm the lucky one." He gets up and starts walking toward me. There's a swagger to his step that I've never seen before, a smoothness to his manner as his eyes lock on my face, focusing hard on something that I can't discern, and he licks his lips. When he reaches me, he lifts his hand and pushes back my hair.

My always messy white-blonde hair. Not like the blonde from school. She styles her hair. Chocolate doesn't stain her clothes, and she probably wore a dress to the party, whereas I'm wearing light jean shorts which have rips in them and a plain white T-shirt with my Chuck Taylors.

I'm really dolled up as always.

His eyes search mine. What is *he* thinking? What is he looking for? The air in the boat is practically nonexistent, and

I swear the room got hotter. His hand trails my face, and my stupid cheek turns into his embrace. He inches closer to me, tipping my chin up to him, and locks his eyes onto mine. "You have no idea what you do to me, do you?"

Huh?

My eyes dart back and forth, trying to read his face.

What is happening?

"Oh, Amelia, *you're* my best friend. You're the one who got me through everything. *You're my home*." He presses his other hand against his heart. "You're the one who makes it all better."

Trying to catch up, I whisper, "You're my best friend too, Nate."

Nate's lips dip in a smirk. "You still don't get it, do you?"

I shake my head, begging him to tell me what I'm beginning to think but am too scared to voice.

Nate's blue eyes soften, and his thumb grazes against my lower lip. A shock skitters down my neck. "The song is about you. I'm in love with *you*. I'm pretty sure I always have been."

Eyes growing wider, I can't make my mind work. "You're what now?"

"I'm going to kiss you, Amelia. So, if you don't want me to, please tell me now." His eyes search mine, waiting for my reply. When I don't, he inches closer, pressing his lips against mine. Heat travels through my body, and when his tongue parts my lips and he presses his hand against my back, pulling me closer, practically holding me up since I'm about to collapse from the shock of this moment, I moan into his mouth and feel him smile against my lips.

Wrapping my arms around his neck, I open my mouth wider. I'm finally experiencing the boy I've been dreaming about, and I'm lost in his taste, in his soft kisses, in his hunger for me. *Me.* Pulling back, he whispers into my mouth, "Of course, you taste like chocolate." His smile melts me further into a puddle.

A giggle escapes my lips, and my eyes grow wide in embarrassment. *I don't giggle*. "What just happened?"

He smiles again. "I'm pretty sure I kissed you. You want me to do it again just to make sure?"

Smacking him softly with my arm, I glare. "Don't joke around right now, Nate. Is this for real? Everything you just said. Am I dreaming?"

His eyebrows raise in surprise. "Is this something you dreamed about?" I let my eyes drift to the other side of the room, afraid to be honest. Nate pulls on my chin again, forcing me to meet his gaze. "Hey, don't do that. I just bared my soul to you. Wrote a song for you. Tell me the truth; is it all one-sided? Did I just ruin our friendship?"

I close my eyes, focusing on his touch, unable to lie to the only boy I've ever loved. "You could never ruin our friendship… and it *isn't* one-sided."

His face lights up. "Yeah?"

Easily, I smile again. "I feel the same way, Nate. Always have."

Nate pulls me against his chest, hugging me tightly. "Oh,

baby, I can't tell you how happy that makes me."

I cringe at the nickname. *Baby*. Yuck.

He must see my annoyance because he laughs. "Don't like the name? It sounded odd the second it came out. Sorry, Cookie."

I roll my eyes. "Yeah, I'm not crazy about that one either."

With his forehead against mine, he replies, "Too bad. You're my Cookie. My something sweet. So, unless you want me to call you sweetheart or *baby,* Cookie it is."

I sigh. "Why can't you just call me Amelia? That's my name, you know." He raises his eyes to me like a puppy dog begs for a damn cookie. There's that word again. Inward eye roll. "Fine, Pearson. But just because you kissed me and we're doing whatever it is we're doing does not mean I'm going to be calling you any cutesy nicknames. Understood?"

He laughs and places a quick kiss against my lips. It's surprising how quickly he's adopted this ability to kiss me. Like we've both accepted that this is what we do now. Before, we would cuddle in the alcove, and one day we started holding hands. And after the first time it wasn't weird, it was just something *we* did.

Apparently, now we kiss.

Nate raises his eyes to mine. "I wouldn't expect anything less from you, *Amelia*. Pearson it is. Or Nate. Because you know that's *my* name." I roll my eyes at him. He's so annoying. "So, what is it that we're doing?"

I practically shove him. Why is he acting like such a girl?

"Clearly, we are kissing. And hugging. And holding hands. What does it look like we're doing?"

He laughs again. "My feisty girl."

"*Your* feisty girl?" I cock my eye up at him in a dare.

Please say I'm your girl. Confirm it. I know I make it difficult, and I tease him relentlessly, but this is what we do, and I can't change me to be with him. I hope he's prepared.

He smiles wider. "Yeah, *my* feisty girl. You got a problem with that?"

I nuzzle into his chest and whisper, "No. I kind of like it."

"So, you going to tell me why you were upset before?"

Oh, I forgot about that.

Now that I feel completely justified in my anger, I let him have it. "Oh, you know, I just found out that you were *kissing* Heather last week at a party. A party I knew nothing about." My eyes are laser focused on his reaction. This is the first time I have had the right to get angry at him, and although I'd rather it not be five seconds after he just poured his heart out to me, it doesn't change that we need to deal with my feelings. Unfortunately, I have them no matter how much I try to act like the calm, cool chick when I'm around the boys.

Nate doesn't flinch, which I appreciate. "Your brother begged me not to tell you about it. Claire's parents were away, and he wanted to spend the night at her house after the party. I'm sorry."

Oh, Jack is so dead. I am totally telling my mother.

"You just gonna brush past the kiss accusation?"

Nate pulls me closer. "No. Heather kissed me. I tried to like it. Honestly, being in love with you isn't all it's cracked up to be. I had to face telling your brother, and I needed to know it was real before I pulled off that Band-Aid."

My mouth twitches. So many things were just said in that sentence. "Being in love with me isn't all it's cracked up to be?"

Yeah, we're going to start with that one.

Nate turns his head and looks at me like, *is this a serious question.* "Your brother is my best friend. *We* are best friends. Our families are best friends…and your dad is scary."

I mean I didn't get this glare from my mom. My dad *is* scary. Although in this situation I would think Jack is the one to fear.

"So, you kissed Heather."

"Yes. And the whole time, I was thinking about you. Which is why the next day I took your brother out to lunch and told him how I felt."

My eyes almost bug out. "You talked to Jack already?" This isn't the 1600s. Neither my brother nor my father determine whether *I* am interested in a boy. Whether *I* want to date a boy. Obviously, my face shows my anger because Nate palms his face nervously.

"Before you freak, just hear me out. Obviously, Jack doesn't get to decide whether you date me. *You* decide that. But I felt I owed him the truth. He's been my best friend since we were in diapers."

Love & Tequila Make Her Crazy

I guess that's fair. "Well, how did he take it?" I can only imagine that Jack had quite a lot to say about this topic.

"He said he's glad I finally realized what everyone else knew years ago, that he'll kill me if I hurt you, and that he wished me well because you weren't going to make this easy." Nate smiles and raises his eyebrows at me. I bite my lip to hide my own grin. That is not at all what I expected Jack to say. Speechless, I faceplant against his chest. "Still mad at me?" he whispers into my hair.

I shake my head. "From now on I'm the only girl you kiss, right?"

Without hesitation, he lifts my chin up and makes an insane promise. "Forever."

CHAPTER 7

Amelia

As soon as I said the words, "I'm not your home," I swear my heart broke a little. Why is this so hard? It's been almost three years since I last laid eyes on that man, two years since I finally got up the courage to ask for a divorce, and a year since I recognized that it was time to move on and try dating.

After a few lackluster dates I decided to put that on the backburner. Watching my brother Jack with his fiancée, Charlotte—and hearing about her disastrous dating stories—made me realize that I didn't just want to *date*, I wanted the real thing.

Although I'll never admit it, I think I just decided to shelve the idea of dating because I'm still broken from Nate.

How is that possible? How after three years am I still broken?

Correction. Two and a half years. For the last few months, I had started to finally feel like myself again.

Working at the flower shop with Karen was the first step. In Nashville I'd owned an old Volkswagen Beetle Van. Nate painted the words "Amelia's Flowers" in beautiful pastel colors on its sides, helping me create my own little business. He would help me in the early mornings, then nap during the day until it was time for one of his many gigs. We had this perfect little life, until we didn't.

Leaving Nashville, my van, my business, and Nate had been the hardest decision I'd ever made. When Karen said she was opening a flower shop this year I was jealous. It was exactly what our town needed, and I hadn't even realized it. She asked if I could help her get the store up and running, and somehow in doing that, I started to heal. I finally started feeling like *me* again.

Right when life was finally starting to settle, and I was busy enough to at least numb the loss of the man who had always been my home, he walks back into my life and sets my world on fire.

"Dammit!" I throw the lemon I've been trying to slice for tonight's crowd. It's a foggy day, and the sun never came out. Perfectly fitting for my mood.

Hailey walks into the bar and the skin on her forehead creases as she stares me down. "Can you stop murdering the lemons?"

In defiance, I stab my knife into the next lemon. "Don't test me today."

She laughs, walking over with her hands up in the air, and takes the knife out of my hand gently. "Take the night off."

My defenses rear up. I *cannot* stop moving. That would give me too much time to think, and I *cannot* think right now. "I'm good. I won't murder any more fruit." I manage to give her a smile which only makes her more concerned.

"You're going to scare away the customers with that face. Please go home. Or go out. Honestly, I really don't care what you do, but you're not staying here."

Although I'm prepared to argue, my buzzing phone steals my attention. As soon as I see it's my cousin Belle, I put it on speaker. "Hey, Belle, what's up?"

"I need you. I'm in deep." She laughs like a crazy person, and my ears perk up. Finally, I can focus on someone else's disaster.

"Just tell me what you need."

In the background, Hailey screams, "She's on her way. I'm sending her home." I roll my eyes, throw my apron on the counter, and flip her the bird. She laughs and waves me off.

"Am I meeting you at the nursing home?" I ask as I walk to my car, waving at the cook as I walk out. He seems to mimic a question as to where I'm going, and I point upstairs to Hailey and act as if I've been guillotined. Let Hailey explain how she fired me. That should keep her busy for a while.

Belle groans. "No. I need you to meet me at the golf range. You know how to golf, right?"

"You are seriously turning into an old lady. First you move into that place and now you want to golf."

Belle moved into a fifty-five and over community accidentally. It's something that happens to her often—she accidentally does really ridiculous things, and I absolutely love teasing her about it.

Love & Tequila Make Her Crazy

Belle laughs. "Just stop. I can't handle your teasing right now. I need you to meet me at the golf range and teach me. So please, oh wise one, my favorite cousin, *the prettiest one of us all*, agree to help me."

Oh, she's laying it on thick.

"Fine," I say as I walk to my apartment to change. I live next to the restaurant. I scored an awesome apartment when I started working with Karen. It's right above the shop, and I believe I have Karen to thank for that as well. She knew I needed out of my parents' house last year. I think everyone could see I was spiraling. She said she knew the owner, and she was able to negotiate a great monthly rent for me. She's one of the few people who knew about Nate's and my marriage, and although I never told her why we got divorced, I'm sure Nate did. Even though I was no longer her daughter-in-law, she helped me, which leaves me unbelievably grateful.

Well, until this week that is. Now she's also on my not-so-nice list. Not quite on the shit one though. That one is solely reserved for her son.

Belle squeals into the phone, "Thank you! You're the best. Okay, I'll meet you there in a half hour."

"You're buying me dinner after," I say before I hang up. I hear her screech "of course" as I toss my phone onto my couch and start peeling off my uniform. My eyes grow wide when I realize that my curtains aren't pulled shut. My apartment sits almost directly behind the bar, and my view looks at the upstairs deck and the bay beyond. Shawn is working behind the bar—Hailey must have called him in to cover my shift—and sitting at the bar, looking awfully chummy, is none other than my ex-husband. As if they can feel my eyes on them, they turn at the same time. Nate's eyes narrow as if he's trying to figure out if I'm real and then they practically double when he confirms that I am in fact naked.

Naked in my living room with a wide-open window wasn't the smartest thing I've ever done. Shawn smiles—he's used to my crazy—and Nate's jaw tightens. Shawn is in for a world of trouble. I wave and Shawn laughs. Then I grab my phone quickly and shoot Shawn a text.

Me: Told Nate you're my boyfriend. Play along for me please. I'll owe you big!

Shawn reaches into his pocket, and I see him read my text. He shakes his head, smiles, and nods back at me. That will definitely piss Nate off even more. Now he thinks we're exchanging cute messages while I'm naked. I bite back a smile imagining a jealous Nate.

It shouldn't make me this happy. I shouldn't feel this alive. *He* shouldn't be able to conjure any of these feelings anymore. But unfortunately, he does.

Scurrying into my bedroom, I grab a pair of shorts and a T-shirt, then make my way into the bathroom to check out my makeup and pull down my hair. At work I always keep it up. It looks more professional. Having it pulled back gives me horrible migraines though, so the second I can, I always pull my almost-white locks down and shake out my hair to give it some volume. Unlike my cousin who has full, long, absolutely drool-worthy hair, mine is cut to my shoulders and thin. Any volume I give it will likely disappear in the heat, but it's better than doing nothing.

Grabbing my phone and keys as I head out the door, I see a text from Shawn.

Shawn: Your boy is not happy. Pretty sure he's going to break a tooth from clenching his jaw so tight. I hope you know what you're doing.

Rolling my eyes and twisting my lips, I hum to myself. Yeah, I have no idea what I'm doing. But knowing he's as miserable as I am is a consolation.

Me: He's not my boy. You are. ;)

Shawn: Haha. Whatever you say. You better give Charlotte and Jack a heads-up before they blow it for you.

Me: Jack and Nate don't talk. I think we're safe.

Shawn: Okay. Have fun tonight. And close your curtains, you're getting Old Earl here too excited at the bar.

I laugh to myself thinking of the toothless man. His grin is creepy enough. I definitely don't want to picture him smiling at me while I'm naked. A chill runs down my spine, and I do a little nervous dance in the hall. While I'm happy I gave Nate a show tonight, I'll make sure to avoid doing that again.

Being back at the driving range is surprisingly more difficult than I remember. Not the actual swinging of the club—that part is like riding a bike. Every time my club hits the tiny ball from muscle memory it sails, and I feel the same sense of euphoria I did in high school when Nate, Jack, and Peter used to bring me to play. It was always the four of us. Especially after Nate and I started dating. Jack could no longer claim I was following him; everyone just accepted that I was following Nate. Or more accurately put, Nate was bringing me with him because he never wanted to do anything without me. Man, how times have changed.

Belle, on the other hand, can't hit the ball to save her life. And she is the one who actually needs to. She got herself into a bit of a pickle by accepting a job she's not qualified for, and somehow golf is the answer to keeping the job. How it involves golf I'm still not sure, but I'd rather focus on anything other than Nate, so I'm trying to help.

"Belle, you really need to angle your body toward the ball and not toward the net." I step behind her and angle her again, but as soon as she hits the ball she goes right back into the wrong stance.

"Okay. I'm seriously terrible at this," Belle says as I swing and send my ball into the distance again. "Way to make me feel even worse."

Shrugging, I say, "I used to play with Jack, Peter, and Nate."

Dropping her club, Belle walks over and takes me in her arms. "Sorry, Ames. I know you still miss him."

I'm not used to having someone touch me. It sets off an emotional roller coaster that I've been biting down since I first saw Nate again. Honesty pours from my lips. "I miss them both."

I never told anyone why Nate and I broke up. Hell, I never told my family Nate and I were married. We did it on such a whim. Or at least that's what I tell myself now. At the time none of it felt spontaneous. It felt like something I needed as much as my next breath. Becoming his wife was the only role I ever knew without a doubt I wanted to play.

At the time, my brother and Peter were in the Air Force. With them overseas, we wanted to wait for a big wedding, but we didn't want to wait to become husband and wife. Tragically, Peter died and then our marriage crumbled. I quietly slunk back to town, divorced Nate, and acted as if we'd just drifted apart. Plenty of high school sweethearts break up. I'm sure my family wondered, but Belle never pushed, so I never explained. I never broke down. Oddly, I feel dangerously close to breaking down now.

Part of me wants to confess everything. I want to tell my family about my marriage, how we got divorced, *the reason that we got divorced*, and the fact that I'm now a divorced woman whose ex-husband is back in town and making me reconsider everything. But I don't even know how to start the conversation.

As if she can sense that I'm going to cry, and unaware how to handle it since that isn't an emotion I express freely, Belle changes tactics. "Okay. So, teaching me to golf is obviously a bad idea."

No. Hugging me was a bad idea, but I'll let her think it was the golf.

"Why don't we go grab a beer?" she offers.

To break the tension, I laugh. "You need to learn to golf to keep this job, right?"

Shrugging, she gives me a devilish look. "I've still got my looks. If all else fails, I'll charm them with my hips."

She certainly does have her looks.

"I could go for a beer. But I also want to hit something. How about the batting cages?" Picturing Nate's head as the ball speeding toward me is precisely what I need.

"Put me in, coach!" my cousin screams.

Oh, she's so not athletic. This might be a disaster. Shaking my head, I put my arm around my cousin as we walk. "You are going to need so much help. So. Much. Help."

Hours later as I lie in bed replaying the last few days, I can't help but cringe again at my words to Nate. When things ended, we never so much as fought. I stormed out and when I came back, he was gone, and we never saw each other again. Our decades-long friendship was over in a matter of minutes, our twelve-year love affair tossed out to sea, and our brand-new marriage nothing but a memory. He promised me forever and then he didn't even make a backward glance in my direction when he left.

Nate

Hating how things ended with Amelia on the boat this afternoon, I decide to stop by the bar to apologize. I just want her to know that I'm sorry. That I'm not here to make her life harder, and if she wants to pretend she's dating Shawn, I'll give her that satisfaction for a while. In the end I know Amelia and I are what forever is made of. We got sidetracked, and our pride got in the way of happiness, but I'm not going to let that happen again.

As I sit down at the bar, Shawn looks at me with a pensive face. Maybe they really are dating? Why does the guy look so nervous? *Fuck.*

"Hey, Nate is it?" he asks as he puts a napkin in front of me.

I extend my hand to shake his. "Yeah. Is Amelia working tonight?"

He shakes my hand. "Nope. Hailey sent her home. She was apparently doing a number on our fruit."

Cocking my brow, I try to figure out if that is a literal thing or if she figuratively was having a problem.

He laughs when he sees my clear confusion. "The lemons didn't stand a chance." He picks one up and tosses it on the bar. I see the stab marks throughout.

Chuckling, I pick it up. "Yeah, I'll have to apologize to the poor lemon. I'm pretty sure she was picturing me when she did this."

Closing my eyes, I wince again at the memory of her words. *I'm not your home and you aren't mine.*

"Don't sweat it. We've all been on the wrong side of Amelia's wrath. Just be happy you didn't catch her with her flower shears; those things can be deadly."

He laughs again and his familiarity with my wife leaves me feeling all sorts of anxious. His eyes flash, and I turn to see what he's looking at. I'm not sure what I expect to find, but Amelia's naked frame in the window never factored into the equation. My eyes grow wide, taking in every inch of the body I've missed these last few years. She is far enough away that I have to squint, and then I feel shitty for doing it when Amelia clearly has no idea we're watching.

We.

My head snaps back to Shawn just in time to see him look at his phone, laugh, and look back at my wife with a smile.

Did she do this intentionally? Grant him a peep show as a preview of what's to come? Amelia was never shy with her body, but I also thought that had more to do with us being each other's firsts. Our one and onlys. The idea that this man has touched her in that way makes me want to take the bottle sitting on the bar and throw it.

I did this to us. I'm the one to blame. Somehow knowing that doesn't change the outcome though. I'm miserable, and my wife is apparently screwing the guy sitting across from me. Before I lose my shit, I offer him a curt nod and leave the bar. While I'd love to stalk over to her apartment and give her a piece of my mind, I know that won't end well either. I lost that right years ago. So instead I text Jack and head to Aiden's to wait for him.

"Man, you look like you might kill someone right about now." Jack slaps me on the back at the bar, and I grimace before remembering how long it's been since I last saw my best friend and get up to clap him on the back in a burly man hug.

"Your sister has me a bit off-kilter, but man am I happy to see you." Jack hugs me back and then we both sit down at the bar, giving each other a once-over and smiling. "You look good."

Jack smirks. "Just because you can't get one Fitzpatrick in bed doesn't mean you have a shot at me."

Through gritted teeth, I say, "She ain't a Fitzpatrick anymore."

Jack laughs and slaps me on the back. "Yeah, try telling her that. I'm all caught up on your bullshit." He eyes the beer in my hand, and I stiffen. "You good now?"

I nod once. "I know I put you through a lot of shit over the years, but I'm not the same guy I was."

Jack winces, and I know, like me, he is returning to the past. The months after Amelia left when I spiraled out of control. When alcohol and fights were all I had to get me through every day. "You saved my life," I say to him.

"So, you're not worried about a relapse?" he asks honestly.

I meet his eyes. "I'm good, Jack. I got the help I needed because of you. I'm not an alcoholic; I was drowning in depression. Alcohol was just how I coped. Right now, I'm not coping, I'm living. I promise."

Jack nods once, seemingly accepting that I have worked through my demons. If not for him, I'd probably be dead or in jail right now, so I understand his concern. "Well, if that changes, I have a friend, Kyle, who owns a tattoo shop in town. He's also a therapist. He was in the service too." He slips out his wallet and hands me a card with the tattoo artist's information.

Jack knows the significance of my ink. I swallow my pride and thank him. As much as I'd like to believe I have everything under control, it doesn't hurt to have support. In fact, it's what I learned was necessary over the last few years away from Amelia. She was the one person who supported me my entire life until she couldn't.

Needing to find out the truth about Amelia's relationship,

I change the subject. "So, this brother-in-law of yours, is he a good guy?"

Before Jack can respond, the bartender approaches and asks if he wants a beer. Jack orders a Guinness and then looks at the menu, seemingly ignoring my question. I take the menu out of his hand, motion to the waitress, and order us both burgers with fries. The fries here are crispy potato wedge-like chips. In New England you eat them with salt and malted vinegar. It's the epitome of a perfect pub dinner.

Jack doesn't object, instead shrugging to acknowledge that he doesn't mind my ordering for us both. "Which brother-in-law? The one next to me can be quite a dickhead, but I still like him."

Narrowing my eyes, I watch for his reaction. "The one who is currently sleeping with your sister. *Not* me."

Jack's jaw drops open and then he scratches his face. "Yeah, I feel like I'm walking into a trap here. If I answer one way, you'll kill me. If I answer another way, Amelia will kill me. So, I'm going to plead the fifth for the time being."

So much for childhood friendship. I guess I can appreciate his concern about getting on Amelia's bad side, though. I'd been living on it for quite a while, and it isn't fun. "How 'bout you just go with the truth. What do you think of Shawn?"

Jack relaxes his shoulders. "Great guy. Moved here a few months ago, after the engagement. Come to think of it, that was when he first met Ames. Shit, I never put two and two together. Charlotte will be thrilled." He goes to text his fiancée, and my hand slams over his. This chummy chummy shit ends now.

"She's my *wife*, Jack. My goddamn wife." My heart feels like it's going to explode.

Jack shakes his head. "Then get your head out of your damn ass and win her back."

I run my hand over my face and watch Jack's eyes trail the ink on my arm. "I'm fucking trying, but it seems like she's already moving on. I need you to find out if this is real. If she really likes this guy. If she does, I'll back off. I don't want to make things hard for her again. I know I caused all this shit… everything…I lost everything…"

Jack's arm falls onto my back, and he squeezes, pulling his head close to mine. "You didn't do this. You both did. You got in a fight. It was a damn misunderstanding, and if not for the fact that all of us were messed up over Peter's death, it would have been a blip in this thing we call marriage. Unfortunately, it all spiraled out of control. But you got the help you needed. In the end, you're back and you're going to make it right. Let yourself off the hook."

His words are so undeserved. I did this. I destroyed us. But he isn't wrong that it started from a stupid fight. In the end though, everything is my fault.

"Fuck, I miss him."

Jack leans back in his chair and sips his beer. "Me too, man. Me too. But we're still here. And it would have killed Peter to know that you and Ames broke up because of his death."

Love & Tequila Make Her Crazy

My hand pulls on my face. "I don't know how to make it right. I know what I want. I know I could make her happy. We were so damn happy in Nashville, Jack. I wish you coulda seen us. We were good."

Jack smiles and tilts back in his chair. "I don't doubt it. You were always good. Which is why I never begrudged you falling for my little sister. Even after everything that has happened, I don't blame you, Nate. I know why it went wrong. *I* get it. But that's because I'm as fucked up as you. I was just as destroyed from his death. And you lost more than I did."

The unspoken name lies between us. My father. I lost my father, and Peter and Jack joined the Air Force because it was what they could do to help. They couldn't make me better like Amelia could, but they could do that. Which is why all of this is my damn fault. Peter's death. The end of my marriage. It's all because everyone was constantly trying to make things better for me.

"Shit, I just want to take care of her, Jack. I want to pay you all back for what you've done for me. I want to be worth it." Emotion stings my eyes, and my chest closes up.

Jack looks at me with a pointed stare. "Shut the fuck up. *Seriously.* I love you, man, but you are not the only reason that Peter and I did what we did. And Peter sure as fuck didn't die because of you. Or me for that matter. It took me a long time to come to terms with that, and I'm not going back down that spiraling hell of self-loathing. Prove her wrong. Show her you're worth it. Show her you're not going to disappear. *Stay* and prove her wrong."

I gulp, trying to hear his words. Trying to believe them.

Jack continues. "Listen, Charlotte and I didn't have an easy start. It was rocky. And the only way I was able to win her over was through proving to her that I wasn't going anywhere. Being honest with her. I needed to stop running. And so do you, buddy. Because unfortunately we were both running from the same thing. And it nearly cost me my chance at happiness, and I'll be damned if I let the same thing happen to you. You've always been like a brother to me. Be my brother. Marry my sister."

I offer a weak smile. "I am married to your sister."

"Yeah, well, you gotta be honest about that too. As Ricky would say, 'Lucy, you got a lot of 'splaining to do.' So, get to it."

His words run through my head as the waitress places our food in front of us. Everything he says is true. And although I don't have everything worked out, I do have some of it handled. Unfortunately, I have to play the long game and be patient. Not something I'm exactly great at, but considering I waited two years before sleeping with the love of my life, I'm pretty sure this should be a piece of cake.

Or not.

CHAPTER 8

Amelia
Seventeen Years Old

"I'm so nervous." I spray my perfume on and apply a light gloss onto my lips. Making a kissing noise, I blow one into the mirror, ensuring my pout is prepared for my big ask.

My cousin Belle stares back at me in the mirror and rolls her eyes. "You've been dating for two years. You think he'd say no to going to prom with you? Please." Her black hair swings as she shakes her head, and her blue eyes tell me she thinks I'm being unnecessarily dramatic. Which I never am, so clearly she's wrong.

"He's in college, Belle. He's a nineteen-year-old college man. Why would he want to go to prom in the town where he graduated last year?"

Belle laughs, swinging that luscious hair of hers again. "He's not a man. He's a college boy. He's nineteen, and he laughs when Jack talks about farting and plays PlayStation with Peter. He's barely a step above a middle schooler. He'd be lucky to go to prom with you."

Damn, I knew there was a reason why I kept her around. Hugging her close, I squeeze her and then push her out of my room. "Love you, now go! He's going to be here any minute."

On cue my mother yells up to us both, "Nate's here."

She still doesn't let him come into my room. We've known each other since we were toddlers. I've literally spent more nights sleeping next to him than anyone in my life. Granted, it was on the boat when no one else knew, but seriously, if we haven't had sex by now I think it's safe to say he can enter my room unaccompanied. I bound down the steps and roll my eyes at my mom. "You're so embarrassing, Mom."

She looks up at me affronted. "Nice to see you too. Belle, honey, can you tell your mom I'll see her at Bingo tonight?"

I eye my mother. "*See,* embarrassing."

"Oh, you just wait, girls, one day the big event will be Bingo on a Friday night."

Belle laughs and I grunt. "Yeah, fat chance." Tossing my mom a kiss on the cheek, I run outside to meet Nate in his car. "Woah, what happened to your hair?" I skim my fingers across his head before even saying hello. His beautiful brown locks are missing, and his head is shaved just like Jack and Peter's. For them it makes sense since they're in ROTC. "Is this like a sympathy cut?"

Nate laughs and leans over to kiss me, then he pulls the seatbelt across my lap and straps me in. It's like he thinks I don't take care of myself or something. "A sympathy cut?"

"Or jealous of the boys?" I narrow my eyes. I don't want Nate to get any crazy ideas and go join the boys when they go into the Air Force. Having to worry about my brother doing that is bad enough.

He shakes his head. "I've been told it looks hot."

I fold my arms across my chest. "By whom?"

Daring him to mention any college girls, or really anyone at all, I hold his eyes captive. "*Grant*. He says it's good for the band."

Rolling my eyes, I point to the wheel. "Drive."

Taking the wheel in one hand, he squeezes my thigh with the other. "You look gorgeous, babe. Where to?"

Forgetting about my momentary annoyance, I practically bounce in my seat. "The boat. Where else?"

I need his body against mine immediately. Just because we haven't had sex yet doesn't mean we haven't done other things. And I'm running out of patience. I'm not even sure why we're waiting. We both love each other. We said I love you the first day we got together. We're meant to be together. What are we waiting for?

Nate smiles at my obvious excitement. "Take it you've been missing me?"

"You're so annoying." I bite my lip and look out the window.

We arrive in front of Nate's house within seconds since he only lives a few houses down. He'd just come from campus which is almost an hour away. I hate the distance. For most of our lives he was only a hop, skip, and jump away whenever I wanted him.

Nate rounds the car and opens my door, grabbing my hand in his own to sneak me down to the docks before his mom or Sam can see us. Her new boyfriend is here almost as much as I am. I'm not sure how Nate feels about it, but I don't want to ruin tonight by asking.

With my hand in his, precisely where it belongs, we duck down and run, laughing once we make it past the windows and onto the dock. Throwing both of our shoes aboard, he hurries me into the boat's cabin, toward the big bed. We no longer need to sleep in the alcove. Sam and Mrs. Pearson don't use the boat. It's Nate's. His mom told him he could live on it for all she cared, she just knew that his dad would want it to be his, and he would want it to be used.

Nate's lips are on mine as soon as we breach the door. I'm pawing at his shirt, slipping it over his head, and he does the same to mine. "Oh, babe, you look gorgeous." He's finally stopped calling me Cookie, and we've settled on babe. It's a thousand times better in my personal opinion. He only pulls Cookie out when he wants to drive me nuts. It backfires if he uses it while we're in bed. Not cute to remind me of our middle school years.

His teeth brush against my nipple, and I sigh in pain. A pleasurable pain. "Pants, Nate. Take off your pants."

He struggles to get out of his jeans as I slip mine down.

Finally, with only our underwear left, we fall onto the bed, tangling together. Rubbing against him, I work us into an almost insurmountable frenzy, so close to both hurtling over the edge. "Nate, I want you inside of me." I whisper the words, pleading with him to finally give in. "Make love to me."

Nate stills and pulls back a bit. He lifts his hand to my face and runs his fingers over my jaw. "Amelia, I love you."

I moan. "I love you too. Please, fuck me, Nate."

His eyes grow dark. "The first time we're together, I will not be fucking you."

I close my eyes. I love the man who cherishes me more than I can express, but in this moment, I just want him to look at me like a woman. Like someone he fantasizes about and can't keep his hands off. "*Nate, please.*"

He leans up and kisses me softly. "What's going on? I want this too, but this feels like it's about something more than just that."

Groaning, I slide off him. The moment is over. I feel humiliated. I just want my boyfriend to want to have sex with me. Is that asking too much? I know he loves me, but I'm starting to wonder if he actually *wants* me. What's with the haircut? Is he trying to be hot for someone else?

My mind spins, and I bite on my cheek, aware that I'm spiraling. I shift my head onto the pillow and face away from him, not wanting him to see the insecurity which racks my face. Nate wraps his arm around me, pulling my ass close to him, and shifts his chin onto my shoulder. "Babe, talk to me. What's going on?"

He presses a kiss to my neck, and I feel my resolve weakening.

"It's nothing. I just want to have sex."

He chuckles against my neck. "Same, babe, same. But we've waited this long. I don't want to do it in the heat of the moment. I want to make it special. I want to take you out. Wine and dine you. Make you feel treasured. I want both of our first times to be perfect, Amelia, because to me you are perfect."

My chest relaxes at his words, the nervous feeling releases its hold on my heart, and I am finally able to breathe. I turn into his arms and kiss his chest. "I love you too. I'm sorry. You're right, it's both of our first times. We need to make it special. I'm sorry I got carried away."

He tips my chin up. "Don't ever apologize for wanting me too much." He kisses me softly on my lips. "I think about having sex with you every damn minute of the day. It makes me happy to know you want me even half as much."

I let out an exasperated laugh. "I thought maybe you didn't want me anymore. Now that you're in college, in a band, with a new haircut. I don't know. I know you love me, but I mean, I get it—everything else is new and shiny and you deserve to experience life." I choke on my words, hating how desperate I sound, and hating that I actually believe they may be true.

Nate sits us both up and looks me in the eye. "Amelia, do you remember what I told you after our first kiss?" I puff out a sigh and look at the ceiling. "Look at me." He pulls my chin toward him again and rubs his thumb softly against me, bringing me right back to our first kiss. "Do you remember?"

I shrug.

"I promised you forever. *Forever, Amelia.* You are the only girl I ever want to kiss. You're the only girl I ever want to be inside. You, Amelia, have my heart. My soul. You have everything. You're my home. Hear me?"

Tears stream down my cheeks. I never cry. But like every other emotion in the book, I save them for Nate. I crash against his chest. "Will you go to prom with me?"

His chest rumbles as he laughs. "Is this what all these emotions are about? You were nervous to ask me to prom?"

I hate how well he knows me. And I love it too. I nod. "Yes. I understand if you don't want to come. I can just go with friends, and we can meet up after if you'd prefer."

Nate smiles now, a wide smile, and I see the glint in his eyes. He has a plan. "Or, and hear me out, we could go to prom together. I could wine and dine you, show you off to everyone. Let them see how beautiful my girl is. And then we could come back here, and I'll finally get to lose my virginity at prom." He raises his brows to me in a conspiratorial manner.

I can't help but laugh. "Oh, that's so cliché. Losing your virginity at prom. Seriously, Nate Pearson?"

"Be cliché with me. Give me everything I've ever wanted. My girl. Prom night. Forever."

"Okay, Nate Pearson. I'll go to prom with you."

"That wasn't my question."

I laugh again. "Oh, Pearson, you want forever?"

He nods with the biggest smile on his face.

"Forever is yours."

Nate
Nineteen

I've never been so nervous in my damn life. Amelia walks down the steps wearing a white jumpsuit which dips dangerously between her breasts. Not a dress. Not something frilly. It leaves her legs looking impossibly long, her cleavage teasing me, and my dick swollen in my suit. To top it all off she's wearing red lipstick on her lips and a smile.

A brilliant, teasing, excited smile that hints at what's to come once prom is over.

Why did I decide tonight was the night? I should have taken her to a hotel months ago and gotten this over with. This is too much pressure. What if I only last a minute? What if I hurt her? Why am I spiraling?

At least Jack and Peter aren't here to witness my complete assholery.

Amelia's eyes meet mine. "Do I look alright?"

Fuck. I'm already failing. "Dammit babe, you look so beautiful I lost my words. I'm sorry." I kiss her gently on the lips, and she wipes the red from mine when we pull apart.

Squeezing my hand, she says, "I love you," calming me instantly.

This is Amelia. It's going to be fine. Screw that, it will be more than fine. It will be perfect.

"I love you too, baby." She cringes at the word and I laugh. "Sorry, I love you, *babe*."

"Just don't call me Cookie tonight and we'll be fine." She walks off before I have a chance to respond, and I shake my head and laugh. She's got me wrapped around her damn finger. Always has.

With my hand around her waist while we take pictures, I use my thumb to rub circles against her hip. She teases me by pushing her ass flush against me, wiggling when no one is looking. I brush a hand across her nipple, and she leans her head back and moans softly.

Before we get into the limo, she whispers in my ear to keep my hands to myself unless I plan on skipping the dance.

"Don't have to ask me twice," I quip without thinking.

Amelia's face registers her disappointment. "We can skip if you want," she says quietly. Damn, I'm an ass. She wants to go to prom. So much so that she was nervous about asking me.

I force her to look at me while the rest of the couples chat loudly. "I want to dance with my girl. I want to show you off.

Then, and only then, do I want to take you to bed. Sorry, I got ahead of myself."

She gifts me one of her quiet smiles, the ones she reserves for just me. "I'm excited too, Nate."

At prom we dance closely to all the slow songs, our bodies glued to one another, our lips offering gentle kisses, and when the music gets loud we sneak to the corner where our table sits, and she sits on my lap and we talk.

We are in our own bubble. We might as well be in the alcove. She's the only one that exists in this world for me.

Long before the dance is over, Amelia asks if we can leave. Thinking ahead, I had left my car at the venue so we're not stuck waiting for her friends.

On the way back to the boat, Amelia is quiet. Although she holds my hand while I drive, her eyes are focused out her window.

"I had a good time tonight," I say nervously, trying to break the ice. I'm not sure why I feel so nervous. This is Amelia. The girl I've loved since before I knew what love was.

Squeezing my hand, she murmurs, "Me too."

I roll the windows down, needing fresh air like I need to breathe. Amelia turns to look at me just as she unclips her hair, and it flows freely, dancing in the wind.

My heart slams into my chest. This girl, my girl, is the most beautiful creature I've ever seen. Heartstoppingly beautiful. It's impossible that I will ever feel this way for anyone else.

I know we're young. I know everyone says we've never

so much as dated someone else, or held hands with someone else, but I know without a doubt she's my soulmate. I think my dad knew it too. Losing him so young makes it so that the ridiculously limited conversations we did have are all engrained in my memory. I don't have years of tape to roll through. Just a few short years which will never be enough. But during that time he imparted more wisdom than most men do in their lifetimes, because he spent every minute he wasn't with my mom or at work, with me.

In all those moments, he was teaching me how to be a good man, how to treat a woman, how to drive a boat, to empty the trash, to mow the grass, to hold a woman's hand in the way he held my mom's, to cherish a woman, like he cherished my mom. And just like I remember all those things, I also distinctly recall how my dad said, *one day this girl*…and he stopped and shook his head. He couldn't tell me at nine that she was it for me, but I think he could tell there was something between us even then.

It's like she was made for me, and there was never a moment in our lives that we weren't working toward this moment. Knowing that our relationship has my dad's blessing, that he loved Amelia like a daughter, makes me sure that she's the one for me.

"Amelia, I love you. Thank you for taking me to prom."

Smiling, Amelia's mood shifts and she leans into me. "I'm more excited about being with you than some silly dance."

I raise my eyebrows to her. "Hm, you seemed quite excited

for some silly dance, Cookie."

Her eyes narrow. "Don't ruin the moment."

Chuckling, I squeeze her thigh. "Sorry, babe. It's a big night for us. Had to get one in."

She rolls her eyes. "Are you nervous?"

We reach a stoplight, and I give her my full attention. "Yes and no. Nervous in the sense that I want it to be perfect for you. Not in a way that I have any doubts."

"Nate, it will be perfect because it's *us*."

See, this is why she's perfect. My shoulders relax, and I kiss her quickly before the light turns green.

As we pull up to my house, I squeeze her leg. "Wait here," I say before hopping out and running to her side to open the door. Her smile grows even wider.

"Nate Pearson, you are too cute."

Sheepishly, I smile. Not necessarily what I was going for, but I'll take it. The lights in my house are dark which means we don't need to run fast past the windows. Not that my mom doesn't know that we use the boat. Hell, most nights that's where I sleep when I'm home from college rather than my room. But for some reason it would feel like we were doing something wrong if we had to run past the windows tonight.

I want to take my time, hold Amelia's hand, and walk slowly to our spot. To the place where we first held hands, to the spot where she held me through my worst hours, where we shared our first kiss, and so many other firsts after that. It's only fitting that this is where I would bring her the first time we make love. Honestly, if I could figure a way to marry the girl on this boat one day, I would.

Earlier, I had snaked twinkling lights around the bow and down below in the cabin. As we walk down, she breathes in, taking in the view of the moon over the dark bay. The dock and boat are lit up from the twinkling lights. Amelia stills. "Nate, what did you do?"

I wink at her. "Shh, babe, just wait until you see what I've got planned for you." Pulling her into my arms, I bring my lips to hers, bending her slightly so that I'm in complete control, pushing my tongue into her mouth, tasting her, memorizing everything about this moment. The way she smells like cocoa, the feel of her soft skin, her hair blowing around us in the breeze, and the sounds she makes as our kiss deepens.

I pull away before I take her on the grass, and we continue walking to the boat. On the dock, I hold out my hand to her so she can balance as she takes off her heels. Then she steps onto the boat like a pro, and I hear her sigh as she sees the surprises I left for her.

"Chocolate-covered strawberries, Nate?"

I know my girl is excited now. "And champagne," I say, pointing to the bottle chilling in the sink.

She wrinkles her nose. "I've got a few surprises in store for you too." She ducks around the corner into the alcove and disappears. Listening, I hear her shimmying around in there and almost peek in to see if she needs help. Before I have the chance, she scoots out, and my tongue practically hits the floor. White lace lingerie covers her pink nipples and holds her breasts up high. It hugs her curves, and leaves her legs looking like they are eight feet long. I run my hands over my head, trying to control myself, begging myself not to come just at the sight of her.

Groaning, I walk to her, pulling her into my arms. "Babe, I'm never going to last with you in this outfit."

She raises her brows suggestively. "Then I guess we'll just have to take it off pretty quickly."

I shake my head. I want her naked, but I also want her in this. I can't decide what I want more. My fingers trail over the fabric, and her nipple pebbles against my hand. Lowering my lips to her breasts, I bite down, pulling her pert nipple into my mouth. She hisses in pain.

"Too many clothes, Nate."

Quickly, I slip off my black jacket and throw it to the side. Amelia unbuttons my shirt, and I begin undoing my pants. My hand attaches to her ass, and I squeeze her closer to me so she can feel how hard I am for her. "See what you do to me? I can't believe I'll finally get to feel you." My forehead meets hers. "Amelia, I love you so damn much."

She takes my hand and moves it between her legs. The lingerie is wet to the touch. "See what *you* do to *me*."

Unable to wait another second, I pick her up and walk us to the bed. After plopping her down, I walk over to open the

Love & Tequila Make Her Crazy

champagne. She watches in silence as I pop the bottle—expertly may I add—and pour the cool liquid into two champagne flutes I stole from inside the house. Handing her one, I meet her eyes and clink our glasses. "To forever."

She smiles. "Forever." We both take a sip, and it burns my throat on the way down. I've had beer in college, but this is something else. Not exactly expected but not bad either.

Unlike me, Amelia chugs it like a champ and then pops up to grab a strawberry. She bites down and moans when she tastes the milky chocolate. I was smart enough not to try to make them and bought the strawberries from her favorite bakery instead.

She offers me the other bite of her strawberry, and I take it, nipping at her fingers when I do. The mixture of the chocolate, champagne, strawberry, and Amelia leaves me almost dizzy.

"New rule," Amelia says, an excited glint in her eyes. I raise mine to hers waiting for her to tell me what to do. She wins. She controls everything. She can set whatever damn rule she wants. "Whenever we have sex, you need to buy me champagne and strawberries."

I don't even blink. "Done."

She laughs. "I'm just teasing, Nate. I just need you."

Pulling her close, I whisper into her mouth. "Babe, I'll give you whatever you damn want. This fridge will never not be stocked with strawberries and champagne. Mark my words."

She pushes me onto the bed and straddles me as she lays kisses across my chest. "You spoil me."

"Always." Flipping her over, I don't give her a second to react before I'm between her thighs and pushing apart her lips for me, making her legs shake almost instantaneously. We may not have had sex before this, but I've spent plenty of nights exploring this girl's body. I know what she likes and what sends her over the edge. Her hand moves to my head, and she controls my movements.

When it comes to me, she's always in control.

I pull away and sip my champagne and then bring my cool lips to her warm center, and she hisses again and pushes harder against my tongue. "That's right, babe, ride my face." With my other hand, I hold her nipple between my fingers, squeezing and pinching as I feel her body start to fall apart.

"Oh, Nate, I'm not going to last," she cries out as she pulses against me, and my dick swells to an almost painful degree. I move up to bring her lips to my mouth, and she kisses me hungrily. "Now, Nate. I *need* you now."

Never denying my girl, I reach behind me and grab the condom I'd strategically placed under the pillow. Her eyes glaze over as she watches me rip it open and fumble to slide it over my hard length. "Are you sure about this?" I ask one more time. "You're in control, babe. If you want to stop, we stop."

She closes her eyes, and her face relaxes in a soft smile. I stare down at her patiently waiting, hovering above her, ready for whatever she wants.

When a tear floats down her cheek, I panic. My face must

register my concern because she reaches her hand up and softly caresses my chin. "You make me feel so cherished, so protected, and so loved. I want nothing more than this, Nate. You. Forever. *Please*, make love to me."

Leaning down, I kiss her softly, telling her with my lips that she'll always have forever. I'll always protect her. Easiest promise ever. Our eyes hold one another as I push myself inside of her and make us one. Her tightness and warmth surround me, and her cries almost make me lose it. It feels like fucking heaven.

As I burrow deeper into her, pushing my face into her hair, surrounding myself with only Amelia and her scent and her love, she cries out again.

"Am I hurting you?" I ask, pushing her hair out of her face and looking into her beautiful grey eyes.

"Hurts…so good," she sighs. "So good, Nate." Our lips brush against each other, our tongues pushing forward as I begin to move, drawing a moaning cry from her throat. It's almost impossible to control myself when it feels so good to me, but I know that it's stretching her, pulling her open, and *hurting* her. But she meets my movement, kissing harder, pulling me closer, begging me to give her everything, and since she's always in control, my body gives it all to her.

Wanting to make her come again, I try to move my hand between us, to build the pressure where she needs it as I remain inside her, but she pulls my hand up. "I want your chest against me; I don't want any inches separating us. Just hold me, Nate.

Make love to me."

Burrowing myself deep inside her, I give her everything she wants, holding her close and moving quicker, until we are both panting, and the room starts to swirl, a blackness overcoming me as all I see are Amelia's grey eyes and stars.

In that moment, it's solidified in my mind. I will never touch another girl; I will never do this with another girl. Amelia is my forever, and as I come and scream her name, I know with every inch of me that she will always be my home, and inside of her is exactly where I'll always belong.

CHAPTER 9

Amelia

The great thing about living above where you work is the easy commute. The bar is across the parking lot, the charter boats I work off sit at the dock in front of the bar, and the flower shop is one floor below me.

Karen doesn't require a uniform, so I choose a pair of black leggings to go with a grey shirt which I tie at the waist. I pull my hair back in small braids so that my hair remains down, but at least the front wisps, which are never controlled, are out of my face. A bit of Chapstick, a dash of blush, and a few swipes of mascara finish off my look.

Ready in under fifteen minutes—now that's my kind of morning. I make coffee for both of us and walk down the steps, ready to start my day.

I owe Karen an apology. I lost it on her yesterday, and it's not her fault. Hopefully, a coffee and our usual banter will put us back to our normal routine.

I've yet to make sense of anything I'm feeling as it relates to Nate. Fortunately, the next few days are completely booked, and if I can avoid him, I can keep him out of my mind. Or at least that's what I tell myself. He'd been out of my vision for three years and never far from my heart. But one can hope that one day I'll wake up and he'll be nothing more than a bittersweet memory.

Plenty of people move on from their childhood sweethearts. What makes us so different? I'd been naïve to think we were any more special than all those other couples who swore they'd never break up with their first love. Who knows if we even knew the real meaning of love. We'd been kids. We'd never even kissed anyone else. Well, I hadn't.

Of course that's changed in the last few years. I haven't been a nun. And although none of them compared, I know that's because they were all first kisses with a stranger. How could a first kiss compare to any of the kisses I'd had with Nate? We loved each other before we ever touched each other. We were best friends first. One day I will find something to rival that. I'm sure of it.

Resolving to put him out of my mind for the rest of the day, I push open the door with my hip and close my eyes as I inhale the sweet fall day. The sun is shining, and life is looking up.

When I open my eyes, I almost drop my coffee. So much for putting him out of my mind. In the parking spot outside the door sits my pastel Volkswagen Van. The words "*Amelia Pearson's Flowers*" taunt me.

After our wedding, Nate surprised me with the updated

name. He was nervous I'd be upset that he did it without asking, but I'd thrown my arms around his neck and kissed him with the biggest smile on my face. I didn't think I'd ever tire of hearing that name. *Amelia Pearson*. I'd scribbled it on every diary, notebook, and piece of paper I could find for years. Of course, I would want it painted on my business. I wanted everyone to know I was his, and he wanted everyone to know it too.

I close my eyes, exorcising the memory from my mind. "You can do this; it's just a van. You've moved on. *You're moving on*. You've got this." I repeat the words as I walk away from the pastel memories and avoid running my hands across the words the way I used to. Back when I was in awe that I was finally Amelia Pearson, that I was living my dream, owning my own business, and more importantly, Nate Pearson's wife.

"Morning, Karen, you have some explaining to do." I turn my eyes to my ex-mother-in-law, and her sheepish frown melts me. "Ugh, just get it over with. Rip off the Band-Aid so I can focus on work rather than whatever is going on outside in the parking lot."

She smiles nervously. "Remember how you said we needed a vehicle to make deliveries and if we wanted to get involved with weddings? Well, voilà! We have a vehicle."

I turn my head sideways and glare.

"Okay. Well, I know it was yours, so if you don't want us to use it we can get something else." She looks down at her shears and focuses on the roses she's cutting.

I walk over and put my hand over hers, stopping her from her nervous movements. "Nate paid for the van. So technically it's his. We'll just have it repainted." Saying the words hurts, but it's the right thing to do. She's right. We need a delivery van, and I really do want to start doing weddings. For her, of course. It's a great business, and we've already started getting calls after people saw how beautiful our arrangements were at the Linden Place event.

Besides, it might be therapeutic, painting over the words and starting fresh. I'm no longer Amelia Pearson, even if I never got around to changing my pesky license back. I will though. I'll schedule an appointment at the DMV next Thursday. I just need a copy of our divorce decree.

Ugh. I pinch my eyes closed at those words. Why are words so painful? People who say "words will never hurt me" have clearly never had their heart ripped out by them.

"No rush on repainting it. And it's yours, Amelia. Nate bought it for you. You know he never would take it back. We just thought this would be a way you could have something just for you."

We. *We*?

I try to keep my anger in check because I love Karen, but her and Nate making decisions for me is not something I'll take lightly. Enough decisions had been made for me by that man to last my entire life.

Biting back my words, because I know the power of them, I

respond, "That's okay. I'll call Tim at the paint shop on my day off and get a quote." I turn away before emotion pours out of my eyes and sip my hot, bitter coffee. Normally, I use chocolate milk as a sweetener, but nothing will fix this morning, so I don't waste it.

For the next few hours, I disappear in the back and work on arrangements while Karen mans the store front. Any other day, I work on arrangements in the main area because we like to talk and joke around. It makes the morning go quickly. But since I can't control my feelings right now, and I really don't want to yell at Karen—it's not her fault that her son is such a controlling ass—I remain hidden. By lunch time I am starving, and after blasting Taylor Swift for a couple of hours, I feel in control of my anger, so I head out front and offer to grab us lunch.

Mrs. Crowell's smile greets me as I open the door. I start to say hello when I see that she's talking to a man who is holding flowers and working our cash register. My eyes float to the ink on his arms and then narrow as I try to discern the words he has tattooed there. Growling, I pinch my nose and remind myself that the less I know about him the better. I don't know him. I don't know these tattoos. And that is precisely how I need it to stay. "Good afternoon, Mrs. Crowell, how's Meg doing with the wedding planning?"

"Oh, just wonderful! Did you hear Caris opened a winery? We are planning it there. She wants to come in and talk to you guys about doing the flowers. Nate here was just telling me you guys are starting weddings, and I saw the van you got. Too sweet. I'm so happy you guys finally made it official. I didn't realize you'd gotten married. Congrats."

Nate smiles. "Thanks. We still want to plan a big wedding, but life was short, and we didn't want to wait, right, babe?"

Summoning my inner Athena—the goddess of reason, wisdom, intelligence, and peace—I recognize that screeching *I'm not married to him* is not good for business. "Oh, the van is just a joke of Nate's. Not married. Happily single. Actually, I'm dating Shawn Chase, Charlotte's brother. It's a family affair." I wink at her and can practically feel Nate's glare.

Unsure of what is simmering between us, Mrs. Crowell's smile falters, and she looks back and forth between us. We glare at one another and then plaster fake smiles on our faces. "Oh, okay, dear," she stammers. "Well, are you still interested in weddings?"

"Oh yes! How about you and Meg come by Thames tomorrow for lunch? I can bring over a few pictures of wedding packages I put together when I was in Nashville, and we can see if any of them work for you."

"Oh, that sounds lovely, dear. Thank you. Take care, Nate. Welcome back to Bristol!" She heads out the door, and the bell above signals the end of our quiet truce.

I'm seeing red. Angrily, I shout, "Are you kidding me with that? We're married! What would happen if that got out to my family?"

Nate shakes his head. "You really never told them? What did you do—just come back here and act like nothing happened?

Erase me completely from your life?" He doesn't even sound angry; he speaks neutrally, like we're talking about grocery shopping. Which just makes me angrier. He never showed emotion. Never got angry.

Fight with me. Prove to me I matter.

But that's not Nate. He placates me. He tries to reason. Or he just walks out.

"Why would I tell them about our marriage? It was fake. We signed a damn piece of paper in a courthouse. It meant nothing. No more exciting than applying for a business permit. In fact, that took more effort." My words drip with animosity, and I know the scowl on my face leaves nothing to the imagination. Nate turns on his heel and walks out of the store. "Yeah, that's what I thought, leave! It's what you do best," I shout after him.

He doesn't even flinch, just keeps moving. As soon as he's out of my vision I slip down to the floor, lean against the counter, and sob.

I'm so lost to my heartbreak that I don't register when his arms move around me and he lifts me to his chest, holding me close and rocking me. "Shh, babe, shhh. It's okay. I'm sorry. Shhh." The sobs continue, and since I'm unable to steady myself, I lean into his chest and let my body have what it needs the most—Nate's heartbeat against mine.

When the tears subside, I wipe my nose and move to get up. "Let me go," I say tersely as Nate's arms wrap around me tighter. It's beyond embarrassing having him see me this way.

"Just stop for a minute. Dammit, Amelia." His voice has an edge that I don't recognize. It matches the tattoos on his arms. He's no longer a pushover, it seems.

"I'm fine, Nate. Just got a little carried away. And you left again. Just…" I falter, unable to say how I really felt when he walked out. Like the air was sucked out of the room, and I'd suffocate until he came back.

He reaches down and picks up a small blue bag. "Emergency stash. I went to get them from the van."

Chips Ahoy!

I close my eyes and try to keep my breathing tempered. Why is he doing this to me? Why is he here? I can't take it. I can't take that he knows when I'm angry I need sugar to calm me down. I need chocolate. Cookies.

I can't handle that he still has an emergency stash to deal with me. As if he walks around with them. Prepared to be with me again. Prepared to be *us* again.

I glance at the bag, quickly seeing the date and recognizing they are fresh. They aren't leftovers from our past; he just bought them. *Dammit.*

"Thank you," I manage to mumble as he opens the bag and offers me a cookie. I stuff it into my mouth, trying to focus on anything other than this swirling feeling in my stomach as I sit on Nate's lap and listen to his heart pound. When his lips brush against the back of my neck, my body stiffens, and I slide off his lap, not ready to move back so quickly into our old habits.

Love & Tequila Make Her Crazy

Nate smirks as he watches me scramble to my feet. "You feeling better?"

"Fine. Yes. Good. Great. Perfect." I stumble over the words and look anywhere but into Nate's blue eyes and devastating smile. "Where did your mom go?"

Nate shifts and stands. "She had to take Sam to an appointment. I told her I'd help out and close up later."

"You don't have to do that. I'm sure you have other stuff to do. I can handle the store." I mean, it's Karen's store but I'm not going to lie that it doesn't sting a bit that she didn't ask me to cover for her.

"That's okay. Made a promise to my mom. Besides, she said you're busy working on some arrangements for the Blithewold. That's amazing that you've already got them asking you to work with them."

The Blithewold is an old mansion in Bristol on the water with the most gorgeous gardens throughout the property. It was a bit of kismet and a compliment that they asked me to help so soon after the Linden Place event. I really am starting to make a name for myself. I just wish it was my name and not under the Pearson's storefront. I love working with Karen, but it would have been a dream if it was Amelia's just like it had been in Nashville. I bite my tongue to stop the bitterness from dripping into my throat.

Life is good. Karen lost so much. She deserves this.

God, I hate myself for even having to be reminded of that.

"Yeah, I am busy, actually. I was going to grab lunch though. Normally, I go to Thames for your mom and me. Do you want something?"

Just being friendly. This means nothing.

Nate shakes his head. "No. That's okay, you don't have to worry about me. I'll stay out of your way as promised."

He looks down, and I remember the harsh words I said to him only the day before. God, I've been such a bitch. Somehow, I know that girl is still sitting inside me ready to jump on him and yell something else the next time he pisses me off. I can't help it. There is so much anger and hurt swirling inside when I look at him.

But I'd be lying if I didn't admit there were other feelings swirling in there too. I just haven't decided which ones will win. For now, it is just kindness though. I could be kind.

"Wings work?"

He looks up at me with a surprised smile. "Sure. Thanks, Amelia." I nod and walk out before I can think too much about how surprised he is that I'm being nice to him. How taken aback it makes him.

The heat of the sun warms my skin as I walk across the parking lot to Thames. I enter the kitchen to place our orders and the chef smirks. "Thought you were fired."

I laugh as Hailey walks in and quips, "No. But if she walks around naked in her apartment again, scaring away the customers, she will be."

Love & Tequila Make Her Crazy

Shawn trails behind her. When he spots me, he wraps his arm around my waist and plops a kiss on my cheek. "Hi, girlfriend, how are you today?" I slam my elbow into his stomach just hard enough to make a point.

"Girlfriend?" Hailey asks, her eyes darting between the two of us, an obvious air of concern entering the room.

I move away from Shawn and start to speak, "Oh, that's—" when Shawn pulls me close again and stops me.

"Since a few weeks ago. We were testing out the waters, seeing if this was real between us, and now, we've decided to make it official, right, Schnookums?" I turn around to glare at him, and he whispers in my ear, "Just go with it."

Oh. *Oh.* I see he realizes the brilliance of my plan to make Nate jealous and he's deciding to take it out for a ride. Although for him it's to win the girl, and for me it's to keep the guy away.

"Yeah, we're new. But if you ever call me Schnookums again I'll take your balls off. And not in the way you like it." I raise my eyes in innuendo, and I can feel Hailey's jaw drop.

She stutters, "Um, well, congrats guys. I, uh, have some stuff to do for payroll. You working tonight, Ames?"

I nod and smile at her obvious concern over Shawn's change in relationship status. Score one for Shawn. "Yup, see you tonight!" Turning around I press a chaste kiss next to Shawn's mouth, really selling the new relationship. "Sorry, babe, I gotta get lunch back to the shop. I'll see you tonight."

He blushes and smacks my ass before he walks away. Well,

who knew the guy had it in him? Gonna have to tell him to do that when Nate's around. It will make his head explode. I laugh at the image and give the chef our order.

When I enter the shop, Nate is checking out a customer, and I wave for him to come to the back when he's done and flip the sign on the front to closed. In the back, I put his wings on the table and pull out my grilled cheese, placing the fries between us. Then I pull out the two iced teas I bought and set them out as well. When he walks in, I'm just settling down into my chair and popping a fry in my mouth.

Oh, the salt is exactly what I needed. My mind shuts down and I moan.

Nate laughs. "Forgot about how much you love your salt." I open my eyes and give a half smile before I plop another one in my mouth. "Oh, you remembered not to put the sauce on, thanks."

I look down at the wings and realize he's right. I directed the chef to make them how Nate likes them without even thinking about it.

Irrationally, I'm annoyed. Why do I still remember things like that? And why is it second nature for me to make sure it was done right for him? I didn't even think about it.

He sips his iced tea and smiles. "And you squeezed the lemon in." He smirks like he knows the importance of both of these things. Whatever. So I know how he likes his food and drinks. It means nothing. Just that I've known this man my entire life. Obviously, some things don't change. But a lot does.

Love & Tequila Make Her Crazy

We eat in relative silence, me trying to avoid his smirking, and him, well I have no idea what he must be thinking. It's the first meal we've shared alone since the day we received the worst phone call of our lives. Or at least one of the top two worst calls. I guess they are probably tied for me. For Nate, Peter and his father's death are intertwined.

My eyes shut just thinking of Peter and Paul. My irritation with Nate and our entire situation softens for a moment. When I open my eyes, Nate is looking warmly at me with those blue eyes of his. Unable to help myself, I blurt out my thought, "Are you going to the memorial for your father in New York?"

Nate tenses, and I feel horrible for having mentioned it. I know Karen isn't going to New York for the memorial. I didn't ask why, and it probably isn't my place to have asked Nate. He shakes his head. "No, I don't like to memorialize that day."

My head tilts, and I stifle the urge to grab his hand. "It's not about the day, Nate. It's about your dad. If you needed—" I cut myself off. *What am I doing?* I can't offer to go with him. I'm not that person to him anymore.

As if reading my mind and knowing that I'm not actually going to offer, he shakes his head. "My mom and I plan on going out on the boat. She hasn't been out on it in twenty years. It's time."

"Oh," is the only thing I can say. I want to go. I want to be there. But it's not my place anymore. That thought guts me in a way I don't expect. For a moment, I'd forgotten that we were nothing. I'd sunk back into the familiar. The food, the conversation, Nate's scent, his gentle jabs—they'd all left me feeling something I hadn't in a long time. Hope. But hope was a temptress with a match, and I'd just handed her a light.

"It's not a big deal, Amelia," he says, downplaying the significance of it all.

"Nate, it's been twenty years. Of course, it's a big deal."

I don't know why I'm pushing this. It's like I want to be burned.

"It's just another year without my father. Why does one year matter more than another?" Nate runs his hand over the back of his neck in frustration. "I mean 364 days a year most people don't think about it, but on this *one day* everyone wants to commemorate it. Everyone wants to post on Facebook and talk about the tragedy. I live with it the other 364 days a year. I've lived with it the other nineteen years. I don't want to talk about the tragedy. I want to remember my father. I don't need a memorial to remind me of what I've lost. I know every day." He doesn't sound angry; he doesn't even seem annoyed that I'm pushing this. He's just talking to me in the honest way he used to when we were *us*.

What a scary thing, because now I give in. I hand the temptress the gasoline, and I light myself on fire as I reach out my hand to his and squeeze. "He would be so proud of you, Nate."

Nate lets out a stilted laugh. "For what? I've done nothing to make him proud. Jack and Peter joined the Air Force, the Brady brothers became firefighters, Derek became a cop. All these guys we grew up with did these things because of *that day*.

Because of what it inspired…all I did was lose my dad."

I shake my head, willing the tears to remain hidden, and say softly, "No, Nate. You lived. You survived. You followed your dreams. You didn't just exist. You *lived*. Which is exactly what your dad would have wanted." Nate looks up at me and I see that, like me, he is dangerously close to allowing the emotion to spill over. "Nate, he loved hearing you play the guitar, and you'd just started. Your dad lived big, and he wanted the same for you. Just because you didn't do something that you think symbolizes honor doesn't mean that you're not honorable or that your life doesn't have purpose."

Nate's eyes meet mine, and we stare at one another for a moment. "My life had purpose because of you," he admits. I hold my breath. "When I had you, I knew I was making him proud. I was doing the right thing."

The vulnerability in this moment leaves me speechless. I'm a blazing inferno. I pull my hand back before all that is left is ashes and wipe away the tear before it falls.

Seeing that I'm at a loss for words, Nate says, "Thanks for having lunch with me, Amelia."

I sigh, unsure of what else I can say at this point. I want to say that he'll always have me, but it would be a lie. I can't be that person for him anymore. Too much has happened. No matter how badly I wish things were different. Offering false promises would make me just as bad as the temptress. There is no hope left for us. I'm not his salvation; I can't be. There's nothing left for me to give.

"You're welcome, Nate. I'm going to get back to work. I have to head to the bar in a bit, so I probably won't see you before I leave. Did your mom leave you a key to lock up?"

He reaches into his pocket and holds up the pink key his mom had made for the store. She actually let me decorate the store in the pastels that I'd come to love in my floral business. It reminded me of Nashville. Of happier times.

But remembering can be dangerous. Near lethal if I'm honest because it's not the fire that normally kills someone, it's the smoke and the carbon monoxide. It poisons you while you sit peacefully, unaware it's even happening. That's what happier times do to me—remembering—it kills me slowly and yet it never quite finishes the job. It's like someone is continually giving me shots of the deadly gas, but then bringing me back to life before putting me out of my misery.

That damn pink key brought me back to Nashville. I was never a pink and purple girl, but somehow with Nate I was able to be softer. I didn't have to work so hard to fit in with the boys once I was his. It gave me the option to choose things I really liked. And I learned that pastels were one of those things. The pink key is a soft pink, and my key is teal. Unaware that I'm slowly dying in front of him, Nate smiles and replies, "I'm all set. Have a good day, Amelia."

Actively focusing on my ability to breathe, I nod and walk away.

Nate

Well, the van went over exactly as I imagined it would. She's even more stubborn now than before. The crying though—I can't handle the crying. Seeing how much I've hurt her, how much me just being here hurts her, makes me wonder if I'm making a mistake.

But that little glimmer of hope she offered me, allowing me to hold her, to comfort her, and then when she had lunch with me, ordering precisely what she knew I liked…I can't walk away knowing that what we have is right there within reach.

It's like my hands are skimming happiness like a surfer skims a wave with his fingertips. I can feel the way the relationship is turning, and as long as I keep my legs steady, my head forward, and don't throw her for any loops, I think we can ride this out.

After locking up the store, I head down the street, hoping to get some fresh air before heading back to my mom's house. I still have to find a job. And not at a bar. I need a grown-up job. Something that shows Amelia I mean business. That I can put down roots. That I'm not going to disappear at the first call for a music gig. She needs to know she comes first.

A text from Grant is perfectly timed. **Hey, did you give the contract to Amelia yet? She agree to sign???**

I pocket the phone without responding.

"Nate Pearson, say it ain't so!" a tall blonde says as she walks toward me, her mouth wide with a smile.

"Caris Milsom, nice to see you." I wrap my arms around my old high school friend. She "dated" Peter for a short time, or something like that.

Caris holds on to me a bit longer than necessary, and I'm forced to pry myself back a bit awkwardly. If she notices, she doesn't let on. "Heard I'm your new boss," she says with a wink.

I scratch my head. "Oh, right. Your family owns Thames." Her family owns all of Bristol, but that's a story for another day.

Her easy smile remains on her face. It strikes me how different she is from Amelia. While both are tall and blonde, that is where their resemblance ends. Amelia is soft, relaxed, but not cheery. Caris is forced, put together, and always has a smile—although I'm not sure how happy she truly is. It's just a feeling I get. "Yes. Although Hailey mentioned it was only on weekends. What are you going to do with yourself the rest of the time?"

Great question. Something I'm trying to figure out. But not exactly something I need to figure out with Caris in this exact moment. "Thinking about working with Sam." The words exit my mouth without much thought, but as soon as I say them, they don't sound half bad. My non-stepfather has a financial business. He'd offered to bring me on before, and now I know he could use the help. While numbers aren't my thing—or suits and ties—helping Sam would be good, and it would also show Amelia that I was putting down roots.

"Oh, that's wonderful. I'm sure Sam will love having you. Our firm handles some of his work. We send him clients, and he returns the favor. It's a very beneficial relationship. So, I have a feeling if you work with him you and I will become very close." She leans against me, her finger trailing up my chest as if she's flirting. Is that what she's doing? Flirting with me?

I back up again, completely uncomfortable with any woman who isn't Amelia putting her hands on me, and scratch my neck again, keeping my hands and body parts out of her grasp. "Yeah, I guess it's possible. Anyway, I promised my mom I'd pick up groceries. I'll see you later, Caris."

Her face flashes, and I'm not sure if it's annoyance or disappointment, but I don't stick around to find out. Walking quickly, I head to my car. Between Caris and Grant I am exhausted, and it's only three in the afternoon. I've got to get my mind focused and figure out a way to convince Sam to hire me. Then I can rip up the contracts, say goodbye to Nashville for good, and start my life back in Bristol. With Amelia. Hopefully.

CHAPTER 10

Nate
Twenty Years Old

"Man, why are you so nervous? Amelia is going to love this idea." Grant paces in front of me, the high from our last show still evident. The guy has more energy than a bunch of middle school boys at a carnival. He never stops. He's also never dated a girl long enough to learn her middle name, so I'm not taking his advice when it comes to Amelia.

He has no idea how she will react when I tell her I've been offered a permanent gig in Nashville—or at least as permanent as one would hope to find. Grant's cousin is running a bar there, and after coming to visit and hearing our sets he said he could get us at least one night a week. This is huge. People get discovered in Nashville. No one is getting discovered in North Kingstown, Rhode Island, where we go to school.

"I'm asking her to uproot her life and to change all the plans we've been making for years. This isn't just some girlfriend, Grant. We're planning a life together and now I'm asking her—a month before she decides on her college—to move to another state with me and apply to a college there. Even if I can convince her, there's no guarantee we can convince her parents. And I'm not going without her."

I am resolute in my answer. Amelia and I are making plans. I really wanted to get off-campus housing this year and live together, but Amelia wants to try dorm life. She wants to have the college experience. I've had it for the last two years, and it's unfair of me not to go along with that. Now not only am I saying that I'm no longer willing to abide by that plan, but I am also totally flipping the switch on everything, asking her to move across the country and pick a new college, just to follow my music career. If you can even call it that.

Grant stops pacing and kneels in front of me. "I know. But if she wants a life with you, this is your life. Music. This is your chance. Do you really think she'll begrudge you your chance?"

Amelia was working in my mother's garden when I got home. We planned on taking out the boat for the afternoon because it was unseasonably warm for April. Grant managed to grab a bottle of champagne, and I picked up chocolate-covered strawberries as well. I'd been working on a new song, and was hoping between the treats, the boat ride, and my singing, I could warm Amelia up to the idea of our big move.

I hadn't even talked to my mom yet. No sense in worrying her if Amelia wasn't interested. I'd never even left the state because I didn't want my mom to be alone after Dad died. Now that Sam has moved in, and she seems to be doing well, I think it's safe to consider what I really want in life. Peter and Jack have been gone for two years now. I, on the other hand, am stuck in the same spot as when I was twelve. I need this change more than I'd like to admit. I just hope Amelia understands.

Popping into the house to say hello to my mother before we leave, I find her standing in the kitchen staring into the fridge. I lean over and give her a kiss on the cheek, startling her. "Oh, Nate, I didn't hear you come in. Oh, darling, look at you, you look so handsome." My cheeks redden at my mother's attention.

"Thanks, Ma. How are you?"

She pulls me in close for a hug and I squeeze her back. We've gotten extremely close throughout the years. The only two left from our family of three. As much as I rely on Amelia, my mother is also my rock. I find myself pulling her closer, knowing how much I'll miss her when I go to Nashville.

My mother pulls away and gives me another once-over. "I'm good. Really good." Her smile reaches her eyes, telling me this is true. She seems healthier, lighter, like she has a glow that I can't pinpoint. "Can you come into the living room with me for a minute? I wanted to talk to you about something."

Love & Tequila Make Her Crazy

I follow her and notice that the old brown leather couch that my dad loved is no longer there. She replaced it with a light-beige microfiber one. Above the mantel I notice a picture of her and Sam next to the one of her, Dad, and me. It's striking in that it's like she has these two lives which run parallel. Mine will never not include my father. In my mind she will always be my father's wife.

I try to separate these thoughts from whatever is going on right now. I won't react to the couch. I won't be upset with her for parting with an inanimate object. She kept so many things the same throughout the house, throughout my life. Besides, I'm leaving.

Even as I repeat all these things in my head, I feel my hands twisting into fists and my heart beating quicker.

When I spot the diamond on her finger, set in a platinum band and not gold, like my father had given her, my anger wins. "What's on your hand?" My words come out sharp, and my mother practically jumps.

"Nate, Sam asked me to marry him, and I said yes." She looks at me expecting…I don't know what she's expecting because her words are simply on repeat in my head.

My mom is getting married. She'll be his wife. I'll still be my dad's son, but she won't be my dad's wife. What does that make her and me? It feels life-changing.

Before I can stop myself, the words come tumbling out. "Don't marry him, Mom. Please don't marry him." I don't recognize my voice. To my ears, it sounds distant and desperate.

My mother moves next to me and pulls me close.

"Shh, Nate. Don't cry."

Cry? Am I crying?

I feel across my face, and sure enough, it's wet. "Mom, please don't marry him." I wipe away the tears and look at my mother. Her face cracks with emotion.

"Don't you like Sam? I thought you didn't mind having him around." Confusion laces her questions, and I can't even blame her. I do like Sam. He's a great guy. But he's not my dad. I can't explain this sorrow I feel over it all, but I also can't stop myself from responding honestly.

"He's fine. I like him fine. But please don't marry him. Don't replace Dad."

It's like I hit her. She pulls back, sighs, and looks up to the mantel, as if she's picturing her two lives—the one with Sam on the right and the one with Dad and me on the left. Which one she chooses will forever change me, and I know it before she agrees. "I'll never replace your father. And I won't marry Sam if that's how you feel. I'm sorry, Nate, I should have thought about this more. I'm so sorry." My mother pulls me close and continues to whisper in my ear how much she loves me and how sorry she is. I feel the tears pouring from her eyes and know that I should be the one apologizing. She's done nothing wrong. But I don't say any of that. Instead, I whisper to Dad that we're not moving on. We're not replacing him. We'll always be "us three."

I don't have it in me to tell Mom about Nashville. Not when

Love & Tequila Make Her Crazy

I just took away her happiness. "I'm sorry, Mom. What will you tell Sam?"

She looks out to the bay, focusing anywhere but my eyes. "He'll understand. He knows this is a big deal for us. It's just a piece of paper though. We're still going to spend our lives together. You understand that, right? I won't have a wedding, but Sam isn't going anywhere."

I nod. I wouldn't want them to break up. I'm relying on him to be there for my mom. It's the only way I'll ever be able to move on with my life. "I'm happy you have him," I say honestly. "I don't want you to be lonely, Mom, or unhappy, I just…" I falter, trying to explain something that is unexplainable.

Mom nods, the decision seemingly made. "I understand. Why don't you go get Amelia? The water is perfect today. Don't waste it inside with me, worrying about something that we can't change. I'm okay. Are you okay?"

I can hear the disappointment in her voice. Did the wedding mean something to her? Was it her opportunity to start fresh? Am I taking that away from her?

Selfishly, I can't deal with all these emotions right now. I need to convince Amelia to move to Nashville, and we don't have much time. Soon she'll be picking her college—if she hasn't sent in her acceptance already.

I kiss my mom and squeeze her tightly once more, then I leave and head out to meet up with my girl.

I find Amelia outside, kneeling over the hydrangeas, pulling out weeds and biting her lip as she focuses. When she looks up, I spot the telltale sign of a day in the garden, dirt on her face. "Is that chocolate, Cookie?" I tease, swiping at her cheek.

Her eyes narrow. "What did we discuss about that name?"

I laugh. "You forbade me to use it in the bedroom. But last I checked we are outside."

Amelia stands up and pushes me against the house, swarming me with her scent, chocolate, and earth. "If you want to get me in the bedroom anytime today, I'd suggest you keep that name out of your mouth." She pushes her lips against mine, and then she moans as I pull her closer, digging my hands into the flesh of her hips.

"Doesn't seem like I'm going to have to work too hard," I say with a smile as I pull away. "Besides, looks like you need to shower before I go anywhere near you." I teasingly push her back, and she swats at me, taking the dirt on her hands and rubbing it onto my arms.

"I'll run home and shower. Then we can go." She starts to pick up her shears, and I grab her around the waist, throwing her over my shoulder and running to the boat. Her screams and laughter dance with the wind.

"Shower on the boat. No time to waste!" I don't stop until we reach the dock, where I deposit her gently, kissing her hard, allowing her mouth and my need for her to wash away any of the emotions that are still churning in my stomach from the conversation with my mother.

Love & Tequila Make Her Crazy

I need to feel, not think.

I push Amelia backward onto the boat and continue to kiss her until I have her caged against the wall of the cabin. With one arm, I reach into the bathroom to turn on the shower. Then I slip Amelia's shirt over her head and pull her pants off quickly. She stays quiet, letting me appreciate her black matching thong and bra.

"Do condoms work in the shower, Nate?"

"Aren't you on birth control?"

She smiles nervously. I don't want to do anything that makes her nervous, so I slink backward, knowing if I get too close, I won't be able to stop myself.

Amelia moves closer to me and snaps the back of her bra open, exposing her perky breasts. I reach up and run my thumb across her nipple and she moans, tipping her head back and offering it to my mouth. I greedily accept and pull her body onto my knee, offering her friction, and getting harder watching her use me for her own pleasure. "I don't want anything between us, Nate." She stands up and slips off her underwear, looking at me for approval. She doesn't need to ask me twice.

"Are you sure, babe?"

"*Please.*"

I stand up and undress, watching with amusement at how excited Amelia gets whenever I'm hard.

Newsflash—if she's naked, I'm hard. If she's kissing me, hard. Pouting at me, hard.

I lift her up, and she wraps her legs around me, then I walk us into the tight shower. We're barely able to move, we definitely can't have sex in here.

Instead, I wash her quickly, but I take my time rinsing her hair, loving being able to take care of her for a moment, focusing on her needs. She's the girl who makes me feel whole. The one who put me back together. I need her more now than I have in a long time. I need her to make everything better again. I need to focus on anything other than my mother wanting to marry Sam.

As I massage my fingers against her scalp, she moans and drops her head against my chest. I take my time though, getting every last drop out of her hair, playing with every strand, and smoothing away both our worries for the time being.

"I love you," I say as I drop kisses on her neck.

"I love you too. I need to feel you inside of me, Nate. Right now." I finish rinsing her hair, grab a towel, and turn off the water. Then I wrap us both up and lift her legs around me, entering her in one thrust, then pulling her down roughly, giving it to her just like she likes.

"Yes, Nate. Harder." Wasting no time, I bring her out of the bathroom and pull her closer as I walk. Each step feels more erotic. Tighter. Wetter. Never having been bare inside of her, I'm about to explode, but the walking holds off my orgasm. "Oh, Nate, I love the way you feel."

"Me too, babe. You feel like heaven." I lay her down on the bed, and she takes control, angling to get on top. I can feel her every fold, her warmth, her muscles tightening around me. It's almost impossible to focus, let alone think. "Yes, ride my cock, Amelia. Fuck…you're so fucking hot."

Her glazed-over eyes focus, and she leans her hand on my chest as she rides me. She chases every thought from my brain as I watch her move, pulling my orgasm from me slowly, until we are both screaming, and I fill her completely.

As we come down from the high, Amelia falls against my chest, and I run my hand up and down her back, feeling more alive than I've ever felt in my life. "Move to Nashville with me," I say, without thinking. I had a plan, a big speech, an explanation to convince her of why we should move. I was going to work up to the idea, warm her to moving and make it so she couldn't say no.

None of my big plans included springing it on her while deep inside of her, but it is in this moment that I know without a doubt that I can't go without her. If she says she won't go, I'll give up this dream. None of my dreams are worth doing without her.

Amelia looks up at me, her brows shifting in confusion. "What?" She attempts to move off me, but I pull her close. I'm not ready to separate myself from her.

"Grant's cousin offered us a gig. A steady one. It's a real shot, babe. I looked into programs in Nashville for you. The Gaylord Hotel has huge gardens, and students who attend the flower program can intern there. It's a great program. I know it's asking a lot, and you had your heart set on the University of

Rhode Island, but this could be amazing. *We* could be amazing." I squeeze my eyes shut and wait for her to react.

"Nate, that's incredible. You were offered a job?"

I open my eyes, seeing the excitement in Amelia's blueish-grey eyes, which after sex always look a bit greyer. "Yeah. I mean, it's only one place and one night a week. But it's a real chance."

She leans down and kisses me, deeply. "I am so proud of you. Of course I'll come with you. We'll figure it out. As long as we're together, I'll be happy. But I can't believe you already looked into the florist program. Thank you." Shyly, she looks up at me with those beautiful eyes, and I fall even more in love with her than I thought possible. This girl, my girl, is just as in love as I am.

"Really?"

She laughs. "If you think for a second I would have said anything other than 'I'm so proud of you' then you're crazy. I'm crazy about *you*, Nate. Your wins are my wins. Are you sure you want me to come, though? I know this is a big step for you, and I don't know…" She looks away, and I can't help but wonder what she's worried about.

I pull her chin back to me, kissing her softly. "None of it means anything without you, Ames. None of it."

"I know there will be girls at the bars…you're going to make it, Nate, I can tell."

I roll my eyes. "First of all, I don't care about any of that. You are the only girl I even think about. The only one that I want to look at. It's you. You are my home, you are my family, and one day, Amelia, you'll be my wife. None of it means anything without you. Got that?"

Amelia melds herself against my body. "Forever."

CHAPTER 11

Amelia

"So, I'm thinking I need to take things up a notch," Shawn says as he shakes the martini the redhead ordered while giving him a once-over.

"Extra dirty," she says as she bats her eyes at my fake boyfriend.

Before he grabbed the vodka, he nuzzled my neck and kissed me softly. It was odd how a move which used to make me weak in the knees for Nate did absolutely nothing for me when it was Shawn's lips. By any measure, Shawn is a good-looking guy. Taller and wider than Nate, and with chocolate-brown eyes which should have been my undoing.

Truth be told, they just remind me of Charlotte. I only have platonic feelings for him. It's too bad, really, because ever since seeing Nate, I'm craving sex. The fire he lit inside me continues to burn. I'm waiting to become ashes, but every time I think of him or see him, it's like throwing kindling on the flames. I need someone to scratch the itch before I fall back into bed with my ex-husband.

Blowing out a puff of air, I raise my eyes to Shawn. "Take it up a notch?"

"Yeah. Let's go on a date."

I narrow my eyes. "How would that work to our advantage? You want Hailey to be jealous, and I want Nate to stay away. They won't witness us on a date unless we come here, which isn't believable. Who dates in a restaurant where they spend all of their time working?"

Shawn just smiles. "A boat date."

"Huh?" I can't even hide my confusion.

"I heard Nate telling a guy at the bar that he's going to Potter's Cove. Let's find out when he's going and make a day of it. Let's take a boat and spend the day. You invite Hailey. Two birds, one stone."

*Potter's Cove. God, the memories that spot holds. Weekends on the boat, floating, tubing, sex….ugh…*I try to exorcise the thoughts from my mind.

Despite the memories, it actually isn't a terrible idea. It would further sell our relationship to Nate, and maybe he'd leave Bristol. Then I could go back to my life rather than focusing on this empty feeling. As for Shawn, hopefully this little plan will help Hailey realize he exists.

"Perfect idea, Shawn. Let's date." I do a little shimmy, excited for our plan to be put into action.

"Did you guys say date?" Hailey asks, walking up and looking back and forth between us again. Maybe it won't take long after all.

I loop my arm around Shawn's waist, and he pulls me close. "Yeah, we want to go boating while the weather is still nice. Want to join?"

Hailey's face falls. "No. I don't want to impose. As it is you two get no time alone because of work."

Shawn shakes his head. "We get plenty of time alone, right, babe?"

I stiffen at Nate's nickname for me being uttered by another man. No one else has ever called me babe. I shake off the feeling that I'm cheating on Nate. We've been divorced for years.

"Right. We aren't one of those couples who needs alone time during the day."

Hailey shifts uncomfortably. *Yeah, she likes my fake boyfriend.* "Okay, I'll see if Caris is around. We can take her boat out."

"Perfect." I smile widely and remind myself to tone it down when Hailey eyes me oddly.

When I enter the flower shop Tuesday, I'm not surprised to find Nate behind the counter. Karen and I are going to have to chat. I get she wants her son to be happy, but if Nate is sticking around there's no need for me to help out. As much as I love this shop and as much as I missed being a florist, I can't work with my ex-husband every day. It's asking too much of my heart.

"Morning, beautiful," Nate says as he hands me a cup which smells like chocolate. He's wearing a blue shirt the same color as his eyes, and it tightens around his muscles, giving me a full view of his tattoos which I try hard not to focus on. I don't want to know what they stand for. I don't want to know why he chose each one. It's the last thing I need and yet all I can think about.

"Just how you like it, half chocolate, espresso shot, and half coffee." He smiles knowing I won't turn down this treat. Damn him. Normally I miss out on the espresso shot because I don't have a machine to make it.

We used to have one in our apartment in Nashville. Nate would bring it to me in bed, and we'd make love tasting like chocolate. It was the hottest sex in our own little world.

Nate's eyes glaze over, and I realize I'm licking my lips. His mind is clearly wandering to the past like mine. I bite the inside of my mouth, mumble a thank you, and disappear into the back with my coffee where I will lose myself for the next few hours.

At eleven thirty I come out to the front to find Nate talking quietly to his mom. "Hi, Karen," I say with a smile, knowing Nate will leave now that she's back. "If you two want to go to lunch, I can cover the front," I offer, hoping this will speed up my ex-husband's exit.

"Oh, that's okay. I have orders to input. If you're hungry

you can go now. I had a late breakfast."

As I'm beginning to object, Shawn appears in the door. "Hey, babe," he says, offering me a sweet smile. "Hi, Mrs. Pearson," he says to Karen and then nods in Nate's direction. "Nate, good to see you, man. I was hoping to steal my girl for a picnic. Can you take a break, babe?"

Nate's jaw hardens. For a moment I feel bad for this ruse, but when my stomach clenches as I meet Nate's eyes, I know it's necessary. Gravity doesn't exist when he's near me. He sucks all the air from the room, leaving me lightheaded and excited. My body simply can't handle being around him even if my head knows there's no future. It's time to burn everything to the ground so that I can accept there is no rebuilding my relationship with Nate.

I reach out to lock fingers with Shawn. When he pulls me to his chest and brushes a kiss across my lips, I know I've succeeded in leaving nothing but ashes for Nate. If only I felt something other than guilt when Shawn's lips meet mine.

I feel absolutely nothing. No spark. No chemistry. Honestly, I wish I even felt a smidgen of feelings. Even a little stirring of butterflies.

"Thanks, Shawn, so sweet of you," I whisper. Turning around, I avoid Nate's eyes and look straight at a surprised Karen. "I'll be back in an hour." She nods, but her face remains stoic. Poor Karen. This is incredibly awkward. I hate lying to her, but she needs this ruse as much as Nate. They both need to realize I'm no longer a Pearson. If I ever really was one, that time in my life is over.

Shawn and I leave the flower shop holding hands and walk down the docks to Independence Park which sits on the water.

"Did I come on too thick?" Shawn asks as I unpack the bag he brought from the restaurant. "I had chef make you a chocolate shake—figured after seeing Nate this morning you'd be jonesing for some chocolate."

I laugh as I take a sip, moaning as the chocolate hits my veins. Just what I needed.

"Thank you. The 'babe' and the kiss were a surprise, but maybe it will speed up Nate's departure. So thanks. How'd you know he was going to be at the flower shop?"

"Oh, I heard him talking to Caris this morning at the coffee depot. They seemed very friendly. Did they ever date?"

My stomach bottoms out. Nate and Caris? They were in the same class, but I can't picture it. Caris is the exact opposite of me. All beauty products, suits, and smiles. Both of us are blonde with long legs so certainly she would be his type, I guess, but I'd never seen Nate with anyone but me, and quite frankly it makes me sick and incredibly sad. Which is odd because I know he's been with women since we've broken up.

Divorced, not broken up. Divorced is much more dramatic and much more permanent.

Is Caris now his type? Would he really come back to Bristol and settle down with someone else?

It's unbearable. Another shot of carbon monoxide. He needs to leave.

"No. They never dated."

Shawn turns his head thoughtfully. "Hm. They just seemed awfully chummy. If you have any interest in reconciling, I wouldn't wait too long. When Caris sets her sights on something, she goes after it, and it appears her sights have been set on your ex."

My stomach turns because he's right. Caris is nothing if not persistent. Lying through my teeth I say, "Good. Then he'll leave me alone, which of course is what I want."

I bite into my burger and let my mind swirl, knowing I'll never survive Nate staying here with anyone but me. But what choice do I have—there's no future with Nate. I'll have to come to terms with that one way or another.

"So, I noticed Hailey was not too happy to hear about us dating. Two more weeks, tops, followed by a nondramatic breakup where I tell her we both decided we're better as friends because you only have eyes for her, and I think she's yours."

He smiles. "She was there when chef made your shake. She was practically seeing red. It's like she's finally noticing me. Oh, I forgot to mention, Charlotte said she and Jack want to do dinner."

I shrug my shoulders. "Okay, as in a double date or just a regular family get-together?"

I hadn't mentioned anything about this new fake relationship to Charlotte or Jack so I'm assuming it's a family thing, but why would she go through Shawn to ask me?

Shawn appears to wonder the same thing. "Don't know. I just assumed she told me because she knew I'd see you at work. You think it's already spread around town that we're dating?"

I shake my head. Only Nate, Hailey, and now Mrs. Pearson know.

"You think Nate told Jack?" Shawn asks.

"No. They don't talk."

Shawn frowns. "Why don't they talk? I thought you said they were best friends."

"Same reason my marriage ended…and I really don't want to talk about it."

Shawn shifts closer to me. "Talk to me."

I don't talk about this. I never have, which is why my family doesn't know we even got married let alone divorced.

"We got married while Jack and Peter were overseas. We planned to have a big wedding when they came back. We didn't tell anyone. We wanted it to be a surprise, and I wanted to tell them all in person. It was the weekend before we were supposed to come home to tell everyone the news. I was making meatballs, and Nate was pouring a glass of wine for me. He'd just handed me the glass when the phone rang."

I pause, taking a moment to return back to that day. "Even now I can remember every sensation in that moment because it was the last time I knew what perfect felt like. Garlic wafting through the air, Chris Stapleton on the radio, red wine on my lips, and my husband's arm around my waist as he put the phone on speaker when he saw Jack's name on the caller ID. And then two words which changed our lives forever—'Peter's dead.'"

I meet Shawn's wide eyes, not even feeling the tears on my cheeks anymore, my focus adjusting through the wet blur. It feels pretty symbolic of what my life has been the last few years. Trying to see my way through, with no focus, no destination. Just moving from one moment to the next, knowing life will never bring back the perfect I knew in our little home on that simple Saturday night.

Shawn reaches out and pulls me into his lap as I sob against his chest. "I'm so sorry, Amelia." His hands stroke my hair, and I sob harder, remembering Nate's face when we heard Jack's words. His smile fell and he pulled me to him, focusing on my heartbreak, stroking my hair, taking on both of our grief.

I try to force a breath, knowing we are making a scene in the park. "I understand that was devastating, but why did that end your marriage?"

Valid question. I try to ready myself to relive the second worst moment of my life. "Peter's death changed everything. Things were said that can't be unsaid. We both acted out. We both made mistakes." I wipe the tears from my eyes.

My biggest mistake was leaving him. Giving up on us. But what choice did I have? "I can't talk about this. I'm sorry."

Shawn rubs his hand in slow circles against my back. "It's okay. I'm here when you're ready to talk. I'm going to call the shop and tell Mrs. Pearson you're taking the day off."

I wipe the tears and remove myself from Shawn's lap. "No. I'm okay. I'll clean up and be fine. Honestly, staying busy is what saved me."

Shawn hands me a water. "Drink up. All those tears are going to give you a headache."

I take the bottle and stare at Shawn. "How 'bout you take my mind off my drama and tell me what's really going on with you and Hailey?"

Shawn lets out a low laugh. "You don't play fair. I can't say no to a girl with tears."

I pop out my lip in a full pout, really playing up my sadness. It's not hard. *"Please."*

He shakes his head and holds his hands up in defeat. "Okay, okay." He shifts to get comfortable, leaning back on his hands, and faces the sun. "You know how I worked in Tahoe before I came here?"

Shrugging, I take another sip of water. "Yeah, after your famous baseball career."

Shawn winces, and I feel bad having brought it up. Before he settled in Bristol, he was a pitcher on the West Coast. He doesn't talk about it much, but it's impossible not to have heard the story about the famed pitcher whose career came to a screeching halt after a car accident. He wasn't even in the car, just a good Samaritan trying to help out. Look where that got him. "Yeah, after everything that happened, I worked in Tahoe for a while at a bar…and for a year I watched one person after another find love. A guy I was friends with out there, Ryan, he had a best friend…you should have seen these two. They couldn't get out of their own way, but watching two friends fall in love…it just made me realize that's what I want. And what's better than falling in love with your best friend, right?"

The sentiment stabs me in the chest. I know precisely how that felt. This time it was my turn to wince, and Shawn grabs my hand, squeezing. "Sorry, bad choice of words."

I shake it off. "It's fine. So, Hailey…you like her because she's your friend?"

Shawn smiles then runs his hand down his face trying to hide his goofy grin. "Her curves don't hurt either."

Laughter bubbles up, and we both let it burst through, saving the afternoon. He's a super sweet guy, and I'm lucky he's my friend. Hailey will be a lucky girl one day.

Nate

"I wasn't aware Amelia was dating anyone," my mother says as she stares at Amelia and Shawn, walking away hand in hand.

I swallow my pride and the bile that is working its way up my throat after witnessing her kiss another man. Her lips touched someone else's. How many men had she kissed in the last three years? The question makes my stomach turn.

"That's what she says, at least," I mutter, slamming my hand down onto the counter. The loudness grabs my mother's attention. "Sorry."

She smiles sadly. "I told you this wasn't going to be easy."

I raise my eyes to the ceiling, praying for patience. "I just need to focus on something else for a bit. I need to find a job, get an apartment, and prove to her I'm here to stay."

My mom moves closer, squeezing my shoulder. "Are you sure this is what you want? Grant said—"

I interrupt her. "I don't care what Grant said. This is what I want."

My mom looks uneasy. "Nate, she may never take you back. I want you guys together more than anything, but this was your dream. Are you sure you just want to throw that away?"

How could anything be my dream if it meant not being with Amelia in the process? I can't have both things I want. My music career and Amelia. Making the choice to stay here and fight for Amelia isn't even up for discussion. I have to show her she comes first. She gave up everything for me last time, and the least I can do is choose her this time.

"I'm positive. I just need to tell Grant I'm done."

My mom moves away as a customer comes in. "Well, you better do that quickly. And send the contract back. The longer it sits there the more problems it will cause. If you're making a choice, make it." With that she turns to her next customer with a sweet smile.

She's right. I need to rip off the Band-Aid. Remove the last string I have tying me to Nashville. To the other life I had. The one I'd lived without Amelia for three years. None of it made me happy. No one held a candle to Amelia. And somehow I know this is exactly what my dad would have told me to do. This would have made him proud.

CHAPTER 12

Amelia

Walking into work the next morning, I prepare myself to come face-to-face with my ex. I may have spent a few extra minutes getting ready and actually taken the time to style my hair. It's not that I want to be with Nate, but I also don't want to be the disastrous ex-wife of his who always looks like the twelve-year-old who trailed him, Peter, and my brother. Every time I've run into Nate the past week I've been like a doe in headlights, a damsel who needs saving. Not today. Today I am standing on my own two feet. Shawn and I have a plan, and it's going to work. I am going to look put together, I am going to convince Nate I've moved on, Nate is going to go back to Nashville, and I will move on with my life here.

Easy-peasy.

"Morning, Karen," I sing in my most professional and upbeat voice. I hope Nate hears just how fine I sound. Definitely not like a girl who is pining over her ex-husband. Absolutely not someone who is so pathetic she has to fill every minute of her day to keep from thinking about his lips. And positively not someone who never moved on from the way said ex makes her feel. Nope, I sound completely capable, professional, and not like a woman scorned.

"Morning, Amelia. You look beautiful today. Do you have another date with Shawn for lunch?"

See, I do look beautiful. And even Karen is acknowledging my new relationship status. *Winning!*

I shrug my shoulders. "It's possible. He's such a good boyfriend he likes to keep me on my toes."

Even used the word boyfriend without cringing. I look around the store, eyeing behind the counter, and then let my eyes rest on the door to the back where I normally prepare the bouquets. Nate is nowhere to be found. He better not be messing with my arrangements.

The truth is I can't feel him. I know he's not here because the air is light. His heavy fire isn't sucking all of the oxygen from my lungs.

"You know you two have to stop punishing one another."

My eyes shoot up. "Hm?"

"You and Nate. You're looking for him, aren't you?"

"What? No," I stutter, quite unconvincingly.

Karen sighs. "He's not here. He knows being around day in and day out would be too hard. He's not going to be working here, Amelia. Don't worry."

I try to keep the disappointment that he's not here off my face.

The better question though is why am I disappointed? This is what I wanted. For Nate to not come in. My plan was to make it so obvious that I was over him and make it so uncomfortable with Shawn coming around that he stopped showing up everywhere I worked. So now that it worked, why am I upset?

Because he gave up quickly, just like last time. The little voice in my head annoys me because it's right.

Recovering quickly, I reply, "Oh, I wasn't looking for Nate. But that's good that he is doing something else. Great, actually."

Karen's blue eyes search my face, almost like she's trying to laser into my thoughts and change them. It's unnerving, and I'm almost worried that it's working.

"You're both punishing one another for your grief. For how you processed the immense loss of Peter. You both handled it differently, and rather than being there for one another, you pushed each other away. That's why your marriage didn't work. That's why you're miserable now. Maybe I'm overstepping…"

Miserable. *Pft.* Do I look like someone who is miserable? My hair is done, I'm wearing damn blush, and there is mascara on my eyes.

I. Am. Not. Miserable.

I nod vigorously at her. "Yes. You are overstepping."

She pauses, taking in my standoffish appearance—the way I've crossed my arms, pursed my lips, and positioned my feet, as if gearing for a fight. "See, Amelia, that right there. You are always ready to fight. Whether it's on behalf of someone or for yourself. You are always ready to fight. And Nate, he has no fight left in him. *You* were his protector."

My heart registers what she's saying, but my mind remains closed off and angry that she's blaming our divorce on me. She has no idea what she's talking about.

She has no idea what *he* did.

Her eyes dip, and her voice softens as she touches my arm, pulling it from its twisted grip and bringing it to her heart. "Darling, you saved my boy. *Saved him*. He's lost again. And he's going to need you. He does need you. Selfishly, I want you to pick up the pieces because you're the only one who can. You made that your burden and your gift when you were just a child. *I* can't make him better. I can't make you better. You guys do that for each other. And that's why all of us stand on the sidelines waiting. We're waiting for you guys to get this right because you are both floundering. I say this with love, sweet girl, it's time to put down the boxing gloves and grow up."

Anger courses through me. How *dare* she? She has no idea what Nate did to break us. Does she think I wouldn't love anything more than to run to Nate and fix him? But he came back with a smirk and a joking demeanor. That man is not broken anymore. He's healed himself.

I'm the broken one. I'm the ashes. I can't fix anyone, and when I needed him to fight for me—for once to put me first—he failed.

I am the only one who is watching out for me, and I'll be damn sure that I don't risk getting hurt—that I don't wake up the emotions I've learned to quiet—just to go through that kind of gut- wrenching pain again when he decides he's done.

My heart is closed off. It's easier to feel nothing ever again than to risk feeling like you're burning from the inside.

"Karen, I know you mean well, but you just don't understand. Now if you don't mind, I'm going to focus on getting today's orders done." She nods as I prepare to leave, but I can barely look at her. I rush to the back, and as soon as the swinging door closes, the tears pour down my face. So much for mascara. Ever since Nate came back, all I do is cry. *That* should be a clue to everyone—we aren't meant to be.

Before heading to the bar for my shift, I convince Belle to meet me at my apartment so we can lie out in the park for a bit. The weather is still beautiful, and I need sun on my face to bring back some color and lift my mood.

She surveys my outfit when I let her in the door and shakes her head. "Yeah, no."

"Excuse me?"

"Amelia, you have to stop dressing like that. It's depressing." Her eyes scan my outfit, and I look down to see what's so wrong with what I'm wearing. I have on a grey fitted T-shirt and jean shorts. My usual attire.

"What's so bad with how I look?"

Belle laughs. "You look like a hardened woman, a woman who isn't interested in dating, if you catch my drift."

I'm sure I have a stupefied look on my face. "This is how I've always dressed. Why do I need to change now?"

"Yeah, and you had the same boyfriend since you were a teenager. He knew what you looked like naked. He didn't need the subtle cleavage preview."

The what? What is she talking about? And what does it matter if men are interested in me. I'm not looking for a man. Or am I? I can't even keep up with what I want. Being around Nate has totally messed with my brain.

I did want to date again. I was ready for it. Until *he* came back.

Belle continues, "You know, the top that gives just a hint of the skin between your breasts, the spot you can let your hand caress softly, by accident, of course, because just looking at him makes you want to."

"You're insane, you know that?"

"Oh my God. Just put this on." She throws a white floral romper in my direction.

"Where did you get this?"

"I bought it for you. After seeing you at the golf range the other day you looked so...*sad.* It's time for you to start dating again. Nate's been gone for a long time. He's not coming back."

I breathe out, not yet ready to share that Nate is actually

back. I don't want to discuss what that means. I don't want to discuss him at all. "I have started dating again," I say, as I grab the romper out of her hand and resign myself to putting it on.

"Who?" she asks as she follows me into my room. I've learned that I can't change in my living room. No more peep shows for my ex-husband or current fake boyfriend.

"I'm dating Shawn."

"You're dating Shawn?" she mimics.

I pull my shorts off and slip the romper up my thighs. "Yes."

"Shawn Chase?" she asks in apparent disbelief. "As in Charlotte's brother?"

"Yes."

"As in the man who is so obviously obsessed with Hailey?" Belle eyes me, calling bullshit.

I shake my head and purse my lips.

Belle's head falls back, and she lets out a loud laugh. "Yeah, and I'm dating my assistant."

I mimic her laughter. "Well, you want to."

It's no secret that Belle is obsessed with her assistant whom she refers to as the Green-Eyed Monster. At least to everyone else it's obvious. She's still working out her feelings. "I do not."

"Whatever, I'm dating Shawn. Believe me or not—it's true."

Nate

The conversation with Sam went better than I imagined. He did all the heavy lifting for me. Didn't even make me ask for the job, instead making it seem like I'd be doing him a favor. He is honestly a really good guy.

Of course I have no idea how to even use the computers in his office, and I definitely don't own the proper clothes. This is going to be more of a learning curve than I intended.

My mother appears in the kitchen, and seeing my face as I stare at the computer, she lets out a laugh. "Whatchya doing in here, Nate?"

I point to the screen which is covered in suits. How do I even know they will fit? The past few years—okay, my whole life—I'd been a jeans and T-shirt guy. I play the guitar. I'm covered in tattoos. I don't belong in a suit.

But this is for her.

Reminding myself of why I'm doing what I'm doing, I seek my mom's help. "I asked Sam if I could be of any help in the office, you know, while I'm trying to figure out what to do with my life." My mom just nods her head. We both know Sam is the one helping me, not the other way around. My ability to help with financial transactions is limited to suggesting a crowd put a twenty in my tip jar in exchange for a song.

"So you need suits?"

"Yes. I don't exactly think this will pass for his office."

My mom looks down at my outfit and shakes her head. "I'm not sure that even counts as an outfit, Nate. But I have an idea. Follow me."

I close the laptop and follow my mother up the stairs. She can't possibly think that I'll fit in Sam's suits. The man is like the Jolly Green Giant; he's tall but lanky. I'm six feet one, and he's still got at least three inches on me. "Um, Mom, I'm not going to wear Sam's suits."

My mom turns around and frowns. "Well obviously, Nate. That would be weird. Besides, he needs his suits." I like how she recognizes that he would still need them. He may be sick, but he's going to get through it. We're all going to get through it. He has to.

"Right. So...what's your brilliant plan? I promise I won't fit into my first communion suit, Mom."

She rolls her eyes and lets out a laugh. I'm sure she's picturing my large body in the white seersucker. I was adorable back then. Still am. "You're a pain in the ass, you know that?"

I give her my most heartbreaking smile. "But I'm *your* pain in the ass."

"Yes. Yes, you are. Anyway, come in here." I follow her into the guest bedroom and watch as she opens the closet, revealing suits in all different shades. From the lightest of greys to the darkest of blues, it is clear from just looking at them that these are expensive suits.

My mom picks up a light grey one and turns to show me. When I turn my eyes from the suit, I find her blue eyes are glistening. "Your dad always had the best taste in clothes. I could never bear to donate them. And I hoped"—her voice cracks as she pauses—"that one day you would want them." Her eyes flutter down as she takes a moment to control her emotions.

My dad's suits.

Another piece of him. Something else I didn't know existed. Another gift.

"Do you think they will fit me?" I ask quietly, as I move to the closet to see the suits from a closer vantage point.

My mom turns to me and leans herself against my chest and sighs. "You feel just like him. Same height, same build. You are your father's son, Nate." She smiles as she looks up at me.

Choking up and wanting nothing but to lose myself in my mother's embrace, I wrap my arms around her, holding her close and brushing a kiss on her head. "I think I'm a pretty good mix of you both."

She looks up and smiles. "I think you're right about that." Wiping tears from her eyes, she points to the grey one. "Try it on. I'd love for you to have them. What do you say?"

It's nerve-racking trying on the suit, attempting to become the man I admired my whole life. It was one thing to follow the words of his book; it is something else entirely to literally step into his shoes—or clothes. But I am trying to make him proud. Hoping to get it right this time. And I can't think of a better way to start than by dressing the part.

My mother gives me privacy, and I slip the pants on, buttoning them easily. Even the hem falls in the correct place. They fit like a glove. Next, I try the jacket, and like the pants, it fits exquisitely. I walk out of the room and into the hallway where I find my mom gawking at me. "Oh, Nate. You look so handsome."

I grin shyly. "Thanks, Mom."

"I really think this will be good for you. Working with Sam. Settling down. Coming back home. I'm really proud of you."

I bite the inside of my lip. Unlike Amelia, I am a crier. But mom doesn't need to know that. "Okay, I'm going to grab a button-down and head over to Sam's office. Wish me luck." I lean down for a kiss, and my mom plops one on my cheek.

My day is spent learning how to use the computer. I can't even make this up. I legit needed the secretary to show me how to turn on the computer. It's been a while since I've touched one, and I swear they are more complicated than I imagined. She taught me how to navigate their simple website and how to input client information. By midday both Sam's assistant and I are exhausted. Me from staring at a computer screen all day and her from dealing with me.

"I'm sorry I'm so bad at this," I say, apologizing for likely the sixteenth time today.

Fortunately, she is young—in her early twenties—and she seems to appreciate my looks, even if my computer skills are lacking. "Oh, it's okay, Nate. We can work on it some more next week."

My head is pounding. I can't imagine having to do this on a weekly basis. Caffeine seems like a good idea to pass a few more of the hours. "I'm going to run out and grab a coffee, can I pick you up something?" It's the least I can do after monopolizing her time. I'm sure she'll be staying late to finish her actual work now.

"Sure, an iced coffee would be great."

I leave my jacket behind and roll up my sleeves, enjoying the warm fall day as I walk through town. It's unusually busy at Independence Park, overlooking the harbor. Blankets are laid out and children run around. School must have just ended, and energy is bursting from all their little bodies.

I find myself smiling as I watch three boys running in circles, remembering just how crazy Jack, Peter, and I used to be after school. My eyes fall to a leggy blonde wearing a white getup who walks toward me. "Amelia Pearson, we need to stop meeting like this."

Love & Tequila Make Her Crazy

Amelia's eyes go wide as she stares at me. "Na-Nate, what are you wearing?" She practically fans herself. Who knew that a white button-down with the sleeves rolled up would have my tomboy all hot and bothered? Must be the tattoos. Her eyes dance as she studies my forearms.

Definitely the tattoos.

"Just out for a coffee. You?"

Amelia couldn't look more flustered if she tried. Her outfit is also throwing me. Don't get me wrong, Amelia could wear a paper bag and be the hottest woman in the room. But the point is she doesn't need to—a pair of jean shorts and a tank top is *her*. The flowy white, flowery thing she has going on, not so much. "Oh, um…just grabbing a coffee before I go get changed for work."

Unable to hold it in any longer, I let out a breathy laugh. "Yeah, these outfits you keep surprising me with. You know I like you just the way you are, you don't have to go all Martha Washington or Daisy Duck to get me to ask you out on a date. Just say the word, Cookie, and I'm yours." Amelia's lip is between her teeth, and her eyes roam my chest. I wave my hand in front of her face. "Earth to Amelia, you in there?"

Her eyes rise to mine and her cheeks pink. "Oh, sorry. Right. Yes. Wait, what were you saying?"

I chuckle. As much as I enjoy teasing her, when I ask her out on a date, I want her to actually, willingly agree. Not to agree by default because she's not paying attention. Even if it is because she's so attracted to me she's lost her words. "Nothing, Ames. Can I buy you a coffee?"

She looks at me, confused. "Coffee? Who wanted a coffee? Not me. I'm going to work. In the other direction. Over that way. Yes, I've got to go." Without hesitating, Amelia peels off in the wrong direction, leaving me grinning on the sidewalk.

Laughing, I shout, "Ames, the bar's that way." She turns back and looks at me, nods, and then walks off.

CHAPTER 13

Amelia

I luck out when my boss at the charter company calls me to handle a last-minute overnight charter. The girl that was supposed to go got sick, and they needed someone to handle serving and entertaining the guests on the Hinckley that the group was taking over to Nantucket. They were leaving Thursday morning and not coming back until Sunday, so I needed to get coverage at the bar for my weekend shift, but Hailey said she could cover it. Honestly, I think everyone was just saying yes to any of my requests knowing that I needed to get out of town for a few days. Who would think that a town with over twenty square miles would be too small for Nate and me to occupy? But every time I turn around, he's there, whether it was at the flower shop, the bar, or downtown. I couldn't handle it anymore; I needed a break, and the charter came at the perfect time.

For seventy-two hours I lose myself in my job—serving drinks, helping the men figure out how to throw a line, tossing back shots at night with them. The group of guys are a good time, but none of them hold a candle to Nate. It's infuriating. By the time we return on Sunday afternoon, I've declined giving my number to all but one of them. His sister is getting married, and he offered to introduce us so that I have a shot at another florist event, but I'm not positive he's not also looking for a date to said wedding. Whatever. I'm completely single, so it's not like I can't date if I want to.

Each of the guys hugs me goodbye, and Chris, the one with the sister, waves his phone at me and tells me we'll talk soon. I smile and wave goodbye before hopping back on the boat to help clean up before my shift at the bar.

I can feel Nate before I hear his voice. Taking a deep breath, I try to ground myself before my body heats up the thirty degrees he normally inspires.

"How was the trip?" he asks in a throaty tone. It almost sounds like he's nervous. First time he's shown any type of hesitancy since he's been back. Maybe my disappearing act showed him that I haven't just been waiting around town for him to return. I have a life. Albeit a busy work-filled one, but it's how I like it.

Shrugging my shoulders and refusing to turn around, I focus on the task at hand and mumble, "It was fine. Always good to be on the water."

Nate hops onto the boat, and I look around searching for someone to save me. Unfortunately, the captain ran to his car, and the other crew member is below deck. "Nate, you can't be here. What are you doing?"

I finally turn around, and my eyes get stuck on his chest. Last time I saw him, he was wearing a button-down and that did all sorts of things to me, but today might be worse. I recognize the shirt. It's one from a trip we took to Dollywood. It makes me laugh when I look at it—a man wearing Dolly Parton on his chest—but even back when he bought it and he had no tattoos, he looked hot.

"She's a damn good singer," he'd said with a smile. *"And you haven't stopped smiling since we got here."*

I hadn't stopped smiling because we'd gotten married the weekend before and the trip was a mini-honeymoon. I was smiling from all the sex. Just seeing the shirt brings me back to our hotel room, and the stairway, and the van.

Oh shit, the van. Nate had to pull over on the side of the highway.

"You're biting your lip," Nate whispers, moving closer.

"Huh?"

"Amelia," he says with authority, and his eyes grow dark, "stop biting your lip."

My eyes dart from the shirt to his lips and back to the shirt again. He growls, and I swear to God I almost fall backward off the boat. He reaches out and grabs me, pulling my body flush against him, and whispers in my ear, "You thinking about the van? About how fucking naughty you were, unbuckling my pants while I was driving, taking me so deep into your throat that I had to pull the car over…and you *still* didn't stop."

His blue eyes taunt me, and his words heat my skin. Who is this man? Nate Pearson was a sweet-talking boy who made love to me. This—this person standing before me, making my legs quiver and my thighs sweat, is someone else completely.

And I am here for it.

"I—uh—I have to finish cleaning up," I stumble through the conversation and pull back. I can't think about the van. I can't think about Nashville, or sex with Nate, or Nate at all.

Nate smiles his crooked smile, and my heart melts into a puddle.

That's right, just mop me up when you're cleaning the deck, boys. I'm done for.

"See you later, Ames," he says before hopping off the boat.

"Cat got your tongue, Amelia?" a woman's high-pitched voice says. I spin around to find Lucille standing on the dock with a smirk on her lips and a pointed hand on her hip.

I shake my head completely lost as to her question. "Huh?"

She laughs as she walks closer to the boat. "I'd heard rumors that boy was back in town to woo you, but I never would have believed it had I not seen it with my very own eyes. Our little Amelia all doe-eyed and speechless." She clucks her tongue, shakes her head, and smiles a devilish smile. "Don't worry, I won't tell anyone." Her fingers move across her lips as if she's locking away a secret, and I know without a doubt she'll be on the phone with the Bristol Events Committee in the hour. She couldn't possibly let Macy scoop her on this 'story.' I sigh. There's nothing to tell since nothing is going on, but when I go to say that,

I get a look at Nate's smirk as he glances back to the boat, as if he couldn't leave without one more look, and once again my tongue is wagging thick in my mouth and I'm speechless.

"Feeling better, babe?" Hailey asks right before smacking my ass. The guys on the other side of the bar raise their eyebrows to one another, and I shake my head at their obvious excitement. Men are so basic.

I roll my eyes. "Yes, thanks for covering for me this weekend. I needed the break."

"How are things with Shawn?" she asks. I turn to watch him as he takes two women's orders. Their tongues are practically hanging from their mouths. Okay, women are basic too.

"It's good. I mean he's obviously hot and a great guy, so what could be wrong?"

I turn back to gauge Hailey's reaction only to find her staring right at Shawn. Our plan is totally working.

A hush settles over the bar as the guitarist taps into the mic. I look up and meet Nate's eyes. Oh, fuck. What is *he* doing here? I glare at him and then turn to Hailey with my hand on my hip. "Seriously, Hails?"

She laughs sarcastically. "What could go wrong, she

asks. Ha! Thought you weren't interested in your ex-husband anymore, *Ames*?"

I let out an exaggerated breath because I'm mature like that. "You really don't play fair."

She tilts her head and shrugs. "I've got a dog in this fight too. My bet is on the tattooed ex personally. I just don't get you and Shawn."

Perfectly timed, Shawn walks up, grabs my hip, and spins me into his chest before taking my chin in his hand, tilting my lips up to his own, and kissing me. This time it isn't a chaste kiss. His tongue splinters my lips open, and he goes for it. I'm so completely shocked by his moves that I don't resist, and soon I find myself getting into it. Not into it, into it. Not like how I would kiss Nate. God, why am I thinking about Nate while Shawn's tongue is in my mouth? I pull back and stare up at Shawn. He smirks and looks at me as he replies to Hailey, "You were saying, Hails?"

I've got to hand it to him, the man has game.

"Could one of the bartenders grab me a drink?" Nate practically growls into the mic.

Hailey shakes her head and laughs. "Yeah, I still don't buy it. But whatever," she sings the last word, gives Nate a thumbs-up, and gets to work on grabbing his beer.

"Thanks," I mutter to Shawn.

He winks and turns back to the customers. "Kissing you isn't a hardship, Ames."

Love & Tequila Make Her Crazy

I laugh and put a napkin in front of the newest brunette at the bar. "What can I get you tonight?"

The girl giggles and mumbles to her friend, "Uh, the guitarist, please."

"He's not on the menu, but I could make you a cosmo," I offer with a smile. Inside I'm steaming. The kiss did nothing for me. Nate's stinging glare, on the other hand, has my entire body on fire.

"I think I'll just do a wine. Can we get shots too?"

Shots and wine…what a combination. Amateurs.

"What do you think Nate likes?" she asks.

How does she know his name? "The guitarist?" I say, feigning stupidity.

"Yeah. We want to send over a shot," the girl beside her says.

I school my expression. "Chocolate cake shots."

If they're buying, I'm going to make sure he's thinking of me while he downs it.

To be completely fair, I know I am yo-yoing between wanting Nate's attention and wanting him as far away as possible. Part of me would willingly light myself on fire just for the chance to feel his lips against mine again. But the other wiser, cynical, and scared part knows that the possibility of being with Nate again is nonexistent. It still hurts too much to look at him. To be in his presence. And as long as I feel that way, it's impossible for me to try again.

"Those sound good."

"They're the best," Hailey replies, winking at me. "Want me to bring it over to him, Ames? Wouldn't want to take you away from your boyfriend for too long," she teases.

I roll my eyes. Brat.

"Can I take it over?" the girl across from me asks.

I shake my head. "Bar rules—you can't serve alcohol."

Okay, I'm clearly making up rules now. She wouldn't be serving alcohol by delivering a shot to Nate, and Hailey just laughs beside me, muttering, "Bullshit."

"Okay, just let him know Cynthia from the office sent it over," she says with a wistful smile in his direction. He nods his head at her, and she beams.

Cynthia from the office? What office? What is she talking about?

"Where do you work?" I ask, trying to keep my voice neutral. This night is quickly spiraling out of control, and I need to get a hold on it.

"Winsor Financial," she replies. "Nate just started there this week. His stepfather is the owner."

Pieces start to fall together. Nate is working with Sam. *For Sam.* But why? Nate in an office is the most depressing thought. Although I guess that explains the shirt the other day. "Gotcha. And what do you do there?"

"I input the client information. I'm hoping to move up though."

No idea what any of that means. Finances and offices aren't my thing. And they most certainly aren't Nate's. What is he up to?

"Great. Well, I'll make sure to let him know you said hi. Enjoy the show." I hand them their shots and don't waste time watching them.

Moving quickly through the crowded bar, I bring Nate his shot. He's in the middle of a set, and I put the shots down on the deck's ledge and look out at the bay. The sky is set ablaze in a fierce orange and the bay is calm. It's a complete contrast, just like me.

Around me, people sit entranced, listening to Nate's skilled fingers playing Old Dominion's "One Man Band." I turn and meet his eyes, and of course he's staring right at me, singing a song that speaks to my soul. For a moment, I let myself remember the way those lips tasted, the way they sang to me, and the way they made me feel. Against my skin, between my legs, and in my heart.

I honestly don't know if another man will ever be able to touch the places he's branded. Will anyone be able to reach my depths? Would anyone even try? It would be a daunting task to take on, trying to erase the touch of someone who lived within your being. Someone who so deeply intertwined themselves into you that they likely changed your genetic makeup.

Nate shakes his head as if he's answering my question. *No, no one could come close to us. No one gets those parts of you, Amelia—only me. The sooner you realize that, the sooner we can be happy again.*

I hold up the shots, and he motions over to me with his

head as he finishes his song. Sliding the guitar off his lap, he leans it against the barstool he's sitting on and looks up at me. "Tequila?"

"Chocolate cake," I reply.

He grins. "Ah, my girl's favorite."

"Do you mean Cynthia?"

Nate's face falls, and he gives me a blank stare. "Seriously? She's like twelve." I turn to look back at the two women at the bar who are watching Nate and me with unabashed interest. "Wanna give them a show?" he says in a low sexy whisper before wrapping his arm around my waist and pulling me close to him. His fingers dig into the flesh on my hip, and I can practically feel his possessiveness. "You seem to be giving lots of them tonight." He raises his brow and dares me to deny that what happened between Shawn and me only moments before was anything other than a show.

I shrug, pretending that his arms around me do nothing for me. That his breath mingled with my own doesn't make me want to inhale him. That his lips, which are practically a mask against my own, don't make me want to nip out and bite down. "Believe what you want, Pearson. I'm just here to deliver your drink."

He lets go of my waist and holds out his hand to take it, unaffected by my words. We clink our glasses together and down the shots, the whole time our eyes remaining fixed on one another. "So, you're working for Sam?"

A lazy smile spills across Nate's face. "You checking up on

me, Cookie?"

He's impossible. I roll my eyes and wait for him to respond to my actual question.

Nate huffs out a laugh and pierces my heart with his smile again. "Started last week. My last gig as a florist wasn't working. I wasn't able to focus in the hostile work conditions."

"Hostile work conditions!" I practically shout.

Nate remains unaffected. "Yeah, one of the bosses kept staring at me. Made me feel uncomfortable."

"As if," I quip.

"You seem to be doing a lot of staring lately, sweetheart. You know you can touch if you want. I won't stop you."

"Can you be serious for one freaking second? Just answer my question. Why are you working for Sam?"

"Have dinner with me?"

"What?" I practically choke on my own saliva. Why would he think that after this infuriating conversation I would want to spend any time with him?

"If you want to know about my life, have dinner with me." He says the words slowly, emphasizing each one.

"I have a boyfriend."

Nate shakes his head. "You are making this so much harder than it has to be, Ames."

And there it is. Exactly what I knew he was saying before with his eyes. *Give in, Ames. We both know how this will end. Why delay the inevitable?*

Because I'm not ready. Because I don't forgive you. Because I don't want to get hurt again.

"Have a good night, Nate."

He sighs out a long breath. "You too, Ames. Thanks for the shot."

"You can thank your new coworker. Hopefully this job works out for you. It seems you have fans everywhere you go."

As I walk away, I hear him reply, "But you're the only one I want."

Nate

The phone hasn't stopped today with unwanted texts and phone calls. Everyone wants to apologize, extend their condolences, *remember.* But there are only two people I want to see today. Only two people I would give my right arm to spend the day with. One of them sits beside me on the boat, a wistful smile on her face, and the other remains at the flower shop, but I know her heart is with me today.

"It's a beautiful day, Nate. Thank you for making me come out here; I've missed the water."

Somehow my lips manage a smile despite the fact that my

heart is empty. "I feel closer to him when I'm out here."

My mom looks off into the distance. "Have you been reading the journal?"

Every night. Every chance I get. I'm taking every morsel of what my dad wrote, every piece of advice, and trying to figure out how to apply it to my life. So far I've got a pretty good sense of what to do. It's what Jack suggested as well. Prove to Amelia that I'm in this for the long haul. Be patient and prove her wrong. "Yes, thank you again for giving it to me."

My mother's quiet smile is the only response I get. The phone beeps again with another text from some unwanted do-gooder, and I have to hold myself back from picking it up and throwing it into the ocean. But when I lift the phone and see Amelia's name, my heart jumps.

Amelia: You're a good man Nate Pearson. Your dad would be incredibly proud of you. Enjoy the day with your mom. Dinner tonight?

I close my eyes as I let her words settle against my skin, warming me from the inside. It's been almost a week since I asked her to have dinner with me. She's avoided me around town, and last night at the bar she kept her distance. I don't know if it's pity that finally got her to agree to spend time with me—and I certainly feel sort of conflicted over my dad's memory bringing us back together—but I also know Dad would want this. He would want us to make things right, he would want me to lean on her for support, and he would want us both to be happy.

I type up a quick reply and pocket my phone. "Do you think we should say something?" I ask my mom.

She shrugs. "I don't know about you, but I talk to your dad daily. I don't need the twenty-year anniversary to remind me to talk to him."

I laugh. I'm pretty sure I said something similar to Amelia the other day. "Let's do it anyway," I reply.

My mom lifts her eyes to mine, and she grins. "You're right. Let's talk about your dad. We don't do it nearly enough with each other."

We spend the afternoon sharing stories of Dad, laughing about when he dressed up for Halloween as Superman and showed up to work only to find out that they didn't mean that kind of party. And when he snuck me out of school for a Red Sox game on my birthday without telling my mom, and she sent in cupcakes to school only to learn that I wasn't there. He made everything special. *He was special.*

"I had a great time today, Nate. Thanks for taking me out," my mom says as we pull back into the dock. I'd honestly been dreading this day for a while. It felt so permanent. Twenty years since he died. I've lived an entire life without my father. As has my mother. We just keep changing and yet he stays the same in my memory.

But being out on the water, talking about him like he's still in existence, brought a little piece of him back. And maybe that's why people have memorials. To bring the memories to the forefront. To bring your loved one into the present. I want him to know me today. And today I feel like I got to know him a little bit better as well, just from talking to my mom and living in her memories.

Amelia offered to bring takeout down to the boat, and I was both surprised and touched by her offer. Going into town anywhere would have been a disaster. Most people know who I am, and I didn't want to have people approaching to offer their platitudes all night.

But this is dangerous. For her, that is. I'm already an emotional mess of memories today. I've been living in the past for the last few hours, so I don't mind strolling down memory lane, but I know that coming onto this boat and sharing a meal with me in "our space" is going to be hard for Amelia. It makes it even more meaningful that she offered to suck the uncomfortableness up just so she could be here for me. Just maybe this will be the turning point I've been hoping for.

"Permission to come aboard?" she calls as I hear the familiar sound of her feet jumping onto the boat. When she peeks into the cabin, my heart literally skips a beat at the sight of her.

Her blonde hair is pulled back into two braids like she had it at the Linden Place event, and she has a light gloss on her lips. With her signature ripped shorts and a white T-shirt, Amelia is wearing my favorite outfit, and she knows it. She gives me a quiet smile—it's my favorite kind. The one that tells me that she's just happy to be with me. Not because I said something funny or teased her about something—she has different smiles for those—but this one, this one is the Nate Pearson smile, and I fucking love it.

"What's mine is yours, sweetheart. You never have to ask permission."

She rolls her eyes, but her smile remains. "I brought Chinese," she replies, ignoring my flirting.

"Dad's favorite."

Amelia nods. "But if you lay a finger on my Crab Rangoon, I'll cut you." She glares at me, and I laugh. I always pretend to find the entire idea of a pastry stuffed with cream cheese and imitation crab meat as disgusting and then I eat her last one. The truth is I do hate them, but I like riling Amelia up more, so I always swallow the taste just to get a rise out of her.

"As if I would touch them," I say, playing along with our old game.

She rolls her eyes and shakes her head again. It's her go-to response with me these days. "Oh, Amelia Pearson," I sigh out, "have I ever told you, you're my favorite person?"

Amelia's hand stops midair as she puts the food down, and

she stares at me entranced. As if she's really hearing me for once. She closes her eyes and just sits in the moment. I take the opportunity to step closer and remove the bag from her hand, placing it on the table.

"You make even the worst days, my best ones. I would live this day a hundred times over if I could end it right here with you."

Amelia's head tilts toward me, as if my words are an actual caress against her cheek. I lift my hand to her face and rub my thumb against her velvety soft skin. "I love you more than you know, and like you even more than that."

She whimpers in protest and opens her eyes, piercing me with her brokenness. "Nate, please, I want to be here for you tonight, but I can't do this…" She pauses and motions between us. "Let me be your friend."

The raw pain in her gaze, the hurt I see in her expression, slices me. I pull her against my chest and whisper into her hair, "I can be your friend." As I go to pull away, she pulls me back and hugs me tightly.

"You've always been my favorite person," she whispers against my chest.

Tears that have threatened to spill all day break free, and a sob escapes as I realize that I'm finally home.

CHAPTER 14

Amelia

Forgetting the reason for our boat day, I arrive at the docks excited for a day on the water. Ever since I was a child, the ocean has been my happy place. The few years I lived in Nashville, we became lake people because Nate always needed a boat day to decompress, but nothing compares to a day on the ocean. The salty air, the sun kissing your face, the joy of New England in the summer.

A smile hits my lips when I see Nate leaning over and fixing the line, creating a clove hitch, his favorite knot. When he sees me, his eyes light up and they trail my body, appreciating my white bikini which I've paired with my light jean cut-offs. "Hey, Cookie, you coming boating with us?"

Us?

Behind him I spot Caris in a yellow barely-there bikini. Oh, fuck me. I forgot Shawn said Nate was coming on the boat. That's why we planned this damn day. Between the boat charter last week, the unexpected night with Nate the other day, and all the crying I've been doing, it completely slipped my mind. Shawn also mentioned Caris and Nate seemed friendly. How did I miss this? And why is God punishing me? I've been a mostly good person. I don't sleep around. I don't even kiss around. I'm practically a saint. Okay, that's pushing it, but still, I'm kind to animals, I always give money to charity, I help at the food kitchen, I don't jay walk—*I'm a good person.*

Sure, I'm currently lying to my ex-husband about dating my brother's future brother-in-law, but it's a white lie. Work with me here.

I feel an arm loop around my waist, and I look up to find Shawn's strong presence right when I need him. "Hey, babe, ready for our boat day?" He kisses my forehead. "Hey, Nate, glad you could join us. Amelia tells me you're quite competent on the ocean. Maybe you can teach me some things?"

My smile grows when Shawn says *competent*. That'll go right up Nate's ass.

Nate raises his brow. "Competent, huh. I'm surprised you remembered our boat days, Ames. It seems you've forgotten so many things." Under his breath I'm pretty sure he mutters, "like your vows."

I turn into Shawn, nuzzling his chest and providing quite the show. I don't even know why I'm still putting on this show. Nate and I had a good time the other night. After the expected tears, we enjoyed dinner as we reminisced over memories of his father. But none of that changes the past. None of it changes that

I'm still reeling over what he did all those years ago to end our marriage. "I remember everything," I say pointedly. "Which is why I'm surprised to see you on Caris's boat. Never knew you two were friends."

Caris hops off the boat, landing on the dock gracefully, her small breasts barely moving. Score one for me—Nate is a boob guy, and mine are jiggling just from the movement of the docks. Of course that doesn't matter, because I don't want Nate to want me; I just don't want him with Caris. *Totally understandable.*

"Oh, Nate and I go way back, and I needed help with the boat since this is my first year with one and Nate offered."

Of course he did.

She smiles brightly at Nate who looks away shyly. Does he *like* her? Does she make him nervous? When I notice her hand on his arm and watch as redness trails his chest, I have my answer.

Well, fuck if I'm going to make it through this day. Everything is backfiring. Just as I'm about to feign a stomachache, Hailey walks up with a man I don't recognize. "Hey, guys, who's excited for a boat day?" She grips the guy's forearm and smiles proudly. "Guys, this is Kevin. I met him last night, and since he was still here this morning, I invited him." She raises her brows. Behind him she mimes he's huge with her hands. I feel poor Shawn stiffen, but he keeps a smile on his face because he's that nice of a guy, and he shakes Kevin's hand.

"Glad you could join us," Shawn says.

This is a disaster. Boy, did we mess up this fake day date.

My ex-husband and his new crush, me and my fake boyfriend, and his crush with her latest hook-up.

Fuck.

Nate, Shawn, and Caris sit at the wheel captaining the boat. Both Shawn and Caris hang on Nate's every word. In Shawn's defense, his choice was to feign interest in learning how to drive the boat or to sit with me, Hailey, and her boy toy. But Caris gets no pass. She's hanging on my husband like a barnacle, her hand practically attached to his tattooed forearm, making me squeeze the leather seat every time I look their way. Well, my ex-husband, but still.

Hailey's date is napping, and Hailey seems distracted looking between him and Caris, or maybe she's staring at Shawn. Who knows? I'm so over the triangles. After today, I'm breaking up with my fake boyfriend. Who has the energy for these lies?

The ride to Potter's Cove is quick enough. It's a small inlet off Prudence Island which is across the water from Bristol. The town has no grocery store or downtown. A small ferry operates year-round to take the residents to Bristol. A few boats are already moored, and the guys start throwing lines to our other friends, pulling the boats together.

Once the boat engine stops, I spot Charlotte's best friend, Steph, one boat over and jump over to join her, removing myself from the horrible relationship disaster.

"Tell me you have limoncello," I say to Steph as she

screeches a hello. A few weeks ago, we went for Bingo at Belle's nursing home, drank plenty of limoncello, and ended up on a stakeout where we stalked Belle's hot employee that she is trying to pretend doesn't have her all hot and bothered. Obviously, my family has issues when it comes to relationships.

Steph laughs her loud signature laugh. "Oh, you're having one of those days, huh?"

"No talking, just drinking," I say, letting my eyes drift back to Nate who now has a flexible Caris sprawled against his lap in front of the steering wheel where he is showing her the different gears—or whatever excuse he's using.

Steph follows my gaze and whispers, "Who's the guy and why are you growing horns?" This is why I like Steph—she doesn't bullshit.

"My ex," I say. "Now please lead me to the booze." Not ever needing an excuse to drink, even at eleven a.m., Steph leads me away from my personal hell and inside her boat which is conveniently loaded with an impressive amount of alcohol. "Drinking to have fun or to forget?"

Knowing I can't have both, I reply easily, "To forget."

"I got you covered." Steph grabs orange juice off the counter and pours tequila in a red solo cup. "As long as we add OJ it's never too early for tequila."

I smile weakly, grab the tequila bottle, throw back a shot then raise my eyes to her. "I think you misunderstood how badly I need to forget. This is straight-tequila bitterness. A first love, heartbroken kind of drunk, please."

Steph nods, barely reacting to my tequila swig.

Like I said, love this girl.

Two hours later, with my eyes closed as I lie on the bow of Steph's boat soaking up the sun, I feel quite buzzed. My skin feels crispy from the lack of sunscreen, and I know soon I will regret not reapplying some, but the idea of going back to our boat to grab my bottle is not appealing in the least. I'll probably come upon Nate smothering Caris in lotion, pretending to be all friendly. *Bleh.* The thought turns my stomach.

Or maybe it's the tequila.

Someone jumps on the front of the boat, shaking it slightly, and I enjoy the sway. Too relaxed to open my eyes, I grunt a hello and drift back to sleep. A few seconds later—or hours, I'm really not sure—I wake to the feel of lotion being lathered across my chest.

"Jesus, Amelia, you're going to be a lobster," the voice mutters. I think it's my fake boyfriend. I grab his hand and move it onto my breast, and he stills.

"Such a good fake boyfriend. I wish I liked you. Or you liked me. I'm so horny and my husband is hot, but nope, I can't have him because he wants Caris. No one wants me. I'm damaged goods. Old divorcée. I'll probably never get laid again. Help a girl out and just squeeze and make me feel wanted for a minute. I promise I won't tell anyone." I open my eyes to attempt a wink, but the sun blinds them shut.

He moves closer and whispers in my ear, "You're not fucking damaged goods. You're goddamn perfection, and if you don't remove my hand from your perfect tit, I'm going to take your top off and put your nipple between my teeth."

I open my eyes and stare into Nate's cool blue ones which flood with lust.

Oh, shit.

Although, now that my mind is working, I'm not sure if I'd rather Shawn have heard my confession or Nate. Damn tequila, I almost propositioned my brother's brother-in-law to have pity sex with me. Major cringe.

Nate's eyes remain on mine, and he rubs his thumb over my now hard nipple, sending a jolt between my legs. "You haven't moved my hand, Amelia."

I shake my head, unable to make my tongue work. Music blasts around us, and I hear people splashing in the water below, but we are seemingly alone on the boat.

"Why did you call Shawn your fake boyfriend? Are you trying to make me jealous?"

I say nothing, completely transfixed with the way his thumb is passing across my nipple. Involuntarily my hips shift, and he raises his brow. "How long has it been?"

I can't respond. He knows how long. *Three years.* It's been three long years since a man has touched me like this. He leans over and moves his knee between my legs. Pressing it against me, he provides just the right amount of pressure. My eyes fall away from his, and my hips shift sideways, seeking release, chasing it from the only man I've ever wanted with every inch of my body.

Nate pulls my chin to him. "Eyes on me while I get you off, Ames. You don't have to answer my questions, but you have to look at me, okay?" Just the smallest amount of vulnerability enters his voice.

I nod, willing to do anything to keep him where he is.

"Good girl," he says, lowering himself and kissing me softly, his knee pressing harder against my very wet bathing suit. He smirks against my mouth as he feels how turned on he has me. His tongue parts my lips, and he deepens the kiss, as his thumb continues working its magic on my nipple. When he moves the fabric, I hiss as I feel his guitar-calloused thumb touch my bare chest.

"Oh, Nate," I whimper, and I feel his length harden against my stomach.

He comes up for air and looks at me with awe in his eyes. "I never thought I'd hear you say my name like that again."

"Like what?" I pant, actively riding against his knee, feeling the swell building in my stomach. The fire I've been trying to put out for the last few weeks has reached a cataclysmic shift, turning into an inferno. I'd willingly burn just to feel this way one more time.

"Like you could come just from my proximity—like you want nothing but me buried deep inside you. *Forever*." His eyes meet mine at our previous promised words, and I ignore the moment passing between us. I'm chasing my own pleasure; this means nothing.

"Kiss me, Nate," I beg to shut him up, but instead he leans his mouth next to my ear and speaks slowly, transfixing me as I ride the pending orgasm.

"Fuck, babe, I'm still so in love with you. You're all I think about. I see you spiraling, I see you lost, but know that I'll chase you to the end of the earth. I'll fight for us. I'll fight for you. I'm not going anywhere. I love you…"

I shake my head, trying to focus on the feeling. On Nate's warm breath against my skin, his leg between my own, his thumb pinching my nipple. Anything other than his words. But Nate doesn't relent. Not with his fingers, not with his knee, and not with his promises.

"You're the most beautiful woman I've ever seen. And this white bathing suit,"—he lets out a low growl of a laugh—"I'll be dreaming of this for the rest of the week. Now fucking come for me." At his command, the moan leaves my mouth, and he kisses me to keep me quiet, smiling the entire time.

When I stop riding the wave, I feel the heavy realization of what we've just done. With his eyes on me, he shakes his head. "Don't you dare say something cliché like this was a mistake. I'm asking nothing of you but to hold my wife for a few minutes, then you can drift back to sleep and go back to fake ignoring me for a few more days, okay?"

The smile bites at my lips. He knows me so well. Perhaps it's the tequila or the postcoital bliss but I resolve not to fight him, and when he moves next to me, I let my head fall to his chest and wrap my legs into his. We fall asleep, tangled together like we did for years on Nate's boat, and for a few moments I have perfection back.

Nate

Letting go of Amelia is basically the hardest thing I've had to do in the last few months—hell, years. Probably as hard as it was to get on the plane without her three years ago. Because once again—like that day—I have no idea when I will be able to hold her again. I give myself a few more seconds of being enveloped in her scent, kiss her shoulder which is warm from the sun, and shrug her back onto the bow of the boat, placing a towel over her so she doesn't burn anymore.

Making Amelia come had not been part of my plan today, but fuck if I was going to turn down pleasuring my wife when she was so boldly begging for it. It had been three years since I had heard her moan my name. Three years since I had kissed my wife, tasted her, held her, slept next to her. The tequila taste was a surprise, but I guess that's why she was so friendly—my girl never could handle her liquor.

I stare down at her once more, taking in the shape of her breasts under the towel and the way her blonde hair falls over her face. Such a beautiful disaster. Then I hop off the boat and make my way back to Caris. I didn't plan to make Amelia jealous—hell, I wasn't sure I still could. I'm not faking a relationship with Caris like Amelia is with Shawn. Not that I blame Amelia for doing that. She's trying to protect herself the best way she knows how. I just wish the person she was trying to protect herself against wasn't me.

My friendship with Caris has nothing to do with Amelia. I was just trying to be friendly, and Lord knows I could use a few friends right about now. But I won't let Amelia think that I have even a moment of interest in another woman. I never want to give her any reason to be insecure in my feelings for her. The last three years, I failed as a husband. I let her believe that she wasn't worth fighting for. I walked away when she needed me, and now that I'm back, my sole focus is making things right.

Before I can do that though, as Jack said, I need to prove to her that I'm here for good. I'm staying, I'm healed, and I don't just need her to make me better. I am better.

Those weren't just words that I muttered to her. I will fight for her. I will fight for us. I'll love her more as she fights to walk away from me so that she feels it wherever she lands.

"Hey, where did you disappear to?" Caris says as she walks

up and hops onto my lap in the captain's chair.

She has to stop doing this. I lift her up as politely as possible and give her a pointed look. "Caris, you take the captain's chair. I'll stand behind you, and we can test what you've learned today."

She smiles coyly up at me. "Let me guess, Amelia has you wrapped around her finger again?"

I laugh and cover my mouth. "I never untwisted from her. I've belonged to her for the last twenty years. Sorry if you thought this was something else."

Fortunately, she doesn't bat an eye. "You never led anyone on. In high school we all saw how you looked at her. She's a lucky girl. Does she even know how lucky she is?"

I shake my head. "I've put that girl through hell. If I'm lucky enough to get her back, I'll never let her down again, and I hope she'll think she's lucky."

Caris nods over to the other boat where I just came from. "Well, she seems pretty taken with Shawn. Looks like you've got your work cut out for you." I look up to find Shawn helping a very drunk Amelia get to her feet.

Damn, she looks worse than before.

My stomach bottoms out. Will she even remember what happened between us? Did I take advantage of her?

She wobbles, and Shawn catches her and wraps an arm around her as Hailey hops over the bow to help get Amelia across. Just then a tiny brunette appears and starts hollering. Getting nervous about how dazed Amelia looks, I jump out of my seat.

"Hey, what's going on?" My voice sounds angrier than I intended as my nerves get the best of me.

The small brunette glares. "She's too drunk to go back to your boat. My husband and I will take her back."

I shake my head, not giving the idea even a second thought. "Nope. I'm not leaving Amelia out here in the sun without me."

The girl shoots me with daggers. "And who precisely do you think you are?"

I puff out my chest like a goddamn warrior. "I'm her husband. Who are you?" Both Shawn and Hailey's heads whip in my direction.

The feisty brunette seems unfazed. "That's not what she told me. She said you're her ex."

Ah fuck, why does everyone have to keep saying that?

"Her license says Amelia Pearson, so for the moment I win. I'm not leaving my wife here baking in the sun with possible alcohol poisoning."

Shawn shifts uncomfortably and looks to the brunette. "Steph, can you get us back to shore now? If so, I can have Doc stop by the bar to check on Amelia. I'm nervous about her too."

The woman named Steph seems to consider this option. Even though I'm not. "Sure, I'll have Pat take us back now. You call Doc."

Shawn looks at Hailey and whispers something. Then he hops over to our boat. "Man, she doesn't look good. I'll get her back safely. Don't worry. I got her." He pats me on the back, reassuring me, and an understanding passes between us. He knows she's mine. He's not interfering; he's protecting her.

"Fuck," I mutter under my breath. "I'll be right behind you."

He nods. "I know. You're just the only one who can drive this boat back or else I'd let you go with her. But trying to get her across the two boats right now…it's not safe."

I know he's right, but it doesn't make me any happier. But at least she'll be safe. I know he'll make sure of it. And that's all that matters right now.

"Okay, if she wakes up give her water and make sure the doctor is there when we pull in. I'll follow behind so I can help."

He nods again, grabs his keys and phone from the boat, and hops back over. Hailey comes back to our boat and looks at me, her eyes boring into mine. "Damn, the hot pissed-off husband look works for you, you know that?"

Talk about breaking the ice. I almost snort. "Oh yeah, you mind telling my wife that when she wakes up? I could use all the help I can get."

She squeezes my arm and moans. "Oh, shit, sorry. Just so hot. It's the damn tattoos, I think. Did you really not have these when you knew Amelia?"

I shake my head. We don't have time for this. "Another time, Hailey. We need to get to the dock so I can take care of our girl. Okay?"

She smiles. "How come all the good ones are obsessed

with Amelia?"

I give a low chuckle. The girl has no idea how obsessed the tall guy who is faking a relationship with my wife is with her. It was the first thing I noticed the night I saw them at the bar and part of the reason I knew there was no way that Amelia and he were together. Shawn clearly has it bad for Hailey, and the girl doesn't have a clue.

Speeding toward the dock, I don't so much as think, my body is on autopilot as I dock the boat, tie the lines, and run straight to where they have deposited Amelia—who is being examined by a tall, dark man whose brow furrows as he asks Steph what Amelia had to drink.

I listen to Steph recount the way Amelia drank straight from the tequila bottle.

"That's not like Amelia," the doctor says, shaking his head. "She's babysat for Mackenzie. She's got a good head on her shoulders. Was something bothering her?"

Steph thumbs back to me. "You can thank him for that."

Not concerned with being painted as the bad guy, I take the opportunity to ask about my wife.

"She gonna be okay, Doc?"

"And who are you?"

"Her husband." Everyone's heads swirl again. This is getting comical. "Check her license. It says Amelia Pearson." I know Amelia hasn't changed it. Can't do that without a divorce decree, and we don't have one. "Doc, is she okay?"

"Yeah. She needs fluids and sleep. But someone will have to sit with her when she sleeps. It's dangerous for her to be left alone."

We all volunteer at once. Shawn walks over and levels with me. "She doesn't want you around. I know you mean well, but let us take care of her."

Jaw tight, I shake my head. "Not going to happen. You can come, but I'm not leaving her side."

Steph's voice softens. "We get it. But she's in a vulnerable state right now…think about her, Nate."

She's all I'm thinking about. I don't budge. "This isn't negotiable. Believe me, I've nursed Amelia through her first hangover, stomach bugs, the flu…I've seen her at her worst. It's in the vows. I'm not leaving her."

Hailey mutters under her breath, "Finally," and offers me a smile. "Guys, we all know Amelia—she'll tell him to leave when she comes to, and that's how we'll know she's doing better. Let him do this for her. I have a feeling she needs him more than we know."

Touched by her support, I nod toward her. "Thanks. So Doc, can I take my girl home?"

He peers down at Amelia. She is sitting with her head

between her knees, looking pale despite the red burn that cakes her skin.

"Yeah. I'll follow you back to her apartment and get her set up with an IV. It will hopefully spare her the wicked headache."

"Great. Thanks, Doc. Come here, babe." I kneel down next to my wife, whispering softly, "You gonna be okay if I carry you?"

She whimpers softly, "Don't know."

"Okay, we'll go slow." Placing my arms under her knees and behind her back, I lift her up, and she leans her head on my chest, sighing as she inhales. With Amelia in my arms, I feel my heart rate steady, relaxing for the first time since I left her on the boat.

"Call us if you need anything," Hailey says, leaning in and rubbing Amelia's back. "You're gonna be okay, my girl."

Shawn looks anxiously after us. Obviously, the jig is up on their fake relationship, but I have a feeling the ruse may have had a bit to do with his feelings for Hailey too. I don't have the interest to consider the implications of that now. I'm solely focused on getting Amelia settled.

"Wait, how will you get in?" Shawn asks, as if he's finally found a reason to be useful.

"I got a key." I don't explain further. I've been taking care of my wife for the past few years. She just doesn't know it.

I carry Amelia down the docks to her apartment while Doc heads to his car to grab the IV fluid. When I reach the front of the flower shop, my mom peeks out and sees Amelia in my arms. "Hey, how was the boat today?" As she takes in Amelia's condition, her face contorts into one of concern. "Oh my gosh, is Amelia okay?"

Amelia is sleeping against my shoulder but looks terrible. I brush a kiss against her head. "Too much tequila and sun. I'm hurting her, Mom, and I don't know how to make it better."

"Perhaps you just need to give her space. I know you want things to go back to the way they were, but that might not be possible."

I shake my head. "I can't talk about this now. Doc is bringing an IV. Can you wait for him and bring him up?"

My mom nods. "Sure. I'm also going to call Eva. She'll want to make sure Amelia is okay."

I shake my head again. "No. You're not going to call her mother. She's thirty years old, Mom. Please—I got this. Besides, her mom doesn't know we're married—she'll kick me out. And I'm not leaving and I'm not divulging Amelia's secrets, but I will if she comes and tries to kick me out— I'm her husband and I'll take care of her."

Knowing I sound ridiculous and probably more like a child than a grown man, I beg my mother with my eyes to listen to me. Let me do this for her. Let me be the husband I haven't been.

My mom *tsks* her tongue. "You're both such fools with your half-truths. We moms know way more than we let on. But I'm glad to see you're finally acting like a husband. Go take her upstairs, and I'll be up in a few."

I carry Amelia upstairs, dig the key out of my pocket, open the door, and knock it shut with my foot. I look around the apartment where Amelia lives without me, recognizing nothing. Jack packed her clothes and shipped them to her when she asked me to do it. He was intercepting the messages back then, aware I couldn't handle it. When I was finally sober enough to notice, I saw all her clothes were gone from the drawers, but everything else was untouched. Including our photos. Everything is now in a storage unit. I really hope one day we unpack everything together. That we'll live here *together*.

I bring her to the bedroom and cast my eyes to her bed, before gently placing her down. Then I move the curtains closed so the light doesn't hurt her head. When I look back at her, I find her curled in a fetal position. Her breasts spill out of her white bikini top, and her hair is matted to her face.

I reach into the drawers searching for a T-shirt. When I spot a row of shirts I recognize as my own, I shake off a smile. Another sign that she hasn't completely moved on. She's still holding on to my shirts, maybe wearing them for comfort when she misses me. That idea alone brings mixed emotions. Hope because it proves to me that we still have a shot, but damn is it hard to imagine her missing me. I shake off the image of a sad Amelia and grab one of my shirts and sit her up to put it over her body, hiding her breasts and her eventual shame when she realizes all the people who have seen her like this.

Then I lay her back down and leave the bedroom so I can wait for Doc and my mom.

After the IV has been placed, Doc stays to wait for the drip to drain and to take it out. I thank him and politely try to let my mother know it's time for her to leave as well.

"Why don't we order a pizza? Or I can go pick up burgers from the Bean if you want—I know you love their wings," she offers.

"I'll be okay. I'll eat once Amelia wakes up and can keep something down."

"Nathan, let me mother you." Her eyes soften, begging me to let her help.

Resigning myself to her company, I agree. "Okay, Amelia likes the grilled cheese and fries. Do you mind picking it up?"

My mom smiles, clearly loving her caretaking role. For so long, we all took care of her; I'm sure the reversal is welcome. "Yes, I'll let Sam know I'll be having dinner with you."

I smile. As much as I want time with Amelia, I know this means a lot to my mom. While she's gone, I go into Amelia's bedroom to check on her. She's asleep and cuddling the pillow next to her. I had grabbed a pair of sweats off the boat while Doc placed the IV, and now I decide to put them on, removing the board shorts I'd worn all day. A shower isn't the worst idea either.

Moving around the space normally occupied by my wife, I feel strangely at home. Even her shampoo and conditioner are familiar—the same bottles she'd specially ordered in Nashville and that smell uniquely like her.

As I lather myself in her bodywash, I focus on the fact that Amelia was probably naked in this space only a few hours earlier. If not for the worry I feel for her, I'd be able to focus on the sounds she made on the boat this afternoon when I made her come. It felt so uniquely right having her writhing against me again, hearing her moans and tasting her lips.

Instead of focusing on those memories and relieving the slight ache between my legs, I finish my shower, wrap myself in a towel, and walk into the bedroom just in time for Amelia to open her eyes. She looks sleepy and beautiful but still too pale. "Hey, babe, how you feeling?"

I lean against the bed, placing my hand against her head. She's still very warm.

Amelia groans and tries to sit up, but then her facial expression tells me the movement isn't welcome. "Stay where you are, babe. Want me to grab you some water?"

With eyes closed, she barely nods her head. I make myself useful and get her water. When I return, she's asleep again. I leave the water and a bottle of Tylenol next to the bed and put my sweats on.

In the living room, I find my mom setting the table and

placing to-go boxes out. The smell of garlic sesame wafts through the apartment, and the signature smell of the wings stirs my hungry stomach. In the haste of the afternoon's activities, I never took time to eat. It's already seven at night, and my stomach growls.

"Sit, Nate; eat. I'll put Amelia's food in the oven to keep warm." My mom moves with ease around Amelia's kitchen, seemingly familiar with where everything is located.

"You been here for dinner before?" I ask, interested in what my mom's relationship has been like with Amelia.

I asked a lot of her over the last year, trying to line up everything to win back my wife, but it never occurred to me that my mom probably enjoyed the distraction as well, less of a chore to help her son and more that she was taking care of a daughter.

My mom smiles as she sits down and opens her take-out box, pulling out a grilled cheese. I take time to study her. I'd been so focused on winning Amelia back and making sure Sam kept his appointments that I hadn't really had time to focus on her.

Her sandy-blonde hair hangs around her face, littered with greys that she chooses not to hide.

"I'm fortunate enough to get to age," she's said plenty of times. Being so wise is a widow's blessing and curse.

Her blue eyes are still vibrant, but wrinkles dust her face. I'd like to think she got some of them from all the laughter in her life, but I know a lot of them are thanks to the loss of my dad and the worries I've given her over the last few years.

"Amelia had me over to thank me for helping her find this apartment. We had such a good time she made it a thing. We try to have dinner once a month, at least, and we have a rule not to talk shop. Although that's become harder the last few months as she's gotten more excited about the possibility of expanding and doing weddings. She's really great, Nate. You were right when you said she needed this, as did the town. She's filling a niche, and I know she wouldn't have done it for herself."

I beam with pride. Amelia deserves all the praise. She'd built such an amazing business in Nashville, and just when things were really taking off, we lost everything.

"I really appreciate everything you've done. I know it was asking a lot—keeping it quiet, doing it how we did—but you know Amelia. She's stubborn, and if she knew it was me who bankrolled this for her…well, she would have said no."

My mom sighs as she puts down her sandwich. "Eventually you two are going to have to have some tough conversations."

I'm not excited for the prospect, but I know my mom is right. "We just need time. And since I've got forever, we'll get to it."

My mom's eyes grow wistful. "Forever sometimes comes too quickly."

I don't know if she is talking about Dad or Sam. How is it possible that she is once again facing the possibility of losing another partner? "The doctor says Sam has a good chance of beating this, Mom. And I'll be here every step of the way."

My mom wipes away a stray tear. "Oh, I know that. I just…I

don't know. I always thought we'd have more time, and now look at me. I'm fifty-seven and Sam is sixty…and your dad is gone. Sometimes it just feels like it all goes too quickly."

That was the problem. Three years flew by. One minute I was nursing my grief and then suddenly it had been months since I had talked to my wife, and I no longer knew how to reach out. So many things had been said. So much time had passed. I didn't know how to make things right. And then I made things worse. Dug myself into a hole too big to climb out of. When I finally thought I was well enough to fix us, she filed for divorce. Time just kept taking things from me.

Although, I suppose time was often the thief of joy, just as love had a way of memorializing it.

"What time is the appointment tomorrow?" I'd taken Sam to his last appointment, but tomorrow is a big day. We are both going because they'd done another scan to see if the treatment was working.

"It's at three. I figure I can meet you and Sam there if you don't mind picking him up?"

I pat my mom's hand. "Whatever you need." We finish eating, and Mom offers to finish cleaning up while I check on Amelia. She is still sleeping, so I come out to say goodnight to my mom and then lock up.

Eventually Amelia will wake up starving, and until then I'll be here, watching over her, not leaving her side. As long as she allows me to stay, I have no plan to leave her sight.

223

CHAPTER 15

Nate
Twenty-Four years old

Strumming the strings of my guitar, I focus hard on the melody Grant is trying to teach me. Normally, I write the songs, but he'd come up with this one on his own, and it wasn't half bad. Between our normal renditions of "Wonderwall" and "Free Bird," we like to throw in some of our own music, hoping that one day someone will hear one of our songs and tell us they have to have it. It hasn't happened yet, but it feels like we are right on the edge of it all. Like we are one more night away from having everything we've dreamed of.

Amelia opens the door to our apartment, a bright smile on her face, wearing her long white hair down past her shoulders. She'd grown it out since we moved to Nashville. On her legs are jean shorts, Chuck Taylors cover her feet, and her breasts spill out of a tight black tank top.

"Damn, Amelia, you look hot!" Grant crows from the other side of the room, earning a warning glare from me.

Love & Tequila Make Her Crazy

My girl walks straight toward me, ignoring him completely, and I move the guitar off my lap right before she straddles my hips and offers me a kiss they write songs about. "Ugh, get a room, we're practicing!"

I lift my hand up to Grant, offering him a send-off, and pick Amelia up, walking her to our room. "Fuck, Amelia, Grant's right. You look ridiculous in this outfit."

My dick bounces, and Amelia's teeth bite down harder against my lips. "New uniform for the bar. I'm really lucky Grant's cousin was able to get me this job. Between that and the work at the hotel, we'll be able to get our own place soon."

Grant moved in with us after Amelia left the dorms—something her parents weren't happy about. They refused to pay for the apartment. I have enough money in a trust to afford it on my own, but Amelia refuses to let me pay her way, which means we now share a place with Grant that is too small for the three of us when I could have afforded a two bedroom myself. Damn stubborn woman. "I hate that you're working at the bar."

Amelia sits up, working her black top over her head, and reveals a black lace bra. Like a magnet, my hand reaches up, and I rub her pebbled nipple. Amelia shifts against me, riding me as she stares me down. "You play music there, Nate. Why is that okay, but it's not okay for me to work there?"

There is no right answer to this, but I am going to say it anyway. "Because every man in that bar is going to be staring at you and wanting to fuck you, and I don't do jealous well."

Amelia's head dips back as she gives me access to her neck, which I graciously kiss, nip, and bite. "You sure it's not because you don't want me to be there when all the women are throwing themselves at you? I know how these bars are, Nate. I may not be experienced like all of those girls, but I have eyes."

My hands loop behind her back, and I undo her bra, then I move my lips to her nipple, taking it in my mouth while I pull on her other one. "This, Amelia," I say, looking up at her with her nipple between my teeth, "is the only set of breasts that I want. *You* are the only girl I want."

Amelia pants above me, writhing on me and getting me so worked up I almost lose it. "Naked, now." Her words come out needy and breathy. Within seconds we're both naked. She lowers herself down and rides me with reckless abandon. "Harder, Nate. I need it harder."

I push into her, lifting and squeezing my ass, giving her everything she wants. As I feel her tighten above me, contracting and pulling everything from me, the room goes black.

A meteor could collide into earth, and I wouldn't notice the carnage around me. Only the sound of Amelia's heavy breathing, her heart beating, and the feel of her warmth could touch this moment. I am a complete goner for her.

The knock on the door grates on my skin, like heavy metal interrupting a symphony. "Dude, we need to be at the bar in ten minutes."

Before Amelia can hop off, I pull her closer to me and

whisper against her lips, "It's fine; we have time." Loudly, I yell to Grant, "Meet you there. Going with Amelia."

She raises her eyes to me. "You want me to come?"

I told her she didn't have to be at every show. We play almost every night at different places, and I don't want her to sit for hours at a bar by herself. It also makes me anxious that she'll get bored of this life—that she'll want more—so I try to keep the invitations to a minimum.

My eyes soften, and I kiss the top of her head. "Babe, I always want you there. I just don't want to monopolize all your time. You need to be studying and working on becoming the amazing florist I know you will be."

She beams and moves against me, making my eyes roll back again. "I love watching you play. I find it hot. Besides, I can bring my books to the bar, sit in the corner, and just listen to you."

Of course she would do that. It's what she did growing up, sitting at our baseball games with her homework. Or after school while we had basketball practice, she'd wait outside the gym, always with a book in her hand, whether she was reading something for school or just for herself.

"Okay, let's take a quick shower and then we'll head over. I love you." I slap her ass and she laughs against me.

"Love you too, Pearson."

Amelia sits in the corner and watches, now dressed in dark jeans and a tight plaid button-up which is still buttoned one too low for my liking. She's a beautiful distraction in the corner, with her long blonde hair and her head down in her sketchpad. She brings it everywhere she goes, creating floral designs for future bouquets, or just artwork that flows from her hands. Men drinking at the bar stare, and I feel my jaw tick one too many times. But she is oblivious to the attention, never realizing the effect she has on men around her.

How she doesn't understand that every man is attracted to a tall, leggy blonde with a small waist and gorgeous tits like hers, I have no idea, but my girl never did seem to notice the attention she garnered.

I turn back to Grant, waiting for him to announce the next song. We have a few go-to songs, but we like to change the order of them, so it doesn't become monotonous.

The crowd is loud tonight, loving us, throwing twenties in our tip jar and asking for songs that they know we play.

"Okay, ladies and gents, I've got something special for you. Amelia, can you come up here?"

My eyes dart to Grant. "What the fuck are you doing?" I grit

Love & Tequila Make Her Crazy

between my teeth.

Amelia looks up at me, her eyes narrowing as she tries to figure out what's going on. I look back to Grant, completely lost. Under his breath, Grant says, "Wait until you hear this girl sing. You thought she was hot before."

Sing? *Amelia?*

Slowly, she makes her way to the stage, her eyes drifting between Grant and me. Amelia isn't a person who likes crowds—she keeps to her corners, dressing the flowers in the back and listening to the music. She never joins in. What is Grant up to?

"'Dreams' by Fleetwood Mac work for you?" he asks her, ignoring me completely.

Amelia's eyes grow wide. "How did you know?" she whispers.

Grant smiles. "The shower. Amelia, you have an amazing voice. Sing for us."

My pulse quickens, and the room starts to spin. The shower? Why does it feel like a moment just passed between them? My heart hammers in my chest as I try to calm down.

When Amelia takes the mic, and her black lashes flutter shut, time stops. Grant begins on the drums, and my fingers find a way to strum the guitar, as if my entire body knows precisely what is about to happen. When she opens her eyes, the grey irises turn to me, and she opens her mouth to sing, releasing what can only be described as an angelic sound—breathy, deep, and sexy as hell.

Damn, my girl can sing.

She begins to sway her hips as the song gets going, and then as the crowd reacts her hand taps against her hip. She's a damn natural. A performer. She has *it*.

Turning to me, she smiles as she sings the words, and I can do nothing but stare in complete awe, strumming my guitar and tapping my foot to the beat. The bar is dark, and Amelia is lit up by the light like a damn angel. People are actually silent. The rowdy crowd has been brought to their knees, and it's like we are all in this moment together, watching a star come to life.

As the song ends, Amelia's shyness creeps back in, and a redness tints her cheeks. "Did I do okay?" she whispers.

Moving my guitar over my shoulder, I take her in my arms and kiss her harder than I've ever kissed her. The crowd cheers, but it feels like even in the dark bar where the light floods us that we are the only two people in the world. It's as if every moment of our lives has led up to this one moment. "Fuck, Amelia, you did better than okay. Marry me, babe. Please. Marry me and make me the luckiest guy in the whole damn world."

Shock glitters her face as she takes my cheeks between her hands. "Pearson, what are you talking about?"

My heart pounds. "I'm serious, Amelia. Marry me." It isn't even a question. We both know her answer. It'd been written in the stars the moment she put her hand in mine when she was seven. She is mine and she always will be. Hearing her sing made it so I can't breathe without knowing that it's forever though. I need to make her legally mine before someone steals her away because this girl is going places, and I want to be next to her when she does. I never want to be anywhere else.

"Really, Nate?" Amelia's eyes water.

"Yes. Marry me. Please?"

She laughs. "Well, since you sound so desperate."

I squeeze her tighter. "Say yes, Amelia. Say the words. Make me the happiest man in the world."

Amelia's face splits open in a smile. "Yes, Pearson. I'll marry you." I lift her into the air as I kiss her, and she laughs against me as I spin us around, with my guitar on my back and my girl in my arms, in our own little world.

CHAPTER 16

Amelia

Every time I open my eyes, a fog settles over the room, leaving me imagining that Nate is lying next to me, holding me, cuddling me, kissing my forehead, playing with my hair. It feels extraordinary, and also lonely because I know it's all a dream.

I keep my eyes shut, enjoying the hallucination too much. The entire thing feels so real. I imagine I can feel Nate's abs when I run my hands up and down his body in my dream. Even going so far as to take his erection in my hand, exploring him like he is my personal play toy. Clearly my mind is unfair, because in my dream he stops me, placing my hands in his own, not allowing me to take my dream to the next level. "Nate, please," I whimper.

"Shhh, babe, just relax," he whispers in my subconscious mind. I fall back to sleep, hoping the dream will consume me again.

When I wake later, I'm disappointed to realize that it was a dream. Nate wasn't here, obviously, why would he be?

It's just me and a piercing headache.

I spot the water and Tylenol and am impressed that in my apparent drunkenness I'd been smart enough to snag both of these. If only I remembered getting home. Hopefully I didn't make a complete fool of myself. I vaguely remember riding Nate's leg on the bow of the boat while he kissed me.

Groaning, I bring my hand to my head. "Oh, Amelia, what did you do?"

"Hey, you're awake." Nate's voice startles me. Looking between my fingers, I take in my ex who looks absolutely ripped in a pair of low hanging grey sweats which show off his impressive V and no shirt.

I groan. Grey sweats…and when did he get those abs? He'd always been good-looking, but never muscular in this "*eight-pack-abs, glistening body*" way. And I can now see the tattoos don't just cover his arms; there is one right over his heart as well.

I close my eyes, too scared to see what it says. Without even seeing it, I know once I read it, I will find it nearly impossible to hold back from him. The way he kissed me before had weakened me, but the physical was nothing compared to the emotional connection we always had. The only way I have any hope of keeping myself from falling back into his arms is by keeping my distance. Knowing the words he wrote on his body, the meaning behind them, would be impossible to distance myself from.

"My head," I say weakly.

Nate moves closer, and unfortunately, I don't avert my eyes.

Above his heart is my name written within a flower petal. A flower petal I recognize immediately as one of *my* drawings.

He tattooed my artwork on his body.

I bite the inside of my lip, and without thinking, I let my fingers reach out to trace my design.

Nate inhales a breath at my touch. I move to his arms and recognize each of the drawings as one of my own. His entire body has become my personal canvas.

Oh, Nate Pearson, what are you doing to me?

And then I spot the chain around his neck with the simple white gold band on it. *My wedding band.* My eyes shut as I remember slipping it off my finger and leaving it on our dresser almost three years ago...my eyes dip to his left finger where his father's band still sits. We'd chosen to use it as our wedding band. How had I not noticed he was still wearing it? Is he just wearing it because it was his father's or is there more to it than that? And why does he have my wedding band around his neck? And my name on his chest?

I close my eyes as he moves into my space, lifting me up and pulling me against him. "I got you a grilled cheese and French fries. Want me to warm them up, and you can try eating a little bit? Doc said you'd probably be hungry when you woke and that it would be safe for you to eat. Slowly though."

I groan. *Doc*...Doc saw me like this? Oh God, what kind of scene had I made? Nervous to find out anything more, I simply nod.

"Okay, babe, I'm just going to carry you into the living room and get you set up on the couch, okay?"

I really wish he'd stop calling me babe. I shake him off. This is all becoming too much. The kissing, the tattoos, the nicknames, the attention. Nate Pearson broke my heart; I can't let him just waltz back in and sweep me off my feet again. "I can walk. I'm not some damsel in distress that needs saving, and you're not my white knight."

Of course, my knees fail the minute I try to get all high and mighty, and my head lets me know I can do nothing—not take a step or move on my own volition at all.

"Do me a favor," Nate says, a bit of callousness entering his voice. "Just let me take care of you right now. You can go back to hating me in the morning. I know I deserve every ounce of it. Just let me do this for you."

I wince because there is no truth to his words. I don't hate him. I've never hated him. I've loved him. I've been angry at him. I've been hurt by him. But I could never hate him. He owns my heart. Even if I'll never let him know that. But I do recognize that he's just trying to help right now. And I'd used him on the boat. Apparently got so drunk he had to call Doc, and he sat here all night probably watching me like a hawk. The least I can do is be appreciative or at a minimum temper my bark.

Holding out my arms, I let him know he's won. Nate's shoulders relax, and he cradles me. For a moment my eyes stare at my small wedding band, and I almost ask him about it, but

I'm too exhausted for *that* conversation.

Unable to hold up my head, I relax against his chest, which smells like my bodywash. Somehow knowing he'd been in my shower, naked, while I was only a few feet away, doesn't upset me. We keep settling back into one another—lunches, chocolate, showers, kisses. All the walls I've put up, he keeps pulling down.

Nate deposits me on the couch and places a throw blanket around me, warming me before the chill sets in. Then he moves comfortably around my kitchen, easily locating the condiments and plates before he places the delicious smelling grilled cheese before me. He doesn't wait for me to reach for it, instead lifting a piece to my lips.

Nervously, I nibble at it, hoping I don't further embarrass myself by getting sick. As soon as I swallow, I can tell it's precisely what I needed, and my empty stomach rumbles in hunger. I easily finish one half and sip Diet Coke between bites.

"Thank you. I'm guessing I gave you quite the scare."

He chuckles softly. "Yeah, I'm pretty sure I owe all your friends an apology. I was a bit growly."

I find myself smiling. I always liked growly Nate. He only ever got that way about me. In general, Nate is a pretty laid-back guy. Normally, he allows his music to speak for him. He works out his emotions through the guitar strings. But if someone upset me or a guy hit on me in a bar, well, growly Nate got all hot and bothered which always did me in. The quiet man with a jaw tick and a deep rumbling angry voice always turned me on.

"I'm sure they understood," I say quietly, taking another fry.

"Yeah, your fake boyfriend seemed to realize his place." He raises his eyes at me, daring me to challenge his assertion. I just shrug. I don't have the energy to keep up the ruse. And it doesn't matter anymore. Nate and I had always been friends first, and today he had shown that he still cared. I can be his friend, even if it hurts being this close, knowing he isn't mine.

"Like your shirt, by the way," he says, motioning to the T-shirt I'm wearing. I finally look down and see I'm wearing one of Nate's Red Sox shirts. Shit. That's embarrassing.

"It's comfortable," I reply.

Nate laughs and turns his head away before he schools his expression again. Even then, the smirk pulls at his lip. "It looks good on you, Ames. I get it—in Nashville I slept with your pillow every night."

I stare at him dumbstruck. "What…um…that's…" I can't formulate a response.

Nate moves closer, his warm breath hitting against my shoulder. "But here's the thing, sweetheart, you've got the real thing right in front of you now, so if you're looking for comfort, my arms are always open." He leans down, and I think he's going to go in for a kiss but instead he picks up my plate.

"Thank you. I can clean up in the morning. I'm sure you want to get home." I look anxiously to the door. I don't really want him to leave, but there is also no reason for him to stay.

Nate stands up and takes my plate to the kitchen, rinsing it in the sink before placing it in the dishwasher. I thoroughly enjoy watching a shirtless Nate move around my kitchen. Maybe too much.

"I'm not leaving."

Unsure what to say, I just look at him, trying to discern what's the right reaction. I don't like him telling me what to do, but I also do. "Nate, I'm fine."

He shakes his head and waltzes over to the couch, leaning down to lift me up again. When I don't willingly enter his arms, he cocks his brow. "Doc told me to watch you tonight. I'm not risking you getting sick in your sleep."

Biting the inside of my lip, I feel my cheeks grow warm. I really must have been a disaster. "Okay," I begrudgingly agree to be carried. Once he lays me on my bed, I sink into the soft sheets, my eyes growing heavy almost instantly.

Nate shifts off the bed and walks to the living room. "Where are you going?" I ask as he comes back with a blanket.

"I'll sleep on the floor," he says, taking a pillow from my bed and making a mock sleeping area.

This is silly. The man has lived inside of me; he is not going to sleep on the floor. Surely, I can trust myself enough not to get swept up in Nate just because we're sharing a bed. "It's fine. Sleep here." I pat the spot next to me, and Nate looks at me nervously.

"It's okay, Amelia, the floor is fine."

In the sternest voice I can muster, I say, "Pearson, if you don't get in this bed, you can go home. I'm not a poor thing that you have to tiptoe around. And as delicious as you may think your abs are, I am capable of resisting you."

Nate smirks. "Strange, because you couldn't resist riding me this afternoon on the boat."

I narrow my eyes and feel a stirring between my legs. "What can I say, it was a weak moment. It's been too long, and tequila made me do it."

He chuckles softly and moves next to me in bed, pulling me to his hard chest, pressing his abs against me and making me regret the false bravado I just exercised. I absolutely cannot resist these abs. My hand trails them, and he grabs my tiny fingers before I get a chance to get too worked up. "I'm just holding you tonight."

Faking a pout—okay, actually pouting—I ask, "But why?"

Nate stares down at me, his eyes heated and his breath hot against my skin. "Because when I make love to you, I don't want you to blame it on the tequila. I won't take advantage of you, Ames. And, for the record, I know I'm not your white knight, but you sure as hell are mine."

Inwardly I moan. He's making this so hard. Making me fall for him all over again. Reminding me that I loved him. Making me question if I still do. But I keep my voice saucy as I take one last swipe against his abs, before settling into his chest. "Don't worry, Pearson, I was definitely the one who took advantage of you today. Goodnight."

I fall asleep almost instantly, but not before I hear him whisper, "Night, Mrs. Pearson," and damn if the sound of it doesn't still make me smile.

The next morning, I wake to find the spot next to me is empty, and I spread out missing Nate's arms, moving myself onto his pillow where I inhale his scent. It had been so long since we shared a bed, I'd forgotten how amazing it was to be cuddled next to him. How much I loved sleeping in his arms. I slept like a rock and am honestly disappointed we didn't wake up together. When I look at the clock, I'm shocked to see that it's already eleven a.m. Good thing I didn't have a fishing charter today; I absolutely would have missed it.

Next to the bed, I spot a note in Nate's familiar writing… and see my old sketchpad below it.

Stop by the shop when you wake up.

PS You still snore like a trucker, and I loved every minute of waking up next to you, Gorgeous.

I run my fingers over his words and then pick up my old sketchpad. I hadn't picked up a pencil to draw since I left Nashville. I left more than just my husband behind, I left an entire life. And here Nate was slowly bringing each piece back to me. Reminding me of who I was and of the person I could be.

Leaning back into the soft covers, I kick my legs up in the air, this light, airy, happy feeling overcoming me, reminding me of the way I used to feel when Nate and I first started dating. The surprising feeling that he actually wanted me, that he felt the same way I felt, that my best friend was in love with me. Was it possible we could get a second chance?

Unfortunately, the light and airy feeling doesn't remain when I stand up. In fact, I feel a bit like death. Any hope of running down to the store to see Nate, to perhaps thank him by taking him to lunch, is all but forgotten. Even work tonight will be a problem.

My stomach spins, and my head isn't far behind. Lying back down, I resign myself to this position and search out my phone.

When I click on Nate's name, our text string pops up. There's the one from the other day, when I offered to meet him for dinner…and then there's the last text I sent him before that. Just reading the words makes me nauseous.

Me: Mailed the divorce papers, please sign, and file.

I remember debating how to word the text, really wanting to write, "fight for me, fight for us." Or even just, how are you? It killed me that I knew nothing of his life for the last few years. I'd intentionally unfollowed all social media posts about him and his career. Last I knew he was still singing with Grant in Nashville.

Why is he back here? Karen says he's staying, but Nate and

I haven't discussed it. Is he really back for good? Did something happen with Grant, or did he really come back to fight for us?

None of it adds up. The only way I'll find out, though, is if I give him a chance to explain. If I actually *talk* to him. Before I lose my nerve, I type up a quick message.

Hi Nate, thanks for taking care of me last night. Still not feeling great, but hopefully I can repay you with lunch soon.

Next, I shoot Hailey a text.

Please tell me I didn't completely embarrass myself yesterday. I feel like death.

My phone rings almost instantaneously. "Girl, you have some explaining to do!" Hailey hollers into the phone before I even have a chance to say hello.

"Oh, good, I see we've been practicing our inside voices." I roll my eyes as my head throbs. "Please, if you want to talk, just whisper."

Hailey's laughter echoes through the phone. "Oh, you must be feeling all sorts of lousy today. After all that tequila and all that hussy you were practicing."

"Keep 'em coming. Just let me know when you're done, and I'll take you off mute."

She laughs again. "Okay, okay. I'm done. But seriously, how are you feeling today?"

Sighing as I lie back down, I consider her question.

I'm feeling nauseous, embarrassed, and oh-so-confused about the status of my relationship with my ex-husband. Where should I begin? "Feeling pretty lousy to be honest."

"Right. Well, I gotta say, you owe poor Shawn an apology."

Heat inches up my chest. Shit. Nate mentioned that the ruse was up. Does Hailey know what was going on? Can't talk to Shawn and figure it out, so I'm just going to roll with this. "Yeah, we ended things."

"Yeah, I'm pretty sure when he saw you making out with your ex on the boat that was a clue that the relationship was over. Ames, that was pretty shitty. Shawn is great, and he liked you a lot."

The eye rolls are on fire today. Is this girl really this oblivious? "Honestly, it wasn't that serious. I had lunch with him the day before and told him about my confusion over Nate. He understood. Besides, he seems more interested in someone else as well. Believe me, we parted as friends. We're going to be family, after all."

"So you admit there is something going on with Nate?"

Notice how she just glossed right over the Shawn comment. This girl is unbearable. "Yes. Nate and I were married. Clearly, we have a history. Those feelings don't just disappear."

"Right, but you keep going on about how he's your ex. Is it the tattoos? It is, isn't it? They are pretty irresistible."

Laughter hurts my head, but I can't help but giggle when Hailey gets this ridiculous. "Yes, it's the tattoos. They made me lose my panties."

"You lost your panties!"

I palm my face. "No, Hailey, it's a saying. Keep up."

Hailey sighs. "Damn, well, you *should* lose your panties soon if you haven't already…that man is head over heels in love with you."

The smile breaks across my face. It's almost impossible to contain my happiness over having Nate back in my life. Trying to tamp down my excitement, I reply, "Let's not get ahead of ourselves. We're just friends right now. I don't even know why he's back in town."

She sings, "But you're gonna find out! And then you'll lose your panties!"

I laugh. "Okay, I'm going to go nurse my hangover. I'll see you in a few hours."

"Yeah, yeah. Just when the conversation gets good you hold out on me. Whatever, missy. I'll get the truth out of Nate if I don't get it out of you."

"Leave him alone," I say a little too sharply. The last thing I want is my friends filling Nate with thoughts that I'm pining after him. I've been standing on my own two feet for the past few years without him. Just because he's back doesn't mean I'm going to fall for him. He's going to have to work to prove to me that he's back for real. That he's the man I need him to be. Until then, I am going to keep myself grounded, and my panties will remain tightly on my body.

Love & Tequila Make Her Crazy

I wake to the sound of movement in my living room. The hangover must have dragged me back to sleep for a while. When I look at the clock, I see it's already 12:30, so at least I didn't sleep too long. I have a few more hours until I have to get ready for work, but first I have to figure out who is hanging out in my apartment.

Grabbing my robe, I stumble out of my room, adjusting my eyes to the brightness. My bedroom curtains were drawn and the blackout design did its job. "Morning, beautiful. Or should I say, good afternoon."

Squinting my eyes open, I take in the delicious man that owns my heart. "Is that a burger from Le Central in that bag?"

Nate smirks at me, raising his blue eyes to mine in a memory. Burgers from the French restaurant downtown were a secret that we never shared with anyone. Everyone thought it was a small stuffy restaurant meant for only people our parents' age. Not Nate and me, though. We'd discovered that they made the best burgers in town. Hands down, no question. I hadn't mustered up the courage to go there since we split up. "Where else would I get my girl a burger from after she survived her first bout of alcohol poisoning at Potter's Cove?"

I laugh. He makes it sound like a rite of passage. "Hm,

your girl?"

Nate's smile grows wider. "You want your burger?"

I nod. "Yeah, just didn't want you to think I would let that slide. Now sit with me on the couch and let's eat."

Nate winks before grabbing plates and plopping down next to me like no time has passed.

Curling my legs under me, I tuck my robe between my knees, remembering my promise to Hailey that these underwear were staying right where they belong. "So, how are you really feeling?" Nate asks as he hands me half my burger, taking an eyeful of my black robe which isn't doing the best job of hiding my non-bra-wearing breasts.

"Better, thanks to you. Seriously, Nate, *I* wanted to buy *you* lunch to thank you. And then here you are coming to the rescue again. Thank you."

Nate grins and bites into his own burger. Between bites he says, "I knew you'd need one of the magical burgers. Remember the morning after prom when we got them?"

I eye him. "Which prom?"

He laughs. "Mine, you tease. After yours I'm pretty sure we didn't leave the bedroom."

"*Boat*. We didn't leave the boat, Nate."

He smiles wider and points to his head. "Oh, I remember everything. Just testing out your memory. It seems a bit wonky lately."

Rolling my eyes, I focus on the food. "Oh my God," I say,

remembering what he's referring to. "*Peter.*"

We both burst out laughing remembering Peter's face that night. Poor guy had taken a test. I'm pretty sure it was calculus. Nate and Jack went looking for him after school because they were going to get ready together, and we were all taking pictures at the boat. They couldn't find him anywhere, but they eventually found him sitting in class, staring at the wall, a dumbstruck look on his face. He barely registered when they walked in calling his name.

"He couldn't get over how he was going to live with his parents for the rest of his life," Nate says between fits of laughter.

I roll my eyes. "He was always so damn dramatic. It was *one* test."

Nate mimics Peter holding up his hands, looking bewildered. "I'm never going to graduate. I'm going to live with my parents forever. I'll never get to have sex. Sex, Nate, I'll never have sex."

Nate's imitation is so spot on I practically spit out my food. "And then he decided that he wasn't going to waste the night. If he wasn't going to get into college, he was going to smoke and drink and have sex before he lost his chance."

Tears fall down my face as I laugh, remembering how the idiot allowed Stacy Jennings, the girl who always had all the drugs, to give him a shroom. He spent the night waving his hand in front of his face, talking about how dumb he was, and then crying about sex.

"You saved the night though, Nate. You brought him one of

our secret burgers."

Nate beams. "He cried! Over a damn burger."

"It's a good burger," I argue, biting into mine again.

"A damn good burger," Nate agrees, taking another bite himself. We sit silently chewing. "I fucking miss him."

I nod, tears burning behind my lids.

Are we doing this? Are we finally going to talk about it? About Peter? About our fight? I turn to Nate and meet his eyes. They're red with remorse and so much regret. "I miss him so damn much," he says again.

"Nate." I put my burger down, trying to muster up the energy for this conversation.

He shakes his head. "Not now. I just want to remember him. That's all."

My shoulders relax. Me too. For so long, memories of Peter were twisted into the pretzel of my failed marriage. It's nice to focus on just Peter. To replay the memories.

Nate relaxes, and we spend the next hour reliving our childhood. Talking about playing manhunt in the neighborhood, sneaking down to the boat for sleepovers, weekends on Block Island, and even some stories I barely remember because I was so young, but Nate, Jack, and Peter experienced them with me by their sides.

There are so many reasons why Nate and I shouldn't be sitting here like this. I asked for a divorce for a reason. Our fight. The disastrous time apart and then the nail in the coffin of our marriage, when I discovered Nate had moved on while we were still legally married. But right now, sitting here with him, reliving the good, I can't help but wonder if that was all a mistake. We both said things and did things we can't take back, but I know for a fact it was because we were both heartbroken over Peter's death. And we both handled it differently.

Grief and guilt. The strength of those two things overwhelmed our lives and destroyed everything good. Nate is offering me a lifeline, just like I offered him so many years ago when he was drowning from his father's death. If I'm honest, I haven't felt as at peace or as at home in the last three years as I have in the last few hours with Nate by my side, simply talking. Or sleeping in my bed.

"Thanks for bringing my sketchpad back," I say, biting the side of my lip.

"You have any new work I can see?"

Avoiding his gaze, I look down at my hands. "I…uh… haven't sketched in a while."

"How long, Ames?"

I flip my eyes up to his and see him studying me, as if he's bracing himself for my answer. "Since you."

Nate's jaw tightens, and he clenches his fists, as if it physically hurts him to know what my life has been like without him. He breathes through his frustration. "You should never have stopped drawing; you're extremely talented."

"Says the man wearing half my designs on his body," I

tease, trying to lighten the mood.

Nate gives me a false smile, and I ache to make it all better. With our burgers long gone and our drinks empty, we've run out of reasons for him to stay. And yet I don't want him to leave. He sits up, readying himself, and grabs the plates to clean up. Before he can move, I put my hand on his knee, so nervous for what I'm going to say, but more nervous *not* to say it.

I don't want to live in the grief anymore. I don't want to just continue going through the motions of my life. Drinking, working, busying myself just to keep from remembering. *I don't want to just exist. I want to live.* I want to move forward. I want to be happy again. And the man sitting before me seems to be the key to that. He always was.

"Nate, will you go on a date with me?"

Nate looks up at me, clear surprise written all over his face. "Like, a date, date?" he asks nervously.

I square my shoulders and look him right in the eye. "Yeah, I mean I haven't asked someone out in a while, but I think that's what that means."

A shadow falls over his face. Maybe bringing up dating other people isn't the greatest idea. "I'm just teasing, Nate. Yes, a date, date. Unless I'm reading this situation wrong, it felt like you were trying to give us a chance. Did I misread this?" My heart beats wildly below my robe despite the brave face I'm wearing.

Nate's lips turn up. "No, Amelia, you did not misread the situation. I'd love to take you on a date." He moves closer to me, lifting his hand up to push my hair back off my face. As always, my messy hair is getting in the way and becoming a distraction.

"No. I'm taking *you* out. To thank you for everything the past two days. I really appreciate it."

Nate licks his lips. "Babe, the first time I take you out, you are not paying. Nice try though." My eyes flicker, focusing in on the way his tongue brushes so softly against his mouth. It would be so easy to fall back into bed with this man. "Stop looking at me like that, Amelia." Nate's voice is gruff, almost pained.

"Like what?" I ask softly, deciding to throw caution to the wind and moving my hand to the tie on my robe.

"Do not move another inch. Don't you dare touch that string, Ames."

"What, this one?" I ask, holding it in the air and whipping it around, raising my eyes to his.

Nate's arm clamps down on mine. "I'm serious. I want you so damn bad, but I don't have the time that I need to devote to you right now. *Tomorrow.* Tomorrow, I'll take you out and then I'll take you back to my bed and spend hours on that body. Okay, babe?"

My body has no interest in waiting, but I'm also not going to beg. "I work tomorrow."

"Take the night off."

"Can't."

We spar, and it feels like firecrackers zing between us.

"Fine, then I'll woo you at the bar."

I laugh, excited for whatever plan he's concocted in his head. I always loved when Nate surprised me—especially in public. It's hotter than foreplay. "Okay, Pearson. I'll let you woo me." I bite my lip trying to hold back a smile. But dammit, why hide it? It feels good to smile.

Nate lets out a low laugh and pulls me to him. "Thank you, Amelia," he whispers against my ear. "Thank you for having lunch with me. Thank you for talking with me." His voice breaks as he holds me tighter.

Wrapping my arms around him, I pull him closer and whisper into his chest, "Thank you for coming back."

Nate

Pretty sure I couldn't be happier if I tried. I walk into the doctor's office with Sam feeling certain that we will be getting nothing but good news. Today's been a good day. It feels like the race car I was careening in finally slowed down and got back on the track, heading in the right direction.

For years I'd been spiraling in the wrong direction, racing to feel again, trying anything just to stop the pain. All this time the answer had been waiting where I left her. My life made sense when Amelia was in it. I was good enough because I was hers. Why the hell it had to take me this long to recognize that, I'll never understand, but I wasn't going to waste any more time analyzing or stressing over all the time we lost. We're finally on the same page. It felt like old times today. Sitting in her apartment, eating a burger, laughing about our childhood, and teasing one another. For a few moments we were *us* again.

"You seem like you're in a good mood," Sam says as we sit in the waiting room. Before I can respond, my mother walks into the office looking even more stressed than the night before. Circles surround her eyes, and a forced smile greets us.

Standing, I offer my mother the chair next to Sam, and she squeezes my hand before sitting. "How's Amelia?" she asks, looking up, alarmed. "She never stopped by the shop."

I smile. "Sorry, that's my fault. I brought her lunch."

Sam interjects. "Ah, that's why you're smiling."

I acknowledge the truth with my eyes. "Yeah, it was a good day. She's fine, Mom."

My mother breathes out a sigh, and I watch as the stress radiates off her shoulders. The staleness in the office doesn't help. It's like the brackish grey-beige room is meant to further depress and stress you. Shouldn't they have a brighter color, or at least a more calming one? Like a soothing blue.

The nurse walks out of the beige office door with no personality on her face. It's like doom is the only thing this office understands. Not accepting the temperature change, I reach down to my mom's shoulder and squeeze. *We've got this*, I tell her with my touch. She looks up at me and gives me a small smile.

"Mr. and Mrs. Dawson?"

My mom shrinks beneath my hand. "Nope. Just Mr. Dawson. We're not married." I can feel the pain in her voice.

Sam looks to her and then back to the nurse. "They're family. They're coming in."

I smile at him gratefully. He doesn't need to include me, but he always has. Once again, I promise myself to do better by the ones that love me. To *be* better.

We all walk back to the doctor's office, my mother and Sam in front of me, him holding her almost upright and me behind them, feeling like the boy heading to the principal's office.

Had I really been so oblivious all these years to not realize that it still bothered my mother that she and Sam never married? It had been a conversation so long ago, one that while significant at the time, now feels almost like it was had by a different person. A kid. Which is really what I was even at twenty. Not that it's an excuse. I'd stolen over ten years from them. All this time I'd been focused on fixing my marriage with Amelia, and I hadn't even stopped to think about what I'd held hostage from them.

Squeezing my fists tight, I try hard to squash the bout of self-hatred that is rising from my chest. What is wrong with me? Why do I keep proving I wasn't worth it? I'm not worth Peter's death. I'm not worth keeping a couple in love from being married. Amelia deserves a hell of a lot more than me. I run my hand over my forehead as we make our way into the office, keeping my eyes down.

"Sam, how are you feeling?" The doctor stands to greet us. Fortunately, we're meeting in his office, not an examination room. The desk is black and simple, as if he doesn't spend much time in this room. There are a few pictures around the room. A blonde woman and a young boy feature prominently in them. Likely his family. Lucky guy.

Out of the corner of my eye, I see Sam squeeze my mom's hand. "I feel good. Strong."

The doctor nods. "That's wonderful. Karen, it's good to see you. I know this hasn't been easy. And who is this we have here?" he asks, motioning to me.

Sam clears his throat. "This is Nathan. Karen's son."

The doctor smiles. "Oh, wonderful. It's always great to have a supportive family."

His words cut me. *Family*. I've been such an ass. Such a weak jerk. But that ends today. I will make this right. I'm not sure how, but somehow, I will make this up to my mom. And Sam. Lord knows he deserves it.

"Well, let's get right to it. The scans are back. And it's good news. The cancer is shrinking. The treatment is working."

My mother's body begins to shake, and tears stream down her face. My chest heaves watching Sam pull her closer. "Shh, baby, it's okay. It's good news."

The doctor doesn't flinch. He grabs a tissue and hands it to Sam who blots my mother's face. It's too much. Seeing how much pain she is in, seeing how in love with her he is, seeing how much I've stolen from them. And yet, they are getting a second chance.

The sobs rack my mother's body even as she tries to breathe through them and apologize. Her words come out jumbled, and the doctor finally excuses himself for a moment, giving us time to compose ourselves and offering the privacy that it appears she needs.

My mother sinks against Sam's chest. "I...I'm just so relieved," she says between sobs. "You're going to be okay." Finally she breathes and begins to gain control over her emotions. "You're going to be okay."

Sam rubs my mother's back. "*We're* going to be okay."

I slink back to the corner of the room, offering them privacy. It's a miracle to experience true love once in your life. That much I was completely aware of as I'd been lucky enough to find my soulmate. But then I'd gone and thrown it away. Yet somehow I was getting a second chance. Which was beyond anything I felt I deserved.

Some would say my mother was unlucky because she lost her husband so young, and while I know she will always miss him, I can now see how lucky she is to also have found love again. It's rare and special, and while painful, it's a good kind of pain. Because there's a lightness around it. It hurts, but it's good.

Leaning against the wall, I vow to my dad to do better. To help him keep Mom happy by letting her go. By letting her live in the good. Letting us both have a second chance.

After the appointment, my mom asks if I want to join Sam and her for dinner to celebrate. It feels like a pity invite though, like they really want the time alone together, or maybe that's just my guilt playing tricks on me. Either way, I tell them to go ahead without me.

Arriving back at the boat, I crash into bed, finally succumbing to the tiredness and stress from the last few days. First, the anxiousness of dealing with seeing Amelia again, her fake relationship and clear distaste toward me, then the scare on the boat, and staying awake all night to make sure she was feeling okay, and finally the doctor's appointment. I feel like I've been put through the wringer. When my phone rings and Grant is on the other end, I am less than inclined to pick up. He doesn't let it go to voicemail though. He just dials again.

Running my hand over my head, I resign myself to the conversation. "Hey, Grant."

"Hey, buddy. How's it going?"

"It's been better," I say honestly. I don't have the patience to lie at this point. I'm hanging on by a thread.

I hear a door slam in the background. "Oh, shit. I'm sorry to hear that. Your stepdad okay?" Another punch in the gut. He's *not* my stepdad.

I pull on my neck. "Yeah." I sigh out a breath. "We just got good news."

"Oh, that's great, man. So when will you be back? The record label keeps calling."

Kicking the shoe off my right foot, I watch as it sails through the air and hits the door with a thud. "Haven't decided."

I know I need to tell him I'm not coming back, but right now I just don't have it in me.

Grant sighs. "You talk to Amelia?"

The breath comes heavy out of my throat. "Working on it," I grind out.

"Well, don't work too long. We have decisions to make. Things we need to get done. And the label…"

I cut him off. "I know. I got it. I'll handle it. Listen, I gotta go. I haven't slept in two days."

Grant laughs again. "Oh, one of those nights with Amelia. I hear ya. Good for you, man. Tell our girl I said hi." He clicks off before I can correct any of the ridiculous things he just said. I feel like I'm drowning again. The hatred I feel toward myself for keeping my mom from getting married, from leaving my wife for three years and finding her just as fucked up as me, from watching her get so drunk that she actually got alcohol poisoning. It's too much.

I pull out my wallet and grab the card Jack gave me. If there was ever a time that I need the support of a therapist—that I need the pain of the needle—it's right now.

The tattoo parlor is located in an old brick building that used to be a car repair garage. It's on a side street next to the fire station, but when I enter, the entire road is almost deserted. I can't say that disappoints me. I don't want to see anyone right now. If not for the fact that I know I need this right now, I would prefer to be on my boat by myself. But it's because I also would want to down a bottle of tequila while on the boat that I know I need to be here. If I learned anything over the last three years, it's when to ask for help. Right now is a prime example.

"Nate," the man behind the counter says when I walk in. I'm assuming this is Jack's friend Kyle. He has a military buzz cut, massive arms covered in only black ink, and a scar across his face.

I hold out my hand, and he takes it in a strong shake. "Thanks for fitting me in," I reply. "I'm assuming you're Kyle?"

He nods. "Come on back. Do you know what you want done?"

"Yeah, I'd actually like to do Roman numerals of these

dates." I hand him the dates I've written down. Our first kiss. The day we got engaged. Our wedding. And today.

He raises his eyes. "What happened today?"

I clear my throat as I sit in the chair. "Today I decided to take my life back. The last few years have been a disaster for me, but yesterday I saw that it's been just as bad for my wife. I thought staying away was good for her because I destroyed my life and didn't want to take her down with me, but I've since learned that she was drowning too. And today we had a breakthrough. She asked me on a date."

"That's a good thing, right?" he asks as he readies his tools.

I slip off my shirt because I want the tattoo across my ribs, under Amelia's name. "I have a few things I have to make right, but yes, it's a good thing."

"And what is it that you have to work through?"

I sigh. This is the part that's difficult. I want to be with Amelia. I want to be the man she deserves. But first I have to make this shit right with my mom. I need to figure out how to give her back the ten plus years I've stolen from her and Sam.

"My father died on 9/11," I say, trying to put into words something that I still can't wrap my head around. "Selfishly, I asked my mom not to get remarried, and I'm only now realizing how much it means to be married to the person you love. It feels greedy for me to get my wife back and not make it right for my own mother."

The tattoo pen starts buzzing, and I bite the inside of my

cheek as it hits my skin. I watch closely, believing that I deserve to not only feel the pain but watch him make every single mark on my body. Some people would find this masochistic, but it's how I punish myself and it's how I heal. Pain has gotten me through a lot over the last few years. When I couldn't feel anything other than the loss of Amelia, the sting of a tattoo gun made me feel something. Even if it hurt.

"So, what's your plan?" he asks as he focuses on his work.

This is why I came here. I needed to be here to work through this. And I have a plan now. "My friend owns a winery. I'm going to talk to her about a wedding."

"To renew your vows?" he asks.

I shake my head. "No. I mean I definitely think Amelia and I need that, but we are a while away from me getting her down the aisle again. Kind of have to tell her we're still married first," I say with a painful laugh.

Kyle stops his work and looks at me. "She doesn't know you're still married?"

I shake my head. "It's a long story. But no, she doesn't. The wedding would be for my mom."

He cocks a brow. "You think that's your decision?"

I exhale an annoyed breath. "I need to make this right. I need to fix this. I have so much guilt, it's eating me alive. I can't move on with Amelia until I fix this."

He pauses and holds up the gun while he speaks. "Nate, it's about apologizing. I'm sure your mom knows why you asked her to refrain from getting remarried. And she's an adult. It's been years. She could have changed her mind. Should you talk to her about your feelings? Absolutely. Should you explain that it no longer is something that bothers you? Yes. But in the end, she's your mother. She wants you to be happy. Let go of the guilt. The loss of your father is something that most people don't understand, and no one can tell you that your reaction to her moving on was wrong."

I sigh. "No one would say it was right though, either. Honestly, I'm doing this for my dad. He would want her to be happy. It's honoring him to do this. It's something I can do for him, and if I'm honest, part of my guilt over my friend Peter's death is that I couldn't do enough. The reason my marriage went down the tubes is because of that self-loathing. I feel like this is a way forward. A way to honor my dad. A way to honor Peter's sacrifices."

As soon as I say it, I know it's what I need to do. And it appears that Kyle understands because he just nods and gets back to work. With a plan in place, I finally relax and focus on the future, because for once, it feels like I've got something to look forward to.

CHAPTER 17

Amelia
(Almost) Twenty-Three Years old

It's been months since Nate proposed, and we haven't really discussed it. It's not like I expect him to walk around calling me fiancée, but I've almost started to wonder if he regrets his spontaneous question. It's not like I have a ring on my finger, which is totally fine—we're young, in love, and broke. Or at least I am. So I don't know what I expect, but silence on the subject is not it.

Although, I hostess at the bar and get to spend even more time with Nate than usual, the guys haven't pulled me back on stage again. It's not that I thought I'd be part of the band after my one rendition of Fleetwood Mac, but once again, the lack of discussing any of it seems strange. For years Nate and I told each other everything, shared everything with one another, and now suddenly it feels like there is an elephant sitting between us—in the shape of a diamond that isn't on my finger. I feel uncomfortable and nervous *all the time.*

Rather than focusing on whatever is festering between Nate and me, I throw myself wholeheartedly into my job at the hotel and into secretly learning how to write music. I hadn't planned to pick up Nate's favorite hobby, but one day when he was out, I had the urge to run my hands over the strings of his guitar. The urge to remember how we used to be, back when we were still just kids, and I was trying to bring him back to life.

The feel of the chords beneath my fingers hurt at first, but I kind of like the pain. It makes me feel alive and just like I feel with my flowers, that I am creating something with my hands. I will never be a corporate all-star or work in an office, but I can create things. Music. Bouquets. Works of art that are completely different but give me an outlet for all of my balled-up stress from the lack of communication in my relationship.

As happened with my singing, Grant is the one to discover I'd taken up guitar. I am working on a project, a short tune that's been stuck in my head. I know nothing about writing music, but having watched Nate do it for all these years and learning how to strum out a few chords on the guitar has me focused. I want to do something special for Nate. Our communication has been off, and I hope I can express myself through his favorite form of communication—song.

The door to the apartment opens and I practically jump. "Oh, my gosh, you scared me!" I say to Grant, giving him a once-over and noticing his eyes are red, as usual. The guys have late nights often, but I've begun to notice that Grant seems to be extending his hours of inebriation. For the most part I am busy so it doesn't affect me, but if he keeps it up I'll have to mention it to Nate.

"Hey, baby, don't be so jumpy," Grant says, making my skin crawl. I am no one's baby and certainly not his. "Whatchya got there?" he asks, motioning to the guitar in my hands.

Feeling like a cat who has been caught playing with the mice, I place the guitar down on the couch. "Nothing, just playing around."

Grant makes his way toward me, his movements a bit disjointed. To protect myself from him getting too close, I pull the guitar back onto my lap. "I like to play around," he says, sitting next to me and giving me a look that leaves very little to the imagination.

Shit, where is Nate?

Breathing heavily and avoiding his gaze, I hold the guitar closer. "Where is Nate?"

Grant shifts himself closer, flinging his arm behind me, like a teenage boy does at the movies, but with even less skill since he's clearly had a few drinks. "Oh, he had plans. Don't worry, we share everything. He won't be upset."

My stomach drops, a sick feeling settling over me. Nate has been distant the last few months. What is Grant getting at? Nate is out with someone else? Biting the inside of my mouth, I remind myself that Nate isn't like that. And I need to get myself out of this situation. *Fast*.

As Grant moves his hand lower on the couch, he grabs at one of my blonde wisps, pulling it tightly. My eyes go wide, and I screech in pain. "Oh, our girl likes it rough, does she?"

His eyes are wild, and my mind starts to run with where this is going. He's got at least fifty pounds on me, and although I have the guitar in my hand that could be used as a weapon, I would never risk breaking the only thing Nate has left of his father.

When he moves his hand down to my breast and pinches my nipple, I let out a scream, and he takes the other hand to cover my mouth. "Shhh, we both know you want this. I watch how you waltz around this apartment in barely-there clothes, shooting me looks of need and letting these delicious tits hang out."

Fear rattles my insides. He moves to get on top of me, fumbling with his belt buckle, and I know I'm running out of time. My eyes dart back and forth between the door and Grant, and I make a decision to move as quickly as I can. I don't think he expects it, so when I jump up and run for the front door, mumbling something about being late for work, he doesn't follow. He's probably too drunk to even comprehend.

On the other side of the door, my breathing becomes shallow, my heart pounding so loud I can't think. All I know is that I can't go back to the apartment. I can't sleep there.

That was so close…would he really have…?

My mind runs away from me with thoughts I don't even want to entertain. What do I do? I can't tell Nate. But how do I not tell him?

I *have* to tell Nate.

My phone buzzes in my pocket, and as I take it out trying to read the message, the focus is blurry.

Why can't I see what it says?

I wipe at the phone, imagining that maybe the glass is dirty. But the blur remains. As drops of water fall down onto the phone, I realize it's not the phone that's blurry, it's my eyes. I'm crying.

Fuck. I don't cry. I never cry. This feeling that's come over me, this loss of power over my own body, over my own reactions, over my emotions, is so foreign and breath-stealingly painful.

I swipe away the tears, trying hard to focus on the message.

Nate: Meet me at the bar and bring my guitar please. I have a surprise.

The sob that escapes from my throat sounds like a wild animal, and I fall to the floor, clutching Nate's guitar in my last grip on sanity. I *have* to tell him.

Weaving my way through the city, I turn onto Broadway, Nashville's very own Music Row, and hold the guitar to my chest, protecting it from all the bodies that wander, or more accurately stumble, from bar to bar.

Before I meet Nate, I have to get myself cleaned up. He'll

know immediately something is wrong if he sees the remnants of tears on my face. Or maybe he won't since he's probably never seen me cry.

"Dammit, dammit, dammit," I mutter as I walk furiously through town.

A tall blonde walking with a guitar and legs for days is not going to go unnoticed. I know what I look like. My looks get enough comments from people when I work at the bar. Fortunately, a growly Nate, who always makes it clear I'm with him, keeps people I work with away from me, but he can't be around every moment of the day, so clearly I've dealt with drunk men hitting on me.

But that wasn't what today was. Today was so much more. So much worse. I trusted Grant. *Nate* trusted Grant. We let him live with us. What the hell was he thinking?

I reach the door to the bar, say a quick hello to the bouncer, and rush to the bathroom. I look absurd carrying a guitar everywhere I go, but I don't have an option. I don't trust anyone with Nate's baby.

Looking in the mirror, I'm surprised by the person who looks back. In this moment I know one thing; I never want to look like this person again.

Weak. Scared. Sad. Petrified, if I'm honest.

I'm about to destroy Nate's band—his career in Nashville relies on Grant, the guy who he's done everything with since he started college. Is he really going to agree to throw that all away because I say that Grant was inappropriate?

Will he believe me? Did I overreact? My stomach clenches. This isn't me. Doubting myself. I *know* better. I've sat through enough classes. I've been told since I was in high school that women can speak up. That we can tell the truth and be believed. But why with all that knowledge am I still wondering if he'll believe me? Why don't I really even believe myself? Second guessing how I felt, what was said, how his hand felt against my skin and when he pulled my hair and pinched my breast. The way his hand smelled like cigarette smoke and desperation when he clenched it over my mouth to stifle my screams. How I sucked in that scent instead of air. I can still smell it. I can still *taste* it.

It was real. I didn't overreact. I didn't deserve it.

His words echo in my ears. *"We both know you want this. I watch how you waltz around this apartment in barely-there clothes, shooting me looks of need and letting these delicious tits hang out."*

My skin crawls. Did I make him think that was okay? Is it my fault?

Laughter from girls who enter the bathroom, tipsy and happy, is a stark contrast to this existential crisis I'm having. "Oh, honey, he's so not worth it," a short redhead says to me when she sees my face.

Her friend, an equally attractive brunette, puts her arm on my back. When I flinch at her touch, she smiles softly. "We've all been there. Here, I've got makeup in my bag. Can I help you?"

This. This is the moment where I realize what I'm missing from my life. Women. Friendship. There is no one for me to call. I have no friends outside of Nate and Grant in Nashville. Coworkers yes, but not friends. Not like I had at home.

That realization alone sends a shiver down my spine and a new wave of tears pool in my eyes.

Recognizing that what I really need is to focus on these kind drunk girls so I can go to Nate with my wits about me, I allow two women who I don't know, who have no idea what happened to me, help put me back together. Even if it's just makeup, it's exactly what I need at this moment. Their act of kindness, of support, the reminder that women support women, that women *believe* women, reminds me of who I am and what I have to do.

When I finally walk out of the bathroom, with glossy lipstick and pink blush, which are so not me, it's like I've been encased in armor. Almost like the Amelia who just dealt with whatever happened back at my apartment isn't present right now. This is Amelia the actress. I can handle my boyfriend—er, fiancé's—surprise. Now is not the time to break down and tell him everything. But soon. Like, as soon as I get him out of our place of work. I breathe out a fresh breath and look up, searching the bar for Nate.

A waitress who I'm not exactly friends with, but who I know well enough, spots me and screeches, "Oh, thank God you're here! Nate put me on Amelia duty!"

Amelia duty. The words pinch. Am I really so weak that he needs to have people watch out for me?

Yes, Amelia. If we've learned anything from the last two hours of your life, Nate is completely right.

I shrug. "Well, here I am. I've got his guitar. He said he needs it." I hold it out to her.

She claps her hands in excitement. "Yes! Okay, let me have Chandler give it to him. He asked me to get a glass of champagne for your birthday and sit you right here."

Birthday? In all the day's activities I'd forgotten that my birthday is only a few short hours away. Who forgets their own birthday?

Someone who doesn't have friends.

My heart squeezes again. I have Nate. And I will not ruin whatever he's planned by being weak Amelia.

I'm not dressed for a celebration. Just my typical jeans and a black T-shirt. But thankfully, because of the girls in the bathroom, at least my makeup dresses me up a bit.

My heart picks up speed when I realize that Grant may be here. If Nate wanted me to meet him here, and he needed his guitar, obviously he would have Grant here too. But a quick search of the lineup for the night reveals that tonight is open mic night, which is more like karaoke than anything else. Nate uses open mic night to test out new music by himself. My heart slows. Hopefully, Grant is passed out on the couch at this point.

As the singer hands over the mic to Chandler, the bar's

manager, he looks in my direction, finds me, and winks. At that moment the waitress, Sarah, places a bucket on the table with champagne glasses and a bottle of Veuve Clicquot.

Fancy. And so not Nashville. She pops the champagne, pours me a glass, and hands it to me, whispering, "Enjoy the show," before heading back to the bar.

"Boy, do we have a treat for all of you. One of our regular artists Nate Pearson is here, and he has a few special guests for backup."

The crowd cheers, and I squint my eyes, trying to make out the dark figures who stand behind Chandler. There are three of them. Obviously, one is Nate. But who else is with him?

When the light shifts, bringing the three men into focus, I practically fall off my barstool. Behind Nate stands my two other favorite people—Peter and my brother, Jack. Peter gives a goofy wave, and Jack has a big smile. He mouths, "Hey, sis!"

I wave with my mouth hanging open and turn to look at Nate who is wearing his signature smirk. Into the mic he says, "This is for you, babe. I love you."

He strums the guitar, and the familiar bars of John Mellencamp's "Hurts So Good" fill the room. His smile as he stares and sings to me is genuine and filled with joy, hope, and teasing.

Behind him, Peter and Jack sing and do what can only be described as a poor man's Macarena.

The crowd goes wild as Nate hops off stage, and the spotlight follows him until he stops in front of me, flinging the guitar behind his back and reaching into his pocket. When he gets down on one knee, my hand flies over my mouth in surprise.

"Amelia Fitzpatrick, I have loved you my entire life. Since I was a young boy, you have been the one to drive me wild. I know I already asked you this question, but I wanted to make it official, give you a little something so everyone in this room, and everywhere else, knows you're mine. Will you marry me, Amelia?"

I hop off my stool and throw myself at him. We both fall backward, and fortunately for his quick thinking, he moves the guitar before we land on it. Laughing, he looks at me and says, "Is that a yes?"

I kiss him, whispering yes against his lips. "Yes, yes, I'd say yes to you every day for the rest of my life, Pearson."

Nate's smile grows. "You know soon I'll get to call you that too."

"You can call me whatever you want, as long as you call me yours."

Peter and Jack interrupt our little love fest, and champagne is poured as I stare—gape—at the ring Nate bought me. It's perfect. A single solitaire set in a white gold band. "I got a room at the same hotel as Peter and Jack tonight. Figured we need to do a little celebrating, and I don't want any interruptions from our roommate." He raises his eyebrows, and just the mention of Grant sends my stomach into a tizzy. But I refuse to let him ruin this moment.

Biting my lip, I nervously say, "About that. Now that we're

engaged, I'm thinking we need our own place."

"One step ahead of you, Cookie." I glare at his term of endearment, and he throws up his hands. "What? You just said I could call you whatever I want."

I roll my eyes. "But calling me something that won't lead to you getting laid doesn't seem like the wisest thing when you'll have me all to yourself tonight."

Nate kisses me. "That's what I'm trying to say. I'll have you all to myself every night. The guys are here to help us move into *our* new apartment. The one I bought."

"You *bought* an apartment?"

"Yes. I have money, as you know, in a trust. We need our own space, Ames. Tell me this is okay?" His eyes search mine. "It's a condo, and it's close to everything. I think you'll love it."

I throw my arms around him. He doesn't have a clue what this means to me. He doesn't know how he just saved me in a way I'll never be able to explain. We'll be starting fresh, on our own, engaged.

CHAPTER 18

Amelia

The bar is busy tonight. I barely have time to register what time it is let alone pay attention to the fact that I've yet to spot Nate. Okay, that's a complete lie. Even with how slammed we are, my eyes continue to shift to the stairs watching for Nate. Did he change his mind? Decide I wasn't worth all the effort?

The nagging feeling in my stomach doesn't go away even though I know in my heart that Nate wouldn't have come all this way, uprooted his life, taken care of me all night, only to ghost me. Again. That would be too cruel. And although Nate has done some shitty things over the years, he was never intentionally cruel. Just broken. And stupid. And kind of sort of an ass.

Where the hell is he?

"Hey, Princess, stop scowling at the customers. People are starting to leave the bar," Hailey says, hip checking me back to reality.

Painting on my most fake smile, I grit out through my teeth, "Sorry, boss, won't happen again."

Hailey laughs, and then her face goes white, and my eyes follow her gaze. "Fuck," she mutters under her breath. Fuck is right. My husband, or my ex-husband whom I'm kind of sort of dating, walks into the bar with Caris by his side. A hostess seats them at a table directly in my view, and I watch in horror as Nate pulls out Caris's chair and then sits across from her. Is this a date? Is he on a freaking date? As if reading my mind, Hailey nudges me and mumbles, "I'm sure this isn't a date."

Without taking my eyes off them, I reply, "Dinner in a restaurant on the water with a person of the opposite sex. What is a date, for $500, Alex?"

"Okay, I admit it doesn't look good. But there is so obviously an explanation for this. Caris is engaged, and Nate is in love with you."

I give her a haughty laugh. "Caris didn't look engaged on the boat the other day when she was rubbing her ass all over Nate."

Hailey shrugs. "Dan the Douchebag is a loser, and I'd love it if they broke up, but I don't think that's the case. Although you're right, she *was* all over Nate last week. *Hm...*" She taps her finger on her chin.

"As interesting as Caris's engagement status is—*which by the way it's so not*—none of it changes the fact that she's currently sitting across from Nate shooting him googly eyes."

I'm pissed. Shaking mad. Nate seems lost in conversation with Caris, and he hasn't even so much as looked up at the bar to see if I'm here. It's like I've ceased to exist. "I'm waiting on them," I say, sliding out from behind the bar and walking to the table.

Hailey calls out, "You're not even a waitress," but I glare at her, and she shrugs me off.

As I approach the table, Nate looks up and his eyes meet mine. He holds them for a beat too long, sucking me into his soul, holding me hostage with his gaze, and then he gives me a lazy smile, the same kind he used to give me when we'd wake up in the morning, right before he'd lean down and kiss me, with nothing but sex on the brain.

"Caris, Mr. Pearson, how nice to see you both," I grit through my teeth, shaking off the memory of sex eyes.

Caris reaches her arm across the table and smacks Nate. "Oh, she called you Mr. Pearson, you're in trouble now!"

Nate laughs. "It's lovely to see you, *Mrs*. Pearson, although I prefer you with your hair down and a smile." Caris's head falls back in laughter, and I grimace at them both. Of course, I have to be careful. Caris's family owns this restaurant—they basically own the whole town—so being rude to her won't get me anywhere but on the street without a job.

I ignore Nate's comment and take their drink orders, walking away before he has a chance to say anything else. Behind the bar, I pour Caris a glass of Chardonnay and mix Nate a Jack and Coke. Shawn sidles up next to me, watching my every move.

"Can I help you?" I ask, without taking my eyes off Nate's table. He's gone back to conversing with Caris. They are in deep discussion, and my body buzzes uncomfortably watching them.

"Just making sure you don't slip any poison in their drinks," he says with a wink.

"Hadn't thought of it before, but now that you mention it, that's not a bad idea."

Shawn pulls the whiskey out of my hand, stopping my overpour. "Down, Tiger. It looks as fake of a relationship as the one you and I had." Shawn moves his arm around my waist and pulls me in for a side hug. I push away, unable to handle the friendship he's offering, as it will only release the feelings I have swirling inside, rather than the anger bubbling at the surface. I'd rather be angry. It's safer.

"That's just it. We had a fake relationship because I was trying to push Nate away. Nate and I had a long discussion the other night about us, and we had plans for tonight. There's no reason for...*that*," I say, pointing in their direction in complete annoyance. "I was ready to be done with the games," I say softly.

Shawn pulls my chin to look at him. "You have no idea what *that* is. Maybe they're just sharing a meal. Guys and girls can be friends, you know? Just look at us."

I roll my eyes. Nate and I were friends and look where that went. Nate didn't have female friends other than me. Although, I did have a lot of guy friends. "Okay, you have a point. But I don't have to like it."

Shawn chuckles. "No, you don't. Want me to take the drinks over? I don't want you *accidentally* pouring a drink on the owner of the restaurant."

Cocking my brow, I retort, "Stop giving me ideas!" Then I hand him the drinks and send him on his way. It really would be too tempting to douse them both.

My eyes remain on them through dinner, but after an hour Caris gets up, hugs Nate, and leaves the table, before he meanders over to the bar with his eyes focused solely on me.

"Hey, babe, how's your night going?"

With my lips pinched shut, I barely glance in his direction, focusing on the drink orders I'm filling.

"Don't make me call you Cookie," he sings, leaning across the bar and daring me not to look at him.

I don't budge.

"Now is that any way to treat your husband, Mrs. Pearson?" he says with a pout.

Of course, he knows how to get a rise out of me. "Stop calling me that," I hiss under my breath.

"Why? Are you embarrassed of me? Don't want people to know you're my wife?"

Anger pulses below the surface, eating away at my cool exterior, threatening to break through and cause me to snap. "Well, it would be embarrassing if we were married to have you traipsing around town, *on a date*, in front of me."

Nate's calm exterior remains. As always he is able to absorb my jabs without breaking a sweat. "Babe, for the five thousandth time, since I was seventeen, I haven't looked at another woman, let alone gone on a date with one. You're it for me."

The sound of a woman's moans as she screws my husband filters through my mind, but I push it from my memory.

It's in the past. We were separated. He's here now. Be an adult and ask about Caris. Ignore the past.

"Why were you having dinner with Caris?"

Nate's eyes soften, and he grabs my hand again. "Caris and I are friends. I had to talk to her about something. It's a…"—he hesitates and then meets my eyes—"surprise I'm planning. Anyway, I saw her when I got here and figured I'd kill two birds with one stone. You're working, she was about to have dinner by herself, and I figured I could talk to her while we ate. I told you there is only one woman I have ever been interested in. You need to learn to trust me, Amelia, or this is never going to work." Although his words indicate he's giving me an ultimatum, his shaking voice exposes his nerves. "Forgive me?"

I roll my eyes. Tonight was supposed to go so differently. "Whatever."

Nate leans over the bar and grabs my arm, pulling me to him. "Don't say whatever. Say yes, I forgive you, Nate." His hands move down my body, settling on my hips, and his fingers grip the soft flesh below my shirt and send a spark between my legs. "Sing with me tonight?" he asks, his body now fully across the bar and his lips dangerously close to mine.

I laugh nervously into his mouth, succumbing to his lips and kissing him quickly to avoid any discussion of music.

Nate deepens the kiss, his hand moving up my back and

behind my neck, pulling my tongue into his mouth and nipping at my bottom lip.

Holy shit, I'm kissing Nate Pearson again. After three years it really is like riding a bike. Just him being this close to me led my body to react the way it always used to, and everything is familiar. It's the same and yet so different. His kiss is more controlling, his lips rougher. He's not the romantic boy who swept me off my feet back then and yet that person still exists deep down. He's just wrapped in an even hotter package.

A clearing throat reminds me that we're in public, and I'm at work, so I push him back to his side of the bar. "Down, Pearson, I've got a job to do."

Nate winks at me, sending a flutter through my stomach. "Sing with me."

"No." I look the other way, having no interest in discussing this any further.

A customer asks for a beer, and I pop the top, ensuring my eyes don't meet Nate's again.

"When was the last time you sang?"

I shoot him a look, a warning shot, telling him we aren't doing this now. Nate huffs out a breath and walks away. It's fine. I don't want to talk about it. And I definitely won't sing about it. That part of my life is over. Even if I'm willing to give Nate another shot, there won't be any duets in our future.

Fortunately for Nate, my attention is diverted by my girls walking in. My cousin Belle and my brother's fiancée, Charlotte, and her best friend, Steph, plop down at the bar in front of me. Since I don't want Jack to know that Nate and I are speaking again, I avoid looking in his direction. Or at least I try to. It's kind of impossible when my ex-husband looks the way Nate does. He's impossibly good-looking, and when he settles himself onto a stool, pulls out his guitar, and starts tuning it, my eyes practically double in size. He is the sexiest man I've ever seen. I'm not biased; it's the tattoos as Hailey keeps pointing out, along with those long fingers that I know work wonders on my body as well as on his guitar strings. Also his blue eyes keep meeting mine longingly, his black lashes doing nothing to hide his desire.

"*Hellllo*, earth to Amelia," Steph croons, waving her hand in front of my face. I shoot her a look. She knows precisely who I'm looking at, and I don't want to draw attention to him. Of course it's too late. Belle turns and immediately recognizes Nate, and she shoots me a concerned look.

"Wait, what's he doing back?"

Think Amelia, think. Do I admit that we're trying again?

That's what we are doing, right? Trying? Dating? I almost laugh out loud. I'm dating my ex-husband. It's like a Jerry Springer show. Nope, can't admit to that.

"Don't know. He just keeps following me from job to job."

Charlotte's ears perk up. "Who's back?" Steph turns now too.

"Nate Pearson," I say, resigned to the fact that everyone is going to know soon enough.

Charlotte jumps out of her chair. "Oh my God! I have to call Jack. He'll be so excited!"

Before Charlotte can move, I grab her. "Don't you dare."

Everyone stares at me, shocked. "Spill the deets, Ames," Belle says.

Charlotte looks at me concerned, and I can't say I blame her. How had I completely forgotten the biggest hurdle to getting back together with Nate? What does it mean if I give my marriage another chance? Will Jack feel like I'm betraying him for choosing Nate? Will he think I'm choosing Nate? Because I'm not. I divorced him because of my brother.

I *picked* my brother. But honestly the person it hurt the most is me. I've suffered. I lost my husband. I lost my best friend. I bite my lip, hoping that Jack will understand, and I tell the truth. "Nate and Jack haven't spoken since Peter died."

Charlotte's face falls. "I won't say anything to Jack because I wasn't a part of that world, and I didn't know Peter. But you should. If Nate is sticking around, we don't want this to trigger Jack's PTSD."

Dammit. This is worse than I thought. My brother had an incredibly difficult time after Peter died. He blamed himself. And it didn't help that his best friend did as well. Jack has only recently come to terms with everything. The last thing I want is for Nate to send him spiraling back to the darkness that consumed him for so long.

Belle eyes me. "Why do you think he's back? What does he want?"

Steph mouths, "You," to me with a dirty wink, and I shoot her a look to tell her to shut the hell up. Knowing there's only one way to quiet everyone down, I tell them a half-truth. "I don't know. I'm working on trying to find that out. But until then, I'd rather not tell Jack."

Although I know eventually I'll have to deal with that grenade, tonight is not that night. I need time to figure out what exactly we are doing before I gauge whether Jack even needs to know. "The four of us were best friends. Losing Peter destroyed all of us. We all handled it…"

I don't even know how to put into words how we handled it, because in all honesty none of us handled anything.

"We didn't handle it well. But Jack was there. He had it the worst. *Obviously*. I don't want him to go back to that place. If Nate sticks around, I'll make sure to talk to Jack. But for now, who knows what Nate's intentions are."

This is the truth. I don't know Nate's intentions. I believe he wants to give us a shot, and that seems to be what he's saying, but until I find out what his plan is, why he's *really* back here, I need to keep my cards close to my chest.

Fortunately, Steph distracts everyone from the conversation by buying another round of shots. I shoot her a grateful smile, and she winks at me as she downs another. Shawn sidles up behind us and flashes Charlotte a grin. "Oh, look, it's my favorite sister."

Shawn's presence does the trick, and Charlotte beams. "Your only sister, but yes, I can understand why you think I'm your favorite." Charlotte looks at Shawn's arm which is wrapped around my shoulder, and she quirks her brow. "Oh, I'd heard a rumor, but I was hoping this was just that. Are you guys really together?"

I glance at Shawn who gives me a cheeky grin. Oh, he's going to tease his sister. I'm down for it.

"What can I say, we have some good-looking brothers." I smile at Charlotte, and she blanches.

"Ew, don't tell me you think my brother is good-looking. Are you guys sleeping together? Wait, don't answer that. I don't want to know." Charlotte puts her hand over her face and peeks out between her fingers. "Okay, I need to know—hit me with it."

Laughter shakes Shawn and I giggle as well. "Please, Charlotte, I've watched you do Jell-O shots off my brother's chest." I shoot her a look that dares her to protest.

Charlotte smiles wider. "That was vacation Charlotte. We don't talk about her."

We all laugh. After my brother proposed, Charlotte had way too much to drink. It was quite the way to meet the in-laws. I stifle another giggle, relaxing against Shawn. "No, Shawn and I aren't together. He's got his eyes on someone else." My eyes drift in Hailey's direction, and Shawn gazes longingly. Oh, this poor guy is a train wreck.

"I'm not going to lie, it was freaking me out a bit thinking my brother and Jack's sister were dating. Felt a little too Jerry Springer to me."

My insides knot up. She has no idea how ridiculous my life really is. Fake dating her brother while I was actually dating my ex-husband. I have no right to judge Shawn and Hailey; I'm the real train wreck.

As if he feels summoned by Charlotte's words, Nate's voice breaks up our conversation, and he talks into the mic.

"Alright everyone, I'd like to get someone special up here to sing with me. What do you guys think, should our resident bartender come up here and sing?"

My insides buzz, and I feel my body begin to retreat. What is he doing? I told him no singing. I told him I couldn't do it. Why can't the man just listen for once?

When the crowd starts to cheer, I know I'm screwed. I have two choices—get up there and sing my ass off or break down in a puddle and cry. Not interested in having a public meltdown which will definitely make its way through the rumor mill and back to my brother, I do the only thing I can. I throw back a shot of tequila, allowing the burn to coat my throat and loosen my nerves, and launch myself over the bar, sliding across to the other side before grabbing Belle's hand. "We're never talking about this again, but for now you ladies are my backup," I mutter under my breath and drag her with me.

Steph and Charlotte high five behind me and screech, "Yay, backup!"

Thank God all my girls are here. I am going to need them to get through this.

When I reach the mic, Nate looks at me with a devilish grin. "What do you want to sing tonight, Cookie?"

Summoning my inner calm chick, I close my eyes and mutter, "Dreams."

Nate doesn't hesitate. He knew that's what I'd pick. He knows everything about me. And the worst part is that as I start to sing, I know he was right to get me up here. I hadn't lifted a mic since Peter died. I don't even sing in the shower anymore. But as the words fall from my tongue, and my hips start to swing, I feel more like myself than I have in years. I feel alive. The look I shoot Nate is no longer one of anger or irritation over whatever game he's playing. Once again, I'm grateful because this man who I have loved since I was a child is bringing me back to life.

CHAPTER 19

Nate

Watching Amelia interact with her friends is almost as beautiful as watching her sing. *Almost.*

Growing up, Amelia was surrounded by guys. Me, Jack, Peter, and eventually Grant. Never women. Occasionally, she hung out with Belle but that's her cousin. She never had girlfriends.

But watching her tonight, I see that has changed. Between seeing her with Hailey the past few weeks and now singing with Belle, Steph, and a short pretty brunette who I recognize as Jack's fiancée from the pictures he sent of the engagement, it's clear Amelia has found some true friends. It explains why she seems so much stronger now than I remember, even after all I put her through. I have a feeling it's because she's got these women by her side.

She flicks her hair behind her shoulders, shoots me a wink, and stalks back to the bar with her friends, laughing as they harangue her over hiding her insane singing talent. I don't blame them. I felt the same way when I saw Amelia sing for the first time.

Magic. Perfection. Awe.

I'd missed hearing her voice almost as much as I missed her in my bed.

Almost.

I finish playing and the crowd starts to break up. Amelia's friends hug her goodbye, Belle teetering drunkenly as Charlotte grabs her keys and mouths that she'll drive her home. Once I'm positive they are all gone, I saunter over to the bar.

"Fun night," I say, sitting down on a barstool.

Amelia's eyes flick up to mine, and they dance as they travel down my body and up again. "Yeah, I forgot how good it felt to be in front of a crowd. I felt alive."

I smile, a warmth settling over me as she quiets my concerns that I'd pushed too far.

She felt alive.

I sigh out a breath. "You did awesome. And you had quite the backup."

Amelia's face lights up. "I did, didn't I?" She goes back to cleaning the bar top, wiping down the liquor bottles, and collecting the cups, as I watch her every move.

"Do you spend time with them often?"

I want to know everything about her life these last few years. I just don't know where to begin.

Amelia looks up. "You know, lately I have been. Ever since Charlotte and Jack got engaged—" She catches herself and gives me a guarded look.

I reach out to touch her hand. "It's okay, Ames. I know I missed a lot. *Keep talking*."

She winces and looks down at the rag in her hand. "Well, ever since they got engaged…well, we all went to the Azores for it, and I became close with her friend Steph, and now that Belle moved back it's like the four of us have this little group. It's fun. They are a bit crazy sometimes, as you saw tonight, but I think I needed that in my life. I needed *them* in my life."

I nod. "Friendship is important. I'm glad you have them." I smile genuinely at her.

Amelia hesitates again. "I'm sure Jack would love to hear from you."

Now it's my turn to wince. Jack and I never lost touch. He's the one person who understood what I was going through the last few years. He's the one that pulled me out of the darkness. But I really don't want to get into all of that right now. Not when things are so fragile. When we are just trying to find our way back to one another. There will be time for all of that. If we can make this work, there will be a lifetime.

"Right now, I'm focused on one Fitzpatrick," I tease.

She narrows her eyes. "So, you're finally conceding that I'm not a Pearson."

I shake my head. "No, but you'll always be a Fitzpatrick as well. Anyway, plenty of time to talk about all of that. When do you get off? I want to walk you home."

Amelia's eyes soften, and she pulls her lips into a pout. "That's not all you want to do, is it?"

The grin pulls at my lips. "Oh, Amelia *Pearson*, that is definitely not *all* I want to do. But I'm pretty sure detailing my plans on taking all your clothes off would not be workplace appropriate."

Behind her, Hailey laughs. "Right, because we are so prim and proper here at the bar."

Amelia circles her head back to Hailey. "Finish clean-up for me?"

Hailey smacks her ass with a towel, making Amelia yelp. "You got it, babe." Then she turns to me, finger pointed. "You take good care of her."

With my hand over my heart, I reply, "Always."

Amelia grabs her stuff and rounds the bar, slipping her hand into mine. Under her breath, Hailey mutters, "Weird," and to Shawn she says, "I'm never going to get used to this soft side of Amelia."

Amelia leans up and places a kiss against my cheek. "Get used to it," she tosses back.

With my guitar case slung over my shoulder and Amelia holding my hand, I feel lighter than I have in years. If I could freeze frame moments in my life, this would definitely be one of them. Her hair blows in the cool fall air, and the sky is black with thousands of stars, as if they are our own personal decoration, setting the mood for a night I've longed for. Her cocoa smell envelops me as I kiss the top of her head, and I swear if I had to bottle what happiness smells like, this would be it.

Amelia is the girl of my past, she's my childhood, my first love, my first everything, and I hope she will also be my future.

"Is it weird that I'm nervous?" she asks as we reach her door. She turns around and looks at me before entering. "Like, really nervous."

Amelia holds out her trembling hands to me, as if to prove her point.

Her grey eyes meet mine. They are almost silver in the dark hall, the light blue that appears when we are near the ocean nonexistent. "Babe, we don't have to do anything you don't want to. I just want to spend time with you."

She smiles slowly. Deliciously. "Oh, there isn't anything I *don't* want to do."

I laugh softly. "Oh, really? Well, I have to be honest before we go in there. I have things I need to share with you…before we…"

Amelia's finger moves over my lips. "Shhh, I have no interest in talking right now. Just give me tonight."

Slipping the key in the lock, she opens the door and drags me into her apartment. After pushing me against the wall, clumsily and imperfectly, she lifts her lips to mine and wraps her arms around my neck before kissing me until I can't think straight.

My guitar presses into my back, and I shift it off my arm without releasing Amelia, then lift under her hips, pulling her

Love & Tequila Make Her Crazy

legs around me as I hold her, never releasing her mouth.

"Take me to bed, Pearson," she whispers.

There is so much to talk about. So much I have to tell her. But when my wife asks me to take her to bed, all sensible thoughts leave my mind.

We stumble into her bedroom, and Amelia lifts her shirt above her head without my request. I stare at her dumbfounded for a moment. How have I lived for the last few years without her in my life? How did I go over one thousand days without seeing her beautiful naked body? It seems impossible that we wasted all that time without one another. And now, like no time has passed, she's slipping off her bra, exposing her perfect breasts—the only ones I've ever tasted, the only ones I've ever touched—and giving herself to me.

Nervously, she pinches her fingers together at her sides while I stare at her. "I…uh…I don't have any condoms." She looks down, not meeting my eyes. "I don't have sex—well, like ever—so…"

When she looks back up at me, her nerves plain as day, I practically fall over in relief. "Oh, thank God. Amelia, I can't tell you how that…wow."

She hasn't slept with anyone else. I blow out a loud breath. It's been the undercurrent of all my thoughts since I came back. In all honesty it kept me up many nights when we were apart. I had no right to expect her not to date. To not *be* with other people. She asked for a divorce. Hell, she believes we are divorced. But to know that, like me, she's been unable to take that next step with anyone else, it reaffirms my belief in the person I always knew she was and in the love that we share. She couldn't do that with someone else because she's still in love with me.

She chews on the side of her mouth. "So, do you…ugh… have a condom?"

I laugh. "No, I don't regularly walk around with condoms, sweetheart. We haven't used one since you were in high school." Her eyes dart to mine, as if she's trying to work something out in her mind. "Amelia, there's no one else," I assure her.

Her sigh is long, as if she's expelling her nerves. "So, now that we've cleared that up that you and I aren't…with anyone else… ugh," she stumbles through this terribly awkward conversation.

I reach out and pull her into my arms, kissing the top of her head as I stroke her back. "Yes, Amelia, you're it for me. You've *always* been it for me."

Her breathing shallows against my chest, and she holds me tighter. There are so many things I want to say to her. So many things I want to assure her of. I don't want her to ever think that my time away had anything to do with not loving her. Not wanting her. I tip her chin up so that she is looking in my eyes. "Amelia, I've been in love with you since we were kids. I loved you back then, and I never stopped. You are the love of my life."

Tears form in her eyes. They are a silver grey now, turning the same color as the moon in the sky. A tear escapes, and I kiss the saltiness from her face. A fissure of pleasure, a warmth, spreads through my body, sending sparks in all different directions.

"I *love* you, Nate. I love you so damn much, and I've missed you more than I can even explain."

Our lips meet, and our movements become frenzied. I ache to be inside her. Pulling my shirt off, she runs her fingers against my chest, stopping when she reaches the flower petal over my heart with her name in it, and then she stares down at the bandage below it.

It must be strange that I look so different. For years she knew every inch of my body, but now so much of it is covered in her designs. In words and images that got me through the last few years. Inflicting pain to make sure I could feel. Reminding myself that I was still alive, and more importantly, that I still belonged to her. Every single inch is a testament to our life, whether it be the one before my dad died, moments on the boat, adventures with her, Jack, and Peter, our life together in Nashville, our music, or just us.

"What's this?" she asks, pointing to the bandage.

"New ink," I whisper into the dark.

"When?"

"Yesterday."

"What is it?"

I breathe in and out, trying to decide if now is the time to tell her. "Roman numerals," I reply.

"Did it hurt?" she whispers, trailing her fingers against my skin.

I nod. "But I liked it."

Will that scare her—the fact that I survived on pain for the last few years? That I relished in it?

Her eyes dilate, and her lips turn up in a mysterious smile. "Really?" she whispers in what sounds like awe.

My eyes search hers. "Yes."

"Like this?" she asks, as she twists her finger over my nipple, making me grunt in pain.

"Uh-huh," I agree.

Her eyes flash in excitement. "Or like this?" She bites down hard on my lip, and I growl into her mouth. Sex with Amelia was always amazing, but I can already tell this is something else. There's an anger that she needs to work through, and now that she knows she can safely exorcise it without hurting me, I have a feeling we are about to have really angry sex.

I push her back against the bed, leaning over her. "Yes, Amelia, all of those things. Hurt me, pleasure me, it's all the same. As long as I'm with you, it feels good."

Amelia's nails scrape down my back, and she moans into my shoulder. "I need you, Nate. I need you inside me, now." There is an urgency in her voice. I want to take my time; I want to kiss every inch of her body, make her come on my tongue, make her scream my name. But like her, I need to be inside of her more than anything.

I lean up and slide my jeans and boxers off while Amelia watches in fascination. "Fuck, Nate, I forgot how perfect you are." Her eyes focus on my hard erection which strains for her. She licks her lips and then meets my eyes. My fingers fumble with the snap on her jeans, and I slide her pants off with her shimmying assistance, taking her panties with them. I reach down between her legs and feel how ready she is for me.

"Can I taste you first?" she says in almost awe as she continues to stare at my straining erection.

I laugh as I run my hand over my eyes. I forgot how dirty she can be. "Fuck, Amelia, you're the perfect one."

"Please," she says as her eyes remain trained on my cock. I feel it weeping. Crawling over her body, I give her exactly what she wants, slowly feeding it into her open mouth. She grabs my hips and pulls me closer until I hit her throat, and my head falls back in a groan.

"Oh, fuck, Amelia, you can't…" I can't even put a sentence together.

She doesn't listen, instead pushing me farther into her mouth and then pulling out before making a popping sound with her lips that makes me want to flip her over and spank her. But I can't. She owns me. This feeling. The way she's sucking the life out of me. And giving it back. I'm mesmerized by the pleasure on her face as she pleasures me, her gorgeous lips circling my cock, as her hair falls across her face.

I know if I don't gain control of the situation soon, this night is going to end before I even get inside her. I pull back and grab both her wrists in one of my hands, pushing them above her head. "Not so quick, my dirty girl."

She groans as a lazy smile crosses her face. I can see the hazy desire spilling from her eyes. Blowing me turned her on. I slip one finger inside to test out my theory, and she inhales sharply. "Oh, babe, if that's your reaction to my finger, we are going to have to take this slow."

She shakes her head and lifts her hips toward me. "Now, Nate, don't go slow. *Now.* I need the pain too. Make it hurt so good."

Angling myself between her hips, I press against her entrance, almost losing it before I'm even inside her. She hisses as I enter, fast, just as she asked, and I mutter a curse under my breath. "Fuck, Amelia, you feel...*fuck.*"

I've lost the ability to speak. She feels like heaven and hell, burning me with her screams and resuscitating me with her kisses.

Amelia moans as I speed up and slip a thumb over her clit, rubbing her exactly as I know she likes until she's shaking below me. I have to think of all sorts of things to hold myself together. I'm not finishing until she does. Favorite boating knot, favorite number, favorite baseball player, favorite...my mind goes blank when her hand moves behind my ass, and she uses her thumb to put pressure where there never has been.

What the fuck is she doing?

My body betrays me, and we both groan as we come together.

Panting, I fall down on her. I go to get up, to help clean her up, and she pushes me back down and flips over so she's sitting on top of me, lying on my chest. "I just want you to hold me. I want you to remain inside me and hold me. Please, Nate."

I kiss the top of her head. "Of course, babe, whatever you need."

What she doesn't know is her request is everything I need. Being with her, living inside of her, it's the only place I ever want to be. This is a dream. She's my dream come true. And this moment…this moment is damn near perfection.

Amelia

Nate and I fall asleep wrapped in each other's arms, our legs tangled together, our lips likely mid-kiss. When I wake, I momentarily forget where I am. I forget what year it is. Have I stepped back into the past? It feels like all those other mornings, the ones we shared in Nashville, in our condo that Nate bought us, happily engaged and more in love than I ever thought possible.

But it's not. We're not those people anymore. The ink winding its way around Nate's arms and cloaking his chest is a stark reminder that the man who walked out of my life years ago is not the same one lying next to me.

But his heart is the same, his lips are the same, and the way he loves me is the same. It's all-consuming, powerful, and pure magic. It's the same connection we've always shared. And it's the reason why I was always unable to shake him. Unable to move past what I knew we had.

How does one settle for something less than this? Once you've known how it feels to be in the arms of your soulmate—the person who knows every inch of your inner being, not just your body but your essence, the good and the bad, and they still want only you—it's impossible to go out on a date and make conversation about the weather, or sports, or whatever people talk about on dates when you've had something like this.

I kiss Nate's chest, and he stirs against me, pulling me closer to him. If that's even possible.

"Morning, Cookie," he says sleepily. I nudge his side, hating and also secretly loving his words. It's our own little term of endearment, one so engrained in the fabric of our relationship, in the years we've known each other, and yet it still pisses me off. Kind of like Nate. I smile in spite of myself.

"Morning, Pearson. Want to grab breakfast? I have a few hours before I have to head into work. I'm doing a double at the bar."

Nate lifts me up so our eyes meet. "No, you're not."

My brows furrow. "Yes, Nate. I have to work," I say matter-of-factly, like he needs me to say it clearer for him to understand.

Nate kisses my nose. "You're adorable when you're mad."

I poke him in the side. "I'm not mad." Although, my voice definitely hints at agitation. Okay, maybe I am a little mad.

Nate chuckles. "I cleared it with Hailey. We're going boating today. Your ex-boyfriend Shawn is working for you." He wiggles his eyebrows in a clear attempt to tease me.

I roll my eyes and try to find something to stay mad about.

No, Nate can't go and change my schedule on me and tell me what to do. But I actually do want to spend time with him today. And a boat day sounds perfect. And Shawn wasn't really my boyfriend so I can't be mad for him teasing me about that ridiculous attempt to make him jealous. I sigh.

Nate's laughter shakes me. "Trying to figure out how to play this, aren't you, Pearson? You want to come, but you don't like that I've arranged your day without checking." He looks down at me, knowing he's right, and smiles. "Forgive me and spend the day with me, please? I promise I'll make it worth your while."

Unable to hold back the grin, my face breaks open and Nate's eyes crinkle in surprise. "*Fine.*" I bury my head against his chest, not letting him see the huge smile that I can no longer suppress.

"Come on, Pearson, lift up that beautiful face and give me that smile. I earned it," he teases as he tilts my chin up to him and stares down at me, reveling in my happiness.

My smile cracks. "You've got to stop calling me that. It hurts too much." His last name isn't a joke to me. It was an honor to be his wife. All I ever wanted was to be Mrs. Nate Pearson. We are just getting back to a place where I can start wanting that again. Where it feels like there is a possibility that I one day actually will be. But the flippant use of it when I am so clearly not a Pearson only serves as a reminder of the worst time in our lives.

Nate wraps his arms around me. "I never want to hurt you. I want to share some things with you today. But I want to do it once we are both showered, after we've eaten—because a growly, hangry Amelia is not who I want to converse with—and once we are out on the water, because that's our happy place. Okay?"

My heart does a little flip, and my face splits into a smile again. This man knows me so well. I can feel in my bones that he's come back to me and that he's here to stay. I allow myself a moment where I really, truly believe that just maybe we have a real shot and one day I'll be Mrs. Pearson again.

CHAPTER 20

Amelia
Twenty-Seven Years Old

We've been engaged for four years, and life has never been so sweet. I'm not sure if Nate sensed that something had happened or if he just wanted me all to himself, because after we moved out, I rarely saw Grant.

College and working events at the Gaylord hotel kept me busy. Learning about different flowers and creating new designs for events, it was a dream come true. Every time I would create a new bouquet, I would text a picture to Nate, and he'd gush about it for days. He was my biggest cheerleader and my favorite person.

I hadn't touched a guitar though since that fated birthday. I just couldn't get the feel of Grant's hands off my skin. I avoided their sets, and Nate assumed it was just because I was too busy to be hanging at a bar all night, and I didn't have the heart to set him straight.

So when I find them both at our condo, sitting in the living room, practicing a new song, I falter at the front door. Grant's brown hair hangs over his face. He'd grown it out, trying to look like a real musician. To me, he just looked like a Hanson Brother, and if not for the fact that I feared him, I would laugh.

"Oh, hey, Cookie," Grant coos when he spots me. My skin prickles, and I notice Nate's eyes dart at Grant's use of his nickname.

Before I can respond, Nate jumps up and rushes to the door, kissing me softly on the lips. "Hey, babe, sorry to surprise you. We've been working on this song, and we couldn't get it right. I needed a change of scenery from the bar and suggested we come here. Hope you don't mind?"

His eyes rake my face, clearly studying the way my body is reacting to Grant in our home. It almost feels like he can see my thoughts. Like he can see what Grant did to me. But that's crazy. Of course, he can't. Part of me wishes he could though, then Grant would be out of our lives for good.

Grant's drunken drawl enters our conversation. "Oh, Amelia here knows how to write music. Maybe she can help us with this part?" His eyes dance over my body, and I involuntarily whimper. The last thing I want is him anywhere near me. I push myself closer to Nate.

"You write music?" Nate asks, looking at me in an almost accusing manner. Acting as if I've hidden something from him.

I did. I am.

Your best friend tried to rape me, and I never told you.

A sick feeling slithers through my body, reminding me that

I waited too long to speak up. Now it would seem as if I was just covering up something else. I can't respond. I'm powerless against Grant's commentary.

"Oh, she hasn't shared with you her many talents. I'm sure it's just because she wants to surprise you at the wedding, right, Cookie?"

My skin burns at his proximity. Swallowing my fear, I turn to Nate and smile weakly. "Right. It was a surprise," I barely manage to whisper.

Nate's face breaks out in a smile. He hands me his guitar. "Well, show me what you got, Ames."

I stare at the instrument like it might jump out and bite me. Thinking as quickly as I can, I mutter, "How about you play me what you're working on, and I can see if I have any ideas?"

Nate's eyes meet mine, and he pauses for a beat too long. Almost as if he knows. He knows that something happened with Grant. But does he think it was consensual? Does he think I'd ever do that to him? My insides twist.

Please, don't make me say it.

But then I'm almost just as crushed when he doesn't say anything, and instead, he smiles and takes the guitar back and places it on his knee, preparing to play for me. He doesn't know. He doesn't understand.

My heart breaks.

Nate begins playing his song, and I focus on the words, on the way his fingers caress the strings and the way his muscles flex in his arm as he makes the most beautiful music. I listen to the song a few times but offer nothing. "I'm sorry I'm no help," I mutter, walking to the bedroom and waiting for Grant to disappear before daring to come out again.

An hour later the bedroom door finally creaks open. I lie silently in bed, pretending to nap.

"Ames, can we talk?"

My heart pounds in my chest.

He knows.

I nod against the pillow, tears falling now. Nate sits down on the edge of the bed and rubs my back, but I keep my face angled in, hoping he doesn't see the puffy eyes and blotchy streaks.

"I think I know what this is about," he says quietly. "I know Grant drinks too much. And you don't come to the bar because you're busy. But I want you to know just because he is constantly going home with other women, I have no interest in that. I always come home to you."

I bite my lip, drawing blood. Nate thinks I'm upset because Grant is a player. If he only knew. But I still can't find the words to tell him what happened. What if he doesn't believe me? What if he thinks that something more happened? What if he leaves me?

I nod. "I just don't like how much he drinks and how he acts. He's not a good influence."

The words taste bad in my mouth. I'm not a liar. I've never been a liar. And right now I'm lying to the person I love the most. But really, what choice do I have? Would he ever believe me? I waited too long.

Nate crawls over me and curls his body next to mine, pulling me close. "Babe, you are my world. I wouldn't do anything to jeopardize this. I'm going to tell Grant I'm done playing with him."

My breathing hitches in my throat. He can't give up music. He can't give up his opportunity for me. It's too much. I can't ask him to do that. "No, Nate. You can't."

Nate kisses the back of my neck, calm and steady in every movement. "Yes, I can. Amelia, I don't want any of this if it's not with you. Besides, Grant's antics are becoming more of a hindrance. I can start playing by myself. Or maybe my super-hot fiancée, who has an amazing voice and can apparently write music will agree to join me for a few sets. Hm?" Nate's breath is soft against my back, and a warmth spreads through my body, tingling and spreading like little fireflies taking over a nighttime sky.

"Really?" I manage to whisper.

Nate's laugh rumbles against my back. "Is that even a question? Amelia, if I could do the thing I love most with the person I love most…I mean, what could be better?"

I manage to turn my body into his chest, folding my arms around him, and meet his eyes. The blue is almost black in the darkness, but they still shine with so much hope and love that it practically splits me open.

"I…I don't even know what to say," I stutter meaninglessly. How can I find the words to express what this means to me? Not only does he want me to join him on stage, but he is willing to break up his band just to make me comfortable. The sheer force of his love squeezes at my insides, breaks open my chest, and fills me with an undeniable bout of joy and something else that I can't quite describe. I've never felt so whole in my entire life. So complete. So *me*.

"Just say yes, love. And then make love to me."

I smile as I lean into his lips, kissing him softly and whispering yes again and again as he undresses me and makes me feel things I never knew existed.

In the middle of the night, I wake up tangled in Nate's arms, and the song he had been singing is buzzing in my head. I know what it needs. I shake him awake, watching as his eyes crinkle open and he takes in my shadow. A smile creeps across his face.

"Sweetheart," he says in a gravelly voice, "you don't have to shake me awake, just take what you want." He holds out his arms to me, inviting me for a second round.

Playfully, I grab him between the legs. "This is not what I want…at least not right now, Pearson. The song. I think I figured it out."

Like a typical musician, he jumps out of bed almost

instantaneously, nothing more important than his music. He stumbles to the living room naked and comes back holding his guitar in front of him.

The moon shines through the window, casting a glowing shadow across him as he walks back into our bedroom, and my heart slams into my chest. This is when Nate is most perfect. Just barely awake, eyes filled with lust and love, naked, and with his guitar. It's how he was always meant to be. At least for me. I never want to share this Nate with anyone else. Everyone else gets little pieces of him, just like they get little pieces of me, but we save the best, the most perfect parts of us, for each other. Isn't that what love is? In its most perfect form, isn't that how love is supposed to be?

Nate leans over me on the bed and kisses me softly. I don't concern myself with morning breath; it's one a.m., and he doesn't look at me like I'm mussed from our lovemaking. Like me, Nate sees the Amelia that I give only to him. He loves me just the same as I love him. "Show me what you got, Ames."

I sit up and cradle the guitar against my bare chest, the instrument cool against my breasts. Sitting with my legs folded, I lean over, and my blonde hair, which has grown past my shoulders, hangs over the guitar. I press my fingers to the strings, strumming the first chord of the tune he had played for me the night before. Nate's eyes take on a dreamlike quality, watching me as I bite my lip, trying to get it right. I begin to hum the harmony I just heard in my head as Nate's voice croons the words he wrote.

We spend the next few hours like this. Singing and playing, rewriting and making perfect a song that I know he had written for me. A song about growing up, about the love next door, the forever kind of love that hurts so good. As the morning sun trickles in, Nate takes on an almost godlike quality in my mind, and soon I'm unable to play any longer, wanting nothing but his hands on my body, his mouth on my lips, and his cock inside of me.

When we wake up, it's almost noon, and Nate's hips are still locked into mine. "Hey, babe," he whispers against my forehead, kissing me gently. "I forgot; I have a surprise for you."

Before Nate—who am I kidding, was there ever a "before Nate"—at least before Nate and I became official, I never thought I liked surprises. I was always worried that surprises were things I couldn't control, things I couldn't prepare for, and with all that life had thrown at Nate, I wanted to be able to control as many things as possible. But since the first time he surprised me, on his boat when he sang to me and told me he was in love with me, I've loved surprises from this man.

I pull my hands together in a tiny clap. "Oh, what kind of surprise?"

Nate takes my cheeks in his hands and kisses me softly before hopping over me and out of bed. "Be right back."

I lean back in the pillow and sigh, elated and filled with an emotion I can't quite put my finger on. Joy. Fulfillment. Wholeness. What is it? It's like the perfect state that buzzes through your body and warms you from within. Is there a word for that? I can't summarize it into one perfect syllable.

Nate walks back into our bedroom, still naked, *thank you*, with a giant photo album in his hands. Did he make me a collage? I mean, it's sweet but very un-Nate-like. He's creative with his music, but his art skills have never been something to write home about.

"What you got there, Pearson?" I eye it skeptically.

The grin that spreads across his face leaves me breathless. His eyes are almost shy, but the boyish excitement can't be hidden. "Take a look at it."

On the front, the words "Amelia's Flower Designs" are written in gold lettering. The cover is a beautiful soft teal. A squeal I can't contain rises from my throat. "What is this?"

My face breaks out in a smile as I open the book to discover page after page of the photographs of the bouquets I had created over the last few months. I turn each one slowly, looking back and forth between Nate and the book.

"This is incredible. What is this?" I'm still in shock, unable to comprehend that he did this for me.

"I've watched you over the last few years get better and better at these designs. You've been doing this all for other people, but the world needs to know it's you behind these creations. If you want, and it's totally up to you, I think you should start your own business. And hopefully this book will help you do that. And this too." Nate holds up a key which I glance at suspiciously.

I stammer, "Wh-what is that?"

Nate's eyes grow in excitement. "Put on some clothes, Cookie. More surprises." I stare at him deliriously, and he shakes me. "I'm not kidding. Come on."

Nate gets out of bed and throws on a pair of sweats. Then because he realizes that I'm having a hard time keeping up, he rummages through my drawer and grabs me a pair of shorts and a tank top. "Put these on, Ames."

In an almost dreamlike state, I dress and follow an excited Nate, who is still half naked, out of our condo and down the steps of our building. Sitting out front, like the most beautiful piece of artwork I've ever seen, is a light pink van with the words "Amelia's Flowers" written in light purple with different flowers in other pastel colors dotting the van. It's the most beautiful 1970s hunk of junk turned perfection I've ever seen. And yet I still can't seem to figure out what all of this is. "I… Nate, I don't understand." I turn to look at him, and his smile feeds my soul.

"Babe, it's your own business. You need to do this in your name. Start doing weddings, delivering your own custom bouquets, be your own florist. You followed me here without a second thought, and you've been there every step of the way helping me with my dream, now even helping me write music. I just wanted to do something to help you find yours. I'm not sure if I overstepped and if you aren't—"

Love & Tequila Make Her Crazy

Before Nate can finish his sentence, I launch myself at him, jumping into his arms and wrapping my legs around his waist. Nate laughs into my hair as he spins me around. "I take it you like it?"

I look up at him, beaming. "It's perfect. Thank you." I kiss him with as much love as I can muster, trying to convey to him just how much he means to me.

"I really think brides and grooms everywhere are going to love your designs."

"Oh, yeah?" I ask, reveling in this moment.

"Yeah. And I was wondering if this bride and groom could be the first?"

I look at him, confused. "Huh? Who?"

"Us, Amelia, I don't want to wait. Marry me? Now. Let's go to City Hall this week. I can't wait another month to be your husband, another year. It's impossible. We'll do something big when the guys get back, but just for you and me, do this? Please?" His eyes are soft and pleading. And in that moment I know that's the wedding I want. Just the two of us.

Eventually, I want to celebrate in front of our friends and family. I want to have the moment where my dad walks me down the aisle, and our moms clutch hands in excitement. But like our time on the boat, in our own secret alcove, protected from the world, I want this moment just for us. We deserve it. Twelve-year-old Nate deserves it, fifteen-year-old Amelia deserves it, and the two of us, always the two of us, throughout all the years, deserve it.

I nod against his chest. "Yes, Nate. Let's get married."

A few months later

"Put down the whiskey, Jack," I say, losing the battle of trying to grab the drink out of his hand. His eyes are red-rimmed, and his lips sag in a perpetual frown. Nate shoots me a look, shaking his head and warning me to leave Jack alone.

"It's all my fucking fault," Jack mutters for the sixtieth time today. The funeral was rough. Peter's mother sobbed loudly through the entire service. Every time she shrieked, Jack's shoulders tensed, but he stood next to her, his arm holding her own up, taking every squeeze she gave him like he'd been the one to kill Peter himself.

I snatch the drink from his hand, and his head hangs in regret. "It wasn't your fault."

Jack's eyes snap to mine. "I shoulda been there."

Nate is oddly silent. He's gone drink for drink with Jack. Neither of them were ever huge drinkers, so it's clearly gone straight to their heads.

I, on the other hand, have just been standing here watching

them, knowing someone has to be sober enough to drive us home. I'm also waiting for them to both snap. For my husband to finally break down. He hasn't so much as shed a tear since we got the news. He's just been my rock.

We both slipped off our wedding bands before flying home. Now is not the time to tell everyone our news. God, how did this happen? It was always the four of us. I look over at the chair beside Jack's. That's where Peter would normally sit. Peter and Jack on one side, Nate and me on the other. His absence feels even stronger at this table. It's taunting us and clearly driving Jack insane.

"You wouldn't have been able to do anything, Jack. Your base was attacked. He was security. Even if you hadn't been out flying, you wouldn't have been there to help," I try reasoning, but I can tell by Jack's stupor that it's not making a dent into that thick head of his.

"You wanna know the last thing I fucking said to him? The last conversation we had? I bet him he couldn't get this girl's number…she meant nothing to me. I wasn't even interested in her. *He was.* I knew he had been for a while. And I fucking taunted him and threw the number in his face as I walked away and left him to go flying. That's the last time I saw him. The last time he saw me…was me laughing in his face. I don't even remember the girl's name!"

Nate stiffens beside me, his eyes narrowed on Jack. *Say something,* I want to yell at him. *Tell your best friend it's not his fault. Help my brother.* But Nate says nothing, leaving me to deal with this unimaginable scenario. My brother's guilt and grief.

I reach my hand across the table. "Come on, let's get you to bed."

Jack looks at Nate, and I know he is waiting for Nate to say something. To say anything. To tell him it's not his fault. To tell him that Peter wouldn't want him to blame himself. But Nate just looks back at him evenly, almost acknowledging Jack's guilt. Agreeing with it. I feel my insides breaking. Our entire group is fracturing. We are already missing the jokester. The one who always kept us laughing. The balance is off. And now my husband and my brother are looking at each other like they don't even know how to speak to one another. And maybe they don't. How do we continue on as if Peter never existed? Or worse, like he did, and we've moved on. None of us know how to move forward, so silence is all that's left.

We drop Jack off at my parents' house, and my mother takes over and puts him to bed. I know that Peter's death has hit her hard. It's a reminder that her own son is putting his life in danger daily. And he'll be going back on deployment soon. I don't know how she'll manage that. I may need to come visit her more often. I'm sure Nate wouldn't mind making a few more trips home. His mother has been thrilled to have him back. Even if it's for this unimaginable reason. Even if we don't sleep in the house. She'd rather have him here than not at all. And we both know the boat is the only place he ever really feels comfortable in this town.

"You haven't said much," I say to Nate as we make our way onto the boat.

He simply raises his eyes to mine and then looks away. I want him to show emotion. To say *something*. Anything at all. He hasn't cried. He's been like a stone since the moment we found out. It so eerily reminds me of twelve-year-old Nate. The kid who held it all together while he was silently dying inside. He never cried in front of anyone back then. Only me. I want to be that person for him now. I want him to know it's safe to let go.

Even as I start, I know I'm wrong. He's been drinking. Why am I trying to get him to break down? What is wrong with me? I'm so desperate to console him though. For him to need me, like he did years ago. This quiet and steely Nate makes me nervous. Like he could snap at any moment. I can't take the quiet. "Nate, please…we lost our best friend. Say *something*."

Unbuttoning his shirt, he stares in my direction. He opens his mouth once and then snaps it shut.

"You just sat there while Jack blamed himself. He needs us to tell him it's not his fault. He needs *you*." I remain standing next to the door, imploring him to stop undressing and listen to my words. "Jesus, Nate, he's dying inside. You understand that better than anyone. I could have used a little help tonight."

Nate's eyes remain focused on undressing. He doesn't look at me again.

"He's falling apart, you're fucking mute, and I'm spiraling. I mean no one even knows we're married. Everything feels off without Peter. We were supposed to tell them over Thanksgiving. We were finally going to have our moment." At this point I'm more speaking to myself. Clearly my husband has tuned me out. "And now Jack has to go back to that fucking god-awful country. Back to a war that stole our best friend. A never-ending fucking war."

Tears stream down my cheeks as fear takes over. I can't have my brother go back there. He *can't* die.

"Doesn't that scare you, Nate? We've lost one of them already, and now Jack is going to go back there, and his head is a mess. I mean he blames himself. That can't be good. He can't be trusted to fly fucking jets at a million miles an hour when he's blaming himself!" My voice gets higher as the sobs take over. "Fucking say something, Nate. You need to talk to him. You need to convince him—"

Before I can finish the sentence, Nate screams back, "You want me to talk to him? You want me to tell him what I really think? How I really feel? You want to know? Because, Amelia, it's not what you want to hear. And I fucking promise you, it's not what he needs to hear. The fucking truth, Amelia, is that it should have been—"

I hold up my hand to stop him. "Shut up. *Shut up*! Don't you dare say that. Fuck you, Nate Pearson. Fuck you."

We stare at each other for a moment, both shocked by the

anger sprinting between us. I don't think he's ever spoken to me this way, and I most certainly have never spoken to him like that. His chest rises and falls as he pants for breath. "I think we should take a break," he says evenly. "Before we say something…"

I let out a bitter laugh. "That we can't take back? Yeah, pretty sure you just did."

I raise my eyes to his in defeat. I'm not sure how we come back from this. My brother means the world to me, and if Nate can't help get him out of this guilt, if he can't do for Jack what I did for him all those years ago, *because he blames Jack*, well, I don't know how to wrap my head around that. I've looked past Nate's selfishness throughout the years because I've always been happy to give him everything he needed and wanted. He wanted to move to Nashville, so I gave up my plans to stay here and moved without a second's thought. He wanted to chase his dreams of making it big with his music; I kept my mouth shut and didn't tell him what his bandmate did to me because I knew that would be the end of that dream.

I always put Nate first. For once, I wanted him to do that for me. To take care of me. Right now, that would have been helping me get through to my brother. The fact that he once again was putting *his* needs, *his* anger, above what others needed, brought all of those feelings to the forefront. All of the nights I'd sat and watched him and Grant play, my skin crawling, but I did it because I wanted to support him.

I shake my head and let out a sob. "You're such a

disappointment." His eyes flash with pain, and he looks down. "Goodbye, Nate."

I step off the boat, my legs landing with a thud on the dock, and stare back at the place that used to be my safe haven. I'm not sure how I'll ever go back.

CHAPTER 21

Nate

I leave Amelia's apartment with the promise to meet her at the docks in an hour. I have a few things I need to pick up, and I want to check in on my mom and Sam before I disappear for the day.

It's finally time. All the secrets, the living in the shadows, it ends today. Amelia needs to know the truth, and once she does and all the chips are laid on the table, only then will I know if she's truly ready to move forward.

Last night was reckless, but I don't regret a single moment. But knowing that it may be the last time she ever welcomes me into her bed, well, that is not a concern I take lightly.

"Morning, Mom," I holler as I walk into our colonial. She sits at the breakfast table sipping a coffee with Sam. "Morning, Sam, how are you feeling?"

A lump forms in my throat. I have so many things to make up for, and stealing their chance at being married is definitely on that list.

"Morning, Nate, you are just the man we wanted to see. Do you have a minute?" Sam asks, motioning to the chair across from him. I shrug my shoulders and look to my mom. Her face gives nothing away.

"What's up?"

My mom puts her coffee cup down and levels me with a stare before taking Sam's hand in her own. "Sam and I have been talking—we want to retire."

I nod. There's nothing like the notion of facing death to make you realize that certain things in life don't matter. My mom never needed to work. The life insurance money plus my dad's investments would have kept her at home many years ago. Not that Sam needed my mom's finances.

Of course, this doesn't bode well for the job I had taken with him. I'm guessing I'll have to find something else, but that's fine. The only thing that matters in life is family and how you spend your time. If you're lucky, it's with the ones you love. It took me too long to realize that. Too many nights were lost to alcohol and chasing dreams that meant nothing without the ones I loved beside me. I was getting my second chance, and I wasn't going to squander it, and they both deserved to do the same.

"That's great. Really, I'm happy for you."

My mom sighs. "That's not all."

"Okay. Just say it, Mom. Whatever you guys need, I'm here."

My mom smiles and Sam squeezes her hand. "We're going to move."

My stomach drops. She's selling the house.

Dad's house.

His name pops into my head, and my heart sinks with the knowledge that it's time for us to let go. "I can't do this today," I say hoarsely. "I'm meeting Amelia soon."

Sam nods. "We can talk about it another time."

My mom shakes her head. "No. Before you go and start something with that girl, you need to know everything. Nate, I want you to have the house. It's what your dad would want. If you want it, of course." She looks at me nervously, her eyes meeting mine, impressing upon me how much this means to her.

The problem is as much as this house contained all of the memories of Dad, of the three little birds as mom liked to call us, it's also been the place that she's lived with Sam for the last decade, and I can't untangle those two things.

"Let me think about it, okay? It's a big decision, and frankly, it's one that involves Amelia. *Hopefully.*" I smile ruefully. No matter where I live, I want it to be with Amelia. She deserves a say in this decision.

"Speaking of Amelia, you need to tell her about the store. I'm going to be stepping back from it all. Sam and I want to travel. And it was always hers."

Reaching my hand out, I squeeze my mom's small hand in mine. "I'm telling her today. *Everything.* I'm sure she'll want to talk to you too, but I'll make it clear this was all me. I promise."

My mom smiles. "I'm proud of you, baby. And for the

record, it was both of us. It was something I could do for you. I would have done anything to help you get back to who I know you are. I love you."

Feeling dangerously close to crying, I stand up and fold my mom into my arms, squeezing her tightly. "Love you too," I manage to choke out. Then I turn to Sam, and he offers me his hand to shake. I pull him out of his chair and into my arms, hugging him as well.

Life doesn't always give you what you want, and this relationship with this man was never something I would have hoped for, but I'm grateful for it. He's the silver lining. His support and love all these years, from the sidelines and without any expectation for anything in return, is not something to take for granted.

I squeeze him tight and say, "Thank you for loving my mom and me."

When he pulls away, I see tears shining in his eyes. "Nate, I..." he fumbles for words.

I shake my head. "Just saying something that is long overdue. I'm sorry for standing between the two of you for so long. I love you both." With a tight chest, I wait for him to accept my long overdue apology.

My mom wraps her arms around us both in a group hug that doesn't feel as unnatural as one would expect. "We love you too," she whispers against my head.

With a cracked voice, Sam echoes her, "Yes, we love you.

Now go get out of here. Don't leave Amelia waiting any longer than she already has."

I shake my head at the accuracy of those words. She waited. She was never with anyone else. It's honestly the best thing she could have told me. Perhaps I haven't screwed things up as badly as I imagined. I guess I'll know soon.

Amelia

Nate arrives at the docks with a picnic basket in one hand and a beach bag in the other. Just the sight of him, with his inked arms and black board shorts which hang off his hips, and those muscular legs and the warm smile which takes shape as he eyes me like I'm the only thing he wants, makes my stomach flip in nervous anticipation. Trying not to get ahead of myself, I remind myself for the thirtieth time in the last hour that Nate has something to tell me. He has secrets. We are finally going to talk about everything. This makes my stomach drop because I really don't want to talk about the past. Confronting what he did to me, that he gave up on us way before I did—*that he slept with someone else*—makes me choke on my own bile.

I know it's in the past. I know *why* he did what he did. I told him it was over. I left the boat and didn't meet him at the airport for our flight. *I* didn't return to Nashville. *I* said goodbye.

And yet, somehow, I expected him to wait around for me to change my mind. To keep his vows. For better or worse. It's what I did. Even if I didn't realize it at the time. My life has been on pause, waiting for him to walk back in and hit the play button.

I remove the horrible images of Nate in bed with someone else from my mind and look at the man standing in front of me. None of us are defined by one moment. One bad decision. Over two decades Nate showed me who he truly was, and an alcoholic cheater was never it.

This man, the one I've loved since I knew what the word meant, is a good person, a musician, someone who makes me laugh, sensitive, kind, loving, thoughtful. He's shown me countless times that is who he is. In this moment, I make a conscious choice to leave that one night, that aberration in character, in the past. To leave the last three years in the past.

Moving closer to him, I hold my hands out to grab the beach bag. "Here, let me take that."

"Thanks, Cookie, you look beautiful by the way." I smile in spite of his stupid nickname and look down at my bathing suit, the white one that he made such a big deal about the other day.

Meeting his eyes, I reply, "Well, you said you'd be dreaming of it. Figured I'd give you the real thing."

He drops the picnic basket and pulls me into his chest. "Come here, Ames." Nate lowers his lips to my mouth and kisses the hell out of me. My knees go weak as he lifts me up and wraps my legs around his waist, pulling me even closer and giving everyone on the docks quite the show. But I don't care. Being in Nate's arms makes everything feel right.

This moment, the salt in the air wrapping around us like a hug, the sound of seagulls gawking at the sight of us, the feel of his fingers pressing into my head and mussing my hair, is a moment I've dreamt of for years.

Pulling away to take a breath, I meet Nate's eyes. "If you don't put me down, we're going to have to go back to my apartment."

He laughs and leans his head against my forehead. "Okay, I promised you a boat day. Let's get to it."

Nate lifts me over the bow of the boat and then hands me the picnic basket and the beach bag before he starts untying the lines. Someone comes over and offers to help us off the dock, and I settle in next to the captain's chair, right where I belong.

This boat is much smaller than his dad's. It's got a small cuddy cabin below and a bench in the back, along with the captain's chair and the seat that I'm currently occupying. We snake our way slowly through Bristol Harbor, and I focus my attention on the sailboats that are moored here. While I prefer the speed of a smaller boat, there is something beautiful about a sailboat, and I appreciate that so many people enjoy them in our town because they make the harbor look idyllic.

"So, where are you taking me?" I ask, enjoying the eye candy that is Nate Pearson next to me. How is it possible that all of that is mine? I bite my lip remembering our late-night activities. Wouldn't mind a repeat.

"Not far. I want to get to the talking part so we can get to the more enjoyable things I have planned for today."

I smile, knowing precisely what he means, but I goad him anyway. "How do you know there will be more enjoyable things after we talk?"

Nate's eyes dart to mine, and I see nervousness reflected in his gaze. Shit. I really don't want to talk about all of this. "I know it's possible you won't want to be with me after we talk. I'm aware of that." His voice is soft, and his eyes remain trained on mine. "But we can't be us again without going backward and talking about why we are where we are."

I stand up from my seated position and loop my arm around his waist, leaning into him and reassuring him with a squeeze. "Nate, I was there for it all. I know *everything,* and I'm choosing to stand beside you still. There's nothing you can tell me that will make me walk away again. I broke us first by doing that. I'm not going to do that again, I promise."

Nate shakes his head. "I don't deserve you. You, Amelia Pearson, are the love of my life and too damn good for me."

My eyes dip at his words. "I asked you to stop calling me that. For now at least. It hurts because we aren't married, Nate. And losing you, signing those papers, *divorcing you,* was the hardest thing I've ever done."

Nate kisses the top of my head. "Hold that thought. I'm

going to anchor here and then I'll explain."

I let out a slow breath and move away, watching as he stops the boat and hops up on the bow to drop the anchor. Stealing a moment to gain some clarity, I look back to the harbor. The boats bob in the water, and our town looks smaller from this vantage point. But even all the way out here I can still see the bar where I first saw Nate again, I can make out the area where his Dad's boat is currently docked, and Colt State Park where we used to ride our bikes. This town is as much a part of our story as anything, and it seems quite fitting that we're having this conversation with our memories as a backdrop.

Nate sits down and pulls me close and I lift my eyes to his and wait. When he takes my hand in his, I shift to look at him as he speaks, "Here's the thing…*I* never signed the papers."

My mind dances trying to figure out what he means. My eyes narrow, and my tongue pokes against my cheek. "What papers?"

"The divorce papers." He pauses and lets out a sigh before continuing. "I never signed them."

My eyes dart back and forth, trying to read his expression. It's one of honesty. "We aren't divorced, Amelia. I never filed the paperwork." And then because he thinks, *rightfully so*, that I still don't get it, he adds, "We're still married, Ames. You're still my wife."

I don't know what he expects for a reaction, but a burst of laughter probably isn't it. He stares at me as I laugh, covering my mouth and growing silent as my eyes grow wide. "Wait, you're serious?"

Nate rolls his eyes. "Yes. I wasn't going to sign divorce papers when we hadn't even talked. You sent me a text and mailed documents. You refused to pick up the phone. We were together for over ten years, Amelia, friends for over twenty, and you ghosted me. My *wife* ghosted me."

I huff out a breath. Okay, I guess we are doing this. "Nate, I had very good reason to ask for a divorce."

Nate looks at me incredulously. "We were both grieving, Amelia. People get in fights. Say things they don't mean. You don't just up and walk away."

My chest tightens. "Nate, you said you wished Jack was the one who died. What was I supposed to do with that? Hell, you haven't spoken to your best friend since Peter died. It wasn't just me you hurt; it killed Jack too."

Nate's eyes dart to mine. "What are you talking about?"

I remember the moment like it was yesterday. I look at Nate now, trying to figure out why he's trying to spin this. I told him I forgave him. I told him I wanted to be with him. Why are we going backward?

"Nate, I really don't want to talk about this. We're fine. Reliving this is not healthy."

He shakes his head. "Amelia, why would you say I wished Jack was the one who died? I never even *thought* that let alone *said* it. Jack's the one who got me through everything. He's been my best friend my whole life and my brother since we got married. Next to you he's the closest person to me in the world. What are you talking about?"

My stomach bottoms out. "Wait, go back. Jack got you through what?"

"*You!* Your attempt at divorcing me. Peter's death. All of it."

I look away from him, shaking my head. This doesn't make sense. "Nate, you said you wished it was him."

I go back to that moment. I'm positive those were his words.

"No. I didn't."

"*Yes,* you did."

"Amelia, I promise I remember the words that came out of my mouth the moment before you walked off the boat and out of my life. Believe me, I've relived that conversation daily trying to figure out why the one person in the world who promised to love and cherish me for the rest of her life would leave me when things got hard." His voice is filled with anguish, and he lifts his hat off his head and runs his hand over the stubble. The dark barely-there buzz. The blue in his eyes becomes more dramatic without the hat on, and I'm lost staring at him.

Could I have been wrong? Could I have thrown away my marriage over a misunderstanding? No, it's not possible. *I remember what he said.*

"Believe me, I relived that conversation daily too. And that's what you said."

Nate's head drops into his hand. He looks back up at me between his fingers. "No, it wasn't, Amelia. I said 'it should have been'— and you jumped to conclusions. If you had stayed for a half a second longer you would have heard the 'me.'" His eyes are worn, and they sag at his admission.

"It should have been *me*, Amelia. They joined the Air Force because of *me*. Because of my dad. *I* should have signed up. I should have been over there with them. It *should* have been *me*." Nate's shoulders slump, and he leans down, tears filling his eyes.

No. This can't be right. That's not what he meant. That's not what he said. *And it's certainly not fucking true.* I can't imagine my life without Nate. Actually, I can because I lived it for the last few years, and it was hell. But he wasn't gone. He was still reachable. Out there. Capable of coming back. Not like Peter. And the thought of him being gone like that, of him being killed, of mourning him, breaks me.

"I did this?" I ask quietly. *"I* broke us?"

The sick realization that I am the reason why my husband slept with someone else gives me the final hit, and I can barely breathe. I'm catapulted back to that day. To the moment that my marriage ended. And now I see it with totally different glasses. Nate didn't give up on us. I did. *I* walked out of our life and refused to speak to him. When he was drowning, I looked the other way.

How is this possible? How did I do this? I cost us so much time. So much heartbreak.

The worst part is that I can't even tell him why I asked

for the divorce. He thinks it's because he got on that plane, but it's because of me. If I hadn't ignored my husband, turned on him, ghosted our entire marriage, he never would have slept with someone else. That's the reason I asked for the divorce, but I can't even blame him because it's all my fault. I threw Nate away like a piece of trash, and I can't judge how he chose to pick himself up again.

"I'm so sorry, Nate." Tears stream down both our faces, and he looks up at me. "I'm so sorry," I repeat again.

Nate shakes his head. "No, babe, don't cry." He pulls me onto his lap and strokes my hair. "It was a bad time for all of us. I shouldn't have gotten on that plane. I should have fought for you to talk to me. I should have come back sooner. I was drowning and afraid that if I tried to talk to you or Jack, I'd take you down with me. That's why I was silent. That's why I disappeared and drank the next few months away. I should have done a lot of things differently, and I'm so sorry I didn't. This is on both of us. But what I'm trying to tell you is that we get a re-do. I'm here and I still love you. Please, let's try. Work through this with me. Be my wife."

The feel of his hands running through my hair comforts me, but his words are what heal my broken heart. "I'm still your wife?"

I marvel at the insanity of this question. I'm still Amelia Pearson. *Mrs.* Amelia Pearson.

Nate smiles through his tears. "Yes, babe, you're still my wife. And as long as you are willing to keep it that way, I will be by your side. I'll never walk away again, Ames. So what do you say, will you stay married to me?"

I let out a gurgled laugh cry, the sobs taking over my body as all the emotions course through me. Sadness, delirium, happiness, hope, anger, but mostly love. Love for the man who never gave up.

"I'm so glad it wasn't you. I wish it wasn't Peter either, but I'm so glad you're here right now. And you have to know that Jack and Peter signed up for the military for more than just you, and they both knew the risks."

He meets my eyes. "Yes, as your brother has told me before, not everything is about me." He lets out a low laugh, and his eyes shift to the side, ruefully. When he turns back, he reaches behind his neck and slips the chain over his head. My hand goes over my mouth as he drops to both knees in front of me, and I see both my wedding band and engagement ring in his hand. "So, what do you say, Cookie, will you be my wife?"

The smile snakes my face, and I take his cheeks in my hands as I meet the eyes that have always been my past, my present, and most certainly my future. "Yes, Nate Pearson. There is honestly no one I'd rather be."

Nate unclasps the chain and slips both rings off before slipping them onto my finger, and both of us stare down at them in wonder. Then he pulls me against his chest. My *husband* holds me, cradling me, kissing the side of my head, turning my face to his, and kissing me like we never stopped. Like he needs my lips to breathe. And

Love & Tequila Make Her Crazy

I totally get the feeling. It's like I had been underwater for years, waiting for this man to come back and breathe life into me. When we pull apart, Nate looks at me with wonder in his eyes. "Well, I guess I'm glad I brought the champagne."

A giggle bubbles up through my tears. "You brought champagne?"

"And chocolate-covered strawberries," he says, wiggling his eyebrows at me. I snuggle in closer to him. "Let me go grab them, and I can finish telling you everything else."

"There's more?" I sigh. We've covered more than enough.

Nate smiles. "Don't worry, the rest of the stuff is good... well, mostly anyway. No more heavy conversations, I promise." He kisses the top of my head and retreats to the cuddy cabin, leaving me to revel in everything he's just shared.

I'm his wife. We're still married.

A few moments later Nate is back with the treats, two champagne flutes—plastic, of course—and the bottle of champagne. He hands me the glasses and places the strawberries on the bench next to me. Then, like an insane person, he shakes the bottle and pops the cork, sending the fizzing liquid spurting out the top, spraying both of us. "Oh my gosh, Nate!" I laugh as I wipe the champagne off my skin.

He grabs my hand. "Ah, why'd you do that? I was gonna lick it off you." He raises his eyes to me and winks. Dirty boy.

"In the glass, Pearson," I say, holding up my flute to him.

He fills them both and clinks his against mine. "Cheers to

you, *Mrs*. Pearson."

My face opens wide with a smile, the excitement running wild through me. "Cheers to you, hubby."

"Damn, we are going to be insufferable, wifey. I can't wait to tell everyone we know that you are mine."

I roll my eyes. "How about we just focus on us for a bit before we announce to the world we got married years ago, then *kind of, sort of* got divorced and now we're actually not divorced but married again?"

He shakes his head. "Nope. I've waited long enough to tell everyone you're my wife."

I stare him down. "No, you didn't. You basically told everyone you've seen since you got home that I'm your wife. I just thought you were being an ass, and in fact you were."

He laughs. "Well, yeah."

"But seriously, give us some time to figure out what we're doing before we jump with both feet."

I finally take a sip of champagne and let the fizz calm my nerves. It's not that I don't want to tell everyone about us, it's that I need to figure out how to explain to my family that I hid that we got married all those years ago. My mom and dad are going to be sad they missed out on the wedding and hurt that I didn't share what I was really going through these last few years. And I don't exactly blame them.

Nate sighs. "Okay, let me spill the rest of the info and then you can make a decision about what you want to do." Nate shifts the strawberries to the other side of me, offering me one before he starts talking. "Have some chocolate; it always keeps you happier."

I laugh. "Bribing me with chocolate?"

Nate shrugs. "Happy wife, happy life, right?"

Smart boy. I plop a chocolate-covered strawberry into my mouth and moan at the delicious taste. Damn, they're good. "Okay, lay it on me."

"It's about Pearson's—the flower shop."

My eyes crinkle in worry. "Is something wrong at the flower shop?"

Nate shakes his head. "No. Nothing's wrong. In fact, everything is as it should be."

"Yeah, your mom has done a great job with her shop. I'm kind of jealous I didn't think of it sooner to be honest. We have the perfect town for that business, with all the wedding venues and event locations. I mean, how did the town survive without a flower shop before this?"

Nate smiles. "It's not her shop."

"What?"

Nate takes a sip of his drink and meets my eyes. "It's yours, Amelia. I bought it for you. It's your shop."

"I don't understand."

Nate squeezes my hand. "Jack told me you were working at the bar, running yourself ragged, drinking a lot…" He drifts off and looks away. When he turns, I see the immense pain this has caused him. Yes, I drank a lot. It was either drink or work, and I didn't have enough work to stop the drinking. I would have done anything not to think about Nate with someone else. Nate's words cut through my thoughts. "I was drinking a lot too. Or I had been. I was a mess. Jack got me to see how that wasn't fixing anything, and he helped me come up with a plan to help you. I knew you wouldn't welcome me walking back into your life right away, and you weren't in the headspace to deal with me."

I bite the inside of my mouth. It's not that he's wrong, but the scheming he and Jack did—when I thought they weren't even on speaking terms—doesn't sit well with me. I've always been the little sister, the younger one that they all felt they needed to take care of. It's not a role I relish. I stay quiet, hearing Karen's words in my head. *Put down the boxing gloves*. Last time I jumped to conclusions, I lost everything.

Nate frowns. "I can tell this doesn't make you happy. And I'm sorry. Again. Honestly, Amelia, if I could go back to three years ago, I'd fix everything. Do it all differently. But I wouldn't re-do this because buying you that store, asking my mom to hire you, to befriend you and help you through what was obviously a hard time, I would do that ten times again. I couldn't be there for you, but I could help in my own way. I knew you were happiest selling flowers from that damn van."

I smile ruefully at the memory of my van. Thankfully, I haven't gotten around to having it repainted. "So, you bought me a flower shop."

I sit dumbfounded at this news. Karen opened the flower shop last year. And it took months before that to set it up.

"When?"

"When you sent the divorce papers."

My eyes grow. That was almost two years ago. He's been working behind the scenes on this for that long. Why didn't he just come back to me? My mind whirls with thoughts that I can't properly express.

"Wait, you own the building?"

Nate nods.

"So, you're my landlord?"

"Yes."

I laugh uncomfortably. "Nate, none of this makes any sense."

"Amelia, I couldn't just stop being your husband. But as much as you weren't doing well, I was doing worse. I couldn't come back. I had to get better. And then I got nervous. What if I came back and you didn't love me anymore? Or you couldn't forgive what I'd done? So I just stayed away, delaying having this conversation, because as long as I delayed it I could stay married to you. You couldn't force a divorce that you thought had already occurred. I don't know." He shrugs uncomfortably. "I still had hope."

As insane as this explanation is, it also makes sense. The truth is that the last three years, and how we got here, doesn't matter. What matters is that we found our way back to one another. Being angry with Nate won't get me what I want.

Forgiving him, accepting his mistakes, his generous gift of my dream, and allowing him back into my heart is the only way I'll be happy.

I let out a shaky breath, my decision made. "You still have hope, Nate. I'm not crazy about the way you went about all of this, and I'm definitely going to have a talk with my brother, but I guess what I need to say is thank you."

Nate lets out a nervous laugh. "Thank you?"

I smile and lean against him. "Yes. You bought me a store. You reminded me of who I needed to be—*from over a thousand miles away*. When I thought you didn't care at all, you were in the background *actively caring* and doing something about it. Do I wish you'd come back sooner? Of course. I hated being apart. But I love *you*, Nate. And you loved me so much that you did all of this not knowing if I'd ever take you back. It's just"—I falter for words—"just thank you, okay?"

Nate wraps his arms around me. "Okay." He laughs softly against my ear, sending a shiver down to my belly.

"Are we done with the serious revelations now?" I whine.

Nate bites his lip. "Just a few more things."

I sigh. "Oh God. Okay."

"Sam is sick. He's doing better, but he and Mom want to retire. Enjoy life while they can, ya know?"

Oh, poor Karen. And Sam. My heart breaks for them both. "That's horrible. What is it?"

"Cancer," Nate replies solemnly. "But they caught it early,

and have been very private about it. I think it just made them both realize life is too short."

I'm sure Karen realized that long ago, but I don't point that out to him. We've had enough somber conversations today, so the last thing I need to do is bring up his father. I wrap Nate in my arms and look up at him. "Life *is* too short. Move in with me?"

Nate kisses the top of my head. "Duh, I own the place."

The laugh sneaks out of my mouth unexpectedly. "Right. Can we go home now, Nate?" All I want is to go back to *our* apartment, put his clothes in our drawers, make dinner in our kitchen, and make love in our bed before falling asleep in each other's arms.

"Yes, babe, let's go home."

CHAPTER 22

Amelia

My first night back at Thames since I found out that I'm still married, I walk around with a giant smile on my face, freaking everyone out. Honestly, it's kind of fun. "Seriously, you need to tell me what's going on," Hailey says for the fifth time since I've gotten here.

I shrug my shoulders. "Just happy is all."

Hailey laughs. "Yeah, but you're never happy. Not like this." She circles my face with her finger. "You're all smiley. I don't know what to do with it."

I almost burst at the seams, so ready to tell someone, *anyone*, that Nate and I are back together. But I was the one who begged him to keep it quiet, so although Hailey knows it involves Nate, I can't tell her that we're married. Not yet anyway. We need to tell our families first, and I'm so not ready for that inquisition. Besides, Belle just had her heart crushed by her coworker and I don't want to be all smiley while she's miserable.

"Get out of here. Isn't it your day off?"

Hailey shakes her head. "Yes, but I've been summoned by my grandmother. Not exactly something I'm looking forward to!" She walks out of the bar, leaving me to hum to the music in peace.

"Hey, Amelia, you look awfully chipper," Caris says, walking up to the bar and almost ruining my mood. I say almost because no one can ruin my mood, not even the woman who I believe was trying to sleep with my husband.

Because I'm a jealous witch, my grin grows. "Yes, Nate and I are in a really good place. Just happy is all."

So much for keeping my mouth shut.

Caris surprises me when her face registers genuine joy. "Oh my God! That's wonderful. I know how much he wanted to work things out. Congratulations." Then she comes around the bar and throws her arms around me, surprising me even more. Perhaps I had her pegged for someone she wasn't.

Sheepishly, I tone down my smile. "Thank you. So how are things?"

I'm not really sure what to do now that I'm not trying to rub her face in my happiness. I don't know Caris. Not well at least.

"It's okay. Busy with opening the winery. I'm not sure if you heard, but I've been contacted by a matchmaker. She's going to be handling some events at the winery. Ever heard of her? Grace Kensington?"

I shake my head.

"Oh, well, she's a big deal. She works with billionaires to

find them wives."

I raise my eyes. "That's certainly something. Maybe you should sign up with her," I tease. I recently learned that Caris's fiancé had cheated on her. He almost cost her the law firm she owned. But that's a whole other story.

Caris shakes her head. "No. I'm done with rich men." She rolls her eyes. "But I'm hoping her matches lead to weddings which occur at the winery. Speaking of, we could really use a florist for all of our events. Would you be interested?"

My eyes practically pop out of my head. "Are you serious?"

Caris smiles and lets out a soft laugh. "Yes. Nate showed me your work. He's always trying to talk you up. It's exceptional. Honestly, we'd be lucky to be able to refer brides to you."

My cheeks grow warm. Between the Blithewold, Linden Place, and now the winery, Pearson's Flowers is going to have a monopoly on the flower game in this town. As I go to respond, Shawn walks into the bar, whistling.

"Speaking of happy bartenders, what the heck is going on in this place?" Caris says, motioning to Shawn. The smile reaches his eyes. What *is* going on with him?

"Ladies, I finally made my move!" Shawn steps behind the bar and picks me up, spinning me in a circle.

Laughing, I smack him to put me down. "What move?"

Caris leans across the bar with her hand under her chin and a devious smile on her face. "A move on my sister?"

Shawn doesn't even try to hide his excitement. "I saw her

down at the docks about a half hour ago. She looked so beautiful, took my damn breath away, and I thought to myself, what am I waiting for? I walked right up to her, turned her around, and told her I'd been dying to do this for weeks. Then I dipped her and kissed her. And she kissed me back!"

Caris and I both look at one another, trying to make sense of what he's saying. "This was a half hour ago, Shawn?" I ask, staring at the clock.

"Yup. I kissed her and told her to meet me for dinner tomorrow night. Six p.m. at Roberto's. If she shows, I'll know it was more than just the most earth-shattering kiss I've ever experienced."

I shoot Caris a look and then turn back to Shawn. "Right. Wow. Well, that's great, Shawn. The keg is empty. Can you grab one from downstairs?"

Shawn tips his head as if saying, *at your service*, and he leaves us to continue gawking at him. "Um, Caris, Hailey has been with me all afternoon."

Caris looks white. "So, he couldn't have kissed her at the docks?" she asks nervously.

Why is she nervous?

"No. It's not possible. She was standing right there a half hour ago. She was in your exact position until about three minutes before you walked in. This doesn't make sense."

Caris looks like she's seen a ghost.

"What aren't you telling me?"

"I've got to go." Caris barely looks back to me as she

walks away.

Muttering to no one in particular, I say, "If Shawn didn't kiss Hailey, then who did he kiss?"

The Blithewold hosts music on the lawn events where musicians play in the gardens overlooking the bay at sunset. When the manager found out Nate was back in town and still singing, he was offered a gig. Upon learning that Nate would be singing, Hailey volunteered us to handle the cocktails, and fortunately there is no nineteenth-century garb to wear. My only job is to mix margaritas and pour sangria while making small talk with people I've known almost all my life.

I'm tempted to ask Hailey about the alleged kiss with Shawn when I hear a girl mention Nate by name. "Wow, I can't believe Nate Pearson is back," she says to her friend.

Hailey gives me a look that says she doesn't like the girl talking. I feel bad immediately. If Hailey doesn't like you, she doesn't keep it to herself.

The friend responds, "Right! He's so hot. I wonder if he's single."

Hailey eyes me and I shake my head. We are *not* telling people.

The other one replies, "Who cares if he's single! It's not like

Love & Tequila Make Her Crazy

I want to date him, but what I would do to that body!"

Uh-oh. The chihuahua next to me—a.k.a. Hailey—is going to lose her shit. Under my breath, I mutter, "Seriously, I'm not concerned. *Don't.*"

I serve them drinks and smile politely, trying to figure out why they look so familiar. At the last minute, the first girl exclaims, "Oh my God! Amelia! I didn't even recognize you. How are you?"

I raise my eyes in confusion because I still don't recognize her. "Um, hi. I'm good."

"It's Heather. Heather Bonnet. I went to school with your brother. How is he, by the way?"

My mind dances with the ridiculous nature of this conversation. The girl who kissed Nate and made him realize that he wanted to date me, fifteen years ago, is now standing before me after just saying how she doesn't care whether my husband is single because she wants to have sex with him. God, the audacity. I roll my eyes. "Jack's fine."

The girl next to her smiles sweetly, as if they weren't both just talking about my husband like he's a piece of meat. "Is he back in town? Still single?"

I don't hold back. A laugh escapes my throat. "Why would that matter to you? You're only interested in sleeping with hot guys from what I understand."

Fortunately, they have the decency to look embarrassed. "Oh, you know what we meant," the second girl says sheepishly.

"I'm sure a guy like Nate never settled down. Musicians have reputations, you know?"

Do they not remember I dated Nate for years? Sure, maybe they didn't know we stayed together, but they cannot be this clueless.

Nate's voice on the mic ends the little reunion that I was not enjoying. "Evening, everyone. Tonight you're in for a little treat. Ames, you mind coming up here and helping me out?"

His blue eyes meet mine, and I know he's doing this because he saw Heather talking to me. If I didn't love him before—which I totally did—then I'd fall for him all over again right now.

I smile at the girls, hand Hailey the drink I'm mixing, and walk toward my husband.

"Now this girl and I have been writing music together for a long time. I'd like to play one of our originals. What do you say, babe?"

So much for keeping this under wraps. How long will it take for the rumor mill to hit my mom and dad? In this moment, I don't particularly care. I take the mic from Nate's hand and smile. Our eyes don't leave one another as we sing the first song we ever wrote together. It's like coming home. Singing with him, I feel weightless.

Hours later we stumble into our apartment building, unable to keep our hands off each other. Nate spent the entire performance telling me with his eyes precisely what he wanted to do with my body. If there was any question as to who Nate was going home with tonight, he answered Heather's inquiries loud and clear.

I bite his lip now, my hands fumbling with his pants, anxious and desperate to feel his hardness against me. Nate grabs my wrists in one hand and puts them above my head and pushes me against the door of our apartment. "I want you right here."

A shiver runs down my spine, and I arch my pelvis into him, moaning as I get the little bit of pressure between my legs. It's completely ridiculous. There's a bed or a couch or a million other surfaces on the other side of this door and yet the dangerous nature of getting caught, of allowing him to take me against our apartment door because our need for one another is so great that we can't wait another moment, is so hot I might explode.

Nate kisses down my neck, while his other hand unbuttons my pants and slips them off me. His fingers move expertly between my legs, and he smiles when he finds I'm more than ready for him. "So fucking perfect, Amelia."

He slides one of his fingers inside me and then pulls it out quickly, leaving me gasping as he licks his finger with a dirty smile. "So fucking delicious."

The moan that leaves my throat is like a sigh. "Please, Nate," I beg.

He unzips his pants, and within seconds he's plunging into me while still holding my hands above my head. Kissing me as he thrusts repeatedly, giving me everything I crave. My legs shake from the intensity, and I'm left breathless.

"Remember how you stood in front of your window?" he

pants as he thrusts deeper.

I whimper a yes, my eyes closing as I lose myself in him.

"I wanted to bend you over in front of that window and spank you. Show everyone you were mine."

Nate picks my legs up and wraps them around his waist, finally releasing my wrists and taking my ass into his hands as he continues to thrust. With my back against the door, I can do nothing but take his continuous hammering and love every minute.

I laugh at the memory. "Yeah, that wouldn't have gone over well. But imagining it now, it's incredibly hot."

Nate opens the door and pushes us into our apartment, carrying me to the window. "Bend over," he instructs, lowering my feet to the ground, and pulling out before positioning me on the couch.

It's after midnight, and the bar is closed. There's no real danger that anyone would see us, but the moon glistening over the bay offers a light into our apartment, and it *feels* dangerous.

I listen to his orders and shriek when his palm lands on my ass with a loud smack. He thrusts into me from behind without warning, building both our orgasms to an almost unimaginable height. "You stood right here naked…in front of another man, Amelia," he says before smacking me again, sending a warmth zinging through my body. "No one gets to see you naked, Ames, no one."

When I don't respond he tugs on my hair, just hard enough so that I have to look at him. "Tell me, Amelia. Tell me I'm the only one who gets you like this."

There's a fire in his eyes that I've never seen before, and it makes my insides clench with desire. To feel him losing control, watching his calm demeanor disappear because he's crazy with jealousy, is intoxicating. "You're the only one, Nate," I promise.

With each thrust he punishes me and growls obscenities in my ear. "Fuck, babe, you're so fucking tight. I love that I'm the only one that's ever had you this way…and the only one who ever will." He smacks my ass again, and I clench around him. What the hell is he doing to me? Every spank makes me wetter. Hotter. More turned on. His fingers dig into my flesh, and I love the feel of being controlled by him, of being possessed by him.

Against my neck, Nate's hot breath teases my skin as he growls, "I love your sounds, Amelia. I love the way you're squeezing my cock, how fucking dirty you are for me…"

As I start to scream and clench around him, Nate's own orgasm hits, and he practically falls onto me. His warm breath continues to heat my skin as he pants against my back. "Shit…" he mutters, as if he's finally come back to earth. I'm with him. Shit is right.

Nate squeezes my hips, presses his lips against my shoulder, and then pulls out. I feel the loss of him immediately. He walks to the kitchen to grab a towel, and I laugh realizing that he's still wearing pants even though mine were left somewhere in the hall. He comes back to me with warm water on a towel and cleans me off.

"Are you okay?" he asks as he gently towels me off.

I meet his gaze and breathe out. "Yes, I am more than okay."

"Was I too rough?"

I shake my head. "I liked it."

His eyes register pure relief. I think we are both surprised by how rough that was and yet I'm still turned on. We may have been together for years, but it was never like that before. And I'm looking forward to what else we can try. Nate gently rubs my cheek. "I never want to hurt you. I only want to make you feel good."

I push myself to his lips, kissing him and biting down on his lip. "I said I liked it, Nate...like, a lot."

His crooked smile spreads across his face, and he kisses me again. Then he disappears to collect my clothes from the hall.

After brushing my teeth and slipping on a tank top, I hop in bed and wait for Nate to return. Nate brushes his teeth and gets in bed with me, only wearing boxers. He pulls me into his chest immediately. "I loved having you sing with me tonight, Ames," he says as he kisses my forehead.

"Me too."

"It felt like old times. Like the nights we spent in Nashville. It was..."

I finish his sentence, "magic."

Nate smiles down at me. "Exactly. Play with me again? Let's do this, Ames. All of it. It was amazing having you next to me tonight."

Love & Tequila Make Her Crazy

It *was* amazing singing with him. It honestly felt empowering and just...*right.* But that's not who I am anymore. "Nate, I'm a florist. I'm...that was fun. And it will be fun to randomly join you, but I mean, that's your thing. The broody hot musician. People don't want to see your wife next to you singing. They want the fantasy."

"What are you talking about? The crowd ate it up tonight."

I sigh. "Yeah, because it was a family night. At a bar, in a club, in a stadium—where you really belong—that's when people just want you. I'm the backup singer, the side voice; you're the musician. You are who they come to see. I'm just there for show."

"Are you kidding me right now? Amelia, you're talented. And you're gorgeous. Half the time in Nashville I was sure people were there to see you more than me."

I roll my eyes even though I know he's not entirely wrong. When it was just us two on stage, there were just as many people screaming for me as there were for him. We didn't pay attention to anyone though. It was just us, enjoying the music, enjoying time together, and making decent money. It was us running my floral business together during the day and then singing at night. Could we really have that here? I bite my lip as I hesitate. "I don't know."

Nate lowers his head so we are nose to nose. "Just think about it, okay, Cookie?"

I laugh and push against him. "Okay, Pearson, I'll think

about it."

"I love you."

I smile. "I love you too. Now go to sleep. We have an early morning tomorrow at the shop."

Nate

My stint working in an office ended before it began. I apologized to Sam, and he laughed when I said it just wasn't for me. Amelia needed help in the store since my mom was retiring, and between that and music a few nights a week, I'd be busy enough. After word got out how amazing Amelia's arrangements were at the Linden Place event, we were getting calls almost daily for more events. I'd never seen her so excited. It was like everything was falling into place.

Across the room she talks to a customer, slipping out the book I made for her with all of her previous arrangements and showing off potential options to a bride and her mother. Smiling, I lift the phone which is buzzing in my pocket to my ear, saying hello without taking my eyes off my wife.

"Hey, man, how's it going?" Grant's voice sends a jolt to my system.

Love & Tequila Make Her Crazy

Fuck.

I lift my eyes to Amelia and motion that I'm going to take the call outside. She nods and returns her attention to the customers.

Outside, I pace down to the docks, wanting to get as far away as I can from my idyllic life while I have this phone call. "Hi, Grant, what's up?"

He laughs. "What's up? *Seriously*! You've been avoiding my phone calls for weeks, and the label is breathing down my neck asking when you are going to be back to record. Did Amelia sign the papers yet?"

My shoulders tense as I think about the damn contract. I'd completely forgotten about it. I hadn't been back to the boat since I moved in with Amelia, and we'd been busy with the shop and christening every inch of our home and newfound marriage.

"No. And I'm not having her sign anything. I'm out, Grant. I'm not coming back."

A sense of relief washes over me now that I've finally said it. Of course, turning down a record deal sounds insane, but none of it is what I want anymore. This life with Amelia, working together, living together, waking up together—it is all I want.

Our life is here, and it's enough for me.

Grant laughs. "Good one."

"I'm serious, Grant. I'm not coming back. Find another guitarist."

"Fuck you, Nate. It's your songs they want. Your voice. You fucking know the deal is about you. Believe me, if I could replace you I would, but they want *you*. And you're not going to screw me out of this." His words cut through me. It's the person he always was—a complete asshole—and I have no idea why I put up with him for so long.

"Do whatever you want. I'm not coming back. So…figure it out."

"Did you tell Amelia everything? Share with her where you were all that time? Poor little Amelia would never forgive herself if she knew what she did to you."

Hatred burns at the surface. For myself and for the man I thought was my friend for so long. His threat is clear and he's not wrong. Amelia would never forgive herself, and I have no intention of sharing those truths with her. We've been through enough. It's in the past, and that's where it's staying.

"Grant, threatening me is not going to get you what you want."

He laughs on the other end of the phone. "Yeah, it will. Because you didn't tell her. You don't want her to know. Figure out a way to make this work, or I'll tell Amelia everything." He hangs up the phone before I can respond.

Fuck.

I throw the phone into the grass. What the hell am I going to do? If I tell Amelia, it will just put more stress on her. She'll spiral, and shit will go downhill real quick. If I don't tell her, then I'll have to go back to Nashville. None of these options are viable. But reasoning with Grant is useless. The guy is the devil, and unfortunately he holds the keys to my happiness. With one fell swoop he could destroy everything.

I spot Caris walking toward me and wish I could sink into the ground. I don't want anyone to see me like this.

Spiraling. Out of control. Desperate.

But it's hard to miss a grown man having a breakdown, so of course she heads in my direction. "Hey, Nate, everything okay?"

I dust fake dirt off my knees and reach for my phone before standing up. "Yup, just dropped my phone. What's up?"

Caris stares at me for an extra beat then seems to decide not to push. "Just wondering when you're coming by the winery. We have plans to make, remember?"

I close my eyes and nod. Yes. Another part of the plan I put in motion. I just need to keep moving forward. Keep doing the right thing and hope that everything works out.

Readjust karma. Make things right.

"Absolutely. When works for you?"

I can't wait too long. My mom will be leaving to travel as soon as Sam is cleared at his final appointment. But I don't think she'll go anywhere until after the holidays, so it's safe to assume if I plan this to happen before Christmas we're safe. "I'm thinking December. Do you think that's possible?"

Caris bites her lip. "Belle is just getting settled, but I think we can make it work. Come by tomorrow afternoon. I'll make sure Belle has all of your options laid out, and we can sit down and make a plan. That work?"

I forgot Belle had started working at the winery with Caris.

Poor girl lost everything after her boyfriend discovered she'd been lying to him. At least I'll have a friendly face to work with for my mom's wedding. Feeling better already, I smile. "Yes. That works perfect."

As Caris walks off, I know what I need to do when it comes to Grant. I pick up my phone, searching for the correct information, and make my next move in making things right.

CHAPTER 23

Amelia

For the past month we've been able to keep our relationship under wraps. Despite some rumors swirling after the Blithewold event, I was able to chalk it up to another one of Nate's stunts. We've been sneaking around, and I've been intentionally acting mean to Nate in front of people and doing just about anything so that we can make sure we are good before we let everyone in on our relationship status.

I'd be lying if I said I didn't enjoy our bubble. It felt like years ago when we'd sneak around on his boat. But with the holidays upon us, I have no intention of spending them without my husband. Which means it's time to let everyone in on our not so little secret.

Nate sits in the living room strumming the guitar while I prepare the sweet potato soufflé we're bringing to Charlotte and Jack's house for Thanksgiving. We've decided to rip off the proverbial Band-Aid with everyone at dinner.

The Pearsons always joined our family for Thanksgiving. Our families were always intertwined, but no one expects us to come together.

I am positively giddy and also a bit nervous to see everyone's reactions. Especially Charlotte's. We've grown closer over the last few months since she got engaged to my brother, and I know that she loves nothing more than love.

Getting to have a sister, something I always wanted, and getting to share with her that I wasn't this cold, closed-off girl that she'd come to expect me to be, thrills me. We will be raising families together, hosting holidays together, and growing old together, just like we will be with our husbands. I am almost as excited to grow old with my brother and his wife by my side as I am to do it with my husband.

Almost.

It's exactly as I always envisioned my life. It almost feels like we are honoring Peter. Not moving on without him, but living for all of us.

A song Nate's working on drags me from my thoughts. "Hey, play that again, it's beautiful."

Nate's eyes turn to mine warmly. "I'm just fiddling with it. You like?"

The melody is stuck in my head now. I hum to myself as I walk over and sit on the edge of the couch, waiting for him to play it again.

He strums and stops. "I keep getting stuck right here."

I lean my arm out to him. "Can I try?"

Nate smiles and hands me the guitar, waiting for me to adjust my hands properly. When I get myself settled, I try to recreate the melody he was playing, adding in a few different notes. I close my eyes, getting lost in the feel of the strings beneath my fingers, pressing down and enjoying the pain they always inflict on my soft flesh.

Nate's voice takes over as I play, and I harmonize with him, creating something I can only describe as a smooth glass of whiskey on a rainy day. When I strum the last note, our eyes meet, and Nate shakes his head. "I don't think I've ever loved something as much as singing with you. Writing music with you. That was…"

"Incredible," I finish his sentence.

He smiles. "Yes. Can I ask you something?"

Leaning down from the couch, with his guitar in between us, I kiss Nate softly on the mouth. "Anything."

"Will you come to Boston with me?"

I laugh, unsure of where this request is coming from. I shrug. "Sure?"

Nate's forehead creases. "I have an opportunity to record something. I'd like you to come. I want you there to make sure it sounds right. Would you do that for me?"

I hand Nate back his guitar. "Of course, I'll come with you. What's this opportunity?"

Nate looks away as he puts the guitar down and opens up his case to put it away. Inside the case, I spot papers with mine and Nate's names at the top. What's he got in there? Before I can make out the words on what appears to be some type of contract, he pulls it shut and drags me onto his lap. "Oh, just something I'm working on. No big deal."

With my head against his chest, I can't see his face, but his voice sounds uneasy. Not strained, but like he's not exactly telling the truth. I quiet my concern over it, though, because the smell of sugar and vanilla is wafting around us, we just wrote a song together, and we are about to tell our families about our marriage. I don't want my stupid insecurities to ruin our perfect day. The last time I jumped to conclusions, I screwed everything up, and I have no intention of doing that again.

Before I can let it go, I offer him one last opportunity to tell me if something is wrong. "Everything okay, Pearson?"

Nate leans me back against the couch, meeting my eyes as he lowers himself above me, and I am met with a look of pure desire. "Yes, Mrs. Pearson. Everything is just as it should be." I forget all my concerns as he slips his hand below my top and works the sweater over my head, his mouth moving to my nipple and then down my stomach. "And I'm about to show you precisely how it should be."

Nate and I hold hands, staring at Jack and Charlotte's front door which has a wreath with the word *Blessed* across it. Next to the door, a wooden plank has the word *Thankful* painted on it, and orange, yellow, and red mums line the steps. This is precisely how I always pictured Jack's future life. Soon I'm sure there will be mini Jacks and Charlottes running around the lawn, and I can practically see my brother coaching them in baseball and Charlotte cheering in the stands with a cup of pumpkin spice coffee steaming in her hands.

I ache for that future. A future that I now know Nate and I will experience as well.

Nate squeezes my fingers. "You ready, Cookie?"

My head snaps to his, and I laugh. "Way to ruin a perfect moment."

"Let me guess, you were just thinking about how you can't wait until we can have our very own cookie cutter house with some fresh sayings all over it telling everyone how happy and loved we are?"

I roll my eyes. Normally, I'm the sarcastic, unemotional one, whereas my husband wears his heart on his sleeve. Or on his chest, as has become quite clear with my artwork splayed across it.

"Is it so wrong that I'm feeling a bit emotional and happy that after all this time we are finally doing this? Spending our first holiday with our family together as husband and wife."

Nate takes the steaming dish out of my hands and puts it on the steps. Then he cradles my cheeks and looks at me warmly.

"No, Amelia. It's perfect. And you're right. I want nothing more than all of this." He extends his hands toward Jack's house and Charlotte's ridiculous signs. "*With you*. I can't even tell you how hashtag *thankful* I am that we are together. Hashtag *blessed*."

I stifle a giggle as my husband kisses me softly. "I love you, Nate. Thank you for seeing how ridiculous this is and yet still wanting it with me."

Nate pulls me to his chest and squeezes me tight, and emotion catches in my throat. "I want everything with you, Ames," he whispers against my hair. He holds me for a second longer and then kisses me softly once more. I wipe my lip gloss from his mouth, and his eyes sparkle with a smile.

Before I can knock, the door swings open, and the smells of turkey, a warm fire, and sugary desserts waft through the air. My brother's eyes dart to Nate and then to me and then he breaks out in a wide grin. "It's about fucking time." He laughs before pulling me into a hug.

As I remove myself from my brother's embrace, Charlotte rounds the corner and takes in the scene before her. Jack and Nate are hugging, and I'm pretty sure both Charlotte and I tear up. She looks back and forth between Nate and me and mouths, "Did you come together?"

I nod and look around to see if anyone else is here yet. Charlotte smiles as she walks up and hugs me. "You guys are the first to arrive." Then in my ear she whispers, "I need *all* the details."

Love & Tequila Make Her Crazy

When I step back, Nate takes my hand, and I smile up at him. "We are more than happy to share all the details. But the most important one is that we are together, I'm still his wife, *and* we are very happy."

Charlotte claps her hands as she screeches, "Yay! Oh my God! You're married! Are you going to have another wedding? Can I plan your bridal shower? What about a bachelorette party? We could have a joint one! Oh, tell me *everything*!"

Nate laughs, and his breath tickles my ear, sending a thrill down my spine, reminding me of our couch escapades earlier. "I don't even know how to answer those questions because Nate and I haven't really discussed that. We're just happy to be spending the holiday together." Nate pulls me closer, and I get the sense that he has all sorts of thoughts about Charlotte's questions. Quite frankly, so do I.

Jack moves his arm around Charlotte and kisses her cheek. "Sassy, don't start with an inquisition. You've just met the man. Nate, this is my beautiful future bride, Charlotte. Sassy, this is my best friend since diapers, Nate Pearson."

Charlotte shoves Jack playfully. "Oh, I've met Nate. I was a backup singer." Her face is aglow in excitement at finally getting to share her big moment with Jack. My brother eyes both Nate and me, and we just shrug.

"Alright, drinks?" Jack asks, barely reacting to his fiancée's admission that she had hidden meeting Nate. He's used to her antics.

We follow Jack into the kitchen, and I am overwhelmed by the warmth of their house. It's not only the food that smells heavenly, it's the love that so obviously sits in every corner. Pictures of family, of their trip to the Azores where they fell in love, of date nights and boat days, with family and friends. Every inch of the house is welcoming, and with Nate's hand in mine, I genuinely couldn't think of a time I felt more at home.

"So, how do you think Mom is going to take the news?" I ask Jack as he pulls out a pitcher of sangria.

Charlotte pulls out apples. She has whittled out the center and turned them into cups. She pours the Sangria and plops a cinnamon stick into the liquid. "It's a harvest blend, with cinnamon and apples."

Jack kisses her temple. "She cooked the sangria last night. I told her she was nuts. *Hot sangria.* But damn, when I tasted it this morning…it's really good."

I smile as I take a sip. Bursts of apple and cinnamon flavor filter through the sweet wine. "This is delicious. Can we feed it to Mom before we tell her?"

Nate winces. "I'm pretty sure your dad is the real concern."

Jack laughs. "Yeah, I'd definitely be more worried about him if I were you."

My mind whirrs to life. Was this a terrible idea? Surprising our family and announcing that not only are we back together but that we're married. Oh, and we have been for years. Seems like a terrible idea. My stomach aches just thinking how the majority of our marriage was spent apart.

As if sensing my thoughts, Nate kisses the back of my neck. "You're worth it, Ames. I'd deal with the third degree from your dad any day. Don't stress. They will be happy for us…eventually."

I smile in spite of my nerves. Nate makes me so damn happy, and the feel of his warm breath on the back of my neck sends a buzz through my body. I sip the drink again, hoping the liquid courage helps.

Moments later the doorbell rings, and Charlotte's eyes jump to mine. "You ready?" she whispers, squeezing my hand as Jack and Nate head for the door.

I shake my head. "This all feels crazy. Like I'm unbelievably happy that Nate and I found our way back to one another, but it almost feels like this has all happened too easily. Like we just fell back into each other."

Charlotte giggles. "Yeah, I can't imagine it would be hard to fall against that hard chest and those arms. I mean, I never knew that tattoos could be so hot." She fans her face, and I laugh.

"Me neither, sister, me neither. Speaking of siblings, is Shawn coming?"

Charlotte sighs. "Nope, he's helping with something downtown."

I smile. "He's really settled into life as a Bristolian."

"Haven't we all? I mean, it's a magical place." Charlotte smiles wistfully, and I imagine what our tiny town must look like through her eyes. She doesn't have the ghosts of the past haunting her on every corner. She is lucky to just focus on the sparkling bay and the red, white, and blue which litters every street, even during the winter holidays. But the truth is, unlike her, I know the history of this town, and part of that history is Nate and me. We certainly have some ghosts, but we are beautiful just the same. I swallow my pride and walk to the living room, prepared to deal with a few of our ghosts.

My mom and Karen look up at me expectantly as my dad, Jack, Nate, and Sam chat in the corner. Leave it to my dad to not find it strange at all that Nate is here. My mother isn't as fooled. "Hi, sweetie, you are positively glowing."

Charlotte turns to me and gives me a once-over as well. Out of the corner of her mouth she agrees, "Honestly, if I didn't know better, I'd say you were—" I elbow her before she can finish her sentence. My mom's and Karen's eyes both double in size.

The men in the room all turn to look at me, and silence descends upon us. I meet Jack's eyes, imploring him to say something.

Say anything, my eyes plead.

Thankfully, my brother gets the message. "Charlotte made the most delicious sangria. Why don't we go sit at the table, and we can all have a drink and toast the happy couple?"

Okay, anything but that.

I glare at him as my mom's eyes dart between me and Nate, and Dad's gaze turns on my husband. Dad is the first one to speak. "Happy couple?"

I try to formulate words, but Charlotte's statement has my mind spinning.

Glowing. If she didn't know any better.

Oh God, when was the last time I had my period? Nate had been back for nearly three months. We had sex the second week after he came back, or was it the third? I can't remember now.

Either way, the calculation doesn't change. I haven't had my period since we had sex. And I'm not on the pill. How had I been so careless? I'd been completely lost in Nate, and we never used condoms because we never used condoms before. But I was always on the pill. The pill I went off years ago. What was the point of being on birth control when you weren't having sex? Until of course you were.

Oh.

I try to screw my face into any version of someone who is not completely freaking out, but I'm not sure it's working. Nate looks at me oddly and walks over, wrapping his arm around my waist. "Yes, happy couple. Amelia and I wanted to wait until we were all together to tell you. We've gotten back together." He squeezes me to his chest, and out of my peripheral vision, I see my mom and Karen squeeze hands.

You're going to be grandmas, I want to whisper. Best friends and grandmothers. They will be thrilled. It's like I'm in a daze though. I turn to look at Dad, and his smile is wide. *You're going to be a grandfather, Dad,* my mind whispers. I meet Jack's eyes next, and he's grinning sheepishly, clearly embarrassed that he ruined our announcement. *Oh, brother dear, I have a much bigger announcement. Don't you worry. You're going to be an uncle.*

The breath stops in my throat as Nate kisses my temple.

Oh, Pearson, you're going to be a dad.

Tears burn behind my eyes. It's all I've ever wanted. This moment right here. I'm having Nate Pearson's baby.

Nate

Amelia's a bit tongue-tied, but I think it's the right time to set everyone straight. No time like the present, right? I meet my father-in-law's eyes and smile. "John, we aren't just back together."

Everyone's eyes remain on ours, and even my mom looks at me expectantly. I'm not sure why; she already knows that we're married. It's like she thinks there is some other secret I'm going to surprise her with. I turn to Amelia and see uncertainty mars her face. Does she not want me to tell them?

"Well, get to it, Nate," her father implores.

I look at Amelia, and mouth, *you ready?* She nods unconvincingly, but I pull the Band-Aid off anyway. "Amelia and I are married."

Love & Tequila Make Her Crazy

Charlotte claps and squeals in excitement, as if she doesn't already know this news, and my mom beams. I meet Amelia's father's eyes and see the smile growing on his face.

"Well, I'll be dammed." He walks up and claps me on the back, pulling me in for a hug. "Your dad would be so proud."

Emotion stings my throat. Before I can react, he pulls Amelia into his arms. I hear him whisper in her ear, "You better give your mom that big wedding she's been dreaming of. Happy for you, baby girl."

Amelia's eyes dart to her father's and then to mine. She's completely shell-shocked.

Next, it's her mother's turn. She pulls Amelia in for a hug and as they whisper to one another, I step back, giving them a moment. When Amelia looks at me, tears coat her lashes. "I'm okay," she whispers, squeezing my hand. "This is just…" She looks around the room, pausing. "This is just everything I've ever dreamed of."

My mom sneaks in for a hug next, pulling Amelia close. "I'm so glad you're my daughter." If I thought I was close to tears before, watching my mother and wife embrace puts me over the edge. I turn away and focus on Jack who motions to the kitchen. I squeeze Amelia's shoulder, kiss my mother's cheek, and follow my best friend.

"God, that was emotional," Jack says, pulling out a bottle of whiskey and placing it on the counter. "I don't know about you, but I think I need one of these."

I mumble a "Yeah, sure," but my mind is still spinning. Something is off with Amelia. Is it about the recording studio? She seemed to recognize my concern earlier, and as much as I want to share everything with her, I didn't want to ruin this perfect day.

Before I confide in my best friend, Sam and Amelia's father walk in. "Are we doing a celebratory shot?" Sam asks as he clamps his arm around my shoulder.

John takes a glass from his son. "It's a damn good day. Both of my children are happy, both living in Bristol," he says with a knowing smile. I'm sure that is one thing that makes him exponentially happier. We're back here, living in our hometown. Hopefully, one day having grandchildren that he can watch run on the baseball field.

Jack holds up his glass. "To raising future Bristolians."

I laugh but choke on my drink. It dawns on me almost immediately. The glow Amelia's mom mentioned, the look Charlotte gave her, and the calculations Amelia's face wore.

She can't be? She's not? Is she?

The women enter the kitchen, and Amelia settles next to me, leaning her body against my chest. "You okay?" I mutter into her hair, inhaling her chocolate scent and kissing her head.

She nods against my chest. "I'm perfect," she says, raising her eyes to mine, telling me without words exactly what I already know.

We're going to be parents.

I try to corner my wife multiple times during the day, hoping for a moment alone so I can tell her what I'm pretty sure we're both thinking. But it's almost as if she wants to avoid the conversation. She's constantly removing herself from the room, offering to help Charlotte set the table, to serve the food, to clean up. By the time dessert rolls around, I resolve to let it go. It's her body. She's likely got a lot more to come to terms with than I do. I'm thrilled. Fucking ecstatic. If Amelia is actually pregnant, that means I'm getting everything I wanted this year.

A loving husband and father.

It's all I've ever wanted to be, and if I don't feel like a fucking cheesy hashtag in this moment, I don't know when I will. *Blessed.* There is no other word.

After we say goodbye to our family, and I slip Amelia's jacket over her shoulders, I pull her close to me, wrapping my arms around her, and nuzzle into her neck. "I love you, Amelia Pearson. I'm so damn happy."

She pauses, pulling my arms around her tighter. "Me too, Nate."

When we get in the car, I wait for her to say something, but she remains quiet. Back at the apartment, she wanders into the bathroom and disappears for a shower. I'm uneasy because I really don't know the right move here. Do I tell her my suspicion? Give her time to come to terms with it? I'm not an idiot; I can do math. We haven't stopped having sex since that first time. Which means she hasn't had her period in over two months. I'm not sure how either of us missed it this long. There's nothing for us to be ashamed about though. She's thirty, we're married, and we certainly have the funds to support a family. Hell, if anything it makes my resolve regarding the music label even stronger.

I have a plan, and it does not involve Grant ever speaking to Amelia nor does it involve me ever moving back to Nashville. We are having a baby. I am going to give Amelia everything she ever deserved, and we are going to move on from the damn past that has been strangling us for years.

CHAPTER 24

Amelia

Before I totally freak out or scream for joy, I need to make a doctor's appointment. I try to put everything out of my mind because today we are heading to Boston, and I'm thrilled for Nate to finally tell me what is going on with this recording session. He's being very secretive, and that is not conducive to us becoming parents.

Although, to be fair, I'm being freaking secretive too. It's like we're both walking on eggshells, and I hate it.

"Are you excited?" I try, squeezing Nate's hand as we ride on the train to Boston. Parking is never easy in the city, and the day after Thanksgiving could be a nightmare. Nate surprised me with an overnight bag and told me we are spending the weekend.

A long overdue mini-moon, he suggested this morning when we got in the car.

"Yeah. I'm excited to spend the weekend with you," he responds, kissing my cheek. Not exactly what I was looking for, but I'll take it. I stare down at my hands and wonder how long until I'll start showing. If I'm pregnant that is. I haven't even confirmed it. There's a chance this is all just a coincidence. An eight-week coincidence. I mean probably not. I've never missed a period this long. But it's certainly possible. I guess we'll know for sure Monday.

We stop at the hotel before heading to the studio. Nate booked us a room at The Liberty Hotel in Boston. It's an old jail turned hotel. The lobby's ceilings are at least a hundred feet tall. Is this where all the prisoners would hang out during the day and the rooms were the cells? It seems creepy and incredible all at the same time. The restaurant has actual jail bars in it, and Nate asks if I want a drink before we head to the studio. "I'm okay," I reply, not sure how I'm going to avoid drinking all weekend without Nate growing suspicious.

A small smile creeps across his face. Maybe he already has his own suspicions.

The air is crisp in Boston, and it's damp from an early morning rain. We walk the streets, holding hands, with Nate's guitar case hanging on his back. People stare at us, and I wonder what they see. A couple in love? A musician and his groupie girlfriend? A pregnant wife and her husband? Unlikely. And yet we are all of those things. I'll forever be his personal groupie.

The studio is not nearly as grand as I expect. There is black insulation on the walls that I know helps with the sound, a black leather couch in one corner, and a glass partition which contains the microphone and recording equipment. Behind all of that, though, is a room filled with speakers and a few people with headphones resting on their shoulders. "Nate, this is Jen and Clint," a man with a black Metallica shirt says.

"Hi, guys. Ben, it's good to see you," Nate replies, shaking his hand.

Ben—this man does not look like a Ben. He needs a harder name, like Hammer. A laugh escapes as Nate points to me. "This is my wife, Amelia."

My heart constricts at his introduction. *My wife.*

"Hi, guys." I smile and provide an awkward wave.

The woman identified as Jen, who wears black leather pants, red heels, and a smile, motions to me. "Why don't you follow me? I can get you set up on the couch so you can watch Nate in comfort."

Before I walk off, Nate grabs me and pulls me to his chest, kissing me fiercely. It's not a chaste kiss that one would expect in public; it's passionate and filled with hope and excitement. He leaves me breathless.

As I walk away practically seeing stars, Jen eyes me. "Damn, newlyweds?"

I laugh. "We've been together since we were kids actually."

The surprise on her face fills me with pride. "Wow, I imagine he didn't look like that as a boy. How lucky that he grew up to look like that, huh?" I watch as she ogles my husband. It shouldn't be a surprise to me. Nate turns heads wherever he goes. But truth be told, he always has. It's the way he carries himself, like he's got a chip on his shoulder, with his smoldering blue stare and chiseled cheekbones, the strong jaw and muscular arms, but I never really notice those things about him. To me he's soft, sometimes cocky, and just Nate.

I laugh awkwardly at her appreciation for my husband and shrug my shoulders. "Yeah, he's always been pretty hot."

"Oh girl, wait until you hear him record. Watching a guy play the guitar and make music for a record label, wow, you are going to soak through those panties of yours. At least you don't have to worry about the groupies like other wives. I haven't seen many men look at their wives like yours does with you."

Record label?

My eyes dart to Nate. He's settling into the studio and speaking quietly with the other men. The air isn't quite reaching my lungs. Of course this makes sense. Why would we be at a recording studio the day after Thanksgiving unless he had to be. Unless someone *paid* him to be.

I search the studio for Grant, suddenly very concerned that his old band partner—and the person I know he went back to playing with after we separated—is going to show up. My skin crawls, and I want to find a way to get out of my own head and back to Bristol, but I stay rooted in place.

Grant doesn't arrive, Nate plays his songs, takes direction, and the day wears on, uneventfully.

"Let's take a lunch break?" Nate says, walking out and pulling me from the couch. "I'm sorry this is taking so long. I promise to make it up to you later."

I follow him out of the studio into the cold, dreary Boston

day, feeling like I'm walking through a fog. "So what do you think so far? Does it sound good?" Nate asks as we walk.

I nod my head, unable to voice what I'm thinking. Is Nate going back to Nashville? Does he expect me to follow?

My stomach turns over. I don't want to go back there. I don't think it's physically possible to put myself on a plane and walk back into the city where I had my heart broken into a million little pieces.

"Babe, what's wrong?" Nate tugs on my arm and spins me toward him, stopping us both in the middle of the sidewalk.

Before I lose my nerve, I pounce. "Are you moving back to Nashville?"

Nate's eyes crease, and he looks at me for a beat longer than necessary.

Answer the question, Nate, my eyes tell him.

"What? No. I told you I'm here to stay."

The breath catches in my throat. "Then why did Jen say you have a record deal? I'm not an idiot, Nate. We are in Boston, recording an album, in a studio I'm pretty sure you can't afford." My voice is accusatory, and there's a hardness I can't keep out of it.

I wince when Nate tries to brush his hand against my face. "Amelia, I bought you a building, started a business for you, and I don't work. I bought us a condo in Nashville. I have money. Believe me, I can afford this studio session."

I bite the inside of my mouth. *From the trust.* He has money from his dad's trust. I close my eyes, feeling foolish. The last thing I want to do is bring up Nate's dad right now. Or remind him of why he has the money he has. I fall into his arms. "I'm sorry," I whisper as tears threaten to rush my cheeks.

Here I go again, jumping to conclusions and assuming the worst.

Nate brushes my hair with his hands and rubs my back. "No, I'm sorry. I should have told you what we're doing here. I just wanted to surprise you. I want to record all of our songs for our wedding. Will you sing with me this afternoon?"

I look up at Nate, my eyes searching his face. "That's why you asked me to come? You want me to record our songs with you?"

Nate smiles and gives an easy laugh. "Yes, Ames. I thought back to my favorite moments and they are always with you. Writing music, making music, making love. While we can't record the last thing, at least not in public"—he raises his eyebrows—"I want to have our music memorialized. I want to dance with you to our voices at our wedding. Okay?"

I pull Nate's face to mine, kissing him just as fiercely as he kissed me in the studio, making him moan into my mouth. "Let's grab lunch so we can get this session over with, and I can take you back to the hotel, Mr. Pearson."

Nate grins. "Sounds good, Mrs. Pearson."

Nate

After we finish at the studio we get wrangled into drinks with everyone. It's the last thing I want to do. I want to take Amelia back to our room and devour her. Listening to her sing, watching her lips whisper against the mic, and seeing her eyes sneak teasing glances in my direction while we recorded has my dick straining. I'm hard as stone, and Amelia's tight jeans are doing nothing to help the situation. She smiles at me over her soda. I know it's a seltzer even if she had the bartender throw a lime in it to throw me off. The girl doesn't realize that my eyes never leave her. Especially when the bartender had his eyes glued to her chest. Next to me, the woman from the studio, Jen, is laughing at something Amelia just said, but I completely missed it.

Amelia winks at me knowing I'm clueless right now.

"This has been fun, but I'm exhausted. Ready to head up to our room, Ames?" I ask.

We'd settled on drinks at our hotel, and I'm happy we chose that now. Less time until I get her naked and spread out on the bed. My tongue aches to taste her.

Amelia gives me a slight nod and smiles at the others. "This has been fun. Thank you guys." She stands up and takes my hand, and my arm moves around her waist.

Jen's hand moves to cover Amelia's, and she looks at me before her eyes dart back to my wife. "The night doesn't have to end," she says with a clear offer on the table.

I bite back a smile waiting for Amelia's reaction.

"Um, what?" Amelia's eyes dance between mine and the woman who now has her hand moving circles on Amelia's arm.

Jen bites her red lips and looks at me. "If you're willing to share her, that is," she says with no embarrassment at all. Gotta give the girl credit, she has good taste at least.

I grip Amelia tighter, meeting her eyes and ignoring Jen. "Ready for bed, babe?" Amelia seems shell-shocked so I answer for her. "I don't share."

The woman shrugs, but I've already got Amelia moving with me upstairs. When we hit the elevator, a shocked laugh escapes her throat. "What the hell? Did she just proposition us?"

I push her against the cold metal, caging her in, and lick my lips as I stare down at her soft mouth. "Can't say that I blame her. This fucking mouth, Amelia…the things I want to do to it."

She bites her lip, and her lashes flutter before she looks up at me again. "Like what?"

The elevator doors open, and I lift Amelia into my arms. She wraps her legs around me and leans her head on my shoulder as I carry her to our room. As soon as the door is shut, I let her go and unzip my jeans. "On your knees."

Love & Tequila Make Her Crazy

Amelia hesitates for only a moment and then she drops down, like the good girl I know she is. "Now what," she whispers, her eyes hooded and her voice husky.

"Open that beautiful mouth for me." My cock jumps as she does, and I slide between her wet lips, letting out a groan as she glides her teeth across the tip. I wrap my hand around her blonde ponytail, controlling her movements. She fucking raises her eyes and watches me as she sucks. "Oh, you like to watch, my dirty girl. If I felt you right now would I find you drenched?"

Amelia shifts her hips, and I know she's seeking friction, but I'm not giving it to her yet. She moans around my cock.

"Did you think I would actually let someone else near you, Amelia? Let someone else see you like this?"

She moans again.

"Did you want that? Her tongue on you? Is that what you're thinking about while you're on your knees?"

Fuck, just the image has me ready to combust. I pull out, panting, and Amelia reaches out for me, confused.

"On the bed now. Take off your clothes and spread your legs."

I help her up and follow her, watching like a tiger ready to devour my meal. She opens her legs, and her hand moves between them as she waits for me. When I take too long, she starts moving her fingers over her clit, and my eyes watch in fascination. I clear my throat as I speak, "Is that what you did when we were separated?"

She nods as she moans and her head falls back. She's

completely lost to her own pleasure. Her teeth dig into her plump lip, and I start to fist my cock.

"What did you think about when you did it?"

She moans as she moves her fingers faster. "You...always you."

Her voice is breathy, and I can't hold back anymore. I move to the bed and kneel above her, my cock teasing at her entrance. Her fingers continue to move as she stares down at our connection. I slide in just a bit, and she hisses when I pull back out again. The feel of her warmth pulling on me and then the cold hitting me pushes my limits. She groans. "*Nate.*"

"Beg for it, Amelia. I want you to beg for my cock."

"Please, Nate," she purrs as she lifts her hips trying to push me in farther.

I pull back. "Be a good girl and tell me how you want me to fuck you."

Amelia raises her eyes to mine, and she bites her lip again, then she raises her brow in challenge. "Hard, Pearson. I want you to fuck me hard."

I slam into her and she squeals. "Oh, you like that, Ames? Hard. No one fucks you like I do, no one touches you." With each thrust, I brand her. Seeing someone else want her, seeing someone else think they have any shot to get near her, makes me crazy. "I don't care if it's a woman or a man. You're mine."

She starts to clench and I pull out. "Not so fast, Ames..."

She groans loudly and bucks her hips up, desperate for release. "Please, Nate, let me come."

I swat her hand as she tries to touch herself, and she moans as my fingers lightly smack the same spot. Then I lower my lips and circle my tongue. I repeat the move, slapping her clit and licking it. She spasms and cries out, and I lift up, slamming myself into her as she pulses around me. "Oh, fuck, Amelia." I come so hard I see stars.

I fall next to her and pull her close to me, kissing her shoulder. "You okay, sweetheart?"

Her shoulders relax and she pushes her ass against me, making me cuddle her closer. "I'm perfect."

As I drift off to sleep with her in my arms, I'd have to agree. She is absolutely perfect.

CHAPTER 25

Nate

Spending the weekend with Amelia in Boston, away from reminders of our day-to-day life, was invigorating. But nothing compared to the moment she stepped into the booth and sang with me. Knowing that we would be dancing at our wedding to these songs, or playing them in our baby's nursery, made me all sorts of emotional.

I kept the fact that I knew about the baby close to my chest, but I watched how Amelia avoided alcohol all weekend, how she turned down coffee even though she was grumbly and exhausted upon waking up, and I bought her extra chocolate to make up for it.

At night, when she was asleep by my side, I would marvel at her stomach, whispering to our baby like a complete lunatic. I know it's likely too early for a baby to hear me, if babies can even hear from the inside at all, but something about it was comforting. Just like talking to my dad. Maybe he can't hear me, but maybe he can, and if there's a chance that he can, I'll talk all day, hoping to share a few moments with him.

Love & Tequila Make Her Crazy

My plan for the first half of the music that I recorded was to sell it to the label. They were interested in my songs. They could have them, and the money that I made I'd split with Grant and put the rest in a fund for the baby. Amelia's and my music wasn't for sale though.

Monday morning, I wake up in our bed and stare down at my wife, excited to finally be moving past the last few years. All I need is to handle this conference call with the label, sign over my rights to the music, and tell Grant the money is his. Then I'll come back and start planning my future with Amelia—our wedding and the eventual move into our new home. When I mentioned the idea of moving into my parents' house, Amelia, like me, was hesitant. The house has so many memories, and as beautiful as they all are, it just didn't feel like going backward was the way to move forward. My mom would be listing the house in the next few weeks, and she said the money from the sale was ours to buy whatever we wanted. Which means I'll be spending the next few days packing up the house, going through my dad's things, and deciding what we want to hold on to and what stuff it was time to let go. I'm honestly not looking forward to it at all.

Amelia's blonde hair splays across the pillow, and her soft skin creases from sleep. She snores even worse now that she's pregnant, and it leaves me chuckling when I kiss her lips. Before leaving, I lower my lips to her stomach and whisper, "Good morning, baby, can't wait to finally hear all about you. Maybe

Mommy will get around to telling me sometime soon."

I kiss her stomach and she pushes my head, likely thinking I am trying for something else. "That's okay, Ames. Sleep, babe, I'll be back later." She barely stirs, turning over and falling back to sleep.

Before leaving, I stop by the flower shop. My mom agreed to man the storefront since we'd been gone for the weekend.

"Morning, Mom." I kiss her on the cheek, and she beams at me.

"How was your weekend? Everything go as planned?" My mom pushes her hair from her face and lifts her thumb to mine, stroking my cheek.

I meet her eyes. "It was great. Amelia and I did a few songs, and they sounded amazing. I can't wait for everyone to hear them."

She smiles. "How's Amelia feeling?"

Nothing gets past my mother. "She's fine," I say coyly. I certainly can't discuss my suspicions before Amelia and I have had a chance to actually talk about it. Which won't happen until she decides to tell me.

My mom doesn't take the hint though. "She really was glowing on Thanksgiving. Positively radiant."

I give my mom a knowing smile. "That's what happens to a woman in love with Nate Pearson."

My mother smacks me. "Okay, get out of here, you vain boy. You have an appointment, right?"

The excitement bubbles in my chest. "Yes. I'm finally putting everything behind me."

"Good luck, baby."

I walk out of the store, shaking my head and laughing at my mom's term of endearment. I guess you never outgrow being a momma's boy.

"Nate, holy shit, you've been holding out on us!" Jimmy says on the other end of the screen. I asked Sam if I could use his conference room for the video call. There are four other people on my screen, and all of them are from the label, other than Grant's cousin, Vin. He acted as our manager for this deal. I called to let him know my plan, and although he thought I was making a mistake, he couldn't force me to accept a music career I didn't want.

I smile. "I'm glad you like the songs. I hope you have artists interested."

A woman named Candace laughs. "Oh, sugar, *no*. Yes, we loved the songs, but we are only interested in a few artists singing them."

I shrug. I don't care who sings them. I just need the check for Grant. Hell, I'll give him the whole thing if it means getting a clean break. "Just tell me where to sign, and the music is all yours."

Jimmy interjects again. "So, who's the girl?"

I frown. "What girl?"

Candace sighs exasperatingly. "Not girl. Woman. That voice had to belong to a woman. Tell me she is as gorgeous as you are hot, and we have the next *Lady Antebellum*."

The third girl in the room jumps into the conversation, rolling her eyes. "Well, *Lady A* now. And there are three of them. We just want you two."

My shoulders sag. What are they talking about? I look to Vin to make sense of everything, and he finally speaks. "Nate, you sent over music with you and a woman on it. All the songs were duets. Who's the girl? Was that Amelia?"

Oh fuck. I palm my face, rubbing my thumb and middle finger against my forehead. This can't be happening. Shaking my head, I try to speak. "No, I sent the wrong one."

Fuck. Fuck. Fuck.

"Well, we don't want the other one. We want this one. So, what's her name? When can we meet her? Please tell me she looks as good as she sounds."

This time Vin responds. "Oh, she's a hot ticket. You guys will be thrilled." In the background I hear him trying to sell us, *Amelia and me*, as their next big hit. I can't get a word in edgewise. I try over and over again to explain that I sent the wrong songs. That Amelia is not interested. That *I'm* not interested.

"Grant will never go for this," I say finally, hoping that Vin gets the message.

Everyone on the call looks up. "Who's Grant?" Candace asks.

Love & Tequila Make Her Crazy

I look to Vin, waiting for him to explain. He meets my eyes. "Grant was never part of the deal. What are you talking about, Nate? I sold them you. And your music."

Now I'm the one confused. "But the contract…"

"What contract?" Jimmy asks. "Vin, if someone else is interested in them and has already sent over a contract, we need to get ours over to them today. Ours will be better, I promise," he says to me.

I shake my head. "The contract. Grant gave me a contract for Amelia's songs. You wanted Amelia to sign the rights over to her songs so that Grant and I could sing them."

Vin holds up his hand. "I don't know what my cousin has been telling you, but we aren't interested in Grant. I never sent over a contract including him or trying to cut Amelia out. Hell, if I thought Amelia was an option before, I would have sent over a contract for the both of you immediately. She was always part of your magic. You and Grant had something, but it wasn't until you started performing with Amelia that it became clear that you had the *it* factor. The music you two made together, the same thing we heard on that record, Nate—that is pure gold."

I mean, he's not wrong. Everything Amelia touches is like that. She makes it better. She makes me better. But this isn't what she wants. She wants her flower shop in Bristol. She wants to live a simple life, here.

And Grant is blackmailing me. If I don't include him or pay him off, he's going to tell Amelia everything.

Frustrated, I shake my head. "I'm sorry, all I can offer you is my songs."

Jimmy smiles. "Just wait for the actual contract. We'll send it over today. Wait to turn us down once you've read the fine print."

I know what he means. *The fine print*, as in the money they will offer.

I slam my hand against the table. How am I going to explain this disaster to Amelia?

Amelia

My alarm goes off, and I roll over looking for Nate. I have a doctor's appointment this afternoon, and it's time to clue Nate in on why I'm going to the doctor. But he's not here. I find a note on his pillow in place of his head.

Morning, Beautiful, I had an appointment. Dinner tonight? Meet me at the boat, I have something I want to show you. Love you.

My lips twist as I consider whether or not to call and tell him what I'm up to. It feels wrong that I waited this long. I should have told him last night so he could be here for the appointment.

What if they tell me something important today? Like the

sex of the baby? Can you even tell the sex of the baby this early? At most I'm maybe ten or eleven weeks. You can't tell that early—I think.

Frustrated, I stare up at the ceiling. I really screwed up. I don't want to go to the doctor by myself, but I don't want to tell Nate that I'm pregnant over the phone either.

I stare at my phone trying to figure out what to do. A text from Charlotte pops up on the screen.

Charlotte: Hey, how was your weekend with Nate? Let's grab lunch soon I want to hear the real story ASAP.

Charlotte. Hm. I twirl the thought around in my head. She *is* going to be my sister. And she's the only reason that I even realized I was pregnant to begin with. She told me last week she had a personal day today on the schedule so I know she's free.

I bite my lip. Will Nate be mad? I shake the thought from my head. Nate would want me to be comfortable. Yes, he would want to be at the appointment, but he can't be right now, and I can't wait another day to find out if I'm really pregnant and to confirm the baby is healthy.

I'll plan some elaborate way to tell him. The thought makes me laugh. I am so not the type to blow blue and pink smoke out of a container, or to bake a cake that says you're going to be a daddy. And yet, for this I want to be that type of girl. And Charlotte is *so* that type of girl. She can help me figure out a way to tell him.

With my mind made up, I dial Charlotte's number and wait

for her to pick up.

"Hey, future sister!" Charlotte sings into the phone, making me laugh.

"Hi, Charlotte, do you have plans this afternoon?" I bite the side of my thumb hoping she says no.

"Oh, you know, just watching re-runs of *The Office* while I sit in my pj's and relish the fact that I have no kindergartners pulling on my shirt or screaming my name. Why? *Do you have something more exciting you want me to do?*" She sounds positively giddy at the prospect of time with me, which warms my cold heart.

I hesitate before jumping in. This is a big moment. But this woman is going to be family. Hell, she feels like more than family. She brought my brother back from a depression I never thought would end. And my entire family fell in love with her too.

And soon she'd be an aunt to the baby currently sitting in my belly.

That last thought seals the deal. "Would you want to see your niece or nephew's first ultrasound?"

The screech on the other end of the phone cannot be overexaggerated. I'm pretty sure she dropped the phone, cursed, and then picked it up in a rush telling herself to,"*act cool, Charlotte.*"

I laugh again. "I take that as yes?"

Her voice cracks, "Yeah, *yes*. I'd be honored." Then she pauses, clearing her throat. "Does Nate know?"

A twinge of guilt pierces my chest. "No. So you cannot tell Jack! I was going to tell him today before I went to the doctor, but he left before I woke up, and I don't want to tell him over the phone and I *really* don't want to go alone."

I can hear Charlotte smile as she speaks, "Say no more. I'll pick you up in an hour and we can grab lunch before your appointment."

Stupid tears fill my eyes, and I blame the pregnancy. I'm not an emotional person. Although, it seems that I have become one ever since Nate came back into my life, so maybe I can no longer say that. All I do is cry now, whether it's happy tears or sad ones. But lately it's been mostly happy. "Thanks, I'm looking forward to it, Charlotte."

An hour later we are sitting at lunch and brainstorming ways to tell Nate about the baby. Assuming that my lack of a period, over emotional state, and glowing face are an indication that I am with child.

Charlotte scrolls through Pinterest listing off different ways that other more emotionally mature people announce their pregnancies to their spouse. "You could hand him the pee stick," she says, looking at me hopefully.

I purse my lips. "First of all, ew. Second of all, I haven't even peed on a stick, and I doubt they'll give me one at the doctor's office to take home."

Charlotte scrunches her nose. "Yeah, I'm not a fan of that one anyway. Bodily fluid. Yuck. *So not romantic.*"

I laugh. "Well, it doesn't have to be romantic, it just has to be—" I pause, trying to figure out what I want.

"Monumental?" Charlotte offers.

I twist the napkin in my hand. "Maybe. Or like signifying the beginning of a new chapter? A new start? I don't know, maybe this was silly. I should just text him." I go to take out my phone, and Charlotte clamps down on my hand.

"No. Let's keep looking. I'm sure we'll find the perfect way to tell him. Oh, what about this!" she yells, holding out the phone and showing me a card that says, *"My Boobs Are Going to Get Even More Amazing!"* I shake my head. While funny, it's not quite hitting the mark. *"Or,"* she says, staring at the phone again, "a customized chocolate bar!"

I bite my cheek. I mean chocolate is totally our thing, but where would I find a chocolate bar that says *You're going to be a daddy!* And really, chocolate is *my* thing. I want something that is *our* thing. I take the phone from her and scroll down until I find precisely how I want to tell him. "This." I hold the phone out to her. "Do you have any idea how we could get this done today?"

Charlotte looks at me seriously. "Only if you'll let me tell Jack. If so, I can have him put it together while we're at the doctor. What do you think?"

I don't even think about it. I want to do this. And one more person knowing won't make a difference. In the end, this is exactly how I want to share with Nate that he's going to be a dad. This is how I want to start our next chapter. I hope he understands and that he's just as excited as I am.

CHAPTER 26

Amelia

Charlotte delivers me home after the appointment with a promise to have Jack drop off the surprise in an hour. That will give me just enough time to get to the boat and meet Nate for dinner.

I stare down at the thin black paper in my hand with the words, *Pearson, Amelia, 11 weeks 3 days* and an image of my gummy bear.

That's what I've named him slash her—*Bear*—because that is precisely what the little one looked like on the screen, a gummy bear.

Every time I stare at the image, tears burn and my breath gets caught in my throat. And forget it when I imagine Nate's reaction to the news. His blue eyes glistening at me with wonder. The smile that will undoubtedly cross his face. I cannot wait!

I kiss the image and put it on the counter so that I don't forget it on my way out. Before I can walk into the bedroom, a knock on the door stops me.

"Coming," I yell, imagining Charlotte forgot her keys or something else in my apartment. I look around but see nothing she could have forgotten before I open the door. "Hey, what'd you forget?" I ask, as I look into the hall and meet Grant's eyes. My stomach drops as all the air is sucked from my throat, and I slam the door shut.

Grant's hand is quicker, and he stop it and puts his foot in the door, wedging his way into my apartment. I back up quickly, and the tears that were already swirling beneath the surface over the emotional day fall.

"Wh-what are you…doing here?" I stutter. It has been years since I last saw Grant, and it hadn't been a pleasant encounter.

"Hey, Cookie, good to see you too. Nate here?" Grant peers around the apartment, and smiles when he discovers I'm alone. My hands reach for the phone in my pocket, ready to dial, but he grabs it before I can get a grip on it. Wanting to protect the baby, I wince and don't fight back.

It's going to be okay. He's not going to hurt you.

Instinctively my hand moves over my stomach, and I plant my feet.

He does not have power over you. You're a grown woman. You're going to be a mother. And Jack taught you how to fight. You've got this.

I breathe heavily and wait.

"Cat got your tongue?" he whispers, moving closer.

The sound of my heart echoes in my ears. Even swallowing sounds hollow. "Nate should be home any minute. What do you want, Grant?"

He smiles. It's a mean smile—a crooked smile that doesn't quite meet his eyes—and he stumbles forward. I smell the alcohol on his breath, and my stomach turns. Everything about this moment is wrong. "Did he give you the papers yet?"

I look to the ceiling trying to keep the tears from pouring out. "What papers, Grant?" I say, trying to steady myself and hoping that the quicker I get this conversation over with the quicker he gets out.

Grant laughs. "Oh, I take it he hasn't given them to you then. Because if he did, you'd know precisely what I was talking about. Good thing I brought another set." He tosses the papers in my direction, pushing them against my chest. Because I want to protect my stomach, I grab them and stumble in the other direction, away from him.

I have no intention of even looking. I'm sure it's all fabricated bullshit. That's all Grant does.

"Read them in front of me, Princess. I want to see your reaction."

I roll my eyes. I'll play his stupid game if it means getting him out of here. I glance down, and my eyes scan the words, not really taking them in. "Property Distribution, blah blah blah." I mime words and read further. "I, Amelia Pearson, hereby agree to grant all my right, title, and interest in the following songs to Nathanial Pearson pursuant to the property agreement in exchange for all right and title to Pearson's Flowers…" my voice stops.

This is an agreement for the division of our property for the dissolution of our marriage.

"I see you're finally putting two and two together," Grant says evenly. I don't dare look at him. This is just a lie. Grant made these papers up to fool me so I'd jump to conclusions. *Again*. I'm not going to fall for it.

"You can go," I say, pointing at the door.

"I didn't draw these up, Amelia. Nate did. That's why he came back. We have a record deal. They wanted your songs. The ones you and Nate wrote back in Nashville. He figured if he bought you a flower shop, you'd agree. Something for you, something for him."

I shake my head. *No*. Everything he's saying is not true. He's using Nate's good acts to turn them into something that will benefit his version of events. This isn't Nate. *Nate wouldn't do this to me.*

"The thing is," Grant interrupts my thoughts, "it backfired. Because when he got here you looked so hot. I can see why he wanted to get you in bed one more time. You look good, Cookie. And he never could keep his dick in his pants, as you know." His eyes cruelly flick to mine, reminding me of the last time I saw him, and my resolve weakens.

I shake my head, swallowing hard. Putting the images out of my mind. The closed door. The noises. "No. It was a misunderstanding just like this is. You need to leave."

Grant laughs. "Is that what he told you? That you misunderstood when he was sleeping with Gina? How about when he was with Jenna? Or Heather? Were those *all* misunderstandings?"

The bile works its way up my throat, and the room starts to spin. "We were separated, Grant," I choke out.

"Oh, but you're back together now. Did he tell you that he submitted the music you guys made to the label? They want the three of us to record in Nashville together. It's going to be wonderful—you, me, and Nate back together again."

My face falls. Everything up until this moment I could explain away. But how did Grant know we recorded in Boston? How did he know I'd sung with Nate? And Nate had acted so guilty. So shifty about the whole thing. We didn't go out and drink like we normally do. Which was fine with me since I'm pregnant, but Nate doesn't know that. He probably worried if he got drunk, he'd slip and the truth would come out.

And then I remember the papers in Nate's guitar case. The ones with our names on top. He slammed the case shut before I could see them. *He was hiding something.* I knew it even then.

My eyes meet Grant's, and he knows he has me. "Let's be honest, you don't want to play in a band with me. I mean, Nate and I share everything, but you were never up for that." His words, *the words he used the last time I saw him*, are my undoing.

"Sign the papers, Amelia. Give us the music, stay in this town with your little shop, and let Nate become the star we both know he's meant to be. You'll only hold him back if you don't. Right now he thinks this is what he wants because he's surrounded by all the ghosts. His dad, your friend Peter, your marriage. But they're all dead. And eventually Nate will realize that, and he'll hold it against you for keeping him here. He was happy in Nashville. He was good. Why do you think he stayed away so long? The only reason he came back was because he needed you to sign these forms and then he got a little wrapped up in, well, *you,* because you look like *that.*"

Grant moves closer, and his hand trails my arm, sending a chill down my spine. *I need him gone. I need him out of here.*

"Fine. Fine. I'll sign the stupid fucking forms. Just get out, Grant. Get out!" I scream and storm toward the kitchen to find a pen. There's one sitting right next to the sonogram. I stare at the image, apologizing to Bear for ever trusting that Nate would stick around. For being so fooled and for giving our baby such a shitty father.

I sign my name and stare at the spot where Nate's signature will go. "Tell him to file it this time." I toss the papers in Grant's direction and storm into the bedroom as soon as he is gone, collapsing on the bed and trying to forget that Nate Pearson ever existed.

Nate

I pace the boat, fully aware that time has run out. I need

to tell Amelia everything. The truth about what happened in Nashville, the truth about why I came back, and the news about the mistake with the label. I can't have Grant holding this threat over my head. Eventually, Amelia will find out. It's better coming from me. It's the only way.

We are going to have a baby. I need to reassure her that she and the baby are all that matter to me. The past is the past. It's going to hurt. Her and me. Knowing how things happened. I don't want her to blame herself. And I know she will. *Fuck*. It's the last thing I want.

But that's always been our problem. We never want to hurt one another so we don't talk. We hide things. We don't fight. Unfortunately, I have a feeling this is going to cause a huge fight and I'm not looking forward to it.

I stare at the clock. Six p.m. Where is Amelia? She should be here by now.

Her phone goes straight to voicemail, and panic settles in. What if she got in a car accident? Or what if something is wrong with the baby? I grab my keys and head toward the door of the boat when I hear footsteps on the dock. A long breath escapes my throat in relief. Finally. But when a loud thump lands on the boat, I know for a fact that it isn't Amelia. She's too tiny to make that sound, and too steady on her feet. Especially on this boat.

The drunken voice crows out a hello, and a shiver goes down my spine. *Grant.*

I meet his eyes as he stumbles inside. He wears a smug

expression and carries a pile of papers which are turned in all different directions. He throws them at me.

"Handled it," he says with a devious smile.

Oh fuck, this guy is drunk. I need him out of here before Amelia gets here. Coming clean about everything is one thing. Doing it with Grant here is another. That will not go over well. "Uh, thanks," I reply, putting the papers down on the counter and trying to steady him. "How'd you get here, Grant? You shouldn't be driving."

"Look at the papers, buddy. She signed. You're free."

I shake my head, not making sense of his words. "What? Listen, I talked to the label. I'm selling my music. You can have all the money. I'm out."

Grant's laugh reverberates through the cabin, almost like a villain in a Disney movie. The ridiculousness of this comparison is not lost on me. "Nope. No need, my man. She signed. You're divorced. She gave you the rights."

"What are you talking about?" I say before looking down at the papers.

"It's the divorce papers. She signed. You're free. The shop is hers; the music is ours."

For a moment I think he's bluffing, but when I look down at the paper, I recognize the curl of the *A* in her signature. Even in anger, and believe me I can see she wrote this in anger, she has the same curled *A*.

My heart breaks. She gave up. She jumped to a fucking

conclusion again, and she gave up.

Again.

I feel myself losing control. Life is repeating itself. I had everything within reach—my wife, a new life, a *baby*—and it's all slipping away.

"Get the fuck off my boat." My voice is low and menacing. I have nothing left. She took it all from me. Everything. It's all gone.

"Buddy, don't be like that. I saved you." Grant stumbles toward me, but when he meets my eyes, it appears he remembers what I did the last time Amelia broke my heart, and I think it clicks.

Pain. I need the pain.

And if he doesn't get the fuck off my boat, I'll be happy to lose myself in the pain by beating the shit out of him. He holds up his hands and backs away slowly. "Just, uh, call me when you've calmed down."

He disappears as a bitter laugh escapes my throat. When I've calmed down. I'll never calm down. It's not worth it. *I'm* not worth it. But damn, do I wish that I were.

CHAPTER 27

Nate
Twenty-Nine Years Old

The room spins, and my fist lands hard against the object in front of me. Was that an object? Or maybe a person? My hand pulses but it isn't enough. I keep pushing forward. Right arm, left arm, right fist, left fist, until I can feel nothing but the pain.

"Is there someone you want to call?" a gravelly voice asks. A piercing pain tears through my brain.

Someone?

There's no one. I have no one left.

I dial the only person I know in Nashville. Wanting to inflict more pain. That's all my time with him had been. Pain.

"Hello," Grant's voice echoes through the black phone. It is warm against my ear. Probably from all of the other prisoners before me. My stomach rolls at the thought. Or maybe it's from the lack of food and the insane amount of alcohol.

Or the punches that the other guy landed to my ribs.

"I need bail."

When Grant arrives at the station, I don't have to tell him what happened. He doesn't care. He knows she's gone.

He drives me back to my condo, and I grab some things. "You can't stay here, man. Her stuff is everywhere. You need a fresh start. Come back with me. We'll get the band back together."

I don't want to play music. I don't want to go anywhere with him. But he's right. I can't stay here. I follow him home.

"Dude, you have to stop fighting people. You're going to get yourself killed."

I glare at Grant as he picks me up from the station again. Third time this week. My stomach rolls, and I lean out of the car to throw up. With every heave, I feel better because I feel worse. It's what I deserve.

"You just need to sleep this off. Get back to playing music. My cousin got hired by a label. This could be our big break. You just need to stop fighting and focus on the music."

I don't even look at him.

Music. There is no music without her. I don't want to live without her. I'll give myself a few hours of sleep and then I'll be back at the bar, looking for another fight. Someone will put me out of my misery.

"What the fuck are you doing, man?"

I keep my head down, unable to meet his eyes.

"You are going to go to prison. Not jail, Nate, prison. Peter wouldn't want this. Amelia—"

I meet his eyes with a death stare. "Don't say her fucking name to me."

"She's my goddamn sister, Nate. And you broke her. She's *broken*. And you're beating the shit out of everyone you see. Drinking until you can't feel. I see it. I get it. I was *there*. But this isn't the way to live," Jack's voice breaks.

Why is he here? Sitting across from me in this tiny room with my hand shackled to the table. A guard in the corner watches our every move. There is no way that Grant called him. Grant doesn't give a shit about me.

I can't sing. I can't play. My fingers can barely bend because I've broken them so many times in the last few months. It's what I deserve though. And now, since I can't get drunk, I just

Love & Tequila Make Her Crazy

have to remember.

If I piss off someone enough in prison, maybe they'll put me out of my misery. I don't have any fight left.

"Tell her to move on. I'm not worth it." I hang my head. Resignation and defeat control my movements.

Jack's hand moves to mine, and the guard hollers, "No contact."

He moves his arm back and tries a low voice. "*You are worth it.* You have always been worth it. So am I. So was Peter...and so was your dad." His voice is strong but filled with emotion. I can barely raise my eyes to meet his. When I do, I see the emotional toll these past few months have put on him.

He *found* Peter. He saw with his own eyes what this war did to him. And he's still standing. But he was always so much stronger than I am. And Amelia's got his genes. She'll be fine.

I shake my head, unable to respond.

"You'll kill her if she finds out this is what happened to you. She's broken now, but this will *kill her.* Do you understand that? If you can't do it for you, and you can't do it for Peter or your dad, think of Amelia. Think of everything she gave up for you. Think of all the times she sat with you on your boat, making you better, when none of us could. Now think, right now she's at home, and no one can make her better. None of us can do it. You're each other's person. You *owe* this to her. And you owe this to me. *You promised you wouldn't break her heart.*"

I can't bear to listen to his words. I look up at the guard, signaling it's time to go. "I'm no good for her. She'll move on.

She'll find someone better."

Jack's jaw hardens. "What about your mother? Does she deserve this? To lose her husband and now you?"

Mom. What I would do to just crawl into her lap. What I would do to go back twenty years, sitting at the dinner table with her and dad, planning our next adventure. I meet Jack's eyes. "They deserve better."

Jack shakes his head. "That's the thing about love though, isn't it? You can't pick who you love. And Amelia and your mom, they love *you*."

"I can't go back there," I say honestly.

Jack's face relaxes. "We agree on one thing. You're right. You can't. *Yet.* You have work to do."

I bite my lip, relishing the pain. "I don't even know where to start."

Jack levels me with a stare. "Easy. You accept the plea deal. You go to rehab like the judge is offering. The system understands. Which is crazy because it normally feels like everyone is against you, but your lawyer did a damn good job explaining everything you've lost, and we all really believe if you put in the work—go to rehab, do community service, stay out of fights—you'll come out the other side of this. You'll be on probation for two years. You can't leave the state. But you won't be serving two years in prison. You'll have a real shot, Nate. And then you can be the guy they both deserve."

I'm not sure I can do it. If anything he says is even a

possibility. Will Amelia even want to see me when this is all over? Will she have moved on? Will I have broken my mother's heart with all of these arrests? I've disappointed them all.

And Dad.

He can see this, and I know he's disappointed. And yet maybe that's the one thing that pushes me over the line.

He can see this.

Knowing that he's watching me, that one day I'll have to sit across from him and talk to him about all of this, is enough to push me to be better. To *be* worth it.

I give a small nod, and Jack's face lifts in a half smile. I almost imagine I can hear my dad sigh in relief.

Amelia
Twenty-Eight Years Old

My stomach flips as the plane hits the runway, the speed throwing me forward against the seat in front of me. I didn't tighten the seatbelt enough. I *need* to stop being so careless.

I blow out a breath. Healing starts today. I've been stubborn. But so has he. We're married and I need to see him. I considered texting him, telling him I was flying in and wanted to talk, but it felt wrong. How do you text your husband who you haven't seen in almost six months? What do you even say?

No, this has to be done in person. Nate is my person. He's always been my person. And even though he said some terrible things last time I saw him...

"It should have been Jack."

Fuck. Why did he have to say that?

It was the alcohol, Amelia. The emotions and the alcohol and you pushed him.

I rub my forehead, trying to will myself to listen. Being angry with him has done nothing for me. Drinking, crying, and sleeping back in my childhood room, yeah, that's no way to live. It's time to grow up and figure it out.

It's so weird being back in Nashville. I take a taxi to our condo and stare out the window as the city I had come to call home over the last decade passes me by. Our favorite bars, breakfast spots, and parks fill my head in a blur.

Before I know it, we've arrived at my building. I mumble a thank you to the driver, hand him a fifty-dollar bill, and tell him to keep the change. As I step out of the car, I stare up at the place we had called home for the last five years, and emotion clogs my throat.

No time like the present.

I pick up my duffel bag and walk to the steps. I didn't bring a suitcase. All my clothes are still here. I never intended on not coming back last time I left. Somehow, I've managed to survive on a few outfits at home, and since I've mostly been sitting in my bedroom crying, sweats have been sufficient.

As I reach the door, my stomach twists in knots.

Here goes nothing.

I stick the key in the lock and turn, expecting to find Nate in the living room. Or bedroom. Or some sign of life anywhere. But it's dark and empty. No one's here. I walk around without turning the lights on, picking up photographs that line our shelves.

A picture of our engagement with Peter and Jack bookending Nate and me draws my attention. I lift it up, and my hand runs over Peter's face and tears pool. "Oh, Peter, I'm so sorry. I miss you so much." I close my eyes and bite back the memories.

I drop my bag to the floor and walk into the bedroom. Our bedroom. The bed is unmade, and it smells like Nate. I sink into the soft sheets, pull the covers over my body, and fall asleep on Nate's pillow, momentarily forgetting that it's been months since I last held him.

Nate hasn't come home. It's been two days, and I can't keep sitting here wondering when he'll walk through the door. I try his cell phone, but it goes straight to voicemail. I don't leave a message because I don't know what to say.

Hi, I'm home.

Yeah, no. I go to the grocery store, pick two large steaks, baked potatoes, and garlic bread. I grab a bottle of red wine at the liquor store and start to prepare dinner. It's delusional that I think if I make Nate's favorite meal that he'll walk in the door and our life will reset. But I honestly don't know what else to do.

I tell *Alexa* to play country music and sway my hips to Shania Twain while I prepare dinner. At eight o'clock, I have to acknowledge that Nate isn't coming home. It's been three days, and he never once came back to this condo. I gulp down the last sip of wine from the bottle—yes, I drank too much—and cover Nate's plate in tin foil and put it in the fridge.

Nate's plate.

I laugh bitterly to myself. I really am delusional if I think he's coming back to me. I don't know where he is, but somehow I can feel in my bones that wherever it is, he's not mine anymore.

A little drunk, and a lot sad, I stumble down Broadway in search of the bar Nate and Grant used to play at. It had been almost a year since they played together. Nate kept his promise after we married, playing with me instead and leaving that other life behind. I don't know what I expect to find. Would Nate really have left Bristol, hopped on a plane back to our city, and gone back to singing with Grant?

I can't imagine it. And yet I don't know where else he could be.

It takes a few seconds for my eyes to adjust to the light in the bar. It's dark, and the bright lights of the stage blind me. One of my old managers walks up with a smile. "Amelia! Oh my God, it's been forever. How are you?"

I offer her a hug and she squeezes me tight. It's strange because I don't remember us ever being close, but in this moment, I truly need this hug. "I'm actually looking for Nate. Any chance he's here?"

Her eyes flash and I'm sure she knows something. But she just shakes her head. "Maybe try Grant's place? They were here a few months ago. Things got a little out of hand. He was banned from coming back."

My stomach drops. Just as I suspected, Nate had come back to Nashville and went back to his life with Grant. And what does she mean out of hand? I can't bear to ask her to recount my husband's choices to me as if I'm a stranger.

How is it that I have no idea where my husband currently lives and what he's doing?

"Do you have Grant's address?" I hear myself ask.

It's an out-of-body experience because the last place in the world I want to go is to Grant's apartment. It's been years since he assaulted me—almost raped me—and I still can't control the way my hands shake when I remember the feel of his fingers on my back. The way I felt when I thought he would overpower me. It feels stupid that after all these years, when nothing *really* happened, that I still can't get past that moment. There must be something wrong with me.

She provides me with his address, and I'm even more

uncomfortable to learn it's our old apartment. The spot where everything happened. Where Nate and I first started our life together, where we returned after he proposed the first time, where I started my life in Nashville, my love for flowers, my love for music, and where Grant pinned me on the couch and stole a part of me that I'm afraid I'll never get back.

I walk to the apartment in a daze. It's not far from the bar. That was part of the charm of the location, the appeal of choosing somewhere so close to the music scene that made Nate move to Nashville in the first place.

I breathe deeply, preparing myself to enter this space. I'm doing this for Nate. For our marriage. *For our future*. I hope I'm not too late.

Music plays loudly on the other side of the door, and I hear laughter and voices. I hold my hand up to knock and then place it down at my side.

What am I doing? What am I going to find on the other side of this door? Do I really want to know?

But something inside pushes me forward. I can't keep living in this purgatory. If things are over with Nate, then I need to make a clean break. We need to see each other to end it. Or, just maybe, I hope against all rational thought telling me otherwise, he'll be in there just as miserable as I've been. He'll be happy to see me, and he'll want to work this out.

I rap my knuckles against the door. "Coming," I hear a voice shout. The door swings open, and Grant holds the door in his hand, leaning against it as a cocky smile spreads across his lips. "Oh, Cookie, I knew you couldn't stay away."

He reaches out and pulls me against his chest, and before I can stop him, he kisses my neck. I push back hard, panting and angry. "*Don't*. I'm looking for Nate. Is he here?"

In the other room I hear a woman cry out, and my eyes close in realization. Grant watches me and his smile grows. "Oh, that's just Tina. You remember her, right? She went to college with Nate and me. We dated for a bit. I told you Nate and I share *everything*. Why don't you come over here, and I'll make you forget until he's done?"

I shake my head, not believing this can possibly be true, Nate wouldn't do this to me.

But my stomach drops when my eyes follow Grant's to the other side of the room. In the corner I spot the guitar—*Nate's guitar*—and in that moment, I know it's over.

Nate goes nowhere without that guitar.

My stomach turns, and I press my hand to my mouth to hold back bile. Nate's in the other room, making that woman scream. I stumble backward out the door and into the hall. Grant calls out to me, but I hear his laughter as he shuts the door.

I sink to the floor in front of my old apartment and sob, taken back to the same spot so many years ago when I thought my life had changed forever. But I had no idea anything could hurt this much. I clutch my stomach, and the emotions shake my body. I've lost Nate. I've lost everything.

CHAPTER 28

Amelia

I vaguely recognize the sound of banging on my door, the creak as it finally opens, and footsteps stomping heavily around the apartment. I fold myself tightly into a ball, slipping to the ground and hide behind the side of the bed.

Please don't let it be Grant.

I can't take it. I won't be able to fight him off as weak as I am now.

The sobs have drained me, left me weak and vulnerable in a puddle. When the door creaks open and I hear Jack frantically yell my name, my body relaxes and falls into even more violent sobs, the relief and fear washing over me.

Without hesitation, my brother is on the ground, lifting me into his arms and cradling me as he brings me to the bed, holding me against his chest as he comforts me, saying my name over and over again, telling me it will be okay.

I don't know how much time passes, but I vaguely become aware of another figure in the room. It's Charlotte. She hands me a glass of water, and I can see the panic and concern in her eyes. I gulp down the water too quickly and begin to choke on it.

"What the fuck happened?" Jack mutters to her. She shakes her head, lost, and rubs my back.

"What happened, sweetie?" Charlotte asks in a soothing voice. She continues rubbing my back, and I focus on the circles she's making rather than my ever-breaking heart. I don't even know how to get the words out. I don't know how to explain. It goes back years.

Seven years ago, my life changed when Grant put his hands on me, and today I signed divorce papers to get him out of this room. To get him away from me.

What did I do? I didn't give Nate a moment to explain. And Grant probably already ran to him, swinging the papers in Nate's face. I'll be too late to fix things. Just like last time. If there's even anything to fix.

I take a stilted breath. It hurts coming through my throat, my chest constricting and trying to pull the air in and down to my lungs. I said I'd be okay with burning…now I understand the consequences.

A sound akin to a cry, or maybe a sigh, escapes my throat as I try to speak. "It-it was all…it was all a lie."

Charlotte continues rubbing my back. "Shhh, take a breath, sweetie. Take a breath and try again."

I do as told and try to start at the beginning. But where is the beginning?

"Peter died," I say. Charlotte and Jack look at one another

like I've lost my mind. Like they think perhaps I'm having an emotional breakdown and don't know what year it is. Maybe I am. I try again. "Peter died and you blamed yourself, Jack."

Jack nods and sighs. "Yes. Yes, I did."

"Nate and I got into a fight. I thought…" I groan at the horrible misunderstanding. "I thought Nate blamed you as well."

Jack's eyes shoot to mine. "That's why you left him? Because of me?" His voice breaks me.

I nod as tears stream down my face, and then I start to shake my head. "But that's not what he meant. He blamed himself. He thought you and Peter…he thought you signed up for him. Because of Paul."

Jack nods. This isn't the first time he's heard this. "I told him he needs to stop thinking the world revolves around him," he says with a bitter laugh. "It was no one's fault, Ames. It just… happened. We were at war. It doesn't make it easier, but…it just happened." Jack grows quiet, staring at his hands.

I breathe in, gaining courage to continue the story. "I went back to Nashville six months after Peter died. To fix things with Nate. But he wasn't at the condo. I waited for days, and he never came home."

Jack nods again. "Right. He wasn't there."

So, he knows. Jack has known all along. I swallow my pride and continue. "I went to find him at the bar, but he wasn't there. Someone we both knew gave me Grant's address. Suggested I go there to find Nate."

Jack shakes his head. "But he wasn't there, either."

I bite my lip, ready to get to the worst part when I realize what Jack just said. And the way he said it. Like he was so sure of his statement. Like he knew *precisely* where Nate was. "What?" I manage to stammer.

"He wasn't there. You couldn't find him, and you came back, right?" Jack looks at me so sure that this is the sequence of events.

"No. He was at Grant's."

Jack shakes his head. "No, he wasn't."

I feel my cheeks grow red, and anger bubbles. I don't want to talk about this at all, but it is the only way I can explain what happened today.

I *need* my family to understand that I didn't just walk away from my marriage. Nate gave up on us.

"Yes, he was, Jack. He was in bed with another woman. I heard him."

Jack's cheeks grow red as well. "I don't know what you thought you heard, but it wasn't Nate. He was in rehab."

"What? How? What? How the hell would you know that?"

"Because I brought him there. I talked to his counselor daily. He never left. *He couldn't.* It was court mandated."

My mind can't wrap itself around what Jack is saying. "But Grant told me…" I stop talking as realization takes over.

He lied to me. He convinced me that Nate was cheating on me. Just like he lied to me a few hours ago.

Oh my God.

The breath catches in my throat, and I start to hyperventilate. Charlotte rubs my back and orders me to breathe as Jack puts his face in front of mine and says, "Count, Amelia, focus on my face and count backward from one hundred."

I count and make it all the way to thirty-two before I feel calm enough to stop. "Amelia, what happened today?" Charlotte asks. "When I left you, you were so happy."

I meet Jack's eyes. "Grant came over." My eyes close again, remembering his face and the way he smelled and how his hands moved to get close to me. Quietly, and in defeat, I admit, "He tried to rape me."

Jack's jaw locks, and I know my brother is about to kill someone. "Where the fuck is he?" He gets up and starts pacing.

"Not today," I reply. "Seven years ago. The night of the engagement."

Jack's eyes meet mine, and his head tilts to the side, almost like he understands. Like he remembers how broken I appeared, even if I tried my hardest to hide it.

It was the happiest and worst day of my life. Until now that is. Right now, knowing that Nate probably thinks I once again believed a lie, left him without talking, and left my baby without a father—this is so much worse.

"He showed up today. He told me Nate only came back to get me to sign over the music rights. That he bought the store so I would give him the music in the divorce." I laugh bitterly. "If

Nate really wanted the music, he wouldn't have had to give me anything. I would have given him everything. None of it means anything without him."

Jack's eyes soften. "Amelia, no. Nate loves you. He bought this store, had his mother start this business, and came back because he *loves* you. Not because he wanted anything from you."

"Why did he wait so long to come back then? Why didn't he come back years ago? It's only now when he has a record deal that he suddenly wants me. It makes no sense. Grant's story does."

And that's the problem. There's a truth in Grant's story that I can't let go. The way Nate had me sing with him at the studio. The way he acted when I asked what was going on. The papers in his guitar case. How distant he was. How he only came back when this was on the table.

A record deal. *His dream*. I'm the one who stood in the way of it, and he needed to tidy up this last piece before he could walk away again.

Jack runs his hand through his hair as Charlotte and I stare at him. He appears to be weighing his options. Tell me the truth or keep up whatever lie Nate asked him to repeat.

Finally, he relents, looking up and speaking softly, he explains, "He was on probation, Amelia. He couldn't leave the state. And he wasn't okay to come back. He had a lot of issues to work through, just like I did. He didn't want to come back until he was better."

"What do you mean he was on probation? And court ordered

rehab. What are you talking about?"

Jack looks at the ceiling. "This really is his story, but since the two of you are so terrible at communicating, I guess this falls on me." He pauses and then looks up at me with raw pain. "Nate has been my best friend since we were kids. The three of us, me, Peter, and Nate. We were inseparable. Honestly, you were the first crack in our bond."

I twist my lips. This is nothing I don't already know.

"Losing Peter killed him. But losing you, believing that he wasn't good enough for you, believing he wasn't worth Peter's death—it broke him. And he couldn't feel it. He couldn't stand the pain. And unlike me, he couldn't go back to war and lose himself in a job. He just had alcohol and his fists. And he used them both. I honestly think he was hoping someone would take the pain away. Would end it for good." The last part he says quietly, and my stomach churns at the thought of Nate trying to get himself killed.

"He got in one too many fights. Fortunately, he had a good lawyer. Everyone took pity on him. He's lost so much, Amelia. He's so broken. The judge gave him an ultimatum. Two years in prison or rehab and probation. Straight and narrow. He *almost* took the prison sentence." Jack looks down at his hands. "The only reason he changed his mind was because he had an inkling of hope that he could fix himself and then come back to *you.*"

It's almost unbearable to hear what Nate had gone through. Without me. All because of a misunderstanding, a lack of communication, and *Grant*.

"The record deal," I say.

"Honestly, I don't know much about it. You'll have to talk to him. Is it possible that he had a deal? Yeah. I mean, Amelia, Nate had no idea how you'd react to him coming back. Did he keep that ace in his pocket if you turned him down? If things went to hell? Maybe. Did he want that? *No*. I can tell you for sure that he did not want that. I spoke to him almost daily for the last few years, Amelia. All he wanted was to come home to you. It's all he's been working toward. So whatever Grant told you, whatever he made you believe, it's all *his* version. His lie. I assure you, just like last time, this is a misunderstanding. You need to talk to Nate. You guys are going to be parents. You need to stop pushing away from each other and start working together."

My shoulders shake as the tears start again. Tears of relief, tears of sorrow, and tears for our baby. We are going to be parents, and I need to get my shit together.

Nate

I don't even consider going to see Amelia. I don't trust myself. The anger is too hot, my need to hurt someone too great.

It's not that I think I would ever lay a finger on her, but I could see hitting a wall or slamming my car into a pole. All of those things don't feel out of the realm of possibility. Which for the record, I know is a problem. Instead, I dial the number Jack gave me for this situation.

"We need to stop meeting like this," Kyle says as I walk into the tattoo parlor, my jaw set and my eyes bloodshot. Having a tattoo artist on speed dial is coming in handy. Having one that is a therapist is downright brilliant. But right now, I don't want to be psychoanalyzed. I just need the pain.

"I don't want to talk," I say, sitting down in the chair and pulling my shirt off.

"Suit yourself. But you're wasting a perfect opportunity for me to help you while I create a masterpiece."

I grunt and look down, pointing to a spot on my back where he can get to work. "Dealer's choice?" he asks.

The door of the parlor flies open before I can respond. I can feel the heat emanating off whoever just walked in. "Oh, I've got a design for you. Why don't you try this?" Jack asks as he flings a piece of paper into my lap.

I don't look at it, and I don't raise my head to look at him. He's clearly talked to Amelia and thinks he's got everything figured out. Just like her.

"I see the Fitzpatrick family is taking a page out of a familiar book. Hey, Kyle, I'm pretty sure our friend Jack here could use some therapy if you want to use my appointment to talk to him while you work on me."

Jack growls, "Look down."

I pinch my eyes shut like a goddamn child. My maturity is astonishing.

"I really don't want to do this, Nate, but you're leaving me no choice. Look *down*."

I sigh heavily, aggravated that I have to act like a grown-up. "Can you at least start with the needle? I need to feel anything but what I'm feeling right now. Then I'll look down."

The sound of the gun starting sends a rush to my heart, and my pulse relaxes. I feel the first hit, and it's like taking a puff of a cigarette or a drink of whiskey—my body aches for it. I open my eyes, finally ready to deal with Jack, and a groan escapes my throat.

Pearson, Amelia, 11 weeks, 3 days.

The image below her name, the first picture of our child, slams my heart into my chest.

Our baby. My child. Baby Pearson.

"Fuck," I groan.

She really is pregnant. I really am going to be a dad. My eyes clamp shut.

We're quiet for a few moments, the only sounds the buzz of the needle and the music playing in the background.

No one speaks.

Finally, I steal a glance in Jack's direction. He looks exhausted. His eyes are red, his jaw is slack, but his fists are balled. He's just barely holding it together.

Hit me, I want to tell him. I deserve it.

"She gave up on me again," I say instead. I'm so resigned to the fact that we're over—that I've lost everything—I just don't have it in me to fight anymore. The depression eats me alive.

Jack sighs, running his hand through his hair. "You don't have the full story."

I meet his eyes, giving him a *really, buddy* expression.

Jack coughs and clears his throat. "Kyle, stop for a sec."

Kyle turns the instrument off and leans back against the counter, eyeing us both. "Just say whatever you're going to say so he can finish this," I say, motioning to my back.

Jack's eyes dip down and then he looks directly into my eyes, and I see the pain etched in every line around his face. "Grant tried to force himself on Amelia."

I don't know how he manages to grit this out, and I can't quite wrap my mind around the words.

"He what?" I ask, my voice low.

"He tried to rape her, Nate. Years ago. The night you proposed." Jack looks at me like I should understand this. Like anything he says makes sense. "He used her fear of him…from back then…to get her to sign those papers. She didn't…fuck, Nate, she's a mess. A bigger mess than I think either you or I realized. We were so worried about us, about how we handled Peter's death, and I thought her sorrow, her tragedy was just about losing you…but Nate, she's so much more fucked up than that. He convinced her that you cheated. He made her believe that she heard you with someone else. She came back to Nashville for you. She didn't walk away. She didn't send you those divorce papers because of a fight. She sent them because she thought you were with someone else. Because of Grant."

"He tried to rape her?" The words burn my throat. I always thought he was pathetic. A drunk. A loser. But this. This is just so… "Why didn't she tell me? Us? Why didn't she tell any of us?"

Rage hammers through me.

Jack scratches his face as if he's trying to actually scratch the thoughts from his mind. "Probably because of this. Because right now you and I are trying to figure out how this could be true. How we could have missed all the signs. All the clues. I don't know. Maybe because she didn't think you'd believe her? What the fuck do I know!"

I know his anger isn't solely directed at me. He's angry at himself too. If he hadn't kept the secret of my stint in rehab from Amelia, maybe none of this would have happened. If I'd let him talk to her…

Fuck. I feel my anger take over, and just as I'm about to jump up to hit something, I spot the picture on my lap again, and my head falls back.

"I'm going to be a father, Jack. What the hell am I supposed to do now? She gave up on us. She didn't even talk to me. She never trusted me enough to tell me any of this. She still doesn't. *You're the one telling me*. What am I supposed to do with that?"

Jack levels me with a stare. "Do you want to be happy, or do you want to be right?"

I let out a stilted laugh. "Huh?"

"It's an easy question, Nate. And it's marriage. Do you want to be happy, or do you want to be right? Amelia may be wrong in this situation, from your point of view, and you may be wrong from hers, but what does winning a fight do for either of you? What does being right get you? Because from my vantage point you both feel vindicated, but you're both fucking miserable. Happy or right? Make a choice and then live with it."

I hang my head. "I can't make her happy, Jack. She wants normal. I don't know if I'm capable of that. I write music, and I play in bars. I tried the office thing. It's not for me. I'd do it for her, but she'd know…she'd know that I was only doing it for her."

Jack rolls his eyes. "You think she wants someone that you're not. You think she doesn't know who you are. She followed you to Nashville, asshole. She learned to play the guitar. Hell, she has a better voice than you. And she writes music. She's not normal. My sister is many things, but normal, that's definitely not one of them. And for the record, she doesn't expect you to be either. She had this made for you today."

He tosses a guitar pick at me which I catch with ease. Turning it over, I read the message, and a laugh pulls from deep within my chest.

Play me a song, Daddy.

"She knows you, Nate. And you are all she's ever wanted. You have always been enough. So, happy or right?"

CHAPTER 29

Nate

Out of my mind with guilt and anger, I rap on the door, begging Amelia to open up. I won't use my key. I lost that right.

How the hell did I get this all so wrong? The minute I came back to Bristol I should have told Amelia everything. I should have told her we were married. I should have told her about the label. I should have been honest with her, and maybe, just maybe, she would have told me why she really left all those years ago. If she'd told me she thought I cheated on her, we could have cleared this up.

I can't fucking believe Grant put his hands on her. That he touched her. That he convinced her that I would ever touch someone else…

Leaning my head against the door, I continue to knock. Desperate to talk to her. Desperate to apologize. Desperate to hold her again.

The door swings open, and I fall forward, landing on my knees. When I raise my eyes, it's Charlotte peering down at me. "Where's Amelia?"

The pain on Charlotte's face is indescribable. If she looks this bad, I can only imagine how Amelia is handling this. "Shhh, she's lying down. I don't think you should be here." Charlotte crosses her arms and holds her body rigid, as if she thinks her tiny stature is going to keep me from seeing past her and into the bedroom where my wife lies.

I remain on my knees, literally begging her to let me by. "Please, Charlotte, I just need to talk to her. I need to make this right."

Charlotte's face remains hard, but I see uncertainty in her eyes. She shakes her head as if trying to convince herself of my unworthiness. "I think you should go. Amelia can call you when she's ready."

With my hands on my knees, I look down at the floor, taking staggering breaths, trying to find a way to get through to her. "Please, let me make this right. *Please*." A tear falls and then another, and I don't stop them. I'm not sure the last time I cried in front of someone other than Amelia. Possibly when I lost my father? This feels just as debilitating. I can't lose my wife and my child.

It's several moments before I notice that a hand is rubbing my back. I look up to clear my eyes and find it's Amelia kneeling next to me as Charlotte looks down at both of us, as if she's not certain what she should do. "It's okay," Amelia says, looking up at her. "Go home. I'll call you later."

Uneasy, Charlotte glances back and forth at both of us. "Are you sure?"

I fall back on my ass and put my head in my hands, hiding my pitiful tears.

"Yeah, we'll be okay," Amelia says again, but she's stopped touching me. She stands up and hugs Charlotte and walks her to the door. When I hear the click of the handle, I look up to find Amelia leaning back against it and staring down at me.

Afraid to speak and unsure what to say, I simply watch as she sighs and then rights herself before walking to the kitchen. "Would you like a cup of tea?" she asks, as she moves around the small space, filling a kettle with water and placing it on the stove.

I nod my head because I don't want to say no to her. And tea seems safe.

Although I stand up, I remain near the door, still not comfortable making too many movements. She's like a fawn I'm nervous to scare away.

"You can sit down. I'm not going to fall over," she says as she rolls her eyes and huffs out a breath. I finally get the courage to really look at her and study her pale skin which is marred by red splotches. Looks like I'm not the only one who was crying today.

"Amelia, I'm so sorry," I say finally, uttering the only thing I know with certainty to be true.

She holds up her hand. "Just…give me a minute, okay?"

I hang my head in shame and walk over to the counter, sitting down and watching as she pulls out the tea bags, places them in mugs, and then turns to stare at the tea pot. Facing away from me, she begins to speak. "I can't do this again." Her words are like a knife to the gut. I hold my breath as she continues, "I can't lose you again…it's too much." Her shoulders sag, and I watch as they begin to shake with her sobs.

In three steps I'm by her side and wrapping her in my arms. Running my hand through her smooth hair, I try soothing her. "No, babe, you aren't going to lose me. I'm right here. I'm so sorry. I'm right here, though."

Amelia sobs against my chest, her tears seeping through my shirt and searing my heart. Almost as quickly as the she's settled against me, she startles, and pushes back from me. "No, you can't hold me! You…" her voice cracks as she wipes her face and looks away from me.

"I what?"

Through a sob, she replies, "You broke my heart. It's too much. Loving you is too much. It hurts…loving you hurts me because when it's good it's amazing but then…this happens… and it hurts too much."

I grab hold of her face, forcing her to look at me. "Amelia, *this* didn't happen. *Grant* happened."

She flinches at his name, and her skin prickles as if she's cold. *She's scared.*

My stomach rolls over. This is what she's been living with. For years, my wife has been living in fear of a man I considered a friend.

Reaching down, I lift my shirt over my head and pull her

against my chest, getting her as close as humanly possible to my heartbeat, hoping it can calm her and provide a beat to focus on that isn't related to her fear. Grounding her to this moment, to me, and to our life together.

"Breathe, babe," I whisper into her shoulder as I rub circles on her back. When her breathing evens, I inch her away and look down at her. "Do you see this right here?" I ask, pointing to the first Roman numerals below my rib cage.

Amelia studies them quietly, then bites her lip and looks up at me with an openness.

"June 1, 2006, is what it means." I pause to see if she knows the date I'm referring to. Amelia's eyes narrow in confusion, and she stares at it again before looking back to me. "The day you agreed to be my girlfriend. And the date below it, February 18, 2014, the day you agreed to be my wife, a second time…it was the best day of my life." She lowers her eyes and then looks up at me with guilt. "And it was the worst of yours."

Amelia shakes her head. "It was also one of the best." But even as she says it, a tear streams down her cheek.

I cup her face and force her to meet my eyes. "Amelia, I am so sorry that he did that to you. I'll never forgive myself for putting you in that position." It's like chewing steel even talking about it, let alone imagining him putting his hands on her, trying to force himself on her.

But this isn't about me.

Amelia inhales a shaky breath and then looks up at me. "I

should have told you."

I pull her against my chest. "No, you were just trying to survive. I can't even…" my voice cracks as I try to think of the right thing to say. Of how to express to her that I understand, and also, that I'm devastated because yes, I wish she'd told me. I wish we could go back in time and we could have dealt with it then. More than that, I wish I could go back in time and erase the encounter completely…but since I can't, I won't have her blaming herself.

"Amelia, you are the strongest woman I've ever met." Unsure what else to say, I point to the next number. "June 6, 2018."

In a whisper, Amelia says, "The day we got married."

I nod. "Up until now that was the best day of my life."

Amelia raises her eyes in confusion. My hand moves to her stomach, and we both look down at it in wonder. "Finding out I'm going to be a dad, that you are having my baby"—I shake my head in amazement—"Amelia, it's a dream come true."

She huffs out a breath. "You lied to me, Nate. You told me you came back for me. *For us*. But all along you've had that contract in your guitar case. A backup plan." She shakes her head. "I don't want to be an option…a consolation prize…or worse, the thing that keeps you from your dreams. I don't want you to wake up one day and regret staying here with us, regret your life with us."

I hear the goodbye in her words. The surrender in her demeanor. She's got no fight left in her. The woman who always fights, but never fights for me.

I'll fight for us both if I need to. I'll carry our love on my back, I'll wear it on my body, and I will prove her wrong.

"You were never *an* option, Amelia. You were the *only* option. It's no excuse, but I was scared to tell you how bad it got in Nashville. I was scared to admit I hit rock bottom and almost ended up in prison. That I practically threw my life away because I didn't think I was worth it anymore. And I didn't know if you'd ever take me back. But I came back for *you*, Amelia. Not to get you to sign over your songs. I came back for *you*. But if you had moved on, if I thought you were better off without me, I was going to give you the divorce you asked for. That's why I had those papers. Not because I wanted a backup plan. Because I thought it's what you wanted, but dammit, Amelia, when I saw you, I knew I was never going to give you that divorce."

Amelia shakes her head. "I want to believe you, Nate. I want to rip up those damn papers again and slide into your arms and not look back."

"Then do it!" I practically shout as I plead for our future.

Amelia folds her arms over her chest and leans away from me. "It's not just about me anymore. Or you." She looks down at her stomach and then back up into my eyes. "There's been too many half-truths. Too many secrets. You recorded a freaking album for a label and told me it was for our wedding, Nate! It's not as simple as you and me loving each other. I don't know if I *trust* you."

"I was trying to buy Grant off so we could be *free*!"

She flinches again, and I shrink in shame.

"Exactly! Because rather than telling me the truth, that you fucked up in Nashville, you tried to hide it from me. And because I was so devastated by the fact that I misunderstood our conversation on the boat all those years ago and threw away our marriage, I didn't tell you that I thought you fucked someone else. I mean, Nate, we are going to be parents and we can't even have these simple conversations because we are so worried about hurting one another—because that's all we do. We hurt each other. Our love *hurts*." Exasperation and tiredness mar her face. I move to touch her, but she pushes back. "I think you should go."

"No. We need to stay and fight. You need to fight for us."

Amelia's eyelids slowly open, and defeat is all I see. "I'm tired of fighting. Just…" she breathes out. "Let's give it a few days. I need to wrap my head around everything…and you need to figure out if this is really what you want. If you can even accept love. I can't keep showing you you're worthy, Nate; you need to know that you are. I can't worry that if things go wrong, you're going to disappear again…that you're going to crave the pain, or the music, or the fame. And I need to trust that you'll be happy here."

"I don't want to lose you."

She gives me a sad smile. "Then give me space…please."

CHAPTER 30

Nate

Without a clue as to how to prove to Amelia that she and our child are all I need, I throw all of my energy into packing up my mom's house. I don't need time to figure out what I want. I know what I want. But Amelia's right, I still don't believe that I deserve it.

I still don't believe that *I* can make her happy.

I spend days in the attic going through my dad's things, looking at family albums, sorting through my bedroom, packing the kitchen, and working my way to the basement, a spot my dad commandeered all those years ago and that my mom really never let Sam touch.

Walking down the steps, I'm met with a Patriots poster from 2000. Fuck, I know this is the last thing that really matters, but it is utterly ironic and shitty that the year my dad died, his favorite team won the Superbowl and he had no idea that would happen.

Drew Bledsoe is the quarterback on the poster hanging in the basement, and Tom Brady was drafted that year. But the next year he led them to the Superbowl, and the year after that, and

Love & Tequila Make Her Crazy

the year after that. And Dad missed it all.

I hope I have a son I can take to Patriots games.

The thought shocks me. How easily it entered my mind. And instead of feeling like my chest would explode imagining attending a game with my child, without my dad, I just feel…hope.

My eyes turn to the ceiling, and I close them, whispering, "Ugh, even my kid missed out on Brady."

I imagine my dad laughing. My eyes fall on the Red Sox poster, and I mutter to Dad, "You really missed out on the good sports years."

Poor guy was a die-hard fan for Boston sports when it wasn't popular.

I sit down on the couch in the basement, remembering the many nights I spent sitting right next to him, watching a baseball game, him pointing out who was hitting well, me taking every word he said as gospel. I move the pillow next to me on my lap, needing to do something with my hands, and spot a black object stuck in the couch cushion. Lifting it up, I realize it's a book of some kind. When I look at it closer, I see that it's similar to the one my mother gave me a few months ago. It's black, and in gold writing the word *Rules* is embossed on the front.

Inside, in my dad's familiar writing, it says, *Rules for my Son.*

My throat grows dry, and my tongue feels like a foreign object in my mouth, heavy and useless. My fingers move across his words, taking in the power of his strokes which touched this paper so many years ago.

Nathan, as I sit in the room with your mother and you, I'm overwhelmed by a sense of responsibility and love. Your mother was incredible. She handled your birth with a smile, and a few curses, while I was nothing but scared.

We attended birthing classes, I read every book I could find, but nothing prepared me for this. For you.

You'll come to learn that I love rules. I love knowing how things work. But your mom has taught me that sometimes we have to make our own rules. So rule number one, and this one's for me, as much as it is for you, I'll always love you.

Tears threaten to spill at the corners of my eyes. The breath burns in my throat.

That's what it comes down to, doesn't it? *Love.* It really is enough. The book is filled with advice. He wrote in it often.

My first little league game, *Rule # 29 Pull back that arm and don't ever take your eye off the ball.*

My first fishing trip, *Nate, I've never been as excited as I was when you caught that sunny. Rule #54 Always watch the blades on the back of the fish.*

My first crush. *Nate, I think we all know that you have a crush on Amelia Fitzpatrick, maybe I'm wrong but I wouldn't be surprised if in twenty years you're standing at the altar with that girl. There's just something there. Rule #66 Never stop looking at her the way you do now.*

I turn the book back to the first page. *Rule #1 I'll always love you.*

It's the only way to love.

I put the book down and finger the phone in my pocket, turning it around like a card deck. I bite my thumb, considering what to do. Then in a rush, I mutter, "Fuck it," and dial.

"You make a decision?" Jack asks.

"Get her to the winery tomorrow. Five o'clock...*please*."

Amelia

Twelve weeks and three days. That's how pregnant I currently am. It has been a week since he left. Or since I asked him to leave, I guess is more accurate.

I've alternated between crying and sticking out my lower lip, throwing my back straight, and holding my head high, chanting, *I can do this.*

But today is the first day I actually have to be in public. Like real public. We have an event that I have to provide the flowers for. Not only did I design the bouquets, but I also have to deliver them since I have no employees and my husband is off figuring out whether or not he wants to be with me.

And unlike a normal delivery, this one we are doing in the evening, because they had an event planned for earlier in the day. The sun is already setting, and soon it will be impossible for me to even see as I decorate.

I blow out another breath in annoyance, or depression, or anger, mostly at myself. Although there is plenty to go around. I'm angry at Grant. I'm angry at myself. I'm angry at my brother. And I'm angry at Nate.

If Nate and Jack didn't hide his arrests all those years ago, things would have been so different. Or if Jack had told me the truth…or if I'd never jumped to conclusions and left the boat years ago in anger…

Jack hasn't given up though. He appears nightly at my apartment with food, Charlotte, and chocolate. He's a smart man. All three of those things make it hard to be mad. But I'm doing a good job holding a grudge.

Fortunately, both Jack and Charlotte have offered to help make the delivery today.

"Tell me what you need," Charlotte says with a smile, saluting me like a cadet in my florist army, which leaves me smiling. Honestly, she's one of the few people that I can never grimace around. She's just so damn happy. She makes *me* happy. Even in my miserable state.

"Just help me load these into the van and then we can head to the winery." Caris was very quiet over what this was for. I hate not meeting with clients before an event. I want to know who they are, what their style is, what kind of event they are hoping to have. Should I use gold foil, tulle, burlap, ribbon?

Love & Tequila Make Her Crazy

Each can evoke a certain look, and I can make any of them pop, so long as they match the décor and the people. When I'm given as little information as I was for this event, I choose to go with flowers that are in season.

It's winter, almost Christmas, so poinsettias are a focal point in all of my bouquets. I hope the hosts are festive.

I watch Jack load each bouquet into the van. "It's missing something," I say, tapping my chin. "The gold foil!" I shriek, practically toppling poor Charlotte over with my enthusiasm.

I run into the store, grab my tools, and bring them with me to add the appropriate garnish to each design when we get to the winery. I want to make sure it works with the other colors.

As I walk out of the house, I see Lucille cornering Charlotte as Jack packs up the truck. "So where's Nate today?"

Poor Charlotte's brown eyes are wide with anxiety. "Um... he, uh—"

"Leave the poor girl alone," I snap, and Lucille turns her red head in my direction. A smile curves on her lips as she stares me down and looks behind me for my nonexistent ex.

"Well, where is he? Rumor has it that the Pearsons are emptying the house and they're moving. Where will Nate keep his boat? Is he selling that too? Heading back to Nashville perhaps?"

My fingers wrap tightly around the decorations in my hand as I try to hold myself together. I do not need to give this town anything else to talk about. Shrugging my shoulders, I keep a cool face and reply, "You'll have to ask him, Lucille. Now if you don't mind, I have to get to work."

Jack closes the van and looks on with his arms crossed. Some help he's been. Meanwhile, Charlotte's eyes dance between Lucille and me.

"Well, if you're not with him, do you think he has any interest in older women?" she asks with a completely serious face.

Beside me, Charlotte's mouth cracks open, and she openly laughs in Lucille's face. Jack's neutral exterior breaks as well, and he covers his mouth to hide his wheezing. I, on the other hand, remain completely in control. "Don't know, but you should shoot your shot," I reply with a wink.

She beams and walks off, probably daydreaming about Nate's inky arms. The three of us look on after her and then finally my laughter breaks free. "Can you believe her?"

Jack shakes his head with a smile and points to the van. Time to get to work. We crowd into the front seat with Jack driving and Charlotte between us. "Have you heard from him at all?" Charlotte asks quietly. Jack shifts his weight, and I wonder if *he's* heard from my husband. I certainly haven't.

"Nope. For all I know he's gone back to Nashville."

Charlotte squeezes my hand, and Jack glances over at me. It's like he's got something to say. It's on the tip of his tongue, but he bites it back, and we continue in silence.

It doesn't take long to get to the winery. When we pull up, I hop out of the van, averting my eyes from the *Amelia Pearson's Flowers* writing, trying to forget who I am for today.

Love & Tequila Make Her Crazy

Belle is waiting out front with a smile. She started working with Caris a few weeks ago at the winery. She directs us to a small field where she has set up a few chairs with heaters strategically placed to help with the cool December evening. She points to a trellis that she wants us to decorate, and I check out the space. "An outdoor event in December; whose brilliant idea was this?" I mutter under my breath.

I take the extra poinsettias that I brought and wind them through the trellis with greenery, and the result is quite stunning. I snap a few pictures for our wedding book. Or *my* wedding book, I guess. No idea who the "we" would be. It's just me now. Me and the baby.

"Amelia." I turn to see Karen and Sam walking down the path and up the aisle toward me. "What are you doing here?"

"I could ask you the same question," I say, looking around the event, trying to see who else has shown up. So far, it's just them.

"Nate asked us to meet him here. Did you guys decide to look at wedding venues finally? Is your mom coming?"

My eyes dart to hers, and the idea is so preposterous that I can't even respond. Fortunately, Jack walks up and stabilizes me with his hand under my elbow. "Karen, Sam, it's good to see you." He offers a kiss on the cheek to Karen and shakes Sam's hand.

"Do *you* know where Nate is?" Karen asks.

I turn to my brother, but before answering, he waves behind us. "Mom, Dad."

Oh, this just keeps getting better. What the hell?

"Hi Mom, Dad, what are you guys doing here?"

My mom kisses me on the cheek, and Dad gives me a hug. "Jack asked us to come. I figured maybe this is where he and Charlotte want to have the wedding shower?"

Charlotte walks up with a confused face. "What now?"

Apparently, no one knows why they're here. What is going on?

I screw my eyes toward my brother. He's behind this. He better not be tricking Nate into coming so that he can work some magical family intervention. "Don't tell me Nate is going to show up thinking this is an engagement party for you and Charlotte. I will literally kill you if you arranged this to get us back together."

My mother takes a deep breath. "Wait, you're not together anymore?"

My dad looks equally concerned, and Karen just shakes her head in bewilderment.

"Jack, please," I plead with him, miserable at this entire interaction. Next, he'll announce my pregnancy, and I'll have to hear the value of condoms and why I can't raise this baby on my own. I can't sit through this. "I'm out," I mutter, turning on my heels before I have to face the music. Which is quite ironic because behind me is my husband, standing with a guitar strung over his shoulder, staring at me.

"*Cookie*," he says almost breathless. I roll my eyes. I hate that name.

My hand rubs my face. "Pearson, what are you doing here? What is going on?"

Nate walks toward us all, his guitar resting against his hips, and dammit, I can't help but notice how hot he looks. How perfect the instrument falls against his body, how his arm flexes as his fingers strum against the strings.

My body reacts even though my mind is still standing in the *don't trust him* lane.

Nate looks at us all and then he focuses in on his mom. "I've made a lot of mistakes over the last fifteen years." Then he turns his eyes to me. "But loving you was never one of them. Love is never a mistake. Standing in the way of it though, that's a mistake." He reaches our tiny group, and I'm overwhelmed by his presence, his scent, and my heady desire for him.

Damn pregnancy hormones.

"Mom, Sam, I stood in the way of your marriage years ago. I was wrong. You finding your second chance, Mom, that's what Dad would have wanted because he loved you. He always loved you, and me. And he would want you to be happy. And you finding love, and being loved, doesn't hurt his memory; it honors it."

Karen's mouth falls open and Sam steps closer to her, holding her tighter than before. My head darts between Karen and Sam. I never knew they wanted to get married. I never knew Nate stopped it.

What else don't I know?

"I asked everyone to be here today because I want to make that right," Nate says, standing in front of his mom and Sam. Then he turns to Sam, a grin crossing his face, and he moves the guitar to his back before getting down on his knee in front of him. "Sam, will you do me the honor of marrying my mom?"

Uncomfortable laughter breaks out through our group, and Karen smacks Nate playfully before Sam pulls him into a hug. They share words that I can't hear from my vantage point, and Charlotte squeezes my arm. "Oh my God, how romantic was that!" Then she smacks her hands over her mouth and mutters in a whisper, "Sorry, I forgot, we hate him."

I grunt in aggravation. I wish I hated him. But when Nate turns to me with a sheepish grin across his face, I feel myself melt. He walks to me in three steps, determined, with swagger and like a man on a mission. In that moment I know I don't stand a chance.

"Ames, can we talk?" His hand reaches up to my cheek, brushing my messy blonde hair out of my face, and a shudder runs through my body. All I can do is nod.

He holds my eyes for a beat, licking his lips, and his eyelashes flutter closed before they open again, piercing me with a raw love that is palpable. "I know I hurt you, Amelia. Not accepting your love. Not believing that I deserved it, that I was worthy, that I could ever be enough, left walls up that made it impossible for you to penetrate. I should have known better…I should have known that by simply loving you, that was enough. Because Amelia, the way I love you, there aren't love songs to describe it. 'Hurts so good,' 'You're the First, the Last, My Everything,' 'One Man Band'…None of them do our love justice. None of them even hit upon the chord of the kind of love that I have for you. And that's what makes me worth it. That's what makes us special. Love *is* enough."

I nod as a tear slips down my cheek.

"Hurting each other is not all that we do. We write music, we laugh, we boat, we cook." He moves closer and whispers into my ear, "We make love and we fuck." He steps back and looks at me with his crooked smile. "We tease one another, we sit next to each other silently and support each other, we hold hands in the alcove." Nate interlocks our fingers, and I stare down at them for a moment, lost in his touch, but he pulls my attention back with his words. "We're best friends, Amelia, lovers…we're soulmates. The only thing that hurts about our love is when we're denying it…when we're apart."

Nate smiles his handsome smile and wipes the tears from my cheeks. "Keep writing music with me, Ames. I can't do it myself. Be extraordinary with me. I don't have the words without you. I don't have the harmony, the notes, I don't have anything…without you. *You* are my harmony. I *need* you."

And that's when I see the pick. The one I had made for him.
Play me a song, Daddy.

I close my eyes to soak up the moment, and when I open them a conversation passes between us silently.

We're going to be parents. We're having a baby. It's time to grow up. I love you.

Nervously, I reply, "I don't want to hold you back, Nate. You need to be sure you really want this."

Nate's thumb smooths over my lips as he stares down at me. "This is all I want. *You* are all I want. I may not always believe I'm worthy. But I know that our love is. Our love makes me worthy. Our love makes me want to live. And you, Amelia, you make me want to more than live. With you I'm more than surviving. I'm not just existing. I'm living my dream and that makes me worthy."

Accepting his words, I close my eyes and savor the moment. The sky has gone from a brilliant fire to darkness while we stood talking. Within the vineyards, the only light is the candles which line the aisle, twinkle lights which surround the chairs, and the stars above. But the stars don't shine, they burn, just like my love for this man. Maybe burning isn't such a bad thing.

Breathing out a shaky breath, I whisper, "What are you asking me, Nate?"

Nate's voice is strong. He takes my hands, and he doesn't shake as he says, "Be my wife. Be the mother of my child. Marry me. *Again.*"

The words surprise me, and I force a laugh from my throat. "Now?" I squeak.

He smiles, his crooked lip dipping in the cocky way it does when he knows things are going to go his way. "No, not right here. I'd like our own day. And I'd really like to see you in a white dress. We didn't get that last time. I'd like to watch your father walk you down the aisle. We did things a little backward. But we did it our way. Let's do it again. You think you could do that for me? Wear a white dress, walk down the aisle, promise me forever. One more time?"

Tears form in my eyes. "It's not going to be all sunshine and roses, Pearson. I am quick to anger, and sometimes I overreact before I hear the whole story."

He grins. "I know."

"And I want to live in Bristol. I want to raise this baby,"—I grab his hand, pulling it to my stomach, and meet his eyes—"*our baby*. I want to raise our baby *here*."

His eyes soften, and he gives me that lazy crooked smile again. "Me too."

"And I'm going to need chocolate, for like, every meal during this pregnancy. And I don't want to hear anything about it from you."

Nate pats his pocket, letting the blue Chips Ahoy! wrapper peek out. "Got you covered, Cookie."

My eyes narrow. "And you can't—"

"Amelia, *no*. Anything but that."

I smile and roll my eyes. "Fine, you can still call me Cookie."

Nate's smile grows. "Is that a yes?"

I pause and take a deep breath. "Tell me about this record deal."

He shakes his head. "We're having a baby. That's in the

past. We'll work in the shop together, make lots of babies, write music, and I'll play at Thames every once in a while."

He's willing to give up everything for me. But he doesn't understand that his dreams are my dreams. His wins are my wins. And this one we can do together. "I read the contract. The *other* contract. The one that Grant's cousin Vin sent over."

Nate's eyes darken at the mention of Grant's name. A moment passes between us both, acknowledging the horrible things that were done, the things that almost happened, and how much we almost lost.

Almost because we're still standing, together, and if I have my way that won't ever change.

"Anyway," I say, changing the subject, not wanting Grant to ruin this moment or any other moments ever again, "Vin sent over the other deal."

Nate shakes his head. "I didn't ask him to do that. I don't even know how he got your information."

I roll my eyes. "He works for a record label, Nate. They have their ways."

He laughs. "Right."

"It's a good deal. We can have it all. Our music, our baby, our life *here* together, with a few commutes when necessary."

Nate's face brightens with hope, but he almost swallows it down, as if he thinks he's getting ahead of himself. "You'd really want that?"

"To marry you? Make music, have my flower shop, and

raise a family with you? Is that even a question? It's a dream come true because it's with *you*." I squeeze his hands in mine and look up to meet his eyes. They are filled with so much joy, wonder, and love.

"So, is that a yes?" he asks shyly.

The smile bursts across my face, my joy shining so brightly I feel like a damn sunflower. "Yes, Nate Pearson, I'll marry you again. I'd marry you every year for the next fifty years of our lives if you asked. I love you." I fall against his chest as he throws his hand up in the air.

Nate lifts my chin up to him, winking and gives me that trademark smirk as he meets my lips. "I love you too…*Cookie*."

EPILOGUE

Amelia

Nate's mom married Sam on that cool December day in front of my mom, dad, Jack, and Charlotte. Karen asked me to be her Matron of Honor, which made me cry, because pregnancy hormones, and also because she whispered in my ear as she hugged me that I was the daughter that Paul and she always dreamed of.

Nate was Sam's best man. Their relationship has always been a bit unconventional, but that day I saw a healing in my husband, a recognition that this is what his father would have wanted for us all.

I swear the stars shined brighter that night as Karen and Sam danced and ate cake. It was almost as if Paul was offering

Love & Tequila Make Her Crazy

her a special show from above. A love letter written in the stars which reminded her of Rule #1, *I will always love you.*

Nate shared the journals with me, and I laughed realizing how many of the rules he used trying to win me back. Paul always had a way about him, smiling when we were kids, whispering to me that I shouldn't take the boys' crap. It seemed only fitting that he knew even before we did that one day we'd stand at an altar, facing each other and pledging to love one another for the rest of our lives. Not a hard promise—we'd been practicing since we were kids.

Pauline Grace arrived on the Fourth of July, much to the excitement of the town elders. A true Bristolian born on the town's favorite holiday. It didn't get more patriotic, more spirited, and more perfect than that—even if it did mean she was two weeks overdue. I honestly believe that Paul had a little bit to do with the date.

Then on a warm October day, in front of our family and friends, and practically the entire town, we said I do. *Again.*

As promised, I wore a white gown, but it was long and silky and simple. Nate was practically drooling as I walked down the aisle to him. Charlotte carried Paulie, as we like to call her. All twelve pounds of her were dressed in an adorable light pink dress, and Charlotte, my Matron of Honor—she married my brother in August—wore a strapless gown that showed off her gorgeous tan from their destination wedding in the Azores. Paulie had already traveled to Portugal at just six weeks old and then to Italy for

Belle's engagement. Our family just kept expanding.

"What are you thinking about?" Nate asks as he sits in the captain's chair with Christopher in his lap. Chris is two, and five-year-old Paulie is doing twirls on the bow of the boat.

I peel my eyes from our daughter and turn to look at my husband and son. "Just how happy I am."

Nate's eyes grow dark. "I'd like to show you how happy you make me."

"I'd like that too, Pearson."

On the radio a familiar tune starts to play, and Paulie screeches as she bops to the music. "Daddy, turn it up! Chrisssy," she sings in her adorable voice, "this is Daddy's song."

Our two-year-old claps his hands in excitement. I'm not sure he really understands what she's saying, but whenever Paulie talks to him, or calls him by her chosen nickname, he gets excited.

Nate stands, bouncing Chris on his hip, and pulls me from my seated position, taking me in his arms and rocking me against his chest. "And Mommy's song," he whispers in my ear.

"Shhh, that's our little secret. Don't want them getting a big head."

"Oh, we aren't going to tell them that their mom and dad made it on the top ten countdown, for the eighth week in a row," he says with a wink.

I feel my cheeks grow pink. Whose life is this and how lucky am I to be living it?

Love & Tequila Make Her Crazy

"I love you, Pearson," I whisper in his ear.

I meet his eyes and then look at our son. His face is all smiles, and behind him Paulie bounces along to the song. I grab her, and the four of us rock together to the music. This moment right here, this is what life is about.

Isn't that what love is though? A million little moments that make up your life. Fingers intertwined, sharing coffee, sitting quietly on the couch watching TV—or in our case, no quiet moments because we have happy children screeching all the time. Or an evening on the deck sipping wine. In bed making love, fighting because we care too much, traveling the world, writing music together, dancing on the deck of our boat with our children in our arms. Sharing moments that only the two of us have and witnessing one another's lives.

It started when we were just kids, but we've always been that witness for one another. That person for eachother. My first friend, first love, first everything.

With our kids between us, Nate sings in my ear the words to the song we wrote together. A song about love, about life, and about how sometimes it makes you crazy.

ACKNOWLEDGEMENTS

It was hard writing the end on this book because Nate and Amelia feel so very real to me. Young love can be incredibly messy. As an adult I look back on the lack of communication, the inability to fight fair, and the pain my husband and I caused one another when we were first dating. And yet there is no one I'd rather have standing by my side today.

I wanted to capture those emotions, that all-consuming love you feel when you're young and in love, the spiraling out of control, and the eventual heartbreak. I think most people can relate to those strong feelings.

This book was even more special to me though because of Nate's relationship with his father. As someone who grew up during a time when the world fell apart, I wanted to honor the memories of not only those we lost on that horrific day, but the children who were left behind. I hope I did their stories justice.

To my team at Cover 2 Cover Author Services, I am so incredibly proud of how much your company has grown in the last year and so thankful for your friendship, your motivation, your hard work and the dedication you have to my books and my career. Thank you for your belief in me, your encouragement, and your skills. And Monique, this cover…I can't put into words how much I love it.

To my Beta Readers, especially Katherine, Janae, and Marie…what would I do without you? Your love for Nate and Amelia, your encouragement of my craft, and your ideas made this book better. Thank you, thank you, thank you!!!! And to The Cocktail Club, my street team, your excitement for my books surpasses my wildest dreams. Having people believe in me, cheer me on and spend their precious time and energy singing my books praises to all that will listen is how I sell books! Thank you!

Over the last year I have met so many wonderful authors who have not only mentored me but offered amazing friendship daily. And to the ladies who support these authors, who have created a community where we lift each other up in a world that is happy to tear people down, Erica and Haley, thank you.

A special thanks to my author besties, Elyse Kelly, Daphne Elliot, Jenni Bara, Swati M.H. and Amy Alves who are always willing to listen to my questions or my rants. If you haven't read their books, what are you waiting for? With them I created a new community, KU Steamy Romance Reads on Facebook and if you aren't a member you should join. The books these women are writing this year are incredible!

My lovely editors, Ann and Ann of Happily Editing Anns, I can't praise enough. Thank you for loving my characters as much as I do and for your dedication and attention to detail.

Last but certainly not least, my readers, thank you so much for reading this book. There is nothing better than hearing from each of you how a character affected you, or a storyline made you laugh. I love your reviews, your anecdotes, and the notes you send to me. This book was a special one for me. But it isn't the end. We are entering a new series and I cannot wait for you to meet your next book boyfriend. If you're wondering what happened between Shawn and Hailey, don't fret, Shawn's story is coming…but first the Bristol Billionaires will be joining us this summer and let me tell you, it is about to get hot!

If you want to follow along on my writing journey and have sneak peeks into all the characters in Bristol, follow me on Instagram, join my awesome Facebook group, sign-up for my newsletter and follow me on TikTok.

LOVE & TEQUILA MAKE HER CR PLAYLIST

Freedom Was A Highway by Jimmie Allen and Brad Paisley

Tequila by Dan & Shay

Wyd now? by Sadie Jean

Three Little Birds by Bob Marley

23 by Sam Hunt

Love Story by Taylor Swift

Never Say Never by Cole Swindell & Lainey Wilson

Springsteen by Eric Church

One Man Band by Old Dominion

You and Tequila by Kenny Chesney

If I Didn't Love You by Jason Aldean & Carrie Underwood

Written in the Sand by Old Dominion

Hurts So Good by John Mellencamp

Dreams by Fleetwood Mac

Let Go by Frou Frou

Love You Too Late by Cole Swindell

She's Everything by Brad Paisley

Mine by Taylor Swift

Manufactured by Amazon.ca
Bolton, ON